SHADOW SOUL

A DI TUDOR MANX NOVEL

DYLAN H. JONES

First published in 2020 by Bloodhound Books.

www.bloodhoundbooks.com

Print ISBN 978-1-913419-73-8

ALSO BY DYLAN H. JONES

DI Tudor Manx Series

Anglesey Blue (Book 1)

Doll Face (Book 2)

First to read. First to comment. First to say he was proud.
This book is dedicated to Hugh John Jones; avid crime thriller reader,
ex-RAF serviceman, devoted father. 1936-2018

"How can I be substantial if I do not cast a shadow? I must have a dark side also if I am to be whole." — Carl Jung

PART I

KILL STRIKE

PROLOGUE

RAF WADDINGTON, LINCOLNSHIRE, UK.

Flight Lieutenant Bobbie Matthews wasn't the kind of woman who scared easily. But that morning, as she walked across the parade ground, she was hit by a sensation of impending dread that shook her to the bone. To her west, the ground control station appeared to take the shape of an oversized metallic coffin, the flat light of dawn falling across its brutal angular shape like a shroud. The image struck her with such force she imagined the earth would swallow the structure whole; ashes to ashes, dust to dust.

The 'Box', as it had become known to the Royal Air Force's Thirteen Squadron, was a former shipping container. Stripped to the bones, it now housed four banks of high-definition monitors, several rows of back-lit switches, and a pair of joysticks that sometimes in her sleep Bobbie would imagine her fingers were still coiled around, as if for those eight hours she missed their satisfying feel in her hand.

The Box, however, required no sleep. All it required was a constant feed of electricity and the low hum of air conditioning to cool the racks of hard drives and communication systems. It was staffed 24/7 to accommodate the demands of the United

States Joint Special Operations Command at Creech Air Force Base, located in the Nevada desert. Waddington was eight hours ahead and served as an extension of the US Air Force, helping to facilitate round-the-clock surveillance with handovers between Creech and Waddington every twelve hours. The demands of the war on terror, Bobbie had come to learn, were as ceaseless as the war itself.

The day had cast its typical soupiness over Lincolnshire, the sky undecided as to its true intentions, shifting from peaks of blue to murky greyness depending on the wind. To Bobbie's left, the Air Seeker Annex jutted out sharply from the ground, as if the building were constructed in italic to make some kind of point. To her right, the hangars housing the Sentry, Sentinel, and Shadow aircraft loomed wide, and beyond the hangars, the wide expanse of the airfield butted against the outskirts of the RAF families' accommodations from where Bobbie had just driven.

She drew her jacket tight over her flying suit as a regiment of cadets jogged past. "Squintos" – a new batch of intelligence officers in basic training. *They'd need the exercise*, Bobbie thought, as the dull march of their boots faded to silence. Squintos were expected to stare into computer screens for hours, analysing the constant data flow streaming into the command centre. Bobbie herself had spent twelve months as a squinto. She'd left after a year and enrolled in the RAF's Unmanned Aircraft Training programme, which had just opened its doors to non-commissioned pilots. She completed her officer training at RAF Cranwell, then was posted to USAF Creech to compete her formal drone training, graduating with the clunky title of remote piloted aircraft systems (pilot). Six months later she found herself in command of a MQ-9 Reaper Drone as a flight lieutenant. She may still have been sitting behind a desk, but that desk connected her to £20 million of weaponry capable of striking a target with surgical accuracy from 50,000 feet. Bobbie had never felt more alive than when she took control of the drone, 700 pounds of explosive racked in the rails, her finger poised to rain a Hellfire missile on a convoy of insurgents.

As she pulled open the station door, a blast of cold air brushed over her face. Typically, she would have begun visualising the day's mission – slipping herself into the zone – but the same feeling of dread she'd had minutes ago arced through her. She shrugged it off as pre-mission jitters.

"You're late," Officer Cadet Cole Dawson said, smiling.

Bobbie stood by the doorway and took a deep, meditative breath. The sense of something not being quite right lay heavy on her chest. Settling herself into her chair, she glanced at her watch. "Twenty-three seconds late, Dawson. Seriously?"

"Nah," he said, adjusting his neck. "Just pulling your leg, blame it on the boredom."

Bobbie checked her monitors. "If I'd known I was here for your entertainment, I'd have prepared some suitable material."

Dawson chuckled. Thirty-one years old, with a sickly complexion in need of a long holiday someplace sun drenched, Dawson was a sensor operator in command of the Reaper's high-definition camera and tasked with ensuring they had constant eyes on the high value target (HVT). He also controlled the Reaper's laser, which was required to be pinpoint accurate before Bobbie pulled the trigger. If the laser was one degree off azimuth when the missile left the rails, it could mean the difference between striking a HVT right between the eyes or obliterating the convoy of families travelling with him – a mistake he wasn't keen to repeat.

"Don't you know the party doesn't start until I get here?" Bobbie said, adjusting the chair to accommodate her slender, five-feet-nine-inch frame, though in her flying suit she looked shorter, more vulnerable than she wanted to appear.

"They didn't mention that in the mission briefing."

"You don't have it tattooed on your arse by now?"

He smiled and tilted the camera, revealing miles of dirt-brown desert fifty-thousand feet below. "Bobbie's way, or the highway?"

"I respect a man who knows his place." Bobbie secured her headset and adjusted her comms. The voice of the 89th Attack Squadron Reaper pilot broke through the static – Lieutenant Colonel Benton Lowell. She'd trained with Benton back at Creech.

"All's good in the free world, Dazzle's in the Box," Benton said, his voice oozing an easy American confidence. Bobbie had earned the moniker Dazzle when she began customising her headset with imitation gems she bought at a cheap craft store off the Las Vegas strip. At the time, she imagined the gems were some nod to her femininity, but later she began to wonder if she were just trying to infuse a jolt of colour to the drab sandy beige of war.

"Are we clear to match eyes?" Bobbie said, studying the barren desert topography.

"Straight down to it, huh?" Benton said. "You see what I'm seeing?"

Dawson gave Bobbie the thumbs up and rotated the camera. "Brown terrain. Lots of it."

"Yeah, different day, same shit."

"Recon details?"

Dawson slid her a document. "Red card holder approved," he confirmed, pointing at the Base Commander's signature – the final word in authorising kill strikes.

Benton spoke. "We've been tracking a convoy of technicals driving south from Mosul since zero hundred hours, but we've had bugs on the windshield for the past ninety minutes."

"Sandstorm?"

"The goddam mother of. Visibility's returning to situation normal, but the weather geeks predict an encore by sundown."

"Roger that," Bobbie said, scribbling on her notepad. "Any additional intel you lot need to brief us on?"

"You lot?" Benton laughed. "You mean the guys who trained your sorry asses?"

"Correct." If Bobbie had eyes on Benton, he'd no doubt be making a gesture that included lifting one, or both, of his middle fingers to the screen.

"Yeah, we got your intel. Technicals are axle-heavy with metal. Check out the trailer we made earlier." Benton chuckled as he replayed the footage of a convoy of trucks reversing into a narrow entrance to the right of a high-walled compound. "That's some real Mister Bean parking shit, right there," he said, as the trucks took several attempts to reverse into position. "Now, watch this," he added, as a group of men jumped from the trucks and stood in a chain formation at the entrance.

"Anti-aircraft?" Bobbie asked, as the men passed large items of weaponry to each other and onto the truck's flatbeds.

"Fifty-millimetre, standard Russian Army issue, captured from their shitshow in Afghanistan. We counted six weapons stacked like they were heading to holy freakin' war."

"Why didn't you strike before they left the compound?"

"CIVACS," Benton confirmed. "Women and children in the vicinity. We began tracking as soon as they stepped on the gas."

"Copy that," Bobbie said.

"FYI, we're keeping safety eyes on another convoy travelling three kilometres behind," Benton said.

"Friendlies?"

"Unconfirmed, but we scrambled an F15 to keep eyes on them."

"Can you patch me into their comms?"

"Negative. We've got signal blockers along the route. If

they're friendlies, let's hope they've got enough smarts to keep their distance when you rain down the shit-parade. If they're with the HVT, then send the other Hellfire their way, compliments of the US of A."

"Roger that. Assuming control of Reaper in fifteen," she said, folding her fingers gently around the joystick.

"You ready to save the world?"

"Always. Assuming control in ten."

"Don't fuck up our good work now, ya' hear?"

"Good pep talk, Benton."

Dawson nodded at Bobbie. "It's all yours."

"Confirm. I have control of Reaper Craft."

"Have a nice day blowing shit up, Dazzle. Out."

With the Reaper under her command, Bobbie rested the joystick in her palm, her muscle memory kicking in. She sensed herself falling into the zone – the critical mind-space where her mind bonded with the pitch and roll of the Reaper – as it cleaved through the atmosphere 3000 miles away. Lost in the motion, she barely heard her overseer, Flight Commander James Flynt, step in and take position at the rear of the Box. Flynt had a reputation for making swift decisions concerning kill strikes – the more the merrier, seemed to be his default setting.

"Ready to show those Johnny Jihadis some of our Yorkshire mettle, Flight Lieutenant Matthews?"

"I'm from Wales, sir, but yes, I'm briefed and strike-prepared."

"Christ, not the sentimental Welsh type, are you? Cry at the sight of a leek or a bloody daffodil?"

"No, no sentiment at all, sir, just here to do my job," she confirmed, keeping her focus steely-eyed; unblinking.

Flynt swiped the 9-line approval document from the desk. "Estimated strike time?"

Bobbie confirmed the convoy's co-ordinates. "Two miles south there's an open stretch of road, should be a safe strike zone."

"Visibility?"

Dawson checked his instruments. "Significant cloud cover, I could lose altitude, but the HVT might spot the craft."

"Drop thirty angels," Flynt said, as the convoy throttled fast over the dust-ridden road. "At this speed, they've got one eye on the road the other on those seventy-two virgin maidens they've been promised."

Bobbie pushed forward on the joystick, felt herself sinking into the chair as the drone dropped 22,000 feet in seconds.

Flynt jabbed Dawson in the shoulder. "Keep that laser clear of the windows. If they see that little red dot, they're squirting out of there faster than ten pints and a vindaloo."

"Nice image, sir," Dawson said, tracking the laser as it traced past the trucks and to the roadside to avoid any reflections.

"What's our strike azimuth?" Bobbie asked, rolling the joystick left and right so Dawson could match the roll of gyroscopic camera ball with the Reaper's pitch.

"Two degrees. Once they hear the sonic boom, it's bye-bye time."

"Like shooting shopping trolleys in the Manchester Ship Canal," Flynt said, stretching out his back.

Bobbie focused on the laser as it swept ahead of the convoy. "Releasing Hellfire in twenty," she said, bracing herself. A hush fell over the station. "Releasing in ten. Standby."

As he ran his index finger along the rib of the tracker, Dawson turned. "What the...?" he asked, rotating the camera and directing the lens towards a large mass on a collision course with the convoy.

"Shit!" Bobbie said, her eyes scanning across the monitors. "Creech alerted us of sandstorms in the vicinity."

Flynt huffed. "Not going to let a bit of sand fuck up our mission are we, Matthews?"

"No, sir. I'll drop angels, pull down past the cloud cover."

Dawson swung the camera around. "I'm losing eyes on the laser track," he said. "We're fighting a forty-five-knot crosswind from the sandstorm, and it's increasing."

"No time like the present, then, Matthews. You're Red Card Holder approved, make the strike."

Bobbie hesitated. "Sir... I don't think–"

"Right," Flynt interrupted. "You don't think. You carry out the orders as presented. Flight Lieutenant, take the strike."

"Shit!" Dawson said, his voice a pitch higher. He swivelled the camera. "There's another convoy following behind."

"Identification?"

"Visibility's gone to shit."

"More Johnny bloody Jihadis. One stone, two birds, I'd count that as a good day in the Box. Now take the strike," Flynt said.

Bobbie wiped the sweat from her brow. "You don't have all the intel. Creech thinks we have friendlies tailing the convoy."

"Christ!" Flynt said, flinging the document onto the desk. "Make comms contact, find out who they are and what the fucking high-hell they're doing in our strike zone."

"Negative. US Forces planted signal blockers along the route."

"Oh, it just gets better and better," Flynt said, leaning over Bobbie's shoulder. "Dawson, how close are they?"

He surveyed the bank of monitors. "Less than two kilometres, but the HVT's decreasing speed because of the storm."

"What's the blast radius of the Hellfire, Dawson?"

"Fifteen-metre kill radius. Wounding radius twenty metres."

Flynt slapped the back of Dawson's chair. "Then we strike. They'll see the fireworks but they're clear of the kill radius If they're friendlies they can assist with the battle damage assessment, if not, we'll send them the other Hellfire with our compliments."

Sweat oozed from Bobbie's palms as she tightened her grip and dragged her index finger hesitantly along the trigger.

"Matthews, do I have to jump in that seat myself?"

"No, sir!" she said, shaking her head as if she were dislodging the fragments of doubts lodged in there.

Flynt leant close, his mouth inches from Bobbie's ear. "You said you weren't the sentimental type," he said. "Prove it."

Rebelling against everything her body and mind seemed to be telegraphing, she drew back the trigger.

"Three... two... one."

Bobbie's eyes were focused tight on the monitors as the missile sliced effortlessly through the clouds towards its target.

"Rifle, rifle. Hellfire has left the rails," she confirmed.

Silence fell over the Box, all eyes focused on the centre monitor as the ground approached at supersonic speed.

"Contact in ten," Dawson said. "Nine, eight, seven."

Fine. It was all going to be fine. Just another day in the Box, Bobbie mouthed silently.

"Three, two, one..."

The missile ploughed into the heart of the convoy just as the rolling dirt cloud of the sandstorm did the same. A momentary flash of bright white saturated the screens. Bobbie sighed with relief as the trailing convoy came to a stop. Whoever they were, they were safe.

She was about to drop the Reaper to conduct a routine battle damage assessment when the screen seemed to implode in a bleach-white flash. The staff reeled back, as if they could feel the blast from the secondary explosion sear their faces.

It seemed to take an eternity for the screen to clear. When it finally did, Bobbie blinked several times to allow the scene to sink in. Below them a tangle of metal was strewn across the ground. Smoke drifted in thick, black billows, the desert black and scorched as if a huge blow torch had been taken to the earth.

"BDA, now!" Flynt barked.

As the camera swooped over the wreckage the collateral damage was undeniable. Spirals of metal tossed in every direction; human limbs scattered across the road like discarded doll parts. Battle damage assessment: it was the worst part of the job for a Reaper pilot. Maybe the Reaper drone was named for that very reason; you were required to reap what you sowed.

"What the bloody hell just happened?" Flynt said. "There's no way our missile caused that cluster fuck."

A solemn shaking of heads was followed by silence as the camera conducted a secondary recon over the devastation.

"We must have hit the second convoy," Dawson said.

"No. Can't have, we didn't have the fire power," Flynt said.

Dawson directed the cameras high to scour the scene; an apocalypse broadcast in 1080p high definition.

Bobbie sat bolt upright. "Zoom in, there," she said, gesturing to the lower third of the screen.

Dawson focused on a truck door flung several metres from the road, smoke rising from the steel. The camera lingered over a dust-baked cartoon image painted on the side of the door. "Road Runner? Someone's got a sick sense of humour," he said.

A cold slab of stone settled in Bobbie's stomach – the after-shock of the feeling of dread that had overcome her an hour earlier.

"Matthews?" Dawson said, noticing her thousand-yard stare.

Bobbie's words scraped dry over her throat. "It's Danvir–" she said, her voice barely a cracked whisper. "Danvir's regiment."

Dawson glanced at the 6x4 photograph taped to the hard drive closest to Bobbie. "Shit," he said, looking over the snapshot: Six uniformed officers assigned to the RAF Medical Services Branch kneeling by a truck with a Road Runner cartoon painted onto the door.

"You don't even know–"

"A wife knows," she interrupted. She stared down at the joystick – it was slick with sweat. She wanted to wrench it from its foundations, crush it until it was nothing but dust.

"Was he even–" Dawson began.

"Trust me," she said, standing, though her legs felt as if they might betray her at any moment. She pushed away her chair and walked towards the station door.

"Matthews!" Flynt said. "You require your commanding officer's permission to leave this station."

Bobbie wasn't listening. His voice was background noise as she shut the steel door behind her.

She walked to her car, steadied herself, then bent over, hands on knees, and retched. Raising her head, she looked over to the ground control station and wondered if maybe it had all been a bad dream, a nightmare she would soon wake from.

The tears pooling in her eyes and the blackness gathering deep inside her told her otherwise. A wife knew. A wife always knew.

ISLE OF ANGLESY, WALES

12 MONTHS LATER

1

Detective Inspector Tudor Manx had, by the age of forty-nine, come to accept his father's failings; they were all too human, just like his own. He'd forgiven his father for running out on his family when he did. He'd also forgiven him for the missed birthday parties and the Christmas mornings spent waiting for Tommy to recover from another hangover. He'd even absolved him for the paltry child support that arrived every few months, stuffed into thin, dirty envelopes with no return address. Manx suspected his mother had burnt them soon after they were dropped through the letter box. She didn't need the money. The kind of support Alice Manx-Williams required didn't come stuffed in envelopes with "sorry" scribbled hurriedly across them in thick marker pen.

However, the one thing Manx found harder to forgive Tommy for was his parting gift of his midnight blue, 1971 Mark III Jensen Interceptor. Not because it was a hulking, petrol-guzzling steel tank that was as impractical as it was unreliable, but because, try as he might, Manx couldn't bring himself to sell the damn car. It was the gift that kept on taking.

Manx had spent the last hour at Lloyd Lugnut's workshop.

The curmudgeonly old mechanic had lectured Manx on how he should take better care of the "old girl", and he'd guarantee the car would pass its MOT if Manx paid him £2,000 for a set of new tyres and a refurbished exhaust system from a company in Birmingham specialising in manufacturing old Jensen parts. It was at that point, as Manx scraped his jaw up from the floor, that Lloyd had suggested maybe he should consider selling.

"Classic this is. Collectors pay good money for one of these in original condition. Unless you're sentimental about the old girl, attached, like?"

Sentimental? Attached? Manx considered Lloyd's words as he glanced over the cracked leather interior and the bank of gauges – some of which he assumed still worked – set deep into the walnut dashboard. "Sentimental" wouldn't be the first adjective he'd use to describe himself. Manx was practical, that was all. Why throw money away on a new car when the Jensen transported him where he needed to be? At least most days. No, the "old girl" would suit him fine. He'd drive it until one of them gave up the ghost. Most days Manx had the unnerving feeling it would be a close call, with the Jensen having a slim margin of advantage.

This day, however, Manx's state of mind was bordering on the marginally optimistic. The morning was collar-stiff fresh, the sky deep blue with the faintest brush of high clouds. Manx, though, was taking none of this in as he drove, Lucinda Williams's "Righteously" turned up to full volume. He did take some pleasure in noticing the great ball of yellow kicking back over the Snowdonia mountain range – it was a welcome change from the persistent rain and cold of the past few weeks. It was late July, when blue skies and warm fronts were to be expected, but this, after all, was Anglesey where the weather thumbed its nose at such conventions – summers could be as balmy as the

French Riviera or as rain-soaked as a Prague winter; sometimes both in the same day.

The message he'd received an hour earlier from the desk sergeant at Llangefni Station had been cryptic. Someone named Walter Edwards had called with a report of multiple deaths on a minor road off the A55. The desk sergeant had hinted the caller sounded, in his words, "two digestives short of a full pack, boss". Typically, Manx would have left this to one of the young PCs, but the location was on his way back from Lloyd's workshop and there was little else on his docket to take care of this morning other than paperwork and a meeting with DCI Ellis Canton.

"Well, it's hardly a crime scene, is it?" Manx said, as he studied the narrow, hedge-hemmed road and what looked like hundreds of freshly dug molehills scattered across the surface. "Multiple bodies? I could book you for wasting police time."

"Thought it was your speciality," Walter said, cocking his thumbs in the pockets of his dungarees. "Dead bodies." Walter was in his mid-seventies, farmed twenty hectares close to the town of Valley.

"Dead bodies, not dead birds," Manx said, studying the gruesome scene of a hundred or so dead starlings, scattered on the ground as if they'd been thrown from the back of a lorry.

He shook his head – how the mighty had fallen. Ten months ago, Manx was the strategic lead on a high-profile human trafficking case at the Met. Now here he was trying to establish cause of death on a flock of dead starlings. Not that he'd been given much choice in the transfer; it was either a DI position on Anglesey or a swift demotion and a career logging evidence until he was pensioned off. It didn't make his situation any easier to swallow, but he hadn't yet given up on hope that he'd soon be back in London, the city fumes in his lungs; the whole concrete and brick, rotten underbelly, razor's edge splendour of it all under his fingernails. London didn't care who you were or where you came from and Manx loved the city for that. Walking the streets, he was anonymous – nobody's son, nobody's brother – just a copper doing his job and going about his business. He missed that; missed it like he missed the Capital Kebab House at 2am when he was famished and nothing else was open; missed it like he missed the crowds piling out from the pubs onto Camden High Street on a Friday night, and the rush of a well-executed raid and arrest in some murky Soho underground gambling den. There was plenty more he missed about the city, but mentally ticking off that laundry list was a hiding to nothing – he'd been down that road too many times over the past ten months – and anyway, he had the mysterious demise of a hundred starlings to attend to.

"Saw 'em last night," Walter explained, gesturing at the litter of cadavers. "I was driving back from the shops, hundreds of them in the sky doing that murmuration; beautiful it was. Drove past this morning, they're all dead. Never seen anything like it."

Manx nodded. "It's a mystery no doubt, but this kind of thing's handled by the RSPB and Animal and Plant Health Agency."

"But if someone shot them, then it'd be a crime, yeah?"

Manx squatted, found a twig and turned over three of the birds. "No gunshot wounds."

Walter craned his neck up to the cloudless blue sky. "It's like they all committed suicide or something."

"A mass starling suicide? That'd be a first."

Walter beckoned Manx to come closer. "Either that, or it's the bloody RAF. You've got to wonder what goes on over at that base, yeah?" he said, lowering his voice. "Probably some top-secret project they don't want us knowing about killed them."

"Come down to the station and one of our PCs will take your statement," Manx said, getting ready to leave.

"Unsettled me good and proper, this has."

"There's probably a rational explanation. Always is," Manx assured him.

Walter folded his arms tight across his belly. "It's a bad omen, I can feel it in my bones."

Manx wasn't the superstitious type but looking over the carrion carpeting the road, he had to agree with the old farmer – it was enough to send a cold shudder through anyone's bones.

2

"I don't regret killing any of them, if that's what you're asking."
As Bobbie Matthews spoke, a fast jet rattled the windows of the Base Commander's office, belly-rolling low over the RAF Valley airstrip before thundering across the deep green countryside towards the grey outline of the Snowdonia mountains. For the past three days a rare heatwave had settled itself over Anglesey; the sun warm but not searing; the breeze off the Irish Sea cooling but not bracing; the nights balmy but not stifling. Above the commander's desk, the draught from air conditioning wafted down in a steady stream, ruffling the loose papers in his inbox.

Bobbie studied the two men sitting across from her – her former overseer at Waddington, Base Commander James Flynt, who'd been transferred to RAF Valley ten months previously, and Doctor Andrew (Call Me Andy) Pierce.

Pierce was in his late thirties, with a studious, pinched face. He and Bobbie had trained together at RAF Cranwell, but their careers had taken different forks off the same road. Bobbie had found her calling sitting in the pilot's seat with 700 pounds of state-of-the-art weaponry under her command. Call Me Andy had become an RAF clinical psychologist and a chaplain, finding his calling sat behind a desk and dispensing words of comfort at the pulpit. He was the dual-doctorate type the RAF preferred to assign to cases like hers, versed in both theology and psychology – if God couldn't provide the answers, then maybe medical science could.

She'd spent three afternoons a week for the past ten months sitting across from Call Me Andy as he conducted his Trauma Risk Management (TRiM) assessment: required counselling for any drone pilot suspected of suffering from post-traumatic stress disorder. Maybe Flynt had thought she was more likely to bare her soul to someone she knew; a friend.

Bobbie had found the opposite to be true.

Call Me Andy had always made her feel uncomfortable, as if he were constantly studying her, looking for an opening to access her secret doors and passageways. She suspected back at Cranwell he'd had a crush on her but had never made his feelings known. During their counselling sessions, she'd often catch his eyes roaming the hem of her skirt or casting their gaze over her legs when he suspected her attention was diverted elsewhere. If he'd been doing his job, he'd have known Bobbie's attention was never diverted.

Bobbie ran a finger over the plastic gems glued to her headset resting in her lap, rubbing them like a talisman – today she needed all the luck she could get and then some. Call Me Andy had insisted the meeting was just a formality and Flynt was more than likely to keep her combat-ready status as temporarily suspended rather than permanently revoked. Despite his assurances, Bobbie couldn't recall a time she'd felt more anxious, or more powerless.

Flynt peered through his glasses, his ruddy, lean face scrunched in concentration as he studied the report, each flick of the page like the loud pop of a gunshot behind Bobbie's eyes. As he read, she glanced at the photograph on Flynt's desk. The wife, she imagined. A pleasant-looking woman, with a kind smile set across a soft face.

Bobbie had never been soft. She had a more brittle presence that seemed engineered to poke the world in the eye rather than fold unquestioningly to its order. Above her right eyebrow, a small purple birthmark bloomed like an ink blot. People would tell her she had a pretty face, but she'd argue it was more capable than pretty: wide cheekbones, firm chin, and deep, chestnut-coloured eyes. People had also told Bobbie she was too serious, that she should smile more. Those were mostly men, of course. It was pointless insisting that from where she sat the world was a serious place – more serious than they could ever imagine. But men liked to imagine they could fix things, especially her.

A few minutes passed before Flynt set the report back on the table. "I'm not one to mince my words, Matthews. I'll take Andrew's recommendations on board, but as your commanding officer I'm charged with making the final decision."

Bobbie pushed her palms deeper into the crust of gems as Flynt read aloud from the report.

"Flashbacks, insomnia, severe irritation, often developing into anger when questioned about your actions on the day in question, feelings of guilt." He turned to Pierce. "I'm not a doctor, but these are the key indicators of PTSD, correct?"

"Em... it's more complicated. Maybe with more time, myself and Flight Lieutenant Matthews could address the issues more fully," Pierce offered. "I'd highly recommend keeping the temporary suspension in place for now."

"No, I don't think so," Flynt said, shaking his head.

"Don't do this," Bobbie said, her voice barely a whisper.

"And what about all this correspondence?" Flynt stabbed his finger at a thick wedge of papers on the desk. "Twenty-four letters, including transcripts of multiple phone calls to senior officers at Air Command Headquarters demanding what you call the truth about Operation Vanguard. What the bloody hell were you playing at?"

"The report is flawed, sir."

Flynt sat back, and for a moment Bobbie imagined she saw a flicker of hesitation in Flynt's eyes; a deliberate pause to ensure his words came out exactly as he intended. "No, Matthews, it is not flawed." He regained his poise and pointed at Bobbie. "I was there. The only thing flawed in that report was omitting the fact that the bloody Yanks failed to inform us that there were more insurgents in the area. Those bad actors detonated an IED, killed our lads. That, Matthews, is the truth of it."

"With all due respect, sir, you're incorrect. Neither Waddington nor Creech reported sightings of additional insurgents. My husband did not die at the hands of enemy combatants. I will not stop asking RAF Command for the truth of what happened. I owe that to Danvir."

Flynt shook his head. "You do realise you're making this decision a hell of a lot easier for me."

"No!" Bobbie said, her fists bunching. "Please, don't do this."

"Come on, Matthews, this can't be news to you. Any other active combat officer exhibiting these symptoms and I'd have had them marched off-base and into a psychiatric facility months ago."

"I think we should talk about this, sir," Pierce said, turning to face Flynt. "Bobbie's case is complex, she's making great breakthroughs, under my continued counselling–"

Flynt interrupted. "I've given her the benefit of the doubt, that grace period is now over, Pierce."

Bobbie's skin snapped tight around her bones. "You were there that day, sir. You ordered me to pull the trigger."

Flynt's eyes hardened. "And I stand by that order."

"And you were given a Base Commander position while I get

sent off to a psychiatric ward then administrative duties. It's not what I signed up for, sir."

Flynt laid his forearms across the desk. "Flight Lieutenant Matthews, you are permanently relieved of your combat-ready status."

Bobbie's eyes were moist as she turned to Pierce. "Andrew?"

"Sir, this is a mistake," Pierce said, sitting forward. "Flight Lieutenant Matthews has served with distinction. She was one of the few drone pilots to receive a medal in Operation Shader. She's a valuable asset in our war on terror."

"So are the five other drone pilots graduating this month. The RAF thanks you for your dedication and service, but your days flying combat missions are over. I've made arrangements for you to attend a residential veterans psychiatric facility in Liverpool, they're expecting you in two weeks. Maybe they'll succeed where Pierce failed. In the meantime, take some time off."

Bobbie composed herself, kept the tears from flowing. "If it's all the same to you, sir, I'd rather be busy."

"Suit yourself, Matthews, I can't force you to take a holiday, but I will insist you continue your therapy with Pierce. That, as they say, is non-negotiable."

Bobbie stood. "If that's all, sir, I'd like to be excused."

Flynt nodded and dismissed her with a casual wave of his arm.

Outside, the morning held the ominous promise of a bright, warm day – a heavy sky brimming with grey clouds would have suited Bobbie's mood far better. She watched a clutch of fast jet pilots fresh from their flight simulator training walk past laughing and wondered if she'd ever feel anything close to that sense of elation and optimism again. For the past year all she'd felt was a growing darkness, like a shadow casting itself inside her. She heard Call Me Andy shouting her name.

"Bobbie, I just wanted to say–"

"Say what, Andrew?" she said, turning sharply.

Pierce ran a hand through his hair. "I wanted to apologise. Flynt made the wrong decision. I can appeal, write another report."

"Why? Why would you do that, Andrew?"

"Well, I consider us friends, not just colleagues." He paused and gestured to the flag fluttering above the base Welfare Hub. "Remember the motto they drilled into us in basic training?"

"Of course," she said, her hands tapping impatiently on her headset. "*Per ardua ad astra*. Why is that relevant?"

"Through adversity to the stars," Pierce said, placing his hands across her shoulders. "You'll come through this, Bobbie, you're one of the strongest women I know. Have faith... in yourself."

Bobbie winced at the clumsy attempt to bring his god into the conversation. Where faith was concerned, Bobbie's coffers were as good as spent, had been for some time now. When she'd joined the RAF, she'd been young and idealistic with a vague hope of making some kind of difference in the world. That Bobbie Matthews had died twelve months ago on a dust-ridden road south of Mosul and wouldn't be resurrected anytime soon.

"Here, take this," she said, handing Pierce her headset. "I won't be needing it anymore."

3

Stripes, yellow ball nine, gave a satisfying clank as it barrelled into the middle pocket of the pool table. The ancient transistor radio perched on the windowsill played a rousing Welsh folk song. Next to the radio a half-smoked joint fizzled lazily, the ash flaking onto the cracked green enamel of the radiator below.

Melvin Powell set himself up for his next shot. He was in his early sixties, chest thick like a Rottweiler, and a solid beer paunch spilling over his red dragon belt buckle. Back in the day, Melvin was lean and muscular with a hard, chiselled face that seemed sculpted to absorb the force of a well-driven punch. At the age of twenty-one, Melvin had been a fast and wiry welter-weight with enough promise to earn himself the moniker of "The Great Welsh Hope". But those days were long gone, ancient history in Melvin's book, as was the motorcycle accident which had crushed the bones of his right hand and taken him out of the ring for good. Forty years later, he still held himself like the contender he could have been; eyes hard, posture hunched and closed as if he were bracing himself for the next punch to land.

He looked through the window. The pub sign, "The Lantern Arms", swung in the soft breeze. He'd been renting the back room of the pub for two years now. It was a former stable, but Melvin just referred to it as the "shit-hole", and that suited him just fine; people didn't poke their noses around shit-holes. The rent was cheap, and the landlady didn't ask too many questions. He suspected she was sympathetic to the cause, but they'd never talked about it. They'd screwed though, plenty of times, but the subject never came up – some people preferred to turn their backs on shit they rather not know about. Lydia enjoyed the smokes, though, bought at least five joints a week. Maybe she wasn't sympathetic and just liked keeping her dealer close to hand. No matter. So long as he was screwing her, keeping Lydia happy, he was guaranteed free pints and pub lunches most days; a win–win situation in his book.

Lydia was ten years younger than Mel and could still carry off a tight T-shirt and jeans without looking like mutton dressed as lamb. He'd moved in with her to the flat above the pub six months ago with a promise to sign his name on the lease. He was still thinking on it. If he agreed, he wouldn't start pandering to tourists looking for sustainably raised chickens, gin cocktails, and fresh fucking fish platters. He'd keep it real: a pub run by the Welsh, for the Welsh.

Melvin re-chalked and leant low over the table, catching a whiff of stale ash and beer soaked into the baize. He was set to hammer the cue ball when he felt a sharp tug at the back of his head. He spun around.

Ronnie Powell took a step back, held his belly and laughed. "You should see your face, bloody picture it is. By the way, got a call for you." Ronnie raised his mobile as Melvin checked out his reflection in the mirror on the far wall.

"Yeah? Who?"

"1983," Ronnie chuckled. "Says it wants its haircut back."

Melvin smoothed his palms over his hair and tugged on the elastic wrapped around the grey ponytail that hung six inches below his neckline. He adjusted his shirt collar and brushed a dusting of chalk from his dark-rinse Levi jeans. "You're a fuckin' moron. What if you'd been the cops? I could have beat the shit out of you."

Ronnie backed away; his hands held high in mock surrender. "Pigs don't come here, do they? Way off their patch."

"What do you want? You look like a tramp, as bloody usual. You should smarten up, get some bloody decent clothes for a start, show some respect for yourself."

Ronnie shrugged. "I don't feed the corporate fashion machine. Buy all my clothes from the Oxfam shop. Recycling, it is."

Melvin shook his head. His nephew was twenty-three, wiry and hard like Melvin used to be, with a beard he was still growing into. "Make yourself useful and brew us a fresh one," he said, gesturing at the sorry collection of stained and chipped mugs on the table.

Ronnie pulled on the joint. "I'm not your errand boy."

Melvin ran the cue tip along Ronnie's chest, applying a small amount of pressure. "Got yourself a better offer? A job?"

Ronnie shrugged, looked to the floor.

"Didn't think so. Kettle, teabags, mug. Even you can't fuck that up. And don't forget to use the right bloody socket," Melvin said, snapping the joint from the lad's lips.

Ronnie parried away the cue. "All right, but only because you're an old fart and I feel sorry for you." He unplugged the radio and connected the kettle plug to the only working socket in the room. Mel's mobile chirped to life.

"That her?" Ronnie said. "Thought you were done doing favours, it's not like she's family."

"Tea. Now," Melvin said, brushing off a flurry of cue chalk from his shirt and stepping outside.

As Ronnie threw the teabags into the mugs, a twist of anger cast itself in his gut. Or was it envy? Sometimes it was hard to tell them apart. All he knew for certain was that he'd been loyal to Mel for years, been like a son to him, and this was how he repaid him.

It had been weeks since he and his uncle had gone out lamping together. He missed it; missed the camaraderie of two men against nature, driving into the dead of night on the Arctic Wildcat Quad Bike Mel had bought, though he rarely drove these days, preferring to let Ronnie take the driving seat. Ronnie hardly cared if they shot anything; he lived for the thrill of the hunt. If he was lucky and skewered a perfectly aimed bolt in the warm belly of a rabbit or a fox, so much the better, it was something to brag about later over a few beers. Those were the moments he hunted for; Mel and him watching the dawn breaking through the tree branches, a chorus of birdsong heralding the sunrise over the island.

Mel had first taken him lamping when Ronnie was a teenager, taught him how to tune his senses to the forest floor, trained him how to rig his crossbow in the pitch dark, showed him the importance of double-checking his range estimation before firing the bolt; insisted that the best nights for hunting were those when the dark was thick with blackness and the wind rustled in hurried, whistling gasps through the trees and hedges.

But his uncle had also taught him much more.

Mel had taken Ronnie in when he was most in need of a steady guiding hand – even if that hand would sometimes clench to a fist that found a fast trajectory to Ronnie's cheekbone. He never doubted he deserved it when Melvin snapped him with a punch he'd never see coming. His father, Dafydd Powell, was a fan of the more drawn out approach to punishment. Most nights, Dafydd had come home full of bile and beer, itching for a fight he'd been unable to kick-off in the local. Ronnie had learnt not to put up a fight; it was easier that way. Melvin had taken him away from all that, raised him as near to a son as any man could, just the two of them sharing the old cottage near Church Bay. But since Yoko fuckin' Ono had come on the scene she'd upset the dynamic. Not that she was Japanese, Ronnie just called her that behind his uncle's back; it made him feel better, like he had some control over the situation.

Mel returned a few minutes later, unlocked the cupboard and took out both Ten Point Titan crossbows, laying them on the pool table. "Clean these. Remember to check the retention spring and lubricate the flight groove."

Ronnie reached for an old rag. "More fuckin' favours?"

"She's a friend, met her at the pub, she needed my help, end of," Melvin said.

"Lydia know about her, then? This fancy woman–"

Before Ronnie could finish, Melvin stepped forward with the speed of a prize fighter, wrapped his thick fingers around his nephew's neck and pushed him up against the wall. "You keep that big mouth of yours shut, got it?"

"All right, calm down, give yourself a heart attack," Ronnie mumbled. He glanced at the tattoo on the back of Melvin's hand: *Cymru am Byth* – Wales Forever; it pulsed with the throb of his thick veins. Ronnie would often forget how strong his uncle was – like a prize bull, all muscle and coiled-up energy.

Melvin leant in close. "You want to keep working for me? Earn your beer money? Keep it shut," he said, cupping his fingers into a tight grip around his nephew's chin.

"Yeah, yeah, keep your hair on."

He released his grip. "The lads all set for tomorrow night?"

"Yeah, told them to be here by seven."

Melvin leant against the pool table. "It's a fucking plan this is. A real plan."

"The brotherhood know about this plan of yours, then?"

"They'll know when they need to know."

"If you ask me, they won't want to take things this far."

"Good job nobody's asking you, then," Melvin said. "You got that tea brewed yet?"

Tea? Errand Boy? Ronnie's blood peaked to boiling for the second time that morning. Only this time he kept his mouth shut, kept it locked down.

"Three sugars, yeah?" he said, grabbing the cue ball and shooting it down the green baize. It rattled against one of the corner pockets before dropping into the net.

He'd bide his time, just like his uncle had taught him back in the woods, waiting for rabbits to bolt from their warrens and into the blinding glare of the spotlight. Yeah, there'd be plenty of time to prove Melvin Powell wrong, surprise the old bastard with a plan of his own one day.

4

The road's narrow gulley came fast as Bobbie throttled over the rough country lanes. Nine fifteen at night, the final remnants of dusk vanishing into the darkness. Sleep had been hard to come by lately and tearing her Golf GTI through the roads Bobbie had known growing up was as therapeutic as any medication or empty words Call Me Andy had proffered.

Ahead, a tight right-hand corner. She slipped into second, powering down on the accelerator as she exited the apex of the curve. The back end of the Golf twitched, before snapping back into line for the upcoming straight. The needle nudging seventy-five, the headlights caught something blocking the road some twenty metres ahead. Bobbie braced herself and slammed the brake pedal. The tyres skidded on the muddy surface as if it were made of ice. Nineteen metres later, the car came to a sharp stop. She looked up. Staring back at her, two soulful eyes of a huge black bull that had wandered into the road. Bobbie and the creature locked eyes for a few short heartbeats before the beast seemed to shrug its powerful shoulders and saunter back into the field. She let out the breath she'd been holding on to and slipped back into first gear.

Thirty minutes later, Bobbie found herself in the town of Trearddur Bay. She'd parked across from a large detached house with floor-to-ceiling windows and a distinctive 1970s box-like design. She knew the occupants. She'd been invited here by Flynt and his wife for a housewarming party a year ago. Bobbie had attended with the hope of catching Flynt off-guard, press him on the truth about Operation Vanguard, but the sight of Flynt relishing all the attention had turned her stomach. She'd slunk out through the back door after thirty minutes, figuring correctly she wouldn't be missed.

Why the hell was she parked outside his house? No doubt Call Me Andy would have a few theories, but she had one of her own. Bobbie had always believed peace was only ever achieved through balance. Bad actors needed to be neutralised – it was what kept that balance in check. That's why she'd never hesitated in pulling the trigger, not once, other than her last day in the Ground Control Centre. "I stop the bad guys before they kill the good guys." It was a phrase one of the drone pilots at Creech had said to her one night over beers; it had stuck with her ever since. Since Danvir's death, Bobbie's world was seriously off-kilter, and she was sure Flynt held the key to restoring that balance. She'd never bought into the RAF's report on Operation Vanguard and suspected Flynt felt the same, but he'd probably followed the party line in exchange for a fat promotion. He'd also requested Bobbie was transferred to Valley at the same time; far easier to keep an eye on her when she was under his jurisdiction, she imagined.

She made up her mind to knock on his door, demand to speak with Flynt, try to persuade him to reverse his decision, keep her suspension temporary, and allow her to stay at Valley. As much as Call Me Andy irritated her, he was familiar, and he was manageable. She wasn't sick, not in the way Flynt and Pierce insisted she was. It was grief and in time she'd get over it, but for that to happen she needed to find the truth; armed with the truth she could move on with her life, whatever the hell that looked like. But maybe there was never any such thing as closure and death itself always had the last laugh; death, the ultimate closure.

Her hand was on the door handle, her foot ready to step out, when Flynt, wearing his service dress, left the house walked to his car and pulled out from the driveway. A light flicked on in the upstairs bedroom. Bobbie looked up as someone pulled back a slip of curtain. The soft outline of a face appeared behind the glass and stayed there for a minute before stepping back into the shadows. By the time Bobbie looked back to the road, the red blur of Flynt's tail lights had already disappeared into the descending darkness.

5

As Manx entered Benllech town centre, the squeal of worn brake pads against rough steel cut through the morning air. He'd narrowly avoided driving into a family lugging sand buckets, spades, beach blankets, ice coolers, umbrellas, and two large, multi-coloured windbreakers across the road. *Obviously professionals*, he thought, *prepared for whatever the day would bring*. The mother – harried and scowl-faced – threw him a dirty look, grabbed her kids and yanked them towards the hill leading down to the beach.

Manx had forgotten it was the school holidays: with no children of his own, those seasonal measures of time typically passed him by. His sister, Sara, had reminded him of this fact just yesterday, though her statement was more of a complaint than it was information. Her grievance concerned the length of the summer holidays and what she was expected to do with her seven-year-old son, Dewi, for six weeks, and if Manx had an ounce of paternal instinct he would offer to help. Manx agreed; he possessed no paternal instinct. Sara had told him to "grow the hell up" before hanging up. It was the typical ebb and flow of their relationship; his sister expecting more, Manx failing to deliver. One day maybe the tide would turn but he wasn't holding his breath.

A few minutes later, the Jensen parked at the beach, he inched up the windows. At 8.15am, it was already too warm for his regular wardrobe of a black sports jacket, black trousers, white cotton shirt and a thin, black tie knotted loosely so it hung an inch or so below his undone top button.

It was low tide, the sea drawn back to reveal a six-pack torso of sand. Across the sand, a scattering of seagulls and cormorants picked at whatever bounty the ocean had left in its wake. At the entrance, PC Kevin Priddle, arms stretched wide like a scarecrow costumed in a high visibility jacket, tried to appease a pack of dog-walkers complaining about the interruption to their routine.

"Nothing to see here, please move away." Priddle's long, pale face was pulled into a grimace as he sized up the gang, who looked as if they might make a run for the beach at any moment.

A gruff man with a hyperactive border collie at his ankles, spoke. "Why you lot here then, if there's nothing to see?" He craned his neck, trying to peer past Priddle.

"Nothing for the public to see, sir," he emphasised. "Police business. I'm asking you nicely to move away, please. Now."

The man searched for a fresh angle. "We'll just walk on other side," he said, gesturing at a patch of sand under the cliffs. "No one's minding over there."

"You could," Manx said, stepping into the man's personal space. "Then we'd have to arrest you."

The man pulled his dog to heel. At six foot three, Manx had perfected the art of intimidation without needing to lift a finger. "Your choice. Find another beach or I'll have you escorted to the station. We're short-staffed, what with all this activity, so it'll take a few hours to get you processed. But if you're game, I'm game."

The man tugged at his cap and spat on the pavement. "Be on

the news anyway." He yanked on the dog's lead, taking his time walking back to his van, glimpsing over the beach in the hope of a sneak peek of this evening's headline story.

A flush of red bloomed across Priddle's cheeks. "Cheers, like, but there was no need. I was about to read him the riot act myself."

"Balls," Manx said, resting a hand on the PC's shoulder. "About time you grew a pair. Do your job and keep the looky-loos in the car park until we give the all-clear."

Manx turned towards the activity further down the beach.

Detective Sergeant Malcolm Nader marched towards him. "Bread of Bevan's just got here," he said, gesturing to Ashton Bevan, lead CSI, and his team stepping into their over-suits.

"That's going to put a dent in the day's deckchair rentals," Manx said, ducking nimbly under the police cordon. "Details?"

Nader wiped a sop of sweat from his brow. "Dog walker called it in. In a right state she was, took forever to calm her down. She's with Minor getting the full-on victim support."

PC Delyth Morris was on a nearby bench, wrapping a blanket around an elderly woman petting a terrier on her lap.

"Any positive ID on the body?"

"Not yet, but shouldn't take too long, you'll see for yourself."

As Manx stepped over the metal plates the CSI team had set out several metres across the sand, Bevan shot out his arm. "Any closer and I'll have to insist you don one of our over-suits, Manx," he said, barely looking at the inspector.

"Good morning to you, too, Bevan."

Manx looked at the body laid on the sand. Male, the right leg contorted as if it had come loose from the knee socket, his left arm at a right angle to his shoulder, also probably dislocated. From several metres away he could see the man's right temple was bloodied, the skin split open, tendrils of what he imagined was brain matter leaking from the wound. Nader was right: securing a positive ID on the man shouldn't take more than a couple of phone calls. He was wearing a dark blue suit with three stripes on the arms. On the cuffs, a dark band with white stitching. Tracking down the front of his jacket, three brass buttons that ended at the stable belt which was unclipped. His shirt was a lighter blue, fastened to the top button with a black tie in a classic Windsor knot. Above his left jacket pocket, a finely stitched gold emblem of wings and crown surrounded by a blue laurel wreath. Manx recognised it immediately. Royal Air Force service dress.

"The beach is off limits until we give the all-clear," Manx said.

"That'll go down like shit on a doorstep," Nader huffed. "Council'll be on the blower to El Vera before morning's done."

Manx took in a deep inhale of salt-tinged air. Detective Chief Superintendent Vera Troup was top of the food chain at the North Wales Constabulary. Her pale, vampire-like complexion and raven-black hair had earned her the nickname of El Vera amongst the local coppers. She was well connected; a modern breed of DCSIs who liked to cosy up to the local power players; players that included the county council and the more influential business owners and politicians on the island. It was her take on community policing: the closer you were to those wielding power the easier it was to keep tabs on them.

"Put these on, I've got one for each of you," Bevan said, snatching a pair of over-suits from one of his techs. "Unless you clumsy lot have already contaminated the scene, which is highly likely," he added with an ugly smirk that Manx had, on more than one occasion, wanted to smack off Bevan's smug face.

"I think the tide probably beat us to it," Manx said. "Unless you can hold back the sea for a few more hours."

"Aye, or walk across the bloody thing," Nader muttered, just loud enough for Bevan to hear.

Bevan ignored the barbs – they were just noise to him by now. "We'll find something," he said, directing his techs to get to work. "Tide or no tide, if there's human remains chances are some other human's left something of interest."

After Manx instructed Nader and Morris to begin the necessary drudgery of door-to-doors, he noticed a car parked across from the beach. It was the only vehicle in the car park. He crossed the road, walked around the silver Audi A7, and peered through the windows. The keys were still on the centre console, the doors unlocked. On the passenger seat, what Manx recognised as a blue RAF officer's cap.

6

Detective Chief Inspector Ellis Canton's desk was typically a cluttered affair. Today, however, DI Manx was struck by its neatness. No scattering of papers, half-eaten packs of mints or illegible notes littering the desk, just a large white gift box wrapped with a thick black ribbon which Canton was in the process of snipping with a pair of pruning shears.

"If you're feeling inspired," Manx said, settling into the chair. "Mine could do with a bit of a clear-out."

Canton smiled as if he were in the midst of some meaningful meditation from which Manx had just disturbed him. "Happiness, Manx, is a place between too little and too much," he said, reading a quote from a card he'd slipped from inside the box, before tucking it carefully under the fold of ribbon.

"Is it your birthday? I don't remember signing a card."

Canton shook his large, bald head, which in the heat seemed to have garnered an extra patina of shine. "Study material," he said, dragging the box closer. "Arrived this morning."

"Looks a bit fancy for the force, or are they upping their game in the continuing education department?"

Canton brought his palms together. "Do you know it takes six years of training to become a Bonsai Master, Manx?"

"Better get on it then, Ellis, you're not getting any younger."

"None of us are." Canton tapped a finger on the box. "Bonsai Master in six months or my money back."

"Do you get a certificate or something?"

"Several," Canton confirmed. "I've already made space." He gestured to a blank space on his wall. "Positive thinking. Make space for the things you desire, and they will appear."

"Oh, right. So, if I leave out an empty glass it'll get filled with single malt scotch? That kind of positive thinking?"

"You've never felt the urge for enlightenment, Manx?"

"Can't say I have, Ellis."

"Hm," he said, looking at the inspector as if he were searching for something of value but had come up empty-handed. He pushed back his chair. "Vera's already been chewing my ear off about this business down at Benllech."

"To be expected."

Canton pulled himself up in a series of groans. "Closing down the beach? I told her you must have had a bloody good reason. Convince me I was right."

"Dead body, Bevan's on the fence on the COD. We'll get a clearer picture once Hardacre's completed the autopsy."

Canton brushed the leaves of an azalea Bonsai tree. "ID?"

"The victim was wearing RAF service dress. Nader's following up with Valley to see if they're missing an officer. If not, we'll contact the administrative base at High Wycombe."

"Good man," Canton said. "Now, take a look at this," he added, sliding a slip of paper from his inbox. "Preliminary fire investigation origin and cause reports came in this morning."

Manx glanced at the document. "The holiday homes?"

"None of them were occupied at the time, though I'd put that down to good fortune rather than good planning."

"So, what are we looking at, arson?"

"Appears so," Canton agreed. "The fire inspector's at the location of the latest one this afternoon. Might be a good time for you to introduce yourself."

Manx laid the document back on the table. "Any link between the homes? Same owners? Management company?"

"Nothing conclusive, other than they were all available on those holiday home listing sites. None of them were owned by anyone living on the island, except the latest one, which was owned and managed by Logan Collins."

"Should I know him?"

"Local politician, running for election. Conservative."

"Well, there's your motive right there," Manx said, smiling.

Canton narrowed his eyes. "Best keep an open mind, eh? And give the investigators any help they need."

"Anything else?"

Canton slid open a drawer and took out an A4 poster which he flattened across his desk. "Since you ask."

Manx checked out the lettering, which was colourful and in a bold, capitalised font. "What in God's name is a Food Slam?" he asked, turning over the paper and hoping for some further clarity on the flip side. There was none, just a roll call of names and logos of a handful of local businesses sponsoring the event.

"Somewhere you need to be this Thursday evening. Vera requested you, specifically."

Manx sensed another Canton ambush. "To do what, exactly?"

"Be the friendly face of the North Wales Constabulary. Bring Morris along, add a female touch to the proceedings."

"I'm a bit busy, Ellis, what with all this–"

"Three hours at most. Hand out a few leaflets, play nice with the locals and tourists. It's Vera's big summer initiative, she's even got a catchphrase for the whole shebang."

"A catchphrase? Do I want to know?"

"Just Ask A Copper," Canton said, grimacing.

"That's original. Can't you–"

Canton's cheeks quivered as he shook his head. "I'd hate to disappoint my boss. She doesn't respond well to the word no."

"I know the feeling," Manx said, folding the poster and slipping it in his pocket.

Canton rubbed his hands together. "That's the spirit."

"You owe me, Ellis."

"Put it on the tab. And close the door on your way out, my trees require a constant temperature."

"Yes… master," Manx replied, drawing the door closed with a reverent and graceful pull.

7

"Busy afternoon ahead," Manx said, sitting on the edge of his desk. "Any uplifting news to share from the door-to-doors?"

DS Nader shrugged. "Dead-end. We interviewed seventy-two people; nobody saw a bloody thing."

"Load of tourists not too happy being woken up first thing," Morris said. "Same with the locals. Nobody noticed anything suspicious, except for this one pensioner who reckoned he saw something unusual in the sky that morning."

"And?" Manx prompted.

"Told me it was big, yellow and shiny, until I realised, he meant the sun."

Nader chuckled. "Good one, that."

"There's a couple in every pack," Manx said. "Now, Bevan's estimate puts our victim in the water for at least twelve hours. Hardacre should give us a more definitive cause of death, but in the meantime take another shot at the door-to-doors. Ask if anyone saw anything suspicious on Sunday night not just this morning. Someone must have seen or heard something. We have no CCTV of the beach, and until we get a positive ID on the victim, very little to go on."

"So a dead-end, boss," Nader said. "Now what?"

"We keep looking until we find something that isn't a dead-end. We need to find out who the hell this is," he said, pinning a photo of the body to the board. "Morris, pull up any missing person's reports in the past week. Nader, keep on RAF Valley's arse, they must know if they're missing an officer or two by now."

A rumbling of "yes boss" echoed through the room.

"By the way, boss," Nader said, pushing back his chair. "Anything you want me to follow up on those dead starlings over by Valley? Everyone's asking about them."

"Do they have a next of kin we need to inform? IDs we need to verify?"

"Erm... no," Nader said.

"Then we let the RSPB and the Animal and Plant Health lads handle it."

"It's all over the papers," Nader said, showing a copy of today's *Daily Post* front page. "All kinds of theories, the wife's Facebook feed's full of it."

Manx grabbed his jacket from behind the chair. "The press are magpies, Nader, something new and shiny will have caught their attention by tomorrow, so let's get an ID on this victim. Priorities, let's stick to them, eh?"

8

Manx pulled up next to the charred remains of the cottage and glanced over at the camera crew gathered at the front gate. As he exited the Jensen, the crew briefly looked him over, then turned their attention back to their phones.

He checked out the naked shell of the building, which was covered in a layer of black soot. The roof had disintegrated, as had the windows, leaving holes that reminded him of dead men's eyes; empty and cold. The iron beams remained and ran the length of the cottage to meet at the chimney stack which was leaning dangerously sideways.

"Unless you're looking to find out what it's like to be buried under a few hundred pounds of bricks, I'd move back if I were you."

Manx turned as a man with a clipboard approached. He was under five feet tall, wearing a hard hat and possessed an officious manner. "The fire's drawn the moisture from the mortar, so there's no glue holding the structure together. One wrong move and the stack's likely to collapse, right about where you're standing."

Manx complied, stepped back. “Long shot,” he said, “but you wouldn’t happen to be the fire inspector?”

“And you’d be the copper Canton said he was sending over?”

“Detective Inspector Tudor Manx.”

“Rhys Hopkins, Chief Fire Investigator,” he said, flipping up the badge attached to his vest.

“Your report concluded arson?”

“Aye, just like the other four. They used the same accelerant: paint thinner. Just splashed the stuff everywhere and hoped it would catch. Definitely arsonist amateur hour.”

“Any security cameras on the property?”

“They’d be ashes by now if there were.”

“You think it was kids maybe? A prank?”

Rhys tapped the clipboard with his pen. “Kids? Not likely.”

“But you’re convinced the attacks are connected?”

“No doubt.”

“And they were all holiday homes?”

“They were all listed on those online sites, we checked.”

“You’ve lived on the island all your life?” Manx asked.

“Why’s that important?”

“Wasn’t there something similar back in the eighties? Welsh nationalists burning down holiday homes? They set the Britannia Bridge on fire too, if I recall?”

“I’d just signed up for the service,” Rhys said. “Huge bloody fire, the Britannia Bridge, but it wasn’t Welsh nationalists, just a bunch of kids playing silly buggers with matches. The flames caught on the bridge, then when the tar started to melt onto the trees, that’s when the real fireworks kicked off. Nine hours it took us to get it under control. Never seen anything like it before or since.”

“But the holiday home fires, they weren’t kids?”

Rhys shook his head. “Welsh freedom fighters, if I recall.

Nasty buggers too, made bombs too, shoved them through English MPs' letter boxes, miracle nobody died."

"Do you think these new fires could be connected?"

"No idea, but I'll tell you this," he said, rocking back on the heels of his boots. "A fire needs three things to ignite; heat, fuel and oxygen. Take one of those things away, and there's no fire."

"I'm not sure what you're getting at."

Rhys placed his clipboard in the crook of his arm. "If someone's taking up the cause forty years later, you can be sure something ignited that spark, gave it oxygen. People don't usually set fire to houses without a bloody good reason."

The news crew suddenly jumped to action as a car pulled up. A tall, well put-together man exited a grey BMW 5 series, fastened the middle button of his jacket and stood, camera ready, in front of the house.

"The owner," Rhys explained "Logan Collins, Conservative, running for election later this year."

"So I heard."

Manx stepped closer as Collins addressed the camera and spoke with the practised ease of a politician. "I've said this before, but it bears repeating. This kind of criminal activity will not be tolerated. Behind me is what remains of the home my wife and I spent two years of our lives restoring. There are no words to convey our sense of loss, but I assure you, if I'm elected as Anglesey's next Member of Parliament I will make it my priority to work closely with the police to make sure nobody else's hard work and sacrifice ends up in ruins."

"And any messages to whoever did this?" a reporter asked.

Collins turned his face to the cottage, composed himself, and turned to face the camera. "Progress is inevitable. Anglesey is a vibrant community. Don't think you can stop progress, don't think you can roll back the tide, and don't for one second think you'll get away with this. You break the law; you pay the price. It's that simple. Thank you."

Manx watched Collins scuttle back to his car and drive away.

"If he was Welsh, he'd have half a chance of getting elected," Rhys said.

"And because he's not?"

"May as well piss on a bonfire for all the good it'll do him. Right, best be getting off."

As Manx made a final circle of the property, the stench of burnt wood still pungent, he thought on Collins' words. Manx had a deep mistrust of any politician, no matter the party affiliation, but he found himself agreeing with Collins. Wanton property destruction and risking lives in the name of nationalism made him sick to his stomach. He'd always fallen on the side of George Bernard Shaw when it came to that sort of thing: "patriotism is your conviction that this country is superior to all other countries because you were born in it." If that made him less of a Welshman and more of a human being, then so be it. Amongst many of his character flaws, it was one he could comfortably live with.

Manx had left Wales over thirty years ago, hightailed it down to London with a small dream and an Adidas bag packed with clothes and his favourite mix tapes. It had become clear to Manx early in his police career that killers, hardened criminals, or just your average arsehole with a chip on his shoulder and a taste for violence, were, at their core, the same no matter where they came from.

The Glaswegian "hard bastards" always ready with a Doc Marten to the bollocks and a knuckleduster to the nose when the chance came and the price was right; the Belfast drug cartels, all soft brogue and "what's the craic?" until it came time to stab you in the back; the West Indian gangs from Ladbroke Grove housing estates, all patois and laid-back menace as they trained their young roadmen on the finer points of distributing their latest imports; the Ukrainian mobsters trafficking underaged girls for greasy-fingered men with sick appetites. They all had one thing in common; they were born somewhere and that somewhere hadn't made them who they were. That was a choice they'd made, plain and simple. Manx had never been convinced by the argument that circumstances drove people to crime. He'd met enough people who'd suffered unimaginable tragedy and hardships and had come through a damn sight saner and more empathetic a person than he could ever hope to be. There was always a choice; a bad choice road or a good choice road. Whichever road you travelled wasn't dictated by where you came from: it was dictated by the kind of person you were or wanted to become. Crime, Manx has always believed, was a personal choice; the most personal choice of all.

As Manx finished circling what remained of the downstairs bedroom of the cottage, he noticed the charred ruins of a wrought iron bed frame, the mattress shredded and black. Canton was right. So far, it had just been good luck the houses were unoccupied when the fire took.

How long that luck would last was anyone's guess.

9

Manx stood in the chill of the mortuary waiting for the coroner and listening to the rousing drama of an aria he couldn't name but had heard enough times he felt he should know its origins by this time in his life.

"La Traviata," Doctor Richard Hardacre said, shouldering the door open and tying his apron strings around his rotund belly.

"Sorry?" Manx said.

"That look on your face? It's the same one I get when I'm trying to remember where I put my car keys. 'Sempre libera', Act One. Renée Fleming sang it best. I've got the original recording at home. If I could remember where I stored it, I'd lend it to you."

"My loss, then," Manx said, figuring he'd dodged a small bullet. He gestured to the body. "What's the prognosis?"

"Well, death, that's for sure."

"Whatever they're paying you, it's not enough."

"You're not going to like this." Hardacre drew down the sheet, revealing the man's head and upper chest. "Time of death early hours of Monday morning. Cause of death, undetermined." He ran the tip of his scalpel just above the man's right temple. "Multiple bruises and lacerations consistent with a fall. Minimal seawater in the lungs, coup damage to the right side of the temple, contra coup damage to the left."

"In English," Manx said.

"Whatever caused the head trauma was powerful enough to slap the brain against the opposite side of the skull, causing what we call a contra coup injury. The cliffs around Benllech aren't particularly high, but mind you, stumble the wrong way off a kerb and you could end up under this," he said, waving his scalpel.

"Our victim might have been out walking, slipped, bashed his head on the rocks as he fell. He could also have been lying there for quite some time before the tide claimed him. And of course, we have no DNA to speak of, the Irish Sea took care of that."

"Fall or pushed?" Manx asked.

"No way to confirm at this point, however," Hardacre said, slipping the scalpel into the cavity and pulling back the tissue, "I did excavate some rock fragments deep in the wound."

"Excavate?"

"To dig out, Manx, from the Latin, *cavare,* to hollow out."

"Unusual choice of word, that's all."

"Seemed perfectly apt to me. Anyway, I sent the samples to a geologist friend of mine working on a dig site near Llanfair PG. She promised to get me an analysis back in the next couple of days."

"And that would prove?"

"Prove? Probably nothing, but it should confirm if the fragments found in said cavity were from the cliffs around where the body was discovered."

"Got it," Manx said. He scratched the back of his neck. "Benllech is a thirty-minute drive from RAF Valley. Why go out hiking in RAF dress uniform late on a Sunday night?"

"Autopsies don't generally provide those kinds of answers. But if you were contemplating suicide, you might want to wear what's important to you as your last dress change, human vanity being what it is."

"Dress in your Sunday best to meet your maker?"

"It's an important meeting, you'd want to make a good impression. Wouldn't you, Manx?"

Manx was about to reply when the raucous opening chords to Jack White's "I'm Shakin'" echoed through the mortuary. Hardacre's eyebrows arched as Manx checked his mobile. He raised his index finger and took the call outside. He returned less than a minute later as Hardacre was tidying his tray of implements.

"Well, one mystery solved," he said, slipping the phone back into his pocket.

"I'm all ears," Hardacre said, dragging the sheet back over the victim's face.

"Seems RAF Valley's missing a Base Commander."

10

The back room of the Lantern Arms held on to the constant stench of damp and mould like a bad grudge. Melvin could have fixed the damp and replastered the walls, but he'd already done enough for Lydia. His lads had painted the flat above the pub for her last winter for free. He figured doing favours for Lydia was an investment in his future, God knows he had little to show for his life so far. A cottage in Church Bay he'd been renting for ten years, a 1997 Volvo Estate where he kept his supplies, and an old boat with a dodgy outboard motor purchased cheap from a friend with a chronic gambling habit. Whatever government pension he was owed it wasn't going to pay for a bellyful of beer every night and a summer holiday in a static caravan down in St David's, that was for sure.

He slipped a CD into the stereo – one of his favourite Dafydd Iwan tracks. As the song, "Rwy'n Gweld Y Dydd" (I See the Day) hummed through the speakers, he glanced at the flag draped across the opposite wall and felt a thick wedge of pride swell in his chest.

The banner was divided into four equal quarters, each in an alternating yellow and gold colour, an outline of a lion stitched into the individual squares. It was the battle banner of Meibion Glyndŵr – Sons of Glyndŵr – one of four Welsh nationalist rebel factions formed in the late-seventies. Melvin had kept the flag for years, never imagined he'd be inspired to hang it again, imagined even less that when he unfurled the banner and brushed away the cobwebs, he'd feel the same surge of patriotism, as deep and urgent as it had grabbed him back then.

Melvin had been an active member of the Anglesey division of Meibion Glyndŵr for five years. He'd signed up when his older brother, Dafydd, had joined the organisation the year before. They were fighting for Welsh independence, saving the Welsh language from becoming a footnote in history. It was a time when protest singers like Dafydd Iwan were lauded as folk heroes, rallying against the destruction of the Welsh culture. But protest songs and passionate rhetoric only went so far. Any Welshman with a true and unwavering dedication to the cause knew that by the early eighties it was time to lay down guitars and tambourines and ratchet up the pressure. Burning holiday homes owned by the English, was the beginning, followed by a campaign of targeting local MPs with letter bombs and calling in bomb threats to government buildings. By the late 1980s, Meibion Glyndŵr was responsible for fire-bombing 220 English-owned holiday homes in Wales. Melvin himself took credit for eight of those.

Over the decades, he'd let his fealty wane; most of his compatriots had. He didn't feel any less patriotic, it was just that the practicalities of life had got in the way: marriage, divorce, earning money. And besides, political tides had turned in Wales' favour. Come the mid 1990s, Meibion Glyndŵr had all but disbanded. In 1981, Wales was granted its own TV station, and by 2007, the Welsh Government had implemented a strategy that ensured all children attending schools in Wales learnt the Welsh language. No doubt it was progress, but in the past few years he'd felt the old fires of patriotism stir once more. For Melvin, it was unfinished business – the kind of business a man needed to attend to when facing death.

Checking his reflection, he carefully studied the contours of his face for any change. It looked the same to him. A shade more flushed than usual maybe, but he'd been outside yesterday supervising a paint job.

The doctor had cautioned him to take better care of himself now the disease was stepping up its assault. "Small cell lung cancer is extremely aggressive, Mr Powell, and yours is very advanced. We can help alleviate some of the pain, but that's about it."

"How long?"

"A few months, maybe more with intense chemotherapy."

"Fuck cancer," he'd told the doctor. "Fuck the chemo too." That was weakness, staying on the back foot, throwing in the towel for an extra few months drooling into a cup and shitting his bed.

That was no way to exit the world, not for Melvin Powell.

He pulled the elastic around his ponytail – the chemotherapy wasn't going to take his hair, either – a man had to hold on to some dignity. He hadn't told Lydia and wouldn't until it was too late for her to make a fuss. It wasn't the way he'd imagined it would all end, but death didn't play by the Queensberry rules; it fought dirty, scrappy; without mercy.

"All right! You look fuckin' gorgeous. Who's the lucky man?" Melvin turned. Stan Thomas's bulky frame was filling the door frame like a human mechanical digger.

"You smell like you've come right off the building site," he said, looking over Stan's white T-shirt with the faded red dragon flag on the front. He reeked of body odour and dried cement.

"Didn't have time to go home and get myself all dolled up for the likes of you, did I? We havin' a drink or not?"

"I'll put the kettle on."

"Tea? Bugger that."

Stan pulled a bottle from his Lidl shopping bag. "Penderyn Legend, Welsh single malt." He slapped the bottle on the table. "Bet our brothers wish they had this back in the day," he said, gesturing at the photograph next to the flag; seven men standing in front of a stone wall with "Wales Rising" spray painted across its surface.

"Might not have got much done, mind," Melvin said, pouring the whisky into two mugs and handing one to Stan.

"To the cause," Stan said, clinking mugs.

"Land of our fucking fathers," Melvin said. "Time to take back what's ours, no mistake."

11

Bobbie's pace was brisk and determined as she passed the RAF service housing towards Valley town centre. If she walked fast enough the other wives would be less likely to approach her, ply her with questions she had no interest in answering.

The evening was warm, the sky cloudless – what the weather jockeys back at the base would have called "Ginners all the way, Bobbie." She stopped at the small church on the outskirts of town and ran her palm along the rough stone wall. The church had always reminded her of a Hansel and Gretel cottage; rugged walls with a patchwork of stones and a chimney-like steeple shaded by the branches of an old oak tree standing guard over its dominion. All that was missing was a path of breadcrumbs leading to the doorway.

For a moment she lost herself in a memory that was as crisp and fresh as the wedding dress she wore the day she was last here. That was nine years ago. She and her husband of seven minutes, Danvir, had posed for photographs under the ancient oak. If she closed her eyes, she could almost catch the breath of the day, the smell of it; gardenias and trumpet lilies, summer-trimmed grass and the bark from the oak tree still damp from the rain the previous night. She hadn't imagined happiness like that existed before she met Danvir, or if it did, it was meant for other people, not for her.

She missed Danvir more than she was prepared to confess to anyone. She missed his reassuring presence when she sensed the world was slipping from her grasp. When he was away on active duty – sometimes months at a time in some warzone where he couldn't reveal his location – she'd begin to feel untethered, the ebb of his influence gradually unmooring her from everything that made the world right. People had always said Danvir was her rock. They were wrong. Danvir had always insisted she was the moon and he was her gravity, the force that kept her from spinning out from her orbit. She hadn't doubted it for a second.

In certain ways, living back on Anglesey was harder; too many reminders of Danvir. If she were still alive, her mother would have told her: "Have yourself a good cry, then get over it." It was Maggie Matthew's advice for everything from a broken heart to a broken fingernail. Bobbie sometimes saw more of herself in her mother than she cared to admit, but her father? He'd been absent most of Bobbie's life. Maggie had told her she'd met Bobbie's father when he worked as a contractor at the local Wylfa Nuclear Power Station. She'd refused to tell Bobbie his name, "It was a stupid one-night stand, Bobbie. Leave it be, eh?" After a while Bobbie had stopped asking.

Her mother had never married, though she had lived with another man for several years. They'd had a daughter together; Bobbie's half-sister, Tammy. That man eventually left, moved to Dubai promising to bring Maggie and the kids over; he never did. Bobbie often wondered if the stability she found in the predictable routine of the RAF stemmed from her mother's casual approach to child-rearing. Maggie would move her and her sister every few months depending on where her romantic attentions were drawn to at the time. *No doubt Call Me Andy would have something to say about that*, Bobbie thought. After Maggie had died four years ago, Bobbie had found a bundle of tenderly wrapped, yellowing love letters while clearing out her mother's attic.

Maggie had been lying to Bobbie for decades.

Her father wasn't a one-night stand. It was a full-blown love affair, one that continued several years after Bobbie was born. After her transfer back to Valley twelve months ago, Bobbie had made contact with her biological father; it seemed the right thing to do. Excluding Tammy, he was the only family she had left now. She'd never found the right moment to tell her sister. Maybe tonight she'd sow the seeds. But Tammy was more like her mother, and Bobbie could already predict her reaction: "Leave it be, eh, Bobbie." Problem was, Bobbie wasn't very good at letting things be.

As she walked into the pub, the landlady, Lydia Clarke, a bottle-blonde who wore her T-shirts too tight and her lipstick a shade too red, was polishing the hallway mirror. She greeted her with a smile. Bobbie heard her sister's infectious laugh echo off the pub walls as she passed. Tammy was two gin and tonics into her evening and chatting to the young barman as if they were long-lost friends.

She dragged up a stool and sat. "Hiya."

They kissed on the cheek. Tammy wore another one of her expensive perfumes and was dressed as if she were expecting her evening to end up someplace better than here; spotless cream-coloured capri pants, a red summer-weight blouse with a white cardigan thrown across her shoulders, her make-up perfectly applied to highlight the cornflower blue of her eyes.

"She'll have the same as me." Tammy turned to face Bobbie. "You made it then? Expected you to stand me up, again."

"Can't make it an all-nighter, Tam. Got to be up early tomorrow, you know how it goes."

"Not really," Tammy said, leaning into her sister in a conspiratorial fashion. "All top secret, yeah? Bobbie Matthews saves the world," she added, raising her glass and taking a sip.

A year younger than Bobbie, Tammy had married at twenty-three, divorced by twenty-six, but had kept her husband's surname, Povey. Her features were the opposite of Bobbie's; fleshier around the face, blue eyes that caught the light with a playful glint. Bobbie was leaner, pricklier: "You're all bones and right angles, like me," her mother would say. People would never have guessed they were half-sisters; Tammy "the social one," which by default made Bobbie the "anti-social one". They were roles they both had slipped into, each by now expecting the same of the other.

"Like it?" Tammy asked, noticing Bobbie looking at her hair.

"I do. I do like it."

"New stylist over in Beaumaris," she said, flipping a hand under her hair. "Not cheap mind you but worth it, yeah?"

Bobbie had no idea if it was worth it or not. She always had her hair cut at the base salon; a trim every four weeks and the extravagance of a deep conditioning treatment every few months.

Tammy looked around the pub, her lips puckering as if they'd been brushed with something unpleasant. Loose scabs of paint peeled from the walls and the ceiling was yellowed with old cigarette smoke. There was an attempt to appeal to the RAF personnel with photographs of the base taken back in the 1940s when it was first built, and several faded watercolours of the RAF's most iconic planes; Spitfires, Wellington Bombers, Hurricanes. Over the sound system, Heart FM was playing a cheesy eighties pop song by a long forgotten one-hit-wonder. At the entrance, the irritating cha-ching of someone staking their luck on the electronic trivia machine spilled through into the main bar.

"Why didn't you invite me over to the bar on the base? It's like an old people's home in here," Tammy said, pointing at three old men brooding into their pints.

"I'm on the base all day, why would I stay?"

Tammy softened her tone. "Thought you might introduce me to his royal highness, or are you keeping him all to yourself?"

"I'm not affiliated with Air Mountain Rescue," Bobbie said, having maybe caught a glimpse of the Duke and Duchess of Cambridge stepping into their Range Rover one rainy afternoon.

Tammy took another sip. "So, I read about all those dead starlings. Nothing to do with you lot over at the base, was it?"

"Don't believe everything you read in the papers, Tam."

Tammy shrugged and tapped her glossed fingernails on the bar. "We should have gone to Menai Bridge, Bangor even, strike out of your comfort zone."

"I didn't want to go too far, I was sorting Danvir's stuff–"

"Bobbie, love," Tammy interrupted, placing her hand over Bobbie's. "You can't keep doing this to yourself, it's not healthy."

Bobbie snapped her hand away.

"I'm worried about you, that's all. Since you've come back you've been different, like you're not yourself."

"And what is myself, Tammy?"

"I don't know, do I? You just seem more off than usual. And then there's that whole business with Dani."

"I don't want to talk about it."

"Fine." Tammy leant back. "What do you want to talk about, since you invited me to this shit-hole in the first place?"

Bobbie ran a finger across the rim of her glass. "Forget it, this was a mistake," she said, looking at the threadbare carpet, peppered with remnants of pork scratchings and crisps. Tammy was right; the place was a shit-hole – the kind of pub only a local could love. They both turned as a group of four young men – auggies, auxiliary RAF personnel – walked towards the bar.

Tammy nudged her sister gently in the ribs. "This should liven the place up a bit." She caught the attention of the taller of the men. "Couple of ladies here in need of a refill," she said, rattling the ice cubes around her empty glass. "If you're interested."

The man looked Tammy up and down. "Bit forward, int ya?" he said, leaning back. "All you Welsh girls like that?"

"No, I'm one of the special ones."

"Bet you are, love," he said, leaning closer. "Tell me your names, I might buy you a drink."

"We can buy our own drinks," Bobbie snapped.

Tammy ignored her sister. "I'm Tammy, this is Bobbie."

"Tammy and Bobbie? You two country and western singers?"

"I can see why the RAF snapped up a smart one like you," Tammy said, dazzling him with one of her trademark smiles. "I'm named after Tammy Wynette, she's named after Bobbie Gentry."

"You doing a duet later?" he asked. "Karaoke?"

"Not likely, but I'll take a double. She'll have the same."

"I already said, I can buy my own drinks," Bobbie said, setting her glass on the bar.

"Come on, love, cheer up, might never happen."

Bobbie felt the blood thundering in her ears. "You know nothing about me," she snapped.

"Wouldn't mind getting to know you better. Both of you," the man said, smiling. He placed his hand on Bobbie's knee.

His touch was like a shock sparking through Bobbie's veins. Her reaction pure instinct. She spun around, grabbed the man's arm and wrenched it midway up his spine.

"Bobbie! What the bloody hell are you doing?" Tammy jumped from her stool, toppling over the glasses.

"Hey!" the barman called out. "Everything okay over there?"

"We're fine," Bobbie said. "This young man was just about to apologise, weren't you?"

The man took stock of the situation and realised there was no way to come out of this well. He apologised through gritted teeth.

"Good," Bobbie said. "Apology accepted."

The man rubbed his arm. "Jesus, what's your problem?"

"Trust me, you really don't want to know," Bobbie said, slapping a fiver on the bar. "I'll call you, later, Tam."

12

Bobbie circled the car park, blood thumping, fists clenched; skin drawing taut over knuckles, the storm clouds in her head gathering fast. Everything was a sign, it had to be, she thought as she walked in circles, muttering to herself. First there were the starlings: she remembered Maggie – always one for believing in superstition and old wives' tales – once telling her that dead birds were a sign of a new beginning, a rebirth. The bull she'd almost ploughed into must have been another sign; something powerful and masculine blocking her path? The significance was too obvious, but the contained rage and fury of the animal? That was something she could relate to. And the bloke in the pub? Had he been sent to test her? And if so, had she passed or failed?

These thoughts rattling around her mind, Bobbie crossed the courtyard towards the back room. A swatch of yellow light spilled through the window onto the cobblestones. She heard a low murmur of voices from inside. Pushing gently on the door, she walked in and stood off to the side where no one could see her.

Seven men were sat in a semi-circle, the smell of weed and

whisky heavy in the air. Melvin Powell stood and cleared his throat. Bobbie could tell he was nervous; he kept hiking up his trousers and smoothing down his hair as he spoke, softly at first, speaking louder as his confidence grew. "Right, how many of you are still renting your homes or living in the same council house you were thirty years ago?"

Six out of the seven hands shot up.

"And we all know why, right?" he said, his bile steadily rising.

"Too fuckin' right," one of the men barked. "Bloody English buying up our houses for holiday homes. Travesty, it is."

"It's not like our wages have gone up," said another. "My youngest's just married, can't afford to buy a house on the island he was born on. Had to move away, Conwy Valley of all places."

A man stood, his face red and etched with anger. "They closed down Wylfa power because they reckon nuclear's not clean enough, but they don't give us any new jobs. When the site's decommissioned the place will just about run itself. Even if that Chinese company buys it and starts generating, we'll still have to apply for the same jobs we've been doing for twenty years."

Another voice. "They'll probably put us all on zero-hour contracts, like they own the bones of us."

A muttering of agreement hummed through the room.

"That's why we can't sit on our arses anymore," Melvin urged. "If Plaid Cymru and the local council won't do nothing, then it's up to us, yeah? We take the fight to them, get them to take notice, make some bloody changes of our own."

"God helps him who helps himself," another man offered.

Melvin paused. He doubted the existence of any god, benevolent or otherwise, but decided against engaging in theological discussion. He had their attention and wasn't about to risk losing it. He continued. "The more holiday homes get sold, the higher the prices for us locals. They'll come a time none of our kids or grandkids will be able to afford to buy a house on the island."

Another voice. "It's not fucking right, Mel. Not right at all."

Ronnie raised his hand as if he were back in school. "I heard they're trying to pass some new law. The owners have to prove the house is their permanent residence, or something."

"I heard," another man said. "Too little too fucking late, if you ask me. Damage is already done."

"If that Logan Collins gets elected, he's not going to let that happen; bastard owns at least seven holiday homes on the island."

"One less, now," Ronnie said, with a wide smile.

The room erupted with a crack of laughter – a release of tension Melvin wasn't sure he liked or wanted, but rolled with it anyway.

Another man spoke up. "He's doing all right in the polls," he said. "The more English living on the island, better chance he's got of winning. They vote like for like, that lot. The election's only four months away. He could get even more votes by then, win the whole bloody thing."

"Then it's up to us to make sure he doesn't get anywhere close to fuckin' winning," Melvin urged.

"Oh yeah, and how you going to do that?" Ronnie said. "Use your painting and decorating skills to mess up his election posters?"

Another ripple of laughter. This time Melvin didn't roll with it. Instead, he clenched his fists and stepped into his old boxer stance; right foot slightly back, his posture low and aggressive. "Shut it, Ronnie," he said, his lips curling back over his teeth.

"Hey, calm down there, raging bull, you'll give yourself an aneurism," Ronnie said.

Melvin composed himself. "There's a new plan," he said, gesturing to his nephew.

Ronnie ambled to the front and turned to face the men. "Uncle Mel's right," he said. "New plan."

"What's involved?" one of the men asked.

"Best you don't know. Just me and Ronnie on this one."

"Yeah," Ronnie confirmed. "It's a stealth mission, like."

"But we'll all share in the glory," Melvin said, quickly.

"When's it happening, so we know?" one of the men asked.

"Next Thursday night," Ronnie blurted.

Melvin scowled. "Yeah, maybe, we still got some details to work out," he said. "Oh, and by the way, if anyone knows of an old van we can nick from somewhere, let Ronnie here know, eh?"

Bobbie waited for the men to drift off into the car park before entering the room.

"Jesus Christ!" Melvin said, tugging at the cuffs of his Ben Sherman button-down, his eyes darting around the room nervously. "What the bloody hell are you doing here?" He pulled her to the far end of the room, close to the pool table. "What did you hear?"

"All of it," Bobbie said, checking out the gleaming black crossbow laid out across the baize.

Melvin wiped a hand over his lips. "It's not what–"

"Meibion Glyndŵr," she said, gesturing at the flag. "Were you part of it, back then?"

Melvin shook his head. "Another bloody lifetime."

Bobbie leant on the side of the table and ran her hand down the crossbow's tiller. "And those men?"

"Most of them fought for the cause, apart from Ronnie, he wasn't born then. But he's family and he's committed."

Melvin reached for his glass of Penderyn and took a large slug. "You going to tell the police then? Shop us all?"

Bobbie thought on his question. A few months ago, she

probably would have, but now things weren't as black and white as they once were. "Why? Why now?" she asked.

"You just heard why," Melvin said.

"No. Why is this so important to you?"

Melvin shrugged. "A man's got to go out fighting, or else what's the point of it all?"

Bobbie nodded, satisfied with his answer, and lifted the crossbow, letting it rest in her palms. "Heavier than I thought."

"Kill a fox from twenty metres," Melvin said, taking the crossbow from Bobbie and laying it back on the table. "You want to be careful handling that."

Pinned to the wall next to the banner, Bobbie noticed a brightly coloured pamphlet with the date circled with a thick marker pen. She walked over, unpinned it and held it to the light. "Is this the plan you were talking about?"

Melvin snatched the Menai Bridge Food Slam flyer from her hands and rolled it up. "No offence, but maybe it's best you get going now, eh, it's getting late."

"Late? I don't sleep much, anyway. So, are you going to tell me or not? Maybe I can help."

"Look, love," Mel said, his voice suddenly edgier. "You hardly know me. I can't let you get involved with all this; you've got your career–"

"Had," Bobbie interrupted, drawing a strand of hair from her face. "I had a career. Now I'm just another problem they think they can brush under the carpet. I'm done following orders."

Melvin's eyes narrowed. "This isn't your fight. I'd go back home if I were you. Go on, on your way, I've got the pub to close up," he said, coughing loudly into his fist.

"Didn't you hear what I just said? I'm done with orders. Anyway, seems to me you could do with all the help you can get."

Melvin composed himself, ran a tissue across his mouth. "I don't need your help, don't need anyone's help."

Bobbie shook her head. "Well, you know how to contact me." As she left, Bobbie was sure what she'd just witnessed was another sign. She wasn't sure of its significance yet, but that's how signs worked, they took their time to reveal their intended meaning. She just needed to be wide-awake and responsive when the final reveal made itself known.

13

The temperature reader attached to the air conditioning unit in the incident room signalled fifteen degrees Celsius. That was a lie. It was closer to twenty-two degrees, the air stagnant and dry.

"Should have worn my shorts," DS Nader said, walking in.

"Yeah, air con's on the blink," Priddle said. "Don't understand it, the station was just built a few months ago."

"Just in time for summer, perfect that is," Nader said, drawing up a chair. "Boss here yet?"

"Yes, I am, sergeant," Manx said, entering with an armful of files, which he stacked on the desk.

Nader watched PC Delyth Morris enter the room. "Girlfriend playing rough again, Minor?" he said, gesturing at the bruise around her left eye.

"Got it playing five-aside. Not that it's any of your business," she said, turning to face the sergeant. "Anyway, I told you, my name's Morris, not Minor."

"Until the day I'm obliged to call you ma'am, you'll always be Minor to me, love."

PC Morris, a shade under five feet three with the build of a gymnast, slouched into the chair. Normally, she would have fired a sharp retort Nader's way, but this morning she couldn't muster up the enthusiasm. Her typically bright, intelligent eyes were bloodshot and bleary, but still sharp enough to throw Nader a pointed scowl. "Sorry I'm late, sir."

"We have a positive ID on our victim," Manx said, arranging the scene-of-crime photographs on the incident board. "Base Commander James Brian Flynt. Fifty-eight. Flynt was reported missing on Monday morning when he was a no-show for a scheduled meeting."

"He wasn't on any missing persons reports," Morris said.

"Makes sense," Nader said. "Military like to keep that kind of thing to themselves until they confirm if one of their lads is really missing and not on some weekend bender in Amsterdam."

"Flynt's wife will identify the body this afternoon, after that we'll release the name to the press. Morris, accompany Mrs Flynt and if she's up to it, have her come into the station to answer a few additional questions. Tell her it's just routine, but gently does it."

"Got it, sir," Morris confirmed.

Priddle raised his hand. "Do we know the cause of death?"

Manx attached a slip of paper to the board. "According to Hardacre, COD is still inconclusive. We can confirm the Audi A7 belonged to James Flynt."

"Maybe he was meeting someone," Priddle offered.

"Bevan should get back to us soon on the tyre prints he found next to Flynt's car," Manx said. "But I'm not holding my breath."

"If Flynt left a nice car like that unlocked, with the keys inside, I reckon he wasn't intending on wandering off far."

"Or," Manx said, writing the word *suicide?* on the incident board. "He wasn't intending on coming back." Manx was about to continue when the incident room door swung wide open.

"Nothing like the sound of a well-oiled crime-solving machine in action," Canton bellowed, settling himself on the edge of one of the desks. "Troup's just been on the blower."

"That's the kind of news guaranteed to cheer me up."

"That aside, Manx, she's already spoken with the RAF Valley new acting Base Commander. He's expecting you this morning and has requested our discretion around this matter."

"By which he means keeping our noses out of RAF business?"

Nader stretched out his legs. "If they're anything like the army, they'll close ranks quicker than a tart pulling down her knickers."

"You can't call them tarts," Morris snapped. "It's not the nineteen bloody fifties."

"Oh, yeah," Nader said. "Must have meant sex worker. Quicker than a sex worker pulling down her knickers, boss."

"Nader has a point," Manx said. "Our jurisdiction will be limited on an RAF base."

Canton brushed the errant crumbs from an early morning pastry off his shirt. "With your well-honed diplomatic skills, he'll be eating out of your hand in no time, Manx."

As Canton walked out, Manx turned to face the team. "Right, as our fearless leader says, apparently we're a well-oiled crime-solving machine, whatever the hell that means." He added the final few photographs to the board. "Any luck with the additional door-to-doors yesterday, Priddle?"

"Nah, but we're going to knock on a few more this morning."

Manx nodded. "Canton's approved a floater for the collating and entering of evidence, which leaves you, Morris, free to scour Flynt's bank accounts for any unusual transactions, money problems, gambling addictions. Gently does it with the wife but probe her about Flynt's work; anyone with a grudge, jealous colleagues, the usual drill."

"Got it, sir," Morris confirmed.

"Nader, as you seem to have some background in these military matters, you can accompany me to the base."

"Happy to," he said, scooting back his chair.

Manx addressed the team. "This is the first full day of what could be a murder or a tragic accident. I don't need to remind you, but I will; we'll all conduct this investigation with professionalism, all our Is dotted, our Ts crossed. Anyone got a problem with that?"

A communal shaking of heads and a series of *no bosses* echoed around the incident room.

14

The roar of a fast jet rattled the Jensen's old bones as it passed overhead. Manx and Nader were waiting at the RAF Valley sentry gate while a young corporal checked over their paperwork.

"Bloody impressive, eh?" Nader said, craning his neck as the BAE HawkT2 training jet thundered across the airstrip.

"Bloody noisy," Manx said, squirming the tip of his little finger in his right ear.

The corporal handed back the paperwork. "Park at the red and white checks by the Squadron Building. Nowhere else."

As they pulled up a few hundred metres away from the checkpoint, another serviceman was already waiting.

"Don't want us wandering off on our own, looks like," Manx said, looking up at the vast, L-shaped glass building.

"Probably like this on all the bases these days, anti-terrorist precautions and all that."

"Papers," the sergeant demanded. He double-checked their IDs, clicked his heels sharply and turned. "Follow me."

Inside, the building was cavernous, the ceiling at least thirty feet high and supported by several iron girders. The morning sun streamed through the glass, casting geometrical shapes along the gleaming tiled floor. A wide sliding door fitted with a high-tech security entry system led from the main reception area. The sign above read, "Training School, Advanced Flight Simulator #3".

The sergeant stopped at the reception desk. "Wait here. The commander will meet you shortly," he said, and marched, stiff-backed, down one of the adjacent corridors.

As they waited, Nader and Manx studied the collection of photographs arranged in a perfectly regimented line along the wall.

"Saw that one in the *Daily Mirror*," Nader said, pointing at a shot of William, Duke of Cambridge, smiling from a cockpit. He leant in close, squinting. "You think he's really flying that chopper?"

"He most definitely is." The voice was efficient, clipped.

Manx and Nader both turned.

"And, by the way, choppers are typically single-rotor commercial craft, this is a Sea King 3A Helicopter. American made, but we try not to hold that against them."

"Oh, yeah," Nader said. "I recognise it now."

The man smiled. He was as tall as Manx, late thirties and wearing RAF service dress. His eyes alert, blond hair shorn close on the sides with a razor-sharp parting. "Group Captain Hamish Boyd, Acting Base Commander," he said, extending his hand. "Apologies for all the protocol. With his royal highness on the base, we're on a far tighter lockdown than usual."

Manx shook his hand and introduced himself and the sergeant. Nader almost stood to attention as Manx said his name.

"Welsh Guards eighty-one to eighty-seven. Honourable discharge," the sergeant added.

The commander nodded. "Eighty-one? Falklands veteran?"

"Signed up the November before."

"Oh, bad luck. But you made it back in one piece."

"Yeah, just about," Nader said. He paused for a moment. "But keep calm and carry on, that's what they say, right?"

"Indeed, they do."

"We have some questions concerning Mr Flynt," Manx said.

"Of course, but not here," the commander said. "Let's use the conference room. There's someone there who I think should also be part of this conversation."

"Lead the way," Manx said.

The commander stopped midway down the hallway, pushed opened the door marked "Valley #1" and gestured for them to enter.

The room had floor-to-ceiling windows; the blinds pulled down to diffuse the sunlight. At the far end of the table, Jack Carlisle rested an arm on the back of a chair and smoothed down the front of his tie with his hand. His demeanour suggested he was here under protest and had better, more important places to be.

Manx had been formally introduced to Jack Carlisle ten months earlier when he'd first been transferred to Anglesey – it was standard protocol. The Royalty Protection Group insisted they were introduced to all senior-level police officers assigned to the island. Manx had worked alongside plenty of men like Carlisle during his time at the Met; ex-military types who imagined themselves a cut above regular officers because they rubbed shoulders with some minor royals too fond of partying and having their faces slapped on the gossip pages of the tabloids. Jack Carlisle had been assigned senior royal protection officer to the Duke and Duchess of Cambridge for the duration of the Duke's tour of duty at RAF Valley. Carlisle was in his early forties, square-jawed, clean shaven, and wearing a perfectly tailored black suit with a Union Jack badge pinned to the lapel. The last Manx knew, Carlisle had been promoted to a top-tier position at the MoD in Whitehall some six months ago. The fact he was here now, sitting across from Manx, cucumber cool, staring Manx down as if he were someone to be evaluated and if necessary neutralised, didn't bode well.

Carlisle rose to shake Manx and Nader's hands. "Good to see you again, Manx," he said.

"I thought your tour of duty here was over months ago."

"Whitehall insisted. Just treat me like a fly on the wall, I'm here only as a passive observer."

Manx doubted the veracity of that statement and slipped into the nearest chair.

The commander sat opposite, rested his hands on the perfect crease of his trousers and spoke. "I'm only a few hours into this job, flew in this morning from Brize Norton. I never had the pleasure of meeting Commander Flynt, but I heard he was an exemplary officer and a mentor to the young officers. He'll be sorely missed."

Manx listened to his words with a creeping sense they'd been finely honed, obituary-ready. "Anything more substantial you could add?" he asked, drawing out his notebook.

The commander brought his hands together. "Before transferring, he was stationed at RAF Waddington in Lincolnshire. It was a significant promotion for Commander Flynt."

"What was his previous role?"

"Ah, I'm afraid I'm not at liberty to disclose."

"Why Anglesey?" Manx asked.

The commander tugged at the fringe of his jacket. "RAF Valley is one of our most critical fast jet training bases, we'll take all the seasoned officers we can. The gene pool's not that deep with the kind of expertise Flynt had."

"What about grudges, any enemies on the base?"

"I was under the impression he was well-liked. Believe me, we keep a close eye on any kind of abuse of power these days."

"Changed a bit since my time," Nader said. "Put up and shut up or end up on shit-shovelling duty for the duration."

"We've been fashioned into military operation fit for the twenty-first century," the commander insisted. "What with Home Office oversight and pressure from Counter Terrorism we can't escape the glaring light of culpability, much like the police force."

Manx pointed his pen at the commander. "Except the police force is directly answerable to the public," he said. "We don't work under the protection of the Official Secrets Act."

Nader bristled. "The commander's only saying.'

"No, no," the commander said, raising his palm. "Your inspector is correct. The police force has been subject to more than its fair share of negative publicity, but I like to think we're two sides of the same coin. You protect the public from imminent dangers, we protect them from the dangers no one sees coming."

Nader leant forward, stabbing the air between them with his index finger. "Most people don't know the half of it. It's because of people like us they can sleep in their beds at night."

"Couldn't agree more, sergeant," said the commander.

Manx sat back. "Did Flynt have money problems?"

"None that were brought to my attention."

At the far end of the room, Jack Carlisle stirred as if he'd been poked with a stick. "Listen, Manx," he said, leaning across the table. "We're as keen to solve this case as you are, maybe even more so."

"How so, Carlisle?" Manx asked.

"Let's just underline it as a matter of national security. If you find all this was a tragic accident, then all well and good, I'll sleep better at night. We all will."

Manx gave a tight smile. "I'll be sure to let the widow know."

Carlisle continued. "If, during your investigation, you discover Flynt's death was something more ominous, then that would give us cause for concern. The commander of the base where second in line to the throne is currently stationed is killed–"

"I don't remember mentioning anything about anyone being killed, do you, Nader?" Manx interrupted.

"Em, I expect Mr Carlisle – Jack – is just saying–"

"What was Flynt's state of mind?" Manx asked, quickly cutting off Nader mid-sentence.

"Ah," Carlisle said, sitting back and wagging a finger. "You're reaching now, Manx. Investigating outside the box."

"Commander?" Manx said, steering the conversation back on track.

"You'd have to ask the personnel he worked with."

"And you'll give us access?"

The commander shuffled. "Within reason, yes."

"Within reason? Right you are," Manx said. "And when can I expect a list of these personnel?"

"Would end of day work?"

"The sooner we get those names, the sooner we can clear this up and be out of your hair."

The commander smiled: the kind of smile that hid something less friendly, coarser, beneath its smooth veneer.

Manx closed his notebook. "We'll be interviewing Mrs Flynt later. Maybe she can help us paint a more rounded picture."

"I really need to get on," the commander said, standing and stretching out his hand. "It's been a pleasure, although I wish it were under better circumstances."

"Appreciate you taking the time, sir," Nader said, barely stopping himself from saluting the commander.

"You on the island for a while, Carlisle?" Manx asked.

"As long as my country needs me," he said. "Good luck with all this unsavoury business. The copper's lot, eh, Manx?"

As they drove past the checkpoint, Manx, still irritated at Carlisle's presence, turned to Nader. "What the hell was all that about?"

"Closing ranks, you mean, boss? Always happens."

"No, Nader, you, brown-nosing the Base Commander like you were hoping for a bloody officer commission."

"Nah, weren't like that, boss, just looking for common ground, get him to open up."

"And how did that work out for you?"

"Em–"

"Don't bother. It was fucking rhetorical."

15

The late-afternoon air felt good against Bobbie's face as she ran the narrow track that circled the lake across from the base. Her back was slick with sweat, her breathing measured as she crossed the road and passed the sentry gate. She headed towards the gym where she could shower and change before starting her shift. She noticed a flurry of activity around the Squadron Building. Several Range Rovers with thick privacy glass were parked outside, with two RAF police vehicles next to them.

"Hell of a morning."

Bobbie turned. Call Me Andy was standing next to her, dressed in sweatpants and a grey hoodie.

"What's going on?"

"You haven't heard?"

"I wouldn't be asking otherwise."

"Commander Flynt. They found his body this morning."

Bobbie's blood ran to ice. "How? Where?" she asked.

"Other side of the island, I think. They're not releasing much information at the moment."

"Do they know what happened? How he died?"

"They found his body on a beach, that's all I know."

"Who's that?" Bobbie asked, gesturing at a tall man in service dress stepping out of a Range Rover.

"Acting Base Commander, I expect."

"That was quick."

"Time and tide and all that."

Bobbie took a deep breath. She suddenly felt light-headed and bent over, securing her hands on her knees.

"You okay?" Pierce said, placing his hand on her back.

"Yeah," she said, standing and shrugging off his touch. "It's just a shock, that's all."

"Unexpected, no doubt. But the pressures of running a base this size can't have been easy."

Bobbie stepped back and shook her head. "No, not Flynt, he wasn't the suicidal type."

"Time will tell," Pierce said, handing Bobbie an envelope.

"What's this?"

"Your paperwork for the VA hospital. Routine, nothing to worry about."

Bobbie reluctantly took the envelope.

"I can drive you there, so you don't have to travel alone."

"Or make sure I don't get lost on the way?"

Pierce blushed. "No, it's just–"

"When you find the name of this new Base Commander can you come and find me?" Bobbie said, stuffing the envelope into the back pocket of her sweatpants.

"Yes, I suppose. Why?"

"There's something he needs to know."

16

"Bet you drank here all the time, underage too," Gwen Schofield said, sliding Manx's pint across the bar.

Manx sat on the threadbare stool. "Maybe, but it wasn't like this in my day," he said, cocking his thumb behind him.

The pub was adjacent to Moelfre beach, set a few metres across from the ice cream stand and souvenir shop, and at 7pm was packed with tourists. The locals tended to give the pub a wide berth during the summer, preferring to do their drinking further inland, where the only tourists were the ones hiking their way through Anglesey's ancient druid burial sites, or the kind who had taken a wrong turn on a narrow back county road. For Manx, the Pilot Arms was less than a ten-minute walk from his house; reason enough to call the place his local, no matter the season.

He turned as two young boys on a sugar-high screamed and swung on the fishing nets draped across the window. Their mother, fast on her feet, grabbed them around the waist, dragged them back to the table and ordered them to sit.

Gwen shook her head. "I keep reminding his landlordship they'll be gone in six weeks, then we'll be left with the old boys nursing their pints all night and complaining about the prices."

Manx looked over the rim of his glass as he sipped.

"Present company excepted, of course. Never seen you nurse a pint, probably wouldn't know how."

"I'll take that as a compliment."

"Take it any way you want," Gwen said, leaning over the bar to serve a young man with a strong Scouse accent. "So, did you drink down here when you were younger?" she asked, gathering a stack of damp beer mats.

"Might have snuck a pint or two."

Gwen tossed the mats into the bin. "And the rest."

"Why are you asking? Got someone matching my description wanted for underage drinking thirty-five years ago?"

Gwen wiped the inside of a pint glass. "Just been wondering lately about all this change on the island. It's not like it used to be."

"Nothing is, Gwen."

"I reckon there's more holidaymakers here every summer. And all those new flats they're building? They're not for the likes of us locals at those prices, are they?"

"First sign of old age, nostalgia, Gwen."

"But you came back, you must have missed the place?"

"Oh, this is just temporary until I figure things out, then I'm back down to London, get the grit of the city back in my blood."

Gwen pulled Manx a fresh pint. "Yeah, I suppose we have to tell ourselves stuff like that so we don't go bloody mad. Always somewhere better to move on to, greener grass, yeah?"

As she turned to serve an older couple who'd just walked in, Manx laid out the leaflet Canton had given him across the bar.

"Into Food Slams, now, inspector?" Gwen asked.

"If I knew what the hell that was, maybe I could answer."

"A Food Slam? A load of restaurants from the island come

together to cook in one place. That politician, Logan Collins, is meant to be opening it this year."

"That name keeps cropping up."

"Yeah, wants to be Anglesey's next MP. He's delusional, no bloody clue."

"So, he's more than qualified for the job, then."

"He's English, but thinks he's learnt to speak Welsh. He sounds like that Prince Charles after a few too many pints, nobody can understand a bloody word he says–" Gwen stopped mid-sentence. "Oh, and talking about the English," she said, nodding towards the man ambling towards the bar: Lead CSI, Ashton Bevan.

"They say the old lion never strays far from its watering hole," Bevan said. "Or are you the antelope, Manx? The quarry?"

From behind his left shoulder, Manx heard a familiar voice. "It's not going to be a work evening is it, Ash?" Bevan's wife, Sherry, moaned and set her purse on the bar. "You promised."

"Just five minutes, love. Quick bit of business with the inspector here."

Sherry draped her arm elegantly across the bar, dipping her hand at the wrist as if expecting Manx to kiss it. "How are you, Inspector Manx? Enjoying the warm weather?"

"Not particularly," Manx said, shaking her hand.

Sherry smiled. "Yes, you don't look like the summer-loving type," she said, flipping her blonde hair and checking herself out in the mirror behind the optics. The gesture wasn't required. Sherry always looked as if she'd stepped out of a fashion shoot and tonight was no exception. She wore a tight blue T-shirt tucked into white jeans which accented her taut waistline. She'd pushed her oversized sunglasses over her forehead, so they rested on her hair giving an air of casual elegance; more Euro-chic than Anglesey Food Slam.

And then there was Bevan. Several inches shorter than his

wife and with a fast-thinning comb-over. The middle buttons of his short-sleeved shirt strained as he leant on the bar – more than likely hadn't worn it since last summer when he was a few pounds lighter around the belly. Bevan and his wife were like a puzzle Manx could never figure out; a mismatch made in heaven.

Bevan tapped his wife's arm. "Why don't you grab a table outside, I'll bring the drinks over."

Sherry pulled down her sunglasses and pointed at Bevan. "Five minutes, Ash, or you'll be drinking by yourself. Nice to see you, inspector. Keep in the shade, too much sun can't be good for a complexion like yours."

Bevan ordered. "Two gin and tonics, Bombay Sapphire, not that cheap rubbish. And limes not lemons, if you've got them."

Gwen smiled, gave him a two-fingered salute under the bar.

"So, Bevan, is this social or professional?"

"One and the same in my book, Manx." Bevan slid a tenner across the bar. "Treat the social like the professional, and vice versa, you learn a lot more."

"You should hurry up with whatever it is you need to get off your chest before your wife ditches you for a younger man," Manx said, cocking his head in the direction of the window.

Bevan glanced to the patio. Sherry was being chatted up by two young lads and didn't seem in any hurry to send them packing. He turned to Gwen "Get a rush on with those drinks, eh?" Bevan's brow glistened with a mist of perspiration. "That matter down at Benllech beach. As we all know, our victim was found in RAF service dress."

"Flynt was the Base Commander at Valley. We spoke to the new bloke over there this morning."

"And did he enlighten you as to Flynt's previous role?"

"Flight training, apparently."

Bevan reached into his pocket and showed Manx a printout

of the insignia on Flynt's jacket. "Here's the thing," he said. "RAF wings are typically surrounded by a gold laurel wreath, this one, however, is surrounded with a blue laurel."

"Significance?"

Bevan became increasingly flustered as Sherry's familiar laughter wafted through the open window. "Right," he said, pouring the tonic sloppily over the ice. "Blue laurel leaves are assigned to only one division in the RAF, Thirteen Squadron."

"Which is?"

"Flynt was assigned to RAF's unmanned aircraft programme."

"Drones? The commander forgot to mention that."

Bevan grabbed his drinks. "And guess where the only active British RAF drone programme operates from?"

Manx paused, recalling his meeting with the Base Commander. "Wild guess. Waddington, Lincolnshire?"

"Bingo," Bevan said. "Which makes me wonder."

"Wonder what?"

"What else this Base Commander has been keeping from you," Bevan said, with a thin press of his lips that he could have trademarked as his own personal smirk. "Enjoy your night."

17

The following morning, Bobbie stood in front of the Base Commander, field service cap tucked under the crook of her arm.

"Flight Lieutenant Bobbie Matthews, correct?" Commander Boyd said, looking up from his computer screen.

Bobbie stood to attention. "Sir."

He sat back. "Your reputation, as they say, precedes you."

"I'm not sure I understand–"

"If this is why you're here," he said, gesturing at the same thick pile of letters and correspondence Flynt had as near as spat on three days ago. "I'm afraid I don't have the time to deal with your Enid bloody Blyton *Boys' Own* conspiracies. I have a base to run."

"It's not that, sir," Bobbie said, flinching inwardly.

The commander sighed. "Right. Sit. Make it brief."

"I saw Commander Flynt the night before he died," Bobbie explained, settling into the chair.

The commander arched his eyebrows. "You met with Flynt?"

The moment the words left her mouth Bobbie regretted speaking. She could already tell Boyd was a different breed of commander to Flynt. At least twenty years younger, his accent polished, his mannerisms controlled. Privately educated, Bobbie guessed, top-tier college, followed by officer training and a fast-track to Base Commander. Flynt had his faults, but at least she always knew where she stood with the man. Bobbie sensed a brittle iciness from Boyd; ambitious, but with an edge that suggested he didn't care who he stepped over to get there. At that moment, Bobbie was in no doubt Flynt had been given the Base Commander position in exchange for toeing the line on the Operation Vanguard findings. Men of Flynt's background – recruited directly from school, working-class upbringing, fought his way up the ranks – rarely made Base Commander. Bobbie chose her words carefully as she answered. "I didn't meet with Commander Flynt, specifically."

"Then what – specifically – are you not telling me, Matthews?"

She took a breath. "I was out driving, I found myself outside Commander Flynt's house–"

"What time was this?"

"Just after twenty-one hundred hours–"

"What the hell were you doing outside your commanding officer's home at that time of night?"

"I wanted to speak to Commander Flynt. Off-base."

"About these?" He stabbed the papers. "Did you and Flynt share the same disdain for official reports? I understand you were both in the ground control station during Operation Vanguard."

"I believe Commander Flynt accepted the findings."

"So, you were outside his house to persuade him otherwise?"

Bobbie ignored the question. "I saw Commander Flynt leave the house before I had the opportunity to speak with him."

"Was he with someone?"

"No. Drove off by himself, sir."

Commander Boyd thought for a moment and shuffled forward on his chair. "Have you informed anyone else about this?"

Bobbie shook her head.

"Then let's keep it that way. This stays between us, loose lips and all that."

"What about the police, sir? Shouldn't–?"

"Let me worry about that," he snapped. "I don't want the local coppers stomping their size-eleven boots all over my base. If it's relevant, I'll pass on the information. Was there anything else?"

"No, I don't think so, sir," Bobbie said, standing.

Commander Boyd reached for a slip of paper and quickly scanned its contents. "I understand you're leaving us at the end of the month. I'd recommend keeping yourself out of trouble and out of my hair. No more searching for this damned truth you're so obsessed with. Do not provide me a reason to sully your exemplary record. Are we clear?"

Bobbie's fists clenched. The implication was clear enough. As Base Commander, Boyd had the power to write her service record as he saw fit, ensured she was demoted to a less senior position with less pay and a reduced pension when she was finally discharged.

"We're clear," she said. "But if I don't find the truth of what happened, I can't guarantee someone else won't. Sir."

18

Manx walked past the oak doors at the entrance to St Gerard's and followed the cheers coming from the sports field. Back in the eighties, the school was operated by the Congregation of the Sisters of Mercy as a girls' day and boarding school. Manx knew this because as a teenager he'd ride the Friday bus into Bangor with his friends in the hope of catching a slow dance with one of the girls at the local disco. Convent girls, they'd been told by the older lads, were "boy-crazy", easy pickings under the lights of a mirror ball and went weak-kneed at the smell of Brut aftershave. Like most tales concerning girls, it was false. They were neither boy-crazy nor easy. They were no different to the girls at his school, just richer and more aware of their value when it came to dating boys from the local comprehensive. St Gerard's was now co-ed, but the girls still possessed an innate understanding of their value in the world, Manx guessed, as he passed a huddle of them striking Instagram-worthy poses under the shade of a stoic oak tree.

DCSI Vera Troup had summoned him to the school. It was the last day of the summer term; St Gerard's Sports Day. Her daughter, Angharad, was running in the 400-metre relay. Manx had never given much thought to Vera as a wife, let alone a mother. Her posture and icy demeanour did little to encourage small talk or the exchange of pleasantries beyond anything concerning the North Wales Constabulary, recent arrest rates, and improving public relations – Vera's hot button topic at most meetings.

Manx spotted Vera at the finish line wearing a black T-shirt, jeans, and trainers. A girl, who he guessed was Angharad, crossed the finish line, third place. Vera cheered and hugged her daughter. Spotting Manx lingering on the side lines she whispered to Angharad, who sprinted off to join her friends.

"I thought the schools were all done for the summer."

Vera gestured he should follow her to a quiet spot behind the PA system. "St Gerard's is one of the highest rated schools in North Wales," she explained. "If the pupils sacrifice an extra week of doing bugger all and staring at their phones all day, then so be it. It's a competitive world these days, especially for a young woman."

"No doubt," Manx agreed. "So, I suspect you didn't ask me here to sell me on the benefits of a private education?"

"No. That business at Benllech beach–"

"Ah. I had no choice but to close it down, ma'am. God knows what else we might have found there, or if a young kiddie found something before we did."

"And did you find anything?" she asked, folding her arms.

"Only the body, but–"

"I'm not questioning your decision, Manx, I asked you here to talk about Base Commander Boyd."

Manx stepped into the shade. "Played his cards close to his chest. Not surprising. I've got three officers on the base taking statements from anyone who worked with Flynt."

Vera stood for a moment. "You're a good officer, Manx, but you don't strike me as a patient one. If we have any hope of solving this case, we need the RAF on our side and that's going to take diplomacy. No rubbing them up the wrong way with references to police oversight and the bloody Official Secrets Act."

Manx winced. "He's already spoken to you?"

"Besides the point. Get the job done, Manx, but don't jeopardise the investigation before we're out of the starting gate."

"Understood, ma'am," he confirmed.

Following the dead air of an awkward pause, Manx noticed a tall man wearing a pink polo shirt and a powder-blue sweater looped around his shoulders striding towards them – Logan Collins. His hair was gelled back in what Manx guessed was the "politician style". His smile was equally slick and forced. "Found those thugs who destroyed my holiday home yet, Vera?"

Troup straightened, visibly irritated. "You'll be the first to know when we do, Logan."

Collins huffed like a petulant horse and looked over at Manx.

"This is DI Tudor Manx. Logan's two sons also attend the school," Vera said.

"Two, huh?" Manx said. "That can't be cheap."

Collins ignored the remark, studying Manx closely as he shook his hand. "You look familiar."

"I was outside your house when you gave that impromptu press conference a couple of days ago."

"So, you're working on the case?"

"Amongst others."

"Do you know what I think, DI Manx?" Collins said, pulling back his shoulders as if he were about to deliver a speech. "I think it's just the start. These things have a tendency to escalate. Four holiday homes burnt to the ground. What's next? Setting fire to someone's property when they're home, with kids sleeping?"

"Can't argue with that, Mr Collins. That's the kind of tragedy the North Wales Constabulary is keen to avoid."

Collins was about to reply when a young boy ran up and dragged at his trouser leg. "All right, Marcus, Daddy will be right there," he said, with an impatient snap. "Vera, DI Manx. I hope the next time we meet you'll have some encouraging news to share."

"Again, you'll be the first to know," Vera said as Collins walked way. "That wasn't so hard was it, Manx?"

"Here to serve, ma'am."

She presented Manx with as close to a smile as he'd ever seen her offer, then went back to join the other parents.

Manx walked across the freshly mown grass and found some shade under an alder tree and looked over the handsome, stoic form of St Gerard's. As the sun beat down on the afternoon the thick, grey bricks seemed to absorb the light as if they were feeding from its heat. The clocktower cast a long, deep shadow over the field and across Vera Troup, who was kneeling to attend to a small grass burn on her daughter's knee. It felt like an omen of sorts. He quickly dismissed the idea as an overly suspicious copper looking for meaning, in shadows but finding only darkness.

19

From the window of her flat above the pub, Lydia Jones watched the men spill out from the old barn and walk towards the car park. Three of them, including Ronnie Powell, hung around the courtyard laughing and smoking. She pulled hard on a smoke of her own; a tightly rolled joint, one of a handful she kept in an old jewellery box and supplied courtesy of Melvin's Paint and Plaster.

A roar of laughter drifted up from the courtyard. Another one of Melvin's meetings. *No better than bloody kids*, she thought, as Ronnie and another man jostled with each other under the eaves of the old stable. Didn't they have homes to go to? Better things to do with their time than play at being in a bloody gang like they were ten years old?

She'd expected better of Melvin, but then again, she'd expected better of all the men she'd lived with; expected a hell of a lot better from the one she'd married. But like the rest he'd carved a deep wound in her heart, along with an even deeper one in her bank account. Money was replaceable, it came and went, but the heart? That wasn't so easily repaired. In fact, she suspected it healed a little slower and a little harder with every scar.

At the age of fifty-three, she hadn't expected to fall in love again, had resisted the feeling for as long as she could, but a portion of her heart now belonged to Melvin. Would he turn out to be any different to the others? It was something she preferred not to dwell on. When she was young and stupid, she would have done just that, filled her head with some dream of marrying the perfect man, two kids, summer holidays in Spain. These days, she accepted things for what they were, didn't question where the relationship was going. Mel was good to her, most of the time at least, when he hadn't been drinking. He'd never raised a fist to her, though his silence could be as devastating as a slap in the face; sometimes more so.

"Hand me a smoke, eh, love," Melvin said, throwing himself into the lounge chair positioned in front of the television. By default, it had become Mel's chair: like there was Mel's mug, Mel's pint glass; Mel's side of the bed. Lydia felt she should resent this, but truth was, it was comforting: the more he felt at home, the harder it would be for him to leave. It also meant she didn't have to drive the half-hour to Mel's cottage over in Church Bay. Ronnie was living there by himself these days; God knows what kind of mess the place was in; the lad could barely bend over to tie his own shoelaces.

Lydia took a joint from the box and handed it to Melvin.

"Be a love and light it for me, eh?" he said, slipping off his loafers and laying them next to each other in a neat line.

"And what did your last slave die of?"

Melvin loosened his belt. "She didn't die, I divorced her."

Lydia flicked her lighter. "Aren't I the lucky bloody woman."

He grabbed her wrist, pulled her in for a hard kiss on the lips.

"You been on the whisky again?" she said pulling back and

wiping the back of her hand across her mouth. Lydia had been in the firing line of plenty of drunks in her time – that last whisky shot was typically the trigger pull that led to something worse. She could take the beer, gin and vodka even, but there was something about the malty residue of whisky that turned her stomach, brought back those bad memories. If she had a quid for every man who'd smacked her across the mouth with the taint of whisky on his breath, she'd be a rich woman.

Melvin took a long, deep drag. The smoke hit him like a body punch to the lungs. He coughed hard, his body trembling as if everything inside him was shaking loose.

"Christ! You all right?" Lydia said. "Do you want something?"

Melvin waved his hand. "Leave it alone. Don't bloody fuss."

Outside in the car park there was another cackle of loud laughter followed by a badly off-key rendition of "Delilah".

Lydia walked to the window, flung it open. "Oy! Ronnie! Time you and your mates fucked off. Can't have you lot making noise after hours."

No response, but a few minutes later the commotion stopped, followed by the loud rattle of Ronnie's quad bike accelerating.

"I told you enough times," she said, sitting back down. "I can't have this after closing time. If the neighbours start mouthing off and complaining to the brewery, they could take my name off the lease."

"Leave it be, it's just a few mates having a laugh."

"Yeah, is that all?" she asked. "A few mates having a laugh?"

Melvin took a shorter drag this time, sharp and quick. "Why, you heard different?" he asked, his eyes narrowing.

"Just saying, this pub is all I've got. I can't afford any trouble."

"Won't be no trouble." He pushed himself back in the chair, a glassy look in his eyes. "Only trouble comes when people start poking their noses where they don't belong," he said, pointing at

Lydia; a signal this was the end of the matter: no debate, no questioning. "Could do with a sandwich," he said, his tone a degree or two softer. "I'm bloody famished."

"A sandwich?" Lydia said, shaking her head. "I could do with a bloody holiday too, but I don't see anyone offering to take me on a fortnight to Benidorm."

"Aye, good luck with that," he said, with a half-smile that hung around a fraction too long, as if he'd forgotten it was there.

"Might have something left over from dinner," Lydia said, getting up. "I'll go and check in the kitchen."

"You do that," he said, a lazy drawl to his voice.

When Lydia returned five minutes later, Melvin was already asleep, his head tilted towards his right shoulder. She settled the plate on the table and slipped the joint from his fingers. As she did so, she noticed a splat of red on the cuffs of his white shirt. She ran her finger along the spots. They smeared, still moist to the touch.

She brought a hand to her chest and looked at Melvin. Did he seem smaller? Filling the chair less than he did when he first moved in? His shirt looked looser across the chest; his jeans baggier around the waist. Or was it the weed over-stimulating her imagination? But the blood? That wasn't imaginary, that was as devastatingly real as life got.

She felt her chest tighten. Another scar? She could already feel its first nick someplace deep in her heart. She didn't think she had the space or willpower to take any more of them. But maybe the heart always had room to carry more pain; made room for it, prepared itself for it, even.

20

Three hours after the sun had set and the sky had deepened to a dark, impenetrable blue, Bobbie was running the pathway around the lake across from RAF Valley. A spill of moonlight caught off her reflective vest as she ran, the beam from her LED headlight band helping navigate her way. Not that she needed the help, she could run the trail in her sleep by now; if sleep were ever to come to her again.

The air was still, the countryside rustling with nocturnal life. Invisible in the darkness, the mechanical whirring – like a distant engine – of the nightjar birds filtered through the undergrowth, while a chorus of dragonflies hummed over the grasslands. Bobbie could hear none of this. She had her headphones secured tight around her ears listening to "Brilliant Mistake".

She and Danvir had first bonded over Elvis Costello in the RAF Cosford mess when they were both stationed there. She'd always said she could never date anyone who didn't love Elvis Costello, and Danvir had impressed her with his knowledge and passion for his early works. He'd enticed her back to his place with the promise of a rare bootleg from 1978, *The Last Foxtrot, Live in Frisco*. When they discovered they'd grown up less than twenty miles from each other – Danvir in Bangor, Bobbie on Anglesey – it was like some perfect kismet. After that they were rarely apart. The fact that Danvir was a Muslim, though not a devout one, and Bobbie had been brought up in the Methodist tradition, none of that mattered. They were married four years later. After a brief honeymoon, Bobbie was posted to Intelligence Command in Waddington, and Danvir began a series of overseas postings. Nine years later, at the age of thirty-eight, Bobbie was a widow, the bottom fallen so completely out of her world she could barely find her footing.

As she ran "Everyday I Write the Book" played in her headphones. The song resonated deeper than it ever had before. Danvir's story was done, his book closed. But Bobbie's story? That was still wide open, the pages waiting to be written. It was daunting to think of the courage it would take for her fill those blank pages. In two weeks, she'd be transferred, forced to talk about the incident, face her demons with the goal of being fixed. She doubted there was any fixing what was broken inside her.

Fifteen minutes later, the swirl of her thoughts having carried her the last mile and a half, she turned towards the narrow road that passed the east sentry gate. Her body showed no signs of tiredness; there was an energy, like a charge of electricity, pulsing through her.

With "Pump It Up" blasting, she tackled the first few metres of the hill, her hamstrings straining. If the volume had been lower, or her senses more attuned, she might have heard the car approaching behind her. It wasn't until she saw the flash of headlights catch the wall of hedges that she felt the first troubling twinge of unease.

She looked behind. Two glaring headlights filled the narrow road. She was sure the vehicle would slow down. It didn't. If anything, it was gaining speed.

She ripped off her headphones; the ominous growl from the

engine was loud and persistent, the headlights, two searchlights seeking their target. The road was barely wide enough for one car, the hedges too thick and high to provide an escape path.

She picked up her pace. The vehicle slipped down a gear, notching up the revs, edging closer and swerving from one side of the narrow road to the other.

Bobbie's heart thundered in her chest, all excess adrenalin now flowing to her legs and lungs. She looked for any breaks in the hedge; there were none, just a dense, impenetrable thicket. She had one choice; keep running.

As the car caught up with her, the side draft pushed her off balance. She stumbled into the ditch between the road and the hedge. Her feet lost traction in the gulley of the ditch.

Before she fell, the wing mirror clipped her left shoulder. The last thing she saw was the bright flint of sharp rock sticking out from the earth. She knew without question her head would strike it.

She briefly registered the irony of "Accidents Will Happen" spilling through her headphones before she slipped into darkness.

21

The doctor stood at the foot of Bobbie Matthews' bed and spoke, "She was treated for mild concussion, minor lacerations and a nasty bruise on her left shoulder," she explained. "No lasting damage, she'll be discharged by tomorrow morning."

Manx looked at Bobbie, her face pale and peppered with small cuts. In his opinion, she didn't look like she'd be discharged anytime soon but accepted the doctor's prognosis with a slow nod of his head. "Any idea why she asked to see me?"

The doctor clipped the paperwork to the bedframe. "Not a clue. She was insistent we contacted the 'senior officer on the Commander James Flynt investigation'," she said, reading off a scrap of paper. "But you can ask her yourself." She gestured towards Bobbie, who was beginning to stir.

"Bobbie Matthews?" Manx said, stepping closer. "You wanted to speak with me?"

She opened her eyes and shuffled against the pillows with a groan.

"I'm DI Tudor Manx. I can come back later if you'd prefer."

"No. I'm fine," Bobbie said, reaching for her left shoulder and wincing as she touched it.

"You don't look fine."

"Are you leading the investigation into Commander Flynt's death?" she asked, as she made herself comfortable.

"Do you know something about that?"

Bobbie ran her tongue over her lips. "Pass me the water."

Manx did as he was asked and waited as Bobbie placed the straw to her lips. She seemed wary, Manx thought, as if she were weighing up whether to trust him or not.

"I'll leave you to it," the doctor said, turning to leave. "Don't wear out my patient, inspector."

Bobbie wiped the back of a hand across her mouth and spoke, taking several breaks to wet her throat. She explained she was outside Flynt's house the night he disappeared, had wanted to talk to him, how she'd seen him leave the house and her subsequent conversation with Commander Boyd.

"He didn't tell you, did he?" she said.

"Unless he called one of my other officers."

"How likely is that?"

Manx nodded. "Point taken. And why are you in here? I'm guessing you don't think this was an accident?"

Bobbie stiffened. "The vehicle did not slow down. I was wearing a reflective vest and an LED headband, if they didn't see me, they were either blind or drunk."

"Can you identify the car?"

"It was dark, and it happened so fast. But I'd estimate from where the wing mirror hit me, it had to be something with a high-wheel base, like a van or an SUV."

"That's very observant."

"It's my job... was my job, to be observant."

"Who found you and brought you here?"

"Good Samaritan?" she said, shrugging.

"Have you spoken to anyone else about this?"

"Only Commander Boyd. I should have said something sooner, but I wasn't sure if it was important."

"I think Bobbie should rest now, Inspector Manx," the doctor said, stepping back into the room.

Manx gave the doctor space and slipped his notebook into his pocket. "Hope you feel better soon."

"Oh, she'll feel more like herself tomorrow. We'll have you all fixed up."

"Right," Bobbie said. "Good as new."

As Manx left the room, Bobbie saw Andrew Pierce walk towards Manx and introduce himself. She couldn't hear the conversation, but the body language seemed clear enough. His glances, the serious head nods; the inspector taking notes. Call Me Andy was sure as hell not filling in the inspector on Bobbie Matthews' stellar mental stability. She had little time to dwell on this before sleep claimed her; a deep one, the deepest she'd had in months, induced by narcotics and mercifully dreamless.

22

"If you ask me, it's the jet fuel they're putting in the planes," Nader said. He was holding court across one of the desks in the incident room as Priddle listened intently and Morris stifled a yawn. "It poisoned the lot of them," he added, pointing at the *North Wales Daily Post* headline. "Anglesey Starling Deaths. Mystery Deepens."

"The tox report was inconclusive," PC Morris said. "Verdict's still out as far as I'm concerned."

"That's what they want you to believe," Nader said, tapping the side of his nose with his index finger. "Birds don't just fall out of the sky, do they?"

"Sarge's got a point," PC Priddle agreed.

"Jet fuel?" Morris said, shaking her head. "If that's the case why aren't half the birds on the island dead?"

Priddle shuffled forward. "I heard it's a new weapon they're testing out. Sound waves or something."

"And it only kills starlings? That'll stop the war on terror."

"Maybe it's both," Nader said.

"Oh, like a double threat," Priddle offered. "Makes sense."

"Christ almighty!" Morris snapped, sitting back and folding

her arms. "No, Priddle, it doesn't make sense. You two should start your own podcast; plenty of nut jobs out there happy to listen to conspiracy theories all day long." She leaned forward. "We're coppers. We look at the evidence not some conspiracy theory you heard down the pub. There's a rational explanation, you'll see."

"All right, Minor, calm down. What's got your knickers in a twist this morning?" Nader asked. "Girl problems?"

"No," Morris said, dragging her chair back and moving to an empty desk. "Ignorant arsehole problems."

As she sat, Manx walked in and took his place in front of the board. "Morris, how did it go with our victim's wife?"

Morris flipped through her notes. "James Flynt arrived home at eight that night, then left again at around nine. She thinks someone called him from the base, but she wasn't sure."

"And he was wearing his service dress when he left the house?" Manx asked.

Morris nodded. "Didn't have time to change, apparently. Happened a lot, she said, perks of being a Base Commander."

"Money problems? Gambling? Debts?"

"None. His bank accounts all check out. No large deposits in the past twelve months, no unusual transactions."

"A paragon of bloody virtue," Nader huffed. "Bet you fifty quid the bloke's got a bag full of dirty secrets."

"Other than wild speculation, Nader, do you have anything positive to add?" Manx asked.

"Priddle and me interviewed all the blokes, and girls, on the list the Base Commander gave us. They all said Flynt was tough but fair. No grudges, he didn't owe money to anyone, not on the base at least. Everyone seemed to like the bloke. Well, at least as much as anyone can 'like' the boss."

Manx ignored the pointed remark. "And what about alibis for the night Flynt went missing?"

"The personnel we interviewed were on shift that night. They had a training exercise, so it was all hands on deck, everyone accounted for."

"I checked back with the base," Morris said. "Flynt never signed back in, probably drove straight to Benllech."

"He could have met someone," Manx said. "He left the keys in his car and the doors unlocked, which suggests he knew the person he was meeting and wasn't intending to wander far from his car."

"Maybe," Nader said. "But if you're going to top yourself, you wouldn't need your car keys where you're going."

"Why meet someone if you're going to commit suicide, sarge?" Morris asked. "It's not the kind of thing you want an audience for."

"Let's keep options on the table and minds open," Manx said, pinning two photographs on the incident board. "The forensic analysis from the fresh tyre prints taken next to Flynt's car. Eighteen-inch, Goodyear, standard on several thousand cars and SUVs and sold in just about every garage and tyre shop in the country."

"So, a dead-end," Nader said.

"Only on the tyres," Manx said, writing the name, Bobbie Matthews on the board. "This woman, currently recuperating at Gwynedd Hospital A&E, was parked outside Flynt's house at 9.30pm the night he went missing. She witnessed him leave, insisted she didn't follow him, but several hours later he's fish food in the Irish Sea."

"Why didn't she come forward two days ago?" Nader asked.

"Isn't the more important question what she's doing in the emergency room?" Morris asked.

"You're both right," Manx said. "Bobbie Matthews suffered minor cuts and abrasions after being struck by a vehicle outside the base late last night. She did tell me she'd spoken to

Commander Boyd and informed him she'd seen Flynt leave his home that night. The commander neglected, or forgot, to relay that information to the North Wales Constabulary."

"So, let me get this straight," Nader said. "This woman sees Flynt leaving his house and a few hours later he's dead. She tells the commander, who doesn't tell us, then she's run over two days later?"

"Someone's had their coffee this morning," Manx said.

"Did she work with Flynt?" Priddle asked.

"She wasn't on the list the commander gave us," Morris confirmed.

"Which begs the question, if she didn't work with Flynt what the hell was she doing outside his house?" Manx said.

"Stalking the bloke?" Nader offered. "Maybe they were having an affair?"

"It's possible," Manx said, checking his notebook. "The man who found her and drove her to the hospital is a Doctor Andrew Pierce." He wrote the name on the board. "RAF Valley's clinical psychologist and the base chaplain. He mentioned Bobbie Matthews is his patient but wouldn't get into specifics other than he's treating her for a military-related trauma."

"She was obsessed with Flynt," Nader said. "He rejected her, she killed him, made it look like an accident."

"What evidence do you have for that, sarge?" Morris said.

"Been doing this job long enough to trust my gut by now, Morris."

Morris threw her arms in the air. "Great, we can all go home, case solved."

"Ease off the accelerator, both of you," Manx said. "Morris, dig into Bobbie Matthews' background without stirring up things on the base. We keep this quiet for now. If she was targeted by a hit-and-run, let's not give whoever did this an excuse for a do-over."

"Sir," Morris confirmed.

"Oh, and Morris, this will make your day," Manx said, picking up the Food Slam flyer from under a stack of papers. "Canton and Troup request your participation this Thursday evening."

"Jesus," Nader huffed. "Is this to do with that Just Ask A Copper bollocks? Rather you than me, love."

"Be happy to do it, sir," Morris said, smiling. "DCSI Troup's right. It's important we're seen working with the community."

"Christ, the face of modern-day policing," Nader said. "Kiss El Vera's arse any more and you'll need to reapply your lipstick, love."

Morris pushed back her chair. "I know an arse you could kiss, sarge," she said, grabbing her notebook. "I'll be doing research if you need me," she added before walking out.

"Was that necessary?" Manx said, gathering his papers.

Nader shrugged. "Just some friendly banter. No harm done."

"Watch your step. I don't want to be sitting in HR while you get reprimanded for creating a hostile working environment. Morris is right, the force is changing, and for the better in my opinion."

"Aye, well we're all entitled to our opinion," Nader said, standing. "If you excuse me, boss, I've got a couple of suspects ready to beat a confession out of in the cells."

"You're not funny, Nader."

"So the wife keeps telling me." He marched out of the room.

"Priddle, last man standing," Manx said, as the young PC gathered up his notebook and slipped his chair back under the table. "Call all garages within fifty miles of here, ask if anyone's brought in a large vehicle, an SUV or something of that kind for a driver's side mirror repair."

"Got it, sir," Priddle said, and headed through the door.

Manx turned to the woefully empty incident board. He

looked at Flynt's scene-of-crime photographs and Bobbie Matthews' name. Other than they both worked at Valley, there was nothing else to connect them. He picked up a pen and drew a thin line between them. A second later, he wiped his sleeve over the line, leaving only a faint smudge. He was reaching, forcing tenuous connections. That was never a good sign, especially this early in an investigation.

23

Bobbie had been discharged two days ago. The first day she'd spent at home; "recuperating" the doctor had insisted; it hadn't worked. She'd spent most of the day looking out at the small parcel of the back garden, drumming her fingers on the windowsill, drinking coffee, thinking about everything until it felt as if her head would implode. She signed back onto the base the following day.

She'd been temporarily assigned to writing press releases while the press officer was on maternity leave. She'd already done similar work back in Waddington, and at least it kept her brain from kicking into overdrive at every spare second. She drafted a release detailing Commander Flynt's memorial service, which was to be held in the local chapel, and conducted by Andrew Pierce – the funeral was yet to be scheduled and would take place in Waddington when the coroner had released the body. She then drafted an update on the Duke and Duchess of Cambridge's appearance at the Anglesey Agricultural Show in two weeks, highlighting the Duke's excellent progress in his flight training.

Lunch was taken in the History Room Café, where all she

had the stomach for was a strong coffee and half a sandwich. Lunch done with in less than ten minutes, she headed towards the transport hangar. Outside, one of the civilian contractors, a passenger carrying vehicle (PCV) driver Cadwyn Evans, leaned against the wall, smoking. Cadwyn was young, friendly, and liked to talk.

"Can I bum one?" she asked.

He slipped out a pack stuffed under his T-shirt sleeve. "Didn't know you'd stepped over to the dark side."

Bobbie didn't smoke; or at least she hadn't since she'd met Danvir. Before that, she'd only been an occasional smoker: or, as Danvir had insisted, "You only occasionally put yourself at risk of dying of cancer." Point taken; she'd quit for good soon after that conversation.

"I heard about your accident. Probably bloody tourists. No clue how to drive the roads around here. You okay?"

"I'll survive," Bobbie said, coughing as the smoke sucker punched her lungs.

Cadwyn smiled. "Yeah, if the smokes don't kill you first."

Bobbie dropped the cigarette and ground it with the heel of her boot. "You're in charge of the PCVs on the base?"

"Driver, mechanic, car washer. Keep the fleet spotless, the Base Commanders always want it that way; buffed and polished."

"So you'd notice if any of the cars had any damage?"

"What kind of damage?"

"Like the wing mirror. Driver's side."

"I'd know, straight off," Cadwyn said, then gestured with his cigarette as the penny dropped. "Ah, you don't think–?"

"No. I don't know," Bobbie said. "I was just wondering."

"Don't know who'd want to harm you, mind," he said. "One of the good ones you are."

"You really think so?"

"You're a hell of a lot better than most of those higher-ups I chauffeur around."

"That's a pretty low bar," Bobbie said.

Cadwyn laughed. "Best be off, lunch break over." He ground his cigarette into the wall, flicking the butt into a nearby drain.

With forty-five minutes to kill before she was needed back at her desk, Bobbie found some shade under the awning outside the café and sat as far as possible from her colleagues who were enjoying the afternoon sun.

Was she one of the good ones? She thought on Cadwyn's words. She certainly didn't feel that way; hadn't felt that way since that day in the ground control station when her world had shifted off its axis. It was then – the memory of that day replaying in her mind like it had a million times before – that a flash of an idea came to her. Besides Bobbie and Flynt, there was one other person in the Box that day; Officer Cadet Cole Dawson. She could have kicked herself for not thinking of him sooner. She hadn't talked to him since the incident but was sure he was still stationed at Waddington; it was the only base in the country that required a sensor operator like Dawson in the ranks.

Her head buzzing with some glimmer of hope, she walked back to the Squadron Building to make her arrangements, one nagging thought at the back of her mind. With Flynt dead and herself the victim of what she was sure was no accident, she wondered if she was visiting Dawson hoping for answers, or was she travelling to Waddington to deliver him a warning?

24

At 11am the following morning, Ali Kalpar marched into Llangefni police station, examined the décor and nodded his approval. "You lot done all right with the new digs, yeah?" he said, bounding towards the duty sergeant, Aled Rogers. "Could do with more colour, though. Orange or yellow, something more cheerful."

Rogers glanced up from reading the *Daily Mirror*.

"But I suppose you don't want criminals getting too comfortable. They got a word for that, right?" Ali said, scratching his thick, dark beard. "Oh yeah, counterproductive, innit?"

"How can the North Wales Constabulary assist you today?" Rogers asked, recalling the preferred greeting the NWC Public Relations team had insisted be used for "initial client interactions".

Ali introduced himself. He was wearing a spotless white overall and white wellington boots. A fleshy indent from years of wearing a tight-fitting hairnet ran the length of his brow. "Don't worry, I don't bite, all peace, love and understanding, me, until–" he said, pointing at Rogers, "some bastard steals my van. Then, it's war, yeah? Full on."

Ali took a quick inventory as Manx opened the door and walked into the reception area. "No uniform," he said, pointing. "You the boss man here, then?"

"Not by a long chalk," Manx said, barely looking up. "But I'm sure whatever you need, the sergeant can help you out."

Ali stepped closer. "Some bastard stole my van. My deliveries are all caput. People are relying on me, paying customers."

Manx stuffed his hands in his pocket. "Delivering what?"

Ali rummaged in his overalls and handed Manx his business card. "Halal Al, like it says on the card."

"Your name's Halal Al?"

"No, don't be stupid. Real name's Ali Kalpar. Funny buggers over at health and safety started calling me that, so I said I'm taking that. Good marketing, innit, Halal Al? Put a sign on the van, too."

"The van you say was stolen?"

Ali shook his head. "My customers, they're not going to like this, break my bollocks if I don't deliver."

"When was it taken?"

"I parked it outside the abattoir in Gaerwen last night, came in this morning, vanished."

"Give Evans the details, he'll input them on the system, make sure we're on the lookout," Manx said, turning to leave.

Ali shook his head. "Nah, take too long. I know who took it. You can just go to his place, arrest the bastard, I get my van back and still make my deliveries. Job done."

He handed Manx a slip of paper. "Mohsin Sadiq. Been harassing me ever since I bought the business off him, telling everyone I ripped him off. Shit to him! I paid a fair price, and health and safety made me upgrade all the bloody equipment. If anyone could be bothered to ask, I was the one who was ripped off."

"And you have proof he stole your vehicle?"

"If the bloody CCTV cameras were working, I would."

"Which means you don't."

"Home-grown terrorism, they call it, yeah?" Ali said, proudly, as if he'd delivered a particularly sharp point of observation.

"Home-grown?" Manx asked, confused. "Like vegetables?"

"What? No, I deal with meat," Ali explained. "No such thing as Halal veg, is there? No point."

"I think you meant domestic terrorism," Manx offered.

"Yeah, that's it! The bloke's a danger to society." He lowered his voice to just above a whisper. "All begins with a van, then what? It's all suicide vests and Jihads, innit? Don't even see him at the mosque anymore. You know what that means?"

"Enlighten me."

"Not radical enough. Found some well-radical Iman, prays at home, in his back room so he doesn't look suspicious."

"Again, you have evidence?" Manx asked.

Ali shrugged. "Nah, but obvious, innit."

Manx handed back the paper. "Rogers will follow up."

"And you'll arrest him?" Ali nodded like a dashboard dog, hoping Manx might accompany him in the gesture.

"If he's committed a crime, he'll be arrested."

The answer seemed to satisfy Ali. "Honest businessman, I am. Now, I've got to hire a van and the bloody insurance company won't pay me back that's for bloody sure. It's a fucked-up world, innit?"

"More than you can imagine," Manx agreed, buzzing himself back into the major incident room.

25

Officer Cadet Cole Dawson sat at his kitchen table. It was strewn with the morning's breakfast dishes and foil takeaway containers from the night before; chicken biryani, Bobbie guessed by the smell and crusted detritus of basmati rice. She pulled up a chair and slid the boxes out of her way.

"Yeah, sorry. You should have called, I would have spruced up the place," Dawson said, pulling the ring from a can of Boddingtons. "Sure you don't want one?"

"It's eleven in the morning, Dawson."

"The earlier you start, the earlier you get there," he said, taking a slug.

"Get where?"

"Anywhere but fucking here," he said, spreading his arms wide. His eyes were bloodshot, and he hadn't shaved for several days, his hair long and unkempt, T-shirt crumpled and stained. He was a long way down the road from the bright-eyed joker Bobbie remembered from only twelve months ago. Gone was the goofy smile and the puppy-dog eagerness to please. Cole Dawson looked like a homeless man who, by some twist of good fortune, had stumbled into someone's kitchen.

"What the hell happened?"

"You mean when did it all go wrong? Or when did Sophie take the kids and move back in with her mother? Or when did I find out I liked the bottle better than I did my family? Or all of the above?"

"Jesus, I had no idea."

"Yeah, none of us ever do. So why the house call? Didn't think I'd ever see you again after Operation Vanguard went to shit. Oh Christ!" he said, slapping his forehead. "Danvir, your husband, I'm so fuckin' sorry, Bobbie, I tried to call, afterwards–"

"It's fine," Bobbie assured him. "I wasn't in a good place to talk to anyone. Actually, that's why I'm here."

Dawson reached out for a shot glass and the Absolute Vodka he kept in arm's reach. "If we're taking a stroll along drone strike memory lane, I'm going to need something a little stronger."

"I assumed you read the official report?"

"Yeah, of course, we all did," he said, pouring.

"And you agreed with the findings?"

Dawson slugged a mouthful then poured another. "Didn't know there was an option to agree or disagree."

"But in your opinion?"

"Come on, Bobbie, you know how it goes. We're foot soldiers, we don't get to have opinions."

"Right. But you still haven't answered my question."

Dawson downed another vodka and leant forward. "After Operation Vanguard, they said I was unstable, which was hard to argue. There were only so many dead bodies in high definition I could watch. I started seeing them everywhere. Before I went to sleep, playing with the kids, out shopping with the wife. It was relentless, Bobbie, fucking relentless. Still is, if you must know. But you know how it goes."

Bobbie nodded, though she couldn't completely relate. Maybe she was just better at compartmentalising than Dawson.

He continued. “I was down the King’s Arms on a Friday night. I’d been on late rotation; my head was well fucked up. This bloke, all lumberjack beard and CAMRA T-shirt with a bug up his arse about the RAF gets in my face calling us murderers and terrorists. I know we’re trained to step back from all that, but the bloke was a real wanker, I mean top-shelf, self-righteous, fat fuck muppet. So, we get into it, big time. Before I know it, I’ve got one hand around his throat, the other about to punch the living shit out of him. Took three blokes to get me off him. Turns out one of them was one of our flight commanders. I was disciplined the following Monday, got laid into good and proper from the Base Commander. He put me on admin duties until they’d done a full TRiM assessment. To be honest, I was happy to get away from the line of fire, but it left more time for drinking. Always a silver lining, eh?”

“When was this?”

“Christmas last year. ’Tis the season to be jolly,” he said, picking up the bottle by the neck and swinging it side to side like a handbell.

“They took you off active combat duties?”

“Like I was shit on their shoes. And you?”

“Same,” Bobbie said.

“Well, if that’s all you came for, that’s my story, flight lieutenant. The. End.”

Bobbie slid the vodka bottle to the opposite end of the table. “Listen, there’s something not adding up about this whole thing,” she said. “Commander Flynt. They found his body five days ago on a beach on Anglesey.”

“Flynt?” Dawson’s eyes were alert and focused on Bobbie for the first time since she’d sat down. “How? What the fuck?”

“The police haven’t released any details yet, but it makes sense, right, how it’s all connected.”

“How what’s connected?”

"All three of us were in the ground station that day; we know there were no other insurgents in the area, Creech would have informed us. The findings are flawed, but no one's willing to come out and admit that."

"Politics," Dawson said, swallowing another mouthful. He paused, as if hesitating to say what was on his mind before reaching for a stack of papers on the shelf behind him. "About a week after I nearly throttled that bloke, I tracked him down. I wanted to apologise, or maybe I wanted to check out if he was pressing charges and talk him out of it. But here's the thing, part of me thought he might be right, I wanted to hear him out."

"And did you?"

"He told me to go fuck myself at first, but I can be very persuasive with a few in me. He knew all about Operation Vanguard, been tracking this stuff for years apparently."

"He was accessing classified information?"

"Not exactly accessing. Plenty of dissenters amongst the ranks happy to sling some mud at the RAF. All anonymous, of course. I reckoned the bloke was on the spectrum or something, anyway, he showed me all these charts, newspaper clippings. Bottom line, he's figured out since Operation Vanguard government-sanctioned drone strikes increased over two hundred per cent, and little if no coverage by the tabloids. Once the RAF confirmed our lads – your husband – were killed by insurgents, the narrative changed. It was like they had a free pass to bomb whoever the fuck they wanted."

"What are you saying?"

Dawson took a large swig of vodka, wiped the back of his hand across his lips. "This bloke's one hundred per cent convinced Operation Vanguard was a false flag operation."

Bobbie felt the blood rush to her feet, the roof of her mouth run dry. "He's not serious?"

"He didn't seem the joking type. If what he says is true, that

RAF Air Command colluded with the US Joint Special Operations Command to blow the shit out of that convoy of medics to justify ramping up drone attacks, then what the fuck does that make us, Bobbie, other than complicit?"

Bobbie sat back; the wind taken from her. She'd had a severe lack of imagination where Operation Vanguard was concerned. If it were true, it was hardly surprising the RAF had continued to push back and deny; it had become their default position and now it was obvious to Bobbie why. If this information was leaked to the press, the fallout would be catastrophic. This was the kind of cover-up that brought down powerful people, made governments nervous; shook people's faith in the establishments designed to protect them. Had Danvir and his regiment been sacrificed in the name of continuing the war on terror? The thought made her sick.

"I need to speak to this person."

"Don't think so. The bloke runs on a permanent Nervous Nelly setting. But here." He ripped an edge from the *Lincolnshire Echo* and wrote down a URL. "It's the only way he communicates."

Bobbie took the paper and folded it into her jacket pocket. "Thanks. Is there anything I can do to help?" she asked.

Dawson smiled, and for a second Bobbie caught a flash of the man she remembered. "You can pass that bottle back my way."

A second later, the smile was gone.

26

Come Thursday evening, Ronnie Powell was jittery and anxious, his gut tight, head crackling like fireworks on November 5th. "Get out fast. I'll be waiting for you at the dock," Melvin had instructed. "And wear gloves. You won't have time to wipe down."

Orders. Commands. Ultimatums. By now, Ronnie was dog-tired of the way his uncle spoke to him, like he was speaking to a half-wit. But that had always been the order of things when it came to the men in the Powell family. Ronnie was all too familiar with the tired routine; the older generation passing down their "wisdom" with tough love and clenched fists. As a Powell, you were expected to grow up fast and grow up hard. Ronnie had fallen in line with the family tradition, though he'd never been hard enough nor compliant enough in his father's eyes. Dafydd Powell could barely let a day pass without raising his voice, or, more typically, his fist to his son. Ronnie understood early on you couldn't choose your family, but you could choose who in your family to pledge your allegiance to. For Ronnie, that decision had been made when he was thirteen, when his father laid his fists on him for the last time.

Melvin had walked in on the scene: Ronnie, cowering like a petrified dog in the corner of the kitchen, his father zapping his son's naked torso with an electric cattle prod until Ronnie's skin was puckered raw, the kitchen thick with the stench of scorched flesh. Melvin had knocked three colours of shit out of his brother that day. Crouched in the corner, Ronnie had forced himself to watch the whole, brutal beating, if only to make sure his father wouldn't be rising again any time soon to finish what he started.

The speed and power of Melvin's fists as they pummelled into his dad that day left him in awe. The beating was done in minutes, or was it seconds? No matter, by the time it was over Dafydd Powell was unconscious, his right eye hanging from its socket, Melvin standing over him, blood dripping from his knuckles and onto the dirty yellow linoleum.

Ronnie had left with Melvin that afternoon and was as loyal and compliant as any grateful dog might have been. Not that his uncle was an easy man, he was just the best of a bad batch. The odd slap now and again just to keep Ronnie in line and a sharp right hook when Melvin had considered he'd stepped too far over that line. Compared to living with his father, it was as close to a normal childhood as he could have hoped for. He didn't think they'd spoken after that day, the brothers. The last Ronnie heard, Dafydd Powell was living on the foothills of Snowdonia. *Good riddance*, he thought, *best place for the bastard; out in the backend of nowhere drinking himself to an early grave*. What Melvin didn't finish Ronnie was sure the cigarettes and the scotch would.

Scotch? That would have settled him right down, or a thick joint to calm his nerves. Ronnie had never been the patient type. He guessed he'd inherited that trait from his father; an anger that burned somewhere deep in the bones of him. His uncle had always told him, "You fight that urge, Ronnie, push it right down.

If you don't, that's when your guard comes down and you expose your weakness. And what does weakness do? Gets you hurt, that's what, or worse."

Thinking on those words, Ronnie looked towards Menai Bridge town centre. He'd have felt better if Melvin was here with him. It was his uncle's plan after all, and he was just carrying out his orders; the loyal, grateful pack dog. When Melvin had first proposed the plan, Ronnie had attempted to talk his uncle out of it. It seemed too soon, a step too far. It wasn't like they'd be setting fire to empty holiday homes in the dead of night. If Melvin's plan worked, injuries, or worse, were a given – a necessity even.

He tilted the mirror and checked his reflection. His forehead was glistening. He took a hand to his brow, wiped, then checked again. Christ, he was turning into his uncle. He flipped the mirror back, catching the sun's reflection as it shone off the grey shoulders of the Menai suspension bridge behind him.

From his vantage point, half-a-mile uphill, he had a near-perfect view. The main road running through town was closed to traffic and most of the buildings were, this evening, hidden behind several rows of tented booths and food stalls. The smell of a suckling pig roast drifting from the car park of the Victoria Arms reminded Ronnie he hadn't eaten since before lunchtime – he hadn't felt like it, his stomach was churning with a slop of apprehension and fear.

He checked his watch. Quarter to seven – another fifteen minutes. He stabbed at the radio, hoping for some music to distract him; nothing but static. He tried the CD player. The sound of a woman's voice wailing in some foreign language echoed off the van walls. What he wouldn't give for some Black Sabbath or Iron Maiden right now to put him in the right head-space. Melvin had warned him to keep off the wacky-baccy until later, but Ronnie's nerves were already fired through with bright arcs of electricity.

Fuck Mel, he wasn't on the front line, taking all the risk.

He snapped a joint from inside his jacket pocket, struck his lighter and pulled hard until the blunt fizzled angry and red. Almost immediately he felt the soothing effects of the weed. He checked the crossbow bolt he always carried in his right sock was still there – it was. He pulled down the black full-face fleece mask he always wore when he was lamping, secured his sunglasses, and applied a light amount of pressure to the throttle.

The van moved forward, slowly at first, then gathering momentum as it caught the slope of the hill.

27

Manx watched PC Delyth Morris tear into the Sellotape on a small box and lay its contents across the rickety table.

"Just ask a bloody copper," he said, flipping aimlessly through one of the leaflets the public relations team had delivered earlier that morning. "Do people even read these things?"

Morris shrugged. "Not sure what it even means, 'Just Ask A Copper'? Just ask a copper for what?"

"It means," Manx said, "we've got to stand here listening to questions we don't have answers for and taking abuse from a bunch of drunks who've overdone it on the craft beer."

"Won't be that bad, sir," Morris said, laying out the leaflets. "I wasn't doing anything tonight anyway. To be honest, I was glad to get out of the house."

"You've got nothing better to do on a Thursday night? No five-a-side?" he asked, gesturing at Morris's right eye, which was still a little swollen and purple.

Morris brought her hand to her cheek. "The girls can get a bit overenthusiastic," she said, diverting her gaze. "The centre forward's got a sharp elbow."

"Hope you gave as good as you got," Manx said.

"She didn't score the rest of the match," Morris said with a brief smile. She cleared her throat, as if she might find the right words stuck somewhere in there. "I wanted to say, sir, sorry if I've seemed a bit off lately."

"Hadn't noticed," Manx said.

"It's just my dad," she explained. "He's been ill, so me and my mam have been taking turns looking after him."

"Sorry to hear that," Manx said, glancing down the rows of food stalls as they fired up their grills and set out their wares. "Family," he said. "It's a lifetime sentence."

As Morris set out the rest of the leaflets, a voice made her look up. She stiffened and stood a little taller as DCSI Vera Troup stopped in front of the booth, dressed in a white "Food Slam" T-shirt and black jeans. A sliver of red lipstick was drawn across her lips like two asymmetrical scratches.

She turned to Manx. "Good evening, Manx. Ellis told me you'd volunteered. Your enthusiasm won't go unrecognised."

Volunteered? "Yes, ma'am, my hand was the first one up."

"And PC Morris, correct?" Vera asked.

"Ma'am," she said, nodding.

Vera gestured at the pamphlets. "Do you like the new material?"

Morris and Manx glanced at each other.

"Em... top notch, good quality on the printing," Manx said.

"Yeah, good photos too, ma'am," Morris agreed.

Vera narrowed her eyes. She was well trained in spotting an evasive reply when confronted with one as transparent as this. "Well, the focus groups were very encouraging," she said. There was an awkward pause before Vera spoke again. "I should head to the entrance, catch Logan Collins' speech."

"Police protection? I didn't realise he was that unpopular," Manx said.

Vera narrowed her eyes. "Keep up the good work, both of you." She walked away, back straight, stride purposeful.

"Ugh, he's so slimy," PC Morris said, catching a glimpse of Logan Collins emerging from a side street and shaking Vera's hand with both of his; the palm-over-hand gesture favoured by politicians of all parties. "Wouldn't trust him as far as I could throw him," she added with a dismissive shake of her head.

"I hear his fan base is pretty thin."

"The English on the island like him all right, but the Welsh, they don't want anyone who's learnt the language. He just moved here a few years ago, it's not like he's even local."

"God forbid the good people of Anglesey would vote for anything so radical," Manx said, watching Troup walk Collins towards the entrance.

Three and a half minutes away, Ronnie Powell was following orders, his boot pressed on the throttle, the van hurtling downhill and at the perfect angle to inflict optimum damage.

28

Ronnie had heard of out-of-body experiences – maybe this was one of them. He felt disconnected, his mind floating above his body. He remembered Melvin's words: "Keep a constant speed, not too fast." His uncle had also warned him about collateral damage; done right, it would be minimal, Logan Collins and one of his staff at most. One of Melvin's friends, a sound technician, Owen Porth, had let it slip after one too many pints that Collins would be speaking from a podium with a 500-watt sound system connected to two speakers mounted on stands. "Overkill," Owen Porth had spat. "Who does he think he is? The bloody prime minister or something?"

It would be a clean strike, Melvin had insisted. Take out the podium and Collins, then "get the fuck out of there, quick."

The entrance to the Food Slam less than a hundred metres away, Ronnie took a final puff and flicked the joint through the window. The draft caught the butt, blowing it back into the van. Ronnie didn't notice, he was focused on the target dead in the centre of his windscreen, his mind trying to make sense of why the hell Logan Collins wasn't anywhere near the podium.

29

If Logan Collins was disappointed with the number of people who'd turned out to hear him speak, he didn't show it. That was the politicians' way; whatever the turnout, whatever indifference, you kept on smiling, kept on-message. And this evening his message was concise and simple, as always: "Vote for Progress. Vote Logan Collins."

He'd learnt to keep things simple, speak of things people could grasp in soundbites. Tonight, would be no different. He'd speak to the progress Anglesey had made; how it was now one of the UK's most popular tourist destinations, with some of the cleanest beaches in the country; how off-island investment had attracted more visitors, providing more jobs, putting more money in the pockets of working people. He'd touch on the culinary progress; how the island had rediscovered its own rich, natural bounty; sea-to-table dining that could compete with the best of Britain's coastal restaurants.

Collins wanted to push this progress further, issue more planning permissions for holiday flats and the construction of new hotels; secure an increase in tax breaks for small businesses catering to tourists; incentives for clean energy companies setting up windfarms. He'd argue there was a national security issue too; the Ministry of Defence was looking to buy more land around RAF Valley in preparation for more fast jet training and increase the number of pilots for Air Mountain Rescue Service. Selling that land would provide new jobs, pump more money into the community.

However, the initiative he most wanted to talk about was the negotiations he'd spearheaded with the Chinese energy company, the Gonglu Corporation, to purchase the decommissioned Wylfa Nuclear Power Station. He'd worked in the industry as an energy trader for over two decades and retired three years ago at the age of forty-six to pursue his political career. The deal was far from done, but a delegation from the port city of Tiangin, in north eastern China, was due at the end of summer for a site visit. He was preparing to roll out the red carpet with the full backing of the Anglesey County Council and the UK Atomic Energy Authority. If the purchase was successful, it would mean over 4,000 new jobs during the construction phase, at least 800 when it was operational, and would supply power to over two million homes. That kind of progress didn't just garner him good publicity, it got him votes.

These were all the points Logan Collins had wanted to address before announcing the third Annual Menai Bridge Food Slam open. The fact that this never came to pass was due to one off-message decision he made that night.

The sound engineer who'd set up his PA system was right; 500 watts was overkill for the number of people. There was a better way to handle this; a more personal, man-of-the-people approach. He dumped the microphone on the podium shelf and walked out into the small, tight-knit crowd, his smile wide and bright, his hand grasping at every palm happy to shake his.

By the time he heard the high-pitched whine of the engine, he barely had time to turn around to register the van hurtling towards him and the fifty people gathered in a tight pack around him.

30

The screech of rubber burning against tarmac shattered the still evening air like a siren blast.

Ronnie pulled a hard right. The van's rear end swung around and skidded to a violent stop. People were frozen to the spot, as if they were imagining the whole scene, that this couldn't really be happening here on a summer's evening on Anglesey.

Ronnie shoved open the door, slipped out the crossbow bolt from his sock, and ran towards Logan Collins, cutting the air with the weapon as he neared his target.

"Move away! Now! I've got a bomb under here," he lied, tugging at his jacket. "Anyone tries to be a hero, I'll blow you all to fucking pieces."

No longer frozen, the crowd complied and gave Ronnie the space he demanded. All except Logan Collins, who stood there as if he was about to make a difference – become some kind of hero.

Not on my fucking watch, Ronnie thought as he stepped closer.

Collins lifted his arms in the hope the gesture might save him. It wouldn't. Ronnie quickly span around behind Collins, wrapped his right arm around his neck. He tightened the crook of his elbow around Collins' Adam's apple and poked the sharp apex of the bolt into his neck flesh, just deep enough to draw blood.

"Keep back! All of you! Keep the fuck back!"

The crowd didn't need the second command. Those who weren't filming the scene with their phones were already stepping back or had run to the nearest side streets.

Through the slim opening in his face mask, Ronnie saw a woman moving towards him; tall, thin, raven-dark hair. One of Collins' staff, he reckoned. She held a mobile phone to her ear. *Another fucking hero*, Ronnie thought, as he pulled tighter on Collins' throat and etched another shallow nick in the politician's flesh.

"Please, put the weapon down," the woman said, raising her palms. "Whatever this is about, I'm sure we can work it out."

She was calm; way too fucking calm for his liking.

"You! You... put your fucking phone down," he stammered, waving the bolt as if drawing invisible shapes in the air.

She nodded and lowered her phone, but kept the call open.

"My phone's down. Let Mr Collins go, and we can talk. No one needs to get hurt."

As he looked at the woman's way too calm posture, like she was confronted with this sort of emergency situation on a daily basis, another thought struck him. His plan was only half-formed. He hadn't figured out his next steps. All he knew was that Mel was waiting for him to return, his mission complete and successful.

He sensed Collins push back, his arms flexing as if he were about to make some heroic gesture; Ronnie put a stop to that with a fast, sharp knee to the kidneys. Collins groaned. His legs buckled. Ronnie let him fall to his knees, then struck Collins clean in the stomach with his boot. There was little resistance from Collins after that, but he kept the bolt pressing at his neck for good measure. Collins retched out the contents of his stomach. Ronnie had the power to end this now, or step it up a notch, make his uncle proud. He could stab Collins and make a run for it, or maybe there was a longer game to be played; what Melvin might have called a strategy.

As Ronnie was debating his next move, the woman reached into her bag. By the time Ronnie had registered the movement, she already had the cannister in her hand and was about to press on the nozzle. Working on instinct, Ronnie turned his head as the mist from the pepper spray caught his face. A trickle of spray seeped under his sunglasses and into his eye. The pain was instant; like staring directly into the scorching centre of the midday sun.

Ronnie did what he knew best, did what his Powell family instincts compelled him to do. He lashed out, the bolt cleaving through the air. It found its target deep in Vera Troup's abdomen.

The contact was precise and deadly; sharp steel into soft spleen. She dropped her phone and looked down to her belly where blood was spreading in a reservoir of red across her T-shirt.

Ronnie removed the blood-smeared bolt. He dug his finger under his sunglasses and into his eye; the action only intensified the pain. His anger burned deep as he looked down at Collins recovering from the kicking to his solar plexus and trying to comprehend the river of red spreading fast across the woman's T-shirt.

"Fucking walk!" he shouted, tugging on Collins' collar. "Or you'll get the same as her."

Collins rose slowly, stumbled like a newborn calf before finding his footing, the same blade that had just entered the woman's skin now against his neck. The warm dampness of her blood dripped under his collar as he stood.

Ronnie heard someone shout, "She's been stabbed, she's been stabbed!" He didn't require the reminder. He marched Collins away from the crowd towards the street leading down to the shallow cove, his face sweating under the thick fleece mask as he walked.

From the cove, it was a short few steps up a rocky incline that ended at the private boat slip where Melvin was waiting. Collins stumbled and groaned, stopping several times to empty his stomach. Ronnie hurried him along with the promise of more cold steel in his neck unless he picked up the pace.

In his wake, Vera Troup struggled to maintain consciousness, blood flooding through her fingers and pooling in thick scarlet on the warm tarmac.

31

The pain had made another unannounced visit; the third onslaught in as many days. It was as if it were building up momentum, racing Melvin to the finish. He slowly rose from his knee-bound position and looked in disgust at the red splatters across the wooden slip. Blood. The pattern reminded him of tea leaves clinging to the side of a cup; though he didn't require a fortune teller to predict his future. Like the pain, they were there to remind him that his time was short; death was merely spitting distance away.

Ronnie's voice distracted him from pondering too long on that grim thought. He looked over and squinted. Maybe his eyesight was failing too; he was sure Ronnie was with someone. As his nephew drew closer, the reality of the situation clicked into focus.

"What the fuck have you done, Ronnie?" he said, as his nephew shoved Collins towards the boat.

"Water!" Ronnie said, tearing off his sunglasses and mask. "Give me some fucking water. And keep an eye on him, don't want the bastard making a run for it."

Melvin, momentarily stunned, handed his nephew a bottle.

Ronnie poured the water into his eyeball. He blinked rapidly as he spoke. "Got any of those plastic ties you use for the paint supplies?"

"In the box by the lobster pots," Melvin said, looking at Logan Collins, blood dripping onto his shirt. He didn't look much like a politician now, looked more like a man who'd narrowly avoided death and was unsure as to when the next attack would come and if he'd be lucky enough to survive it when it arrived.

Collins let out a grunt as Ronnie jerked back his arms, wrapped a cable tie around his wrists and pulled until the plastic cut into his skin. He pushed Collins down, forcing him to sit on the centre thwart running the width of the boat.

"Here," Melvin said, handing Ronnie an oil-stained rag. "Unless you want him recognising the both of us."

"Oh, yeah, forgot," Ronnie said, securing himself on the bottom boards and pulling the rag taut behind Collins' head.

Melvin ducked into the cockpit and fired up the engine. "What the bloody hell is going on? Don't tell me you bolloxed this up too?"

"It wasn't like you said," Ronnie stammered, wiping the back of his hands across his face. "I couldn't do it. Too many people, Mel. Would have been a massacre, a fuckin' massacre."

"All right calm down and cast us off," Melvin said. "This was your plan? Kidnapping? Jesus Christ!"

"I had to think quick, like. No time," Ronnie said, reaching over to unhitch the bow line from the cleat. It took him three attempts before the rope fell free. He looped it loosely around itself and threw it under the stern-sheet.

"You couldn't just abandon the mission? Turn around?"

"Didn't want to let you down," Ronnie said, rubbing a thumb at the corner of his eye. "We can keep him our prisoner until they agree to our demands. We'll set a ransom, cut off his finger or something, send it to them so they know we're fucking serious, like."

Collins spoke, a panicked throb in his voice. "Please, let me go. I'm no one, really. I won't tell anyone. I didn't see anything."

Ronnie leant across the boat and edged the sharp point of the bolt closer into Collins' neck until he felt the resistance of soft cartilage. "You saw plenty. Now shut the fuck up."

Collins nodded his compliance.

"Put the bolt down, you're not in some bloody film." Melvin's mind rattled through a list of possible options he should be considering, none of which were good. "Christ, you've really dropped us in it this time," he said, slowly backing out of the slip.

Ronnie stood, walked unsteadily to join his uncle in the cockpit. "It's a good plan. Leverage, like, we've got leverage now."

Maybe the lad has a point, Melvin thought, but this wasn't the time to discuss the merits of any plan his nephew had just pulled from his arse. He spun the boat around, the bow facing the open water of the Menai Strait. "I need some time to wrap my head around what the fuck you've just done, Ronnie."

It wasn't the reaction Ronnie was hoping for. He finger-stabbed Melvin in the shoulder. "Done us a favour, that's what I've done," he said, getting deep into his uncle's personal space.

Mel caught the familiar funk of weed rising from Ronnie's jacket. "Thought I told you, no bloody smoking until the job was done," he said, urging the throttle as fast as the old engine would tolerate. "See, this is what happens. Your brain gets messed up, you make bad decisions."

"What the fuck does it matter, now? I only smoked half."

He grabbed the neck of Ronnie's T-shirt, shoving him against the cockpit's thin walls until they rattled. "Half?" he growled. "And what did you do with the half you didn't smoke, genius?"

Ronnie hesitated. "Erm. Threw it out, didn't I? What do you think I am, stupid?"

Melvin nodded and released his grip. As he directed the boat towards the town of Beaumaris, then piloted the craft around the west coast of Anglesey towards Bull Bay, the burn in Ronnie's eye finally eased to a steady smoulder.

The other half? Yeah, he was a hundred per cent sure he threw it out of the van window. At least ninety per cent sure, or maybe a little less.

32

At the entrance, Manx's sole priority, and one which demanded his urgent attention, was bleeding out on the tarmac, her head supported on the lap of one of the St John Ambulance volunteers who had rushed to the scene.

Manx knelt next to the man. Vera was falling fast into unconsciousness, her breath shallow, her pale skin almost translucent now as the loss of blood drew the lifeforce from her. "What's your name?" Manx asked the volunteer.

"Hugh. Hugh Jones," the man said. He was in his seventies, flush-faced, white hair falling in thin strands over his forehead. His hands were pressing hard on a pack of bandages he'd secured over the wound. It took all of Hugh's strength to keep on the pressure, his hands soaked with Vera's blood.

Manx didn't need to ask the question, Hugh's eyes told him everything he needed to know; if the paramedics didn't arrive soon no number of bandages, pressure, or praying to whatever god Hugh put his faith in would stop the inevitable. Vera's heart would soon stop pumping, and whether that happened in the middle of the street or in the major trauma unit five miles away, would be the difference between life and death.

"Hugh, can you keep her with us until the paramedics arrive?"

"I'll give it my best," Hugh said, wiping an arm across his brow. "We're not really trained to deal with this level of injury."

"Consider it on-the-job training," Manx said, feeling some relief as he heard the scream of sirens. If she could hold on a few more minutes there'd be some hope Vera would make it. Badly injured, but alive.

Behind him, a breathless PC Morris spoke. "Jesus, what happened?" she said, bringing a hand to her mouth.

"Later," Manx said. "Let's make sure she's stabilised, then we take witness statements."

As the sirens neared, he urged the crowd to move back, then stepped away, giving the paramedics the space to do their job. He was surplus to requirements now.

He turned to look at the van parked at a right angle to the entrance. The engine was still running, driver's door open, front wheels straddling the kerb. He walked over, leant in, killed the engine. The sound of jangling sitars and a woman's mournful voice coming from the speakers triggered something in his memory.

He switched the music off and examined the van's exterior. Several strips of masking tape were stuck to the sides and door panels. The number plates had been doctored; something a patrol car wouldn't have noticed from a distance, but from a few inches away the disguise looked amateur and rushed.

Focusing his attention back to the masking tape on the driver's side door panel, he caught his fingernails under one of the strips and peeled it from the metal. He did the same with the other four strips.

The revelation was no surprise. It was just as he'd expected the moment he'd heard the music and caught the metallic tinge of dried blood in his throat.

The lettering, "Halal Al's Meats" seemed to scream at him from the side of the van in a garish, flowery font.

More than screaming, it was taunting him.

PART II

KILL THE MESSENGER

33

"Operation Vanguard? Give me a break," Byron Gates snorted. He snapped his fingertips on the Batman-themed pinball, attempting to smack the malevolent grin off the Joker's face taunting him from behind the glass.

Byron, early forties, thick, unkempt beard he liked to tug at when he was nervous and eyes permanently rheumy from constant exposure to all things digital, was talking through his earphones with someone who gave their identity only as Reaper. This wasn't unusual for the kind of people Byron dealt with; people with valid reasons to conceal their real identities. It had taken him a decade to cultivate this web of informers, military personnel compelled to expose the covert operations of global military and technology complex in which they worked, but still valued their careers as well as their lives. Byron was their conduit, a safe harbour from what they'd refer to as the Triple P Threat: Persecution. Prosecution. Prison.

"Listen," Byron said, grinding his teeth and tracking the pinball as it rolled downwards. "This is some real *Alice in Wonderland* bollocks." He flipped the ball, firing a series of lights and ratcheting up his score. "I'm not going down that rabbit hole. Been there, done that, moved on."

However, the next sentence Reaper spoke made the hairs on his neck bristle like they'd been brushed crossways. His concentration was shot. The ball slipped down the gutters with a cackle of laughter and a menacing "Hurry up and die already, sucker," from the Joker. But Byron wasn't listening. He barely even cared he'd just blown past his personal best score. What he'd just heard beat any pinball high. "Are you one hundred and one per cent sure?"

No response. The air was now dead air. Not that it mattered, Byron's attention was now focused on the insistent voice in his head telling him this was the one he'd been waiting for; the mother lode.

He yanked out his earphones hauled his backpack across his shoulder and looked over the SuperBoss Arcade. The arcade was knee-deep in curated retro nostalgia: flashing pink and blue neon stripes across the walls, eighties synth pop blasting through the speakers, and a selection of vintage video games; *Space Invaders*, *Pac-Man*, *Defender*, *Asteroids* and the like. He'd played them all when he was younger; more than played them, mastered them. Surveying the teenagers hunched over the games, killing time during the summer holiday, he guessed they were too young to have played them first time round. What was the word he'd heard recently? Snowflakes? Yeah, these kids were definitely snowflakes; playing first-person-shooter games while their government committed acts of real violence in the name of the war on terror? Yeah, those kids would disintegrate like snowflakes under the weight of that knowledge; the kind of knowledge truth seekers like Byron Gates dedicated their lives to searching out.

His website, DronewatchUK, had been tracking RAF drone

strikes for several years. The site had suffered several denial-of-service attacks and been served a series of cease and desist orders, all of which he'd ignored. Over the past couple of years that kind of attention had tapered off. The authorities probably concluded an amateur-looking website with little traffic and minimal influence posed little danger to their operations.

It had also become apparent to Byron that the majority of the public felt the same. They cared little about the atrocities committed thousands of miles from home – so long as it wasn't happening on their doorstep. There was even a phrase for it: "War Fatigue". Byron imagined it was far worse than fatigue by now, more like a numbness that compelled people to bury their faces in the nearest device to hand to blot out the bad news. It was a way to hold on to your sanity, he thought, but it came at a price; a price which Byron Gates himself had never been willing to pay.

If what Reaper had said was true, this was the breakthrough story he'd been waiting for. One of his informants had sent him the Operation Vanguard report via a triple-encrypted email server several months ago. *Missile launched. Successful kill strike on a convoy of insurgents, followed by a secondary explosion, detonated by nearby IS enemy combatants that took out a convoy of RAF medics following behind.*

As Byron's mind churned, his phone buzzed. He clicked through his triple-factor authentication to access the message. Reaper wanted to meet. He could barely type his reply fast enough.

Where and when?

Several minutes later, the reply buzzed through. Byron checked the driving time from Waddington to Anglesey; three-

and-a-half hours with no traffic, closer to four-and-a-half with. The request was a no-brainer; a meeting with someone who was in the ground control station the day Operation Vanguard was launched was too golden an opportunity to ignore.

Decision made, he walked out into the warm Lincolnshire afternoon, leaving the Joker's cackles and taunts for another day.

34

Manx walked into the waiting room outside Gwynedd Hospital's intensive care unit. Slumped in a chair, DCI Canton was half-asleep, snoring like a contented dog. He sensed someone standing over him and woke with a grunt.

"The doctors induced a medical coma to assist with the healing," he said, stifling a yawn. "But they had to remove her spleen, which will compromise her immune system for the rest of her life. But I suppose it's preferable to the alternative."

"Christ," Manx said, peering through the glass at the man he guessed was Vera's husband sitting at her bedside, the young girl he recalled from the school sports day sprawled across his chest.

"Aye, when it's one of our own, always makes it harder."

One of our own. Four words that never failed to coat Manx's spine with ice. He'd last heard the phrase three months ago when a colleague of his from the Met, CeeCee Cartwright, was found dead on the tracks outside Shoreditch station. Hearing those words never got any easier, in fact, he suspected it got harder each time.

"Not your fault," Canton said, as if reading Manx's mind.

"Vera," he clarified. "Nothing you could have done to prevent this."

Manx looked through the third-floor window to the news crews gathered below. "No ransom demands?"

Canton rose from the chair. "Not a peep. Apart from the usual nut jobs who seem to think wasting police time is a career choice."

"Why Collins?" Manx pondered. "I understand he's not exactly popular, but kidnapping?"

"Been tying myself in knots over that one too. Why kidnap if there's no ransom demand?"

"What if it wasn't planned that way?"

Canton cocked his head like a curious bird.

"By Bevan's calculations, the length of the tyre marks on the road indicates sudden braking from approximately thirty miles per hour. If the intent was to take Collins hostage, why abandon the van, run into a crowd then lead Collins away with a blade to his throat? It's too public, too many witnesses."

"Where are you going with this, Manx?"

"How many attacks have there been when some terrorist ploughs a van, or a car, into a crowd? It's efficient, sends a big message."

"A terrorist attack with the intent of killing and maiming innocent bystanders? This is Anglesey for God's sake, Manx."

"Collins was meant to be speaking that night," Manx continued, testing the theory he'd been churning over most of last night. "He had a podium and speakers set up at the entrance. All the witnesses state he never used it, walked straight into the crowd. What if the original plan was to drive the van directly at Collins, but that plan changed when they saw Collins wasn't at the podium?"

Canton thought for a moment. "And you think there's a terrorist angle here?"

"Not sure, but the van was reported stolen two days ago from outside the Halal abattoir in Gaerwen. Which could point to terrorism, or more likely someone trying to frame it that way."

Canton sighed. "So, do we have any actual, hard evidence?"

"Bevan retrieved the butt of a marijuana joint from the van, but if the DNA's not in the database we're not much further on."

The sudden and loud shriek of an emergency alarm bouncing off the hospital walls startled them both. Seconds later, a flurry of activity as a doctor and two nurses wheeling a complex array of medical equipment barged into Vera's room.

Canton and Manx stepped back as the team huddled around the bed and worked as one seamless unit; efficient, practised; urgent.

"Are you a religious man?" Canton asked.

"Not particularly."

"Faith in anything?"

Manx gestured at the team attending to Vera. "Medical science, I suppose, at times like this," he said, his mind replaying the dark feeling he'd had that day at St Gerard's as the clock tower cast its deep shadow across the lawn.

Canton didn't reply. But in the manner his lips were moving, Manx guessed he was muttering a silent prayer under his breath.

"Let's hope it's enough, eh, Manx," Canton finally said, his fingers wrapping around each other like a set of worry beads threading into a ball of tight pink flesh.

35

When Manx returned to the station later that morning, the mood in the incident room was sombre; he could sense the tension from out in the hallway. As he walked in, the team turned to look at him, faces expectant, eager for good news, but fearing the worst. He had no good news to give, and relayed what Canton had told him. Unsurprisingly, it did nothing to lift the mood. To steer their attention elsewhere, he stood in front of the incident board, removed his jacket and rolled up his shirt sleeves.

"Right, we still have Flynt's suspicious death, Logan Collins' kidnapping and a violent assault on Vera Troup. What if anything connects all of these?"

Following a brief interlude of shoe-gazing from the team, Morris spoke. "What about the hit-and-run on Bobbie Matthews? Shouldn't we include that too?"

"Fair enough," Manx said, circling Bobbie's name. "Does that help us any?"

"Matthews and Flynt were both stationed at RAF Valley, and Logan Collins is always going on about expanding the airbase, adding more jobs," Morris said.

"It's a stretch. Tenuous."

Manx directed his attention back to the incident board. "Let's take a few steps back. Three weeks ago, we had a spate of holiday home fires. The last house was owned by Logan Collins. According to the fire inspector, they're all connected; same accelerant, same MO. A few days later, we find James Flynt's body. No connection to the fires, or Collins, as far as we know."

He pointed to another photograph. "The van we found at Menai Bridge was owned by Ali Kalpar. Whoever took it knew his security cameras weren't working, which shows premeditation. Also, Kalpar had no connection to Flynt or Collins. I'm not saying there is no connection, just that we haven't found it yet. Morris, care to fill us in on what you dug up on Bobbie Matthews?"

"Not much, sir. She didn't have much of an online profile. No Facebook account, Instagram or LinkedIn."

"Who the hell doesn't have a Facebook page?" Nader asked. "Can't get my gran off the bloody thing and she's eighty-seven."

"Not everyone wants to share their life all over the internet," Morris said.

"That why you won't accept my friend request?" Nader said. "Afraid I'll get to know too much about you?"

"No, sarge," Morris said. "I'm afraid I'll get to know too much about you."

There was a short round of chuckling that lightened the mood for a moment before Morris continued. "According to the electoral register, Bobbie Matthews moved to Valley eleven months ago."

"Moved? Where from?" Manx asked.

Morris checked her notes. "Waddington, Lincolnshire."

Manx reached for his marker pen and redrew the faint line he'd drawn between Flynt's photograph and Bobbie Matthews' name a few days back. "That's our connection. Flynt was stationed at RAF Waddington. He transferred to Valley twelve months ago, Bobbie Matthews follows soon after."

"Yeah, makes sense now," Nader said. "He makes sure she gets transferred to Valley so they can continue the affair. They had a lover's tiff. She asks him to meet her at Benllech, they argue, she smashes the bloke in the head, he falls, ends up in the Irish Sea."

"But why would she confess to seeing Flynt that night?" Morris pushed. "If she killed him, she'd keep that quiet."

"Unless she's playing us," Priddle offered. "Like a double bluff. Saw that on a TV show once."

"Okay," Manx said, sensing the conversation was heading downhill fast. "Our number one priority is finding Logan Collins. Witness statements, CCTV videos, rumblings on social media. Canton's doing a direct appeal to the public for any information. Someone on this island knows who's holding him and where. We find him, we get Collins before it's too late, and we get justice for Vera."

"What if it's already too late, sir?" Morris asked.

A hush fell over the room.

"It's our job to make sure that it's not too late, Morris," Manx said. "Now, let's do our bloody jobs and find Collins."

36

Something about Danica Collins' eyes caught Manx's attention – something more than the expected spiderweb of redness after a night spent fretting about whether her husband was still alive. As she removed the tissue from her face, he realised what had made him look twice; her eyes were slightly different colours, one blue, the other a lighter green hue. It lent her an air of coolness that reminded him of a cat wary of someone trespassing on her territory.

Danica was wearing an oversized grey hoodie; not exactly wearing it, more like lost in it. Her face, bare of make-up and with lost sleep draining it of colour, was undeniably striking; her cheekbones high and those eyes, piercing and other-worldly. Her hair, naturally blonde was pulled in a tight ponytail. She spoke with an accent – Slavic, Manx guessed – but her diction was perfect, probably educated at an expensive British private school.

"Do you know who took my husband, inspector?"

Manx paused. She didn't seem the kind of woman who'd appreciate weak platitudes. "To be honest, Mrs Collins, we're no further than we were a day ago."

"Honesty?" she said, folding her legs under her. "Am I meant to be grateful for that?"

Manx ignored the question, which he took as rhetorical anyway. "Have either you or your husband received any threating letters or emails in the past few weeks? Anything that made you concerned for your safety?"

"We would have informed the police, immediately."

"Understood," Manx said. "But could Mr Collins have kept them from you, so as not to worry you?"

Danica wrapped her arms around herself and sunk back into the huge white sofa. "Logan and I have no secrets, inspector."

"Right you are." If Manx had a pound for each time he'd heard that well-worn cliché from a spouse, he'd be retired by now.

"My husband is running as a conservative candidate; I understand that can stir negative feelings in a place with such a strong Welsh identity. But kidnapping? People are more likely to spill their venom on social media these days, don't you think?"

"Or else burn down your property."

Danica let Manx's words hang for a moment. "And I suppose, honestly, you are no closer to solving that crime, either?"

"I suspect they may be connected."

"Perceptive," Danica said, raising her perfectly plucked eyebrows in an arch of sarcasm.

Manx continued. "We'll need access to all your husband's contacts, work and friends. And if you have a recent photo, we'll need that to circulate to the press."

She nodded to herself several times, as if counting the beats of a music track. "Why did they take my husband? Should there not be a ransom demand? Unless–" Danica couldn't bring herself to finish her sentence.

"Best not to jump to conclusions," Manx said. "It's not unusual, the kidnappers will want to make you anxious."

"Job done," Danica deadpanned.

"There's a task-force in place to intercept any communication. We'll station a service car outside your home at all times, but my guess is that when they do make contact it's going to be less personal. Your husband's a public figure, there's value in that, they'll want to exploit it."

"Comforting," she replied, with a tight feline smile.

"Mrs Collins, kidnappings often resolve with the hostages being returned, unharmed," Manx assured her.

"So you can promise me you'll find my husband alive?"

Manx paused, navigating around the trap she was laying out. "I can promise you I'll do everything in my power to find him."

Danica stretched out her legs and stood. "I suppose I will have to take you at your word. I'll get you those contacts you requested."

Manx sat back and sighed. He'd promised no platitudes, then delivered the woman one, nonetheless. Whoever was holding Collins was taking their sweet time in deciding where to place their chess piece. It was the kind of waiting game Manx had little patience for, especially with Troup fighting for her life and Collins still missing.

"Do the names James Flynt or Bobbie Matthews mean anything to you, Mrs Collins?" he asked as she returned with a printout and photograph.

"No. Should they?" she said, handing the papers to Manx.

"Just a long shot. Thank you for your time," he said.

Outside, Manx took in a breath of air. Two days and still no ransom demand? Danica was right. It didn't look good. Morris's words kept coming back to him. *What if it's already too late?*

37

The old coal shed was six feet high and four feet wide and built from stones left over from the construction of the Lantern Arms. It had been decades since any coal was shovelled in or out, but the walls and floor remained coated in a film of black soot. The air inside was thick, as if it were becoming fat off the remnants of coal dust. Not that Logan Collins could see any of this. He could smell it though; it choked his throat with mildew and dank earth. It was what he imagined the bottom of a grave might smell like.

Collins was blindfolded, with a wide strip of duct tape secured over his mouth, his hands and feet also bound. He had to breathe through his nostrils, which were crusted with coal soot, making his nose run. He couldn't remember feeling this degree of hunger before, but more than food, he needed water; buckets of the stuff. He'd read that the human body could live for weeks without food, but water? That was as basic and life-sustaining as they came.

He shuffled along the floor, lifted his feet and kicked against the door. It refused to budge, but he could see slivers of sunlight and hear voices; the same two men that had taken him; Ronnie and Mel. He'd made a point of remembering. How long had it been since they took him? A day? Two? Time seemed immaterial to him now. Surviving this was his goal now. Whatever this was.

Collins leant his ear against the door, catching snippets of conversation as the men spoke.

"A copper! You knifed a fucking copper?" Melvin said, brandishing a copy of this morning's *North Wales Daily Post* as if it were a weapon, stabbing his finger across the headline: "Senior police officer fighting for her life after brutal stabbing attack."

"I didn't fucking know, did I?" Ronnie said, cowering like a scared dog. "Stupid bitch got in the way."

"You've really dropped us in it this time. You couldn't just follow orders? Run into the bastard like we planned?"

"Already told you, too many people. I didn't have a choice."

"You had a choice. You just made the wrong one, as usual."

The sound of Collins battering against the door startled them.

"Get him out," Melvin said. "Before Lydia gets wind."

Ronnie complied, dragging Collins from the shed and forcing him to stand. Collins shook his head, tried to speak but could only manage a series of incoherent grunts. Melvin stepped forward and ripped the duct tape from his mouth. Collins let out a sharp groan of pain and chugged large mouthfuls of air.

"Water," he said. His words were tinder dry and ripped at his throat like barbed wire. "Please, water."

Melvin gestured for Ronnie to get him what he wanted. As Ronnie shuffled off, Collins felt his lungs filling, his head clearing some. Breathing was good, but he needed to see these men; look into the whites of their eyes, consider their intentions.

"The blindfold? Can you?"

"You must be bloody joking," Melvin said. "You'll get water and food, that'll be it."

Collins nodded. "Small mercies," he muttered, and he meant it. He did feel grateful to the man, Mel, the older sounding one. He'd take Mel's small mercies, as many of them as he could get.

Ronnie returned and shoved the plastic bottle to his lips. Collins swallowed and, like Oliver Twist, dared to ask for more.

"More? I'm not your fuckin' errand boy," Ronnie barked.

Collins took a breath, found some words. "You do want to keep me alive, don't you? For whatever it is you're planning? I'm sure I'm no use to you people dead."

Collins couldn't see, but he guessed Mel had directed Ronnie to fetch more water "What is it you want, money?"

Melvin said nothing, just looked at the man standing in front of him; his expensive clothes covered in dirt, his face smudged with soot and dried blood. What did he want with him? It was a bloody good question. He'd never wanted this but with Collins their prisoner, he needed to figure out something fast. They couldn't let him walk. He'd seen their faces, heard their names, it wouldn't take the police long to track them down, especially on this island.

"Keep your mouth shut, unless you fancy dying in there," Melvin said – a death threat was as good a distraction as any from answering his question.

Collins swallowed. "And are you planning to kill me?"

Melvin felt his patience wearing thin. "Yeah. Yeah I bloody well might if you don't stop fuckin' talking," he said, lunging forward and grabbing Collins' shirt collar.

"Good idea, rough him up a bit," Ronnie said when he returned. "Bastard deserves what's coming."

Melvin watched as Collins drank desperately from the bottle. Good ideas? He was short on those, but he wasn't stupid enough to let Collins in on the fact. "Lock him up," he said.

Collins protested. Ronnie put a swift end to that by ramming a fist into his solar plexus and stood back grinning as Collins vomited most of the water he'd just drunk onto the floor.

"Where you off to?" he asked, as Melvin grabbed his car keys.

"Calling someone," he said. "Don't want him listening in."

Throwing himself into the driver's seat of his car, Melvin felt a deep paralysing shock. It was as if his chest was collapsing in on him, followed by a pain that clawed his insides like a grappling hook. The doctor had warned him about this; a severe bout of pain that would arrive without warning and leave in much the same way. He prayed the doctor was right, that the pain would leave, and soon.

He breathed slowly and deliberately, hoping it might ease the agony; it didn't and made Melvin more conscious of what he was sure was the cancer's intention: to remind him he had no dominion over the disease. Eventually, the pain eased to a dull throb that transmitted pulses of electricity through his stomach; he might have called them butterflies, but that was too pretty a word. They were more brutal; more like bat wings, thousands of them, baffling and beating, trying to find a way out.

He called the number he'd intended to call some ten minutes ago before the blunt reminder of the cancer sucker punched him. The call was picked up on the second ring.

"Hi, love, it's me. Yeah, that help you offered? I might take you up on it after all."

38

Mohsin Sadiq, lived on one of the less desirable housing estates on the outskirts of Bangor. As Manx turned into the dour estate – even the sunlight struggled to grace the houses and lawns with any semblance of warmth – his neck-hairs pricked to attention. It wasn't the sort of place that took to coppers turning up in the middle of the day. The vacant stares from the teenagers drinking their way through the summer holidays reminded Manx he was a visitor here, and the car was hardly helping him blend in. The kids' jaws slacked open as he drove: they were either impressed at the sight of forty-year-old British coachwork entering their territory; or a car with functioning wheels and not sitting on its chassis supported by bricks was a rare sighting in the neighbourhood.

Mohsin's house was the best kept in the cul-de-sac; lawn groomed, rose bushes trimmed, flower baskets well-watered. Manx parked outside the living room window where he could hopefully keep an eye on the car. The kids may have looked impressed, but that didn't mean a butterfly's bollocks in a place like this.

"I don't know what this has to do with us," Mohsin said,

grasping for his wife's hand as they sat. Mohsin and Rida were in their late sixties and as neatly put-together as their front garden: perfectly pressed slacks and ironed short-sleeved shirt for him, a deep green and gold sari for her. They looked at each other, each hoping the other had an answer, and when coming up empty-handed, returned their communal gaze back to Manx.

"I understand. But it's our job to follow up on a criminal accusation."

"What criminal accusation?" Mohsin snapped. "Who made this accusation?"

"Ali Kalpar. He thinks you were involved in the theft of his van, which was subsequently used in a violent crime."

Mohsin flipped open his palms and shrugged. "Why would I steal a van that I already sold to him? It makes no sense."

"I told you," Rida said. "Didn't I say only trouble will come from doing business with that man? So stubborn, you never listen."

Mohsin patted his wife's hand. "Hush now, water under the bridge. What's done cannot be undone."

Outside, Manx heard a cacophony of voices. He glanced through the window; the Jensen was still on four wheels, unmolested. He continued. "Can you tell me your whereabouts on the evening the van was taken? Wednesday July 23rd?"

They both looked at each other, a nervous flicker dancing between their eyes, then glanced to the floor.

"Mr Sadiq?" Manx urged.

Rida slowly rose from the sofa and walked over to a cabinet packed end-to-end with photographs slipped into ornate picture frames. She carefully took one in her hand, sat back and handed it to Manx. "Our son, Danvir," she said, folding her hands to her lap.

Manx checked it out. A chubby-faced young man wearing John Lennon-style glasses and a huge smile – the kind of smile that told the world he was coming, and the world had better take notice.

"He was killed, last year. He was a medic in the RAF."

"I'm very sorry–" Manx began.

"Yes, everyone is very sorry, so many apologies," Rida interrupted, a weary steeliness woven into her voice. "Wednesday was our son's birthday. He would have been thirty-six. We promised to honour him by celebrating his life not his death."

"Well, he died for something important," Manx said, struggling for words. "Serving his country."

"Oh?" Rida said. "What did he die for that was so important?"

"Rida," her husband chided, with a low sigh.

Rida paid no heed. "Oil? Money? Revenge? I loved my son with all my heart, but I cannot pretend he died for something good. I have many relatives who have witnessed this war on terror. I never thought Danvir would..."

She quickly caught herself, working hard to keep the tears dammed in. "To answer your question, on Wednesday we were here with our family remembering our son who died for nothing. That, inspector, is what we were doing the night that bloody fool Ali Kalpar says we stole his van. Shame on him. Shame. On. Him."

Manx wasn't often stuck for words, but Rida had rendered him speechless. She was crying softly, weaving her fingers over and through themselves. Manx rose and returned the photograph to the cabinet. As he did so, he noticed another photo; Danvir's wedding day. The woman standing next to him, his bride, compelled him to look closer. Max had stood by her hospital bed not three days ago.

"I assume this is Danvir's wife?" he asked.

Mohsin looked up. "Yes. Bobbie. She's a good daughter-in-law, always comes to visit, even though..." Mohsin's thought trailed away, evaporating like jet vapor in the air.

"Would it be okay if I took this for a while?" Manx asked.

"Why? Why would you need that?" Rida asked. "Bobbie's not involved with this. No, you cannot take it."

Manx pulled out his mobile phone. "Is this okay?" he asked, switching on the camera function. "It's just routine, that's all, eliminating people from our inquiries."

Rida shook her head. "I suppose I can't stop you. Mohsin, you can see the policeman out," she said, then left the room.

39

"You're late," Bobbie said, as Call Me Andy walked towards her. She'd been standing outside his office on the 2nd floor of the RAF Valley Welfare Hub for the past ten minutes.

"Sorry," Pierce said, struggling to balance a ream of papers in his hands. "My meeting with Commander Boyd ran over. Can you hold these?"

Bobbie took the papers and watched carefully as he entered the five-digit code, taking note of each number as he pressed on the keypad.

Inside, the office air was stagnant and hot, and the desire to run a finger under her shirt collar was strong. But that would have been too much of a "tell", more than Bobbie was willing to surrender. "It was you, wasn't it?" she said.

Call Me Andy looked up from his notes. "It was me what, Bobbie?"

"You found me, drove me to the hospital."

"Do not pass a man in need, for you may be the hand of God to him."

"I don't really relate to fairy stories. What were you doing on the road at that time of night? Awfully late for you to be out driving."

"Are you interrogating me?"

"No, just curious. Seems like a coincidence, my therapist finding me out there."

"Lucky I did find you. If it makes you feel better, I was counselling an AA meeting in Holyhead. I took the back roads back to the base housing."

"Must have been my lucky night."

Pierce calmly sat back. "All this resentment and anger. It's counterproductive to your healing. You're in a very vulnerable place right now. You need to let someone help you."

"You know me, Andrew, I don't do vulnerable."

"Remember what I told you a few months ago when we first talked?" Pierce said, leaning forward.

"You said a lot of things."

"Specifically, about your shadow soul, how it can serve as a vessel for all your repressed negative emotional reactions to your trauma. Fear, resentment, rage, guilt, depression, shame, paranoia–"

"Aren't we paranoid ones the only ones who really know what's going on?" she interrupted.

Pierce continued. "That kind of darkness can be overwhelming, Bobbie, it can be hard to fight against if you don't have the necessary mental tools. Have you felt anything like that? I liken it to brain fog, but it's darker, like you'll never find your way through it."

Bobbie thought on the question. Call Me Andy could have been describing any hours in her life between waking and sleeping over the past twelve months. "If that ever happens, I'll let you know," she said.

"Good. Good to know, Bobbie," he said. "Oh, I thought you might like this back." He reached into his briefcase and placed the headset she'd given him a few days ago on his desk. "I noticed some of the gems were loose, so I glued them back on."

"Why? Why did you do that?" Bobbie said, standing. "I didn't ask you."

"Just a gesture, that's all. I thought it might help."

"You thought wrong. I told you, it's no use to me now."

A few minutes after she left, Bobbie's words still smarting like nettle stings, Pierce ran his hands along the crust of gems. In two weeks, Bobbie Matthews would be out of his sphere of influence. The thought carved a deep hole in his stomach. He'd been naïve to think Flynt would have kept Bobbie on the base, but what pinched his heart most was that he'd failed Bobbie; failed a woman who he'd loved since they'd first met, though had never found the courage to tell her. Bobbie wasn't lost to him yet; he still had time. Time to prove to her that if she couldn't accept God as her saviour, then she'd have to accept him as her saviour.

He looked out to the airstrip, the thud of helicopter rotors cutting through the warm air, and ground his palms into the headset, his thumbs edging under the gems until they began to shed like confetti onto his desk.

40

Byron Gates had checked into the Rose Cottage Bed and Breakfast earlier that day. After setting up his laptop, he logged into his private IP wireless connection and checked his messages; nothing since yesterday – good news, it meant Reaper was still committed to meeting.

After unpacking, he drove to a nearby pub, ordered a shandy and scarfed down a ham and cheese toastie, before heading to the meeting point; a café called Tide on the Halen Môn sea-salt plant.

When Byron arrived, a cluster of be-shorted tourists were being led around the Saltcote visitors centre. He ordered himself a cappuccino from the coffee truck and found himself a quiet table far from the crowds.

As he made himself comfortable, he took in his surroundings. The Saltcote was perched on the banks of the Menai Strait with a breathtaking vista across a green-blue ribbon of water. Byron was struck by the majesty of the view: a bucolic setting of lush fields with speckles of sheep, like cotton-wool puffs, set against the green. Above the green, the sun anointed the knotty spine of the Snowdonia mountains with a hazy glow, and at the shallowest points of the strait the water rushed in white flurries.

As he sat, his mind cleared. He'd been far too tense over the past few days, spent too many hours with his eyes focused inches from his screen. It took his mind some minutes to adjust, as if the real world was too overwhelming, its panoramas too wide, its colours too vibrant and saturated, requiring his brain some time to recalibrate.

He glanced at the crowds and wondered if Reaper was watching, or even if someone might be following him. He'd suffered a severe paranoid episode several months ago when he was certain he was being watched. He had no proof, but what was it they said about paranoia? It's the realisation that everything around you is alive and urgent? That's how he felt now; as if everything around him was dialled up a notch, tweaked to the maximum setting.

Reaper had asked him to send a photograph. Initially, he'd refused, but relented when Reaper threatened to back out of meeting. He'd taken a selfie and sent it via a double-encrypted website he used for transferring documents. Reaper had obviously wanted to make sure Byron knew who was in control. All he could do was wait for him to make the first move and introduce himself.

He didn't need to wait long.

He was barely three sips into his coffee when someone pulled up the chair across from him and sat. Byron's face must have betrayed his surprise.

"Expecting someone else?" Bobbie Matthews said, pulling the bill of her baseball cap low over her forehead.

41

After attaching the photograph Logan Collins' wife had given him to the incident board, Manx turned to the team. "No communication, no ransom, no clue as to where he's being held and who's holding him. We're relying on witness testimony and luck, both notoriously unreliable and illusive."

"All the witnesses say the same thing, boss," Nader said. "The bloke was wearing a face mask and sunglasses. He kicked and punched Collins then led him off with some kind of weapon, maybe a knife, to his neck."

"That tallies with the surgeon's report on Vera's wound," Manx said. "Any updates on the witness footage?"

"Eight people filmed the incident on their cell phones. We looked at all the footage. Nothing that contradicts the witness statements, but this one was interesting." Priddle turned his computer screen to face Manx. "It was taken just before it happened."

Manx watched the brief, shaky video. The white van hurtling down the hill, its nose aimed directly at the Food Slam entrance. The loud squeal of brakes, tyre skids, and the van almost jack-knifing before coming to a stop, the front wheels mounting the kerb. The silhouette of a man running into the crowd.

"No doubt in my mind," Manx said. "Collins wasn't where he was meant to be, the driver notices and deviates from the plan. Now he's lumbered with a hostage he doesn't know what to do with, which is why we're still waiting for the bloody ransom demand. Collins has probably seen his kidnapper's face, so he can't just let him go. He's still figuring out his next move. We're in a waiting game."

"The witnesses only saw one man," Priddle said. "Maybe someone else was waiting for him down a side street."

Manx gestured to the scene-of-crime photographs. "The CCTV footage's been analysed from every angle. Unless he knew exactly where the cameras were positioned, then made a point of avoiding them, he vanished into thin air."

"What if he didn't have a car?" Morris said, almost leaping from her chair and marching over to the incident board.

"Meaning?" Manx asked.

She traced a finger along one of the aerial photographs, following the outline of houses on the Anglesey side of the strait. "There's all these private slips between Menai Bridge and Beaumaris. Someone with a boat could have been waiting for him."

Manx considered her theory. "Knock on some doors first thing tomorrow, see if anyone had their slip used without their permission in the last few days."

"Sir," Morris said, unable to resist a small smile as she returned to her seat.

"Priddle, any luck with that hit-and-run incident?"

"Right, almost forgot, what with all this going on." He flicked through his notebook. "Spoke to all the garages on the island. Nobody's worked on a driver's side wing mirror repair in the last two weeks. I'll extend the search to Bangor and Caernarvon. Don't think they're connected do you, boss?"

Manx pinned the print of Danvir and Bobbie to the board. "Bobbie Matthews' husband, Danvir Sadiq, died last year on a tour of duty in Syria. His parents, Mohsin and Rida Sadiq, used to own the Halal abattoir in Gaerwen until they sold the business, including the delivery van, to Ali Kalpar several months ago. This van is the same one used in the kidnapping and the attack on Vera Troup. It's a tenuous link to Bobbie Matthews, and as far as we know she had no connection to Collins."

"How's Vera doing, boss?" Nader asked.

"Still critical. But don't let that be a distraction. Vera wouldn't want us sitting around twiddling our thumbs and worrying about her. Go out there, do your jobs, solve the case."

His words were met with a thoughtful nodding of heads. They all understood the subtext. Whether she survived this or not, they had to do Vera Troup proud. They owed one of their own that much at the very least.

42

Byron Gates wiped a smudge of foam and chocolate powder from his lips. "Reaper?" he said, taking stock of the woman. Build: slight and wearing too much clothing for the warm weather. Face: sharp and angular, a blot of a birthmark above her right eye and a series of minor scratches which looked recent across her cheeks and brow. Eyes: well, those were hidden behind the polarised sheen of aviator shades tinted so dark all he could see was his reflection in the lenses.

"I'm going to make this brief, Byron."

"Yeah, all right, brief's good."

"The official report they released about Operation Vanguard. Do you think it's a cover-up?"

Byron took a short sip of coffee and made a serious effort to appear nonchalant, leaning back and folding his hands into his lap. "Could be. Not that anyone gives a shit."

"I was there. I give a shit," Bobbie said.

Byron gestured to the papers he'd laid out on the table. "After the initial strike, there was a counter-attack by insurgents that left six RAF medics dead. You have proof that's not the case?"

"Who sent you that report, Byron?"

"I couldn't tell you even if I knew. Most of the information I receive is anonymous, obviously."

"And why did this one make such an impression?"

Byron stroked his beard. "It didn't, not at first. But when I published it, the web traffic went off the charts, and then..." he hesitated, glancing nervously towards the patio as a woman stumbled over one of the chairs, knocking over a coffee cup.

"Then what, Byron?" Bobbie urged.

He lowered his voice to just above a whisper. "I couldn't prove anything, but you know when you get that feeling that someone's watching you? I'd get that every time I left the house. I don't know, maybe I was just being paranoid or something."

"It's likely you were being followed, or at least watched."

"Do you think they're watching now?"

"Watching who? Me or you?"

Byron twisted his coffee cup around. "Em... both I suppose."

"I scouted the area a few hours ago and checked out that Toyota Prius of yours for tracking devices."

Byron's mouth slacked open.

"Don't worry, nothing to report. But the question I'm asking myself is, are you the person I should be talking to about this? Are you a safe harbour?"

"Oh, yeah, no worries there." Byron straightened his back. "My site's triple-encrypted, non-static IP addresses, military-grade firewalls, the works. No one's hacking into that without tripping a series of alarms that'll shutter down the whole site."

"Good to know. Now, Here's the deal, Byron, I tell you the whole story. You post it. But you need to do something for me."

He hesitated. "Like what?"

"You need to take this story to one of the national newspapers, one of the more respectable ones."

Byron grimaced. "It's risky, leaves me exposed. I'm not sure–"

"You're not sure?" Bobbie interrupted. "I'm handing you one of the biggest stories on our government's drone programme you've ever had access to and you're not sure?"

Byron tugged sharply on his beard. "I don't even know if you're legit, you could be setting me up."

Bobbie reached into her bag and took out a copy of the *Daily Post* from three days ago, making sure he could see the headline.

RAF officer found dead on popular Anglesey beach.

"Do you recognise the name?" she said, pointing at the paper.

Byron glanced at James Flynt's name, shook his head.

"Flight Commander Flynt was the overseer, what we called the Boss-Auth, in the station that day."

Byron sensed an arc of electricity pulsing through him. "Do you think they killed him, to keep him quiet?"

"It's possible. It's also possible they might kill me, which is why the urgency in getting this story out there, Byron."

"Jesus," he said, sitting back as if he'd been walloped in the sternum. "If they knew I'd talked to you–"

"You haven't signed the Official Secrets Act. I'm exposed here, not you."

Her words were some comfort to Byron, but he still felt uneasy. There was a detached coldness about her that unsettled him.

She continued. "What is important is that you tell this story and tell it correctly. Those medics were not killed by an enemy strike. A secondary battle damage assessment was conducted after our drone left the strike zone, but that report never came to light. After an official hearing, everyone involved with Operation Vanguard was cleared of any blame, but the command saw fit to permanently suspend my combat-ready status. That, Byron, is not acceptable."

"Yeah, I can see that," Byron said, sensing a surety in her tone that made him think she'd spent too many hours churning this over in her mind – the signs were familiar. He reached into his backpack and retrieved a small voice recorder. "Is this okay?"

She stared at the antiquated device. "Bit analogue, isn't it?"

Byron huffed. "I'd like to see some black hat attempt to hack their way into an off-the-grid strip of magnetic tape," he said, checking the micro-cassette was fully rewound.

"Off the grid? If you say so," she said. "I'd go and grab yourself another coffee: this could take a while."

Byron's tape stopped recording fifty-eight minutes and thirty seconds later; his coffee untouched. Reaper had been good to her word, relayed everything that had happened that day, albeit with an eerie tone of detachment. When she talked about the explosion that took out the medics' convoy, her tone shifted, a perceptible crack in her voice. "Imagine the worst day you could possibly have, then multiply it to the power of ten and you might just begin to get close."

"Aren't you risking everything?" Byron said. "Telling me this? They'll figure out it was you eventually."

"I've already lost everything that ever mattered to me. There's nothing left for them to take away."

Byron clicked off the recorder. He had no idea how to respond to her words, other than avert his eyes and make himself look busy stuffing papers back into his backpack.

"If you've got what you need–" Bobbie said, running a finger under her shades.

Byron guessed she was wiping away a tear but couldn't be sure. "Yeah, yeah, it's great, really good stuff."

Bobbie didn't offer her hand and Byron didn't offer his. They were strangers who had met at a table, talked, then gone their separate ways.

As she slipped through the crowd, Byron sipped his coffee and winced; it was stone-cold. He'd been so engrossed in Reaper's account he'd failed to notice the sun had been beating down hard for the past hour; his face felt as if it had been seared in a hot pan.

He passed the back of his forearm over his brow. Several hundred metres away, a powerful telephoto lens framed Byron's sun-reddened face in extreme close-up. It was file sixty-three taken that afternoon and would become file number 615 in a folder labelled "Byron Charles Gates" residing on a secure hard drive deep in a RAF Intelligence server room.

43

Manx arrived at the cottage just after midnight. His sister greeted him at the door, her face pale, eyes bloodshot. Sara had called him thirty minutes ago. Late-night calls from his sister were rarely good news; in fact, most phone calls he received in the early hours of the morning were rarely harbingers of anything good.

"You'd best come in, they're waiting."

Manx kicked the mud off his boots and entered.

"This is my brother, Tudor," Sara said, as Manx followed her into the kitchen of the holiday cottage, located two fields west of his mother's house.

A thin man with a dark beard shook his hand. "Barry Coleman. This is my wife Diane and our daughter, Juliet."

Manx nodded and sat. Juliet was around nine years old, and was spread across her mother's lap, half-asleep. Diane, a bookish-looking woman with an air of calmness stroked her daughter's brow. "Is your mother okay?"

"As okay as she'll ever be," Sara said.

"So, what's going on with Mam?" Manx asked, his eyes

bleary his breath still smelling of the scotch he'd drank before bed.

"Went off wandering, again," Sara explained. "Came over here and scared the living daylights out of this little girl. Just stood outside her window staring. I didn't even know she'd left the house."

"Your sister explained the situation," Barry said. "I went through it with my own father some years back. It's not easy."

"So, mam left the house in her dressing gown, walked over two fields and stood outside a little girl's bedroom?"

"That's what I just said," Sara said, impatiently.

"Just making sure I've got all the facts."

"As you can tell, my brother's a policeman," Sara snipped. "We only get to see him on holidays and family emergencies."

Manx ignored the obvious barb. "You're renting the cottage?"

"Just for the week," Barry confirmed.

"Any idea why my mother would wander over here in the middle of the night? Did you meet her or speak to her?"

"She was walking on the side of the road when we drove in. She waved at us, I think," Diane said.

Juliet stirred on her mother's lap. "Miriam," she said. "The scary woman kept saying 'Miriam'."

Manx and Sara looked at each other, eyes wide, each sensing a similar cold shiver pass through their bones.

"Are you sure?" Sara asked, bringing a hand to her throat.

Juliet nodded. Manx and Sara both studied the young girl. They hadn't noticed it before, but as they looked closer the resemblance was uncanny enough for them both to catch their breaths.

"Who's Miriam?" Diane asked.

Sara spoke. "Our sister. She died–"

"Disappeared," Manx interrupted. "Thirty years ago.

"And she looked...?" Diane asked, glancing at Juliet.

"Show her the picture."

Manx pulled out an old faded photograph of Miriam from his wallet. "She could be her sister," Barry said, studying the bright-eyed young girl, hair parted in the middle, a smile so eerily similar to his daughter's it made him shiver.

"We're so sorry," Diane said, softly. "It must have been awful."

It was, Manx thought, but "awful" didn't even come close. "Where's mam now?"

"I put her in the car. She won't move: she likes the heated seats."

"Good enough," Manx said, standing. "Thank you, both. I'm very sorry this happened. It won't happen again, I promise."

Sara threw him a look that could have curdled milk.

"Honestly, no harm done," Barry said, seeing them out. "Juliet will have forgotten all about it by the morning, I'm sure. Best of luck with everything," he added, closing the cottage door.

Outside, Sara leant against the car and lit up a cigarette, her hands shaking as she brought the lighter to the tip. "Promise? Who the hell are you to make promises, Tudor?" She took a deep inhale.

Manx looked at his mother in the passenger seat. She glanced back at him and pulled her grey hair away from her face. There was a flicker of recognition, but not enough to keep her interest.

"What was I meant to say?"

Sara crossed her arms and dragged the heel of her slippers along the gravel. "I don't know, Tudor. I don't fucking know."

"You need new locks. I'll send someone over tomorrow."

"Thanks, but I can call a bloody locksmith," she said, exhaling a thick trail of smoke. "Any other bright ideas?"

"Motion sensors, so you'll know if she leaves the house."

"Brilliant. Motion sensors. You're a godsend, Tudor, so glad you're back."

Manx was about to protest when Sara raised her hand to stop him. "By the way," she said. "I'm having a clear-out, getting rid of some old stuff, got a box with your name on it. If you want it come by before the weekend."

"Not much of a one for souvenirs."

Sara shrugged and yanked open the car door. "Right. I've told you, so there, job done."

As his sister drove off, Manx looked across the pasture towards Alice's house, which under the soft glare of the moonlight, looked misshapen, like the cruel curvature of an old lady's stoop.

Cwm Tawel (Peaceful Valley) – the name of the house had more than a hint of irony. Manx had never felt anything close to a sense of peace within its walls. What he did sense, with every bone in his body was the presence of ghosts, waiting for him in the rooms and hallways.

He could feel the dead weight of their greeting each time he walked in, as if they'd missed him and were waiting anxiously for his return.

44

PC Morris stood at the end of the long garden that ended at the slip on the banks of the Menai Strait. Across the water, sunlight broke the surface in sparks of bright white. She looked back at the huge mid-century house behind the shade of oak trees; this, she guessed, was what was known as "a multi-million-pound property", one of many constructed along the Anglesey side of the strait.

"I haven't had a boat since Martha died," Peter Whinstone said as they walked. Peter was in his late-seventies, thin, with a severe stoop. "I never was one much for the water myself; dickie tummy. Tried everything, ended up with my head over the side most of the time, put a real dampner on a day out on the water."

Morris gestured to the slip. "What makes you think it's been used recently?" she asked, with a tone of hurried expectation. She'd been knocking on doors all morning with no luck. When, at 12.10pm, she'd knocked on Peter's door, the shine of the gleaming idea she'd had yesterday was already waning.

As they reached the rim of the decking, the water slapping lazily against the stanchions, Peter pointed. "See the cleats?" he said, directing a shaky, liver-spotted finger at the steel teeth protruding from the timbers. "The ropes were still wrapped around them from when I sold the boat. Couldn't get the buggers off to be honest, so I just kept them. I thought they might protect the cleats."

Morris squatted and examined the metal. The centre bias of the cleat was considerably less corroded than the prongs, which had been left exposed to the elements. "When did you notice this?"

"A few days ago. I didn't think much of it. I thought they'd maybe come off in the winter storms."

"Be a pretty fierce storm to rip ropes off a cleat."

Peter kicked a loop of rope lying on the deck. "You think this is connected to that business over at Menai Bridge?"

Morris focused on an unusual pattern of red spots on the deck. "What colour was your boat?"

"*Martha's Pride*? White and blue. Why is that important?"

"Not sure yet," she said, standing. "Any other access points to the slip other than the garden?"

"There's a pathway down to the cove, then it's a bit of a climb, but a cakewalk for someone half my age and no arthritis."

"Did you notice anything or anyone suspicious on or around last Thursday evening?"

Peter wagged his finger. "So, you do think it has something to do with what happened at the Food Slam," he said, puffing out his chest as if he'd just succeeded in getting one over on the young PC.

"You never know. Did you see anyone?"

"Not that I recall. But it wouldn't be me who saw anything." He gestured to the side wall of the house.

Morris noticed them immediately. Two security cameras pointed directly at the slip. "Do they still work?"

"Better had. They cost me a bloody arm and a leg every month for the monitoring," Peter said. "I expect you'll want to look at the footage, then?"

45

"So, are you going to tell me what that's all about?" Tammy asked, sliding a coffee mug across the table and gesturing to the bloodied cuts on Bobbie's face.

Bobbie hesitated. "I was in the hospital. Just overnight."

"Why didn't you tell me? What the hell happened?"

"Don't fuss. I was out running, a car hit me then drove off."

Tammy shook her head. "Out running at night again? I don't know why you just don't get some sleeping pills."

"They don't work."

"Tell me you at least went to the police."

"Of course I did."

"Christ, Bobbie," Tammy said, sitting back and folding her arms. "You and your bloody secrets."

"I'm telling you now, aren't I?"

"If anything like this happens again, promise you'll call me."

"Promise," Bobbie said, pulling out a ream of paper from her backpack and placing it on the table. "Listen, Tam, in two weeks I'm being transferred to a veteran's hospital near Liverpool–"

Tammy let out a breath and grabbed her sister's hand. "Honestly, that's the best news I've heard for ages, love. After what you did to that bloke in the pub, I was beginning to worry. This will be good for you; you'll get some proper help. And you don't need to ask, I'll visit you, every weekend, if that's what you want."

Bobbie slipped the papers towards Tammy. "I had to name a beneficiary, now that Danvir's gone. You know, if something happens to me. It's just some savings and my RAF pension."

"I don't like you talking like this," Tammy said, moving back, as if wanting to put as much distance as possible between her and the papers.

"It's just a formality. RAF protocol."

As Tammy considered her sister's words, Bobbie's mobile rang. She checked the area code – Waddington. "I'd better take this, might be important."

Bobbie stepped into the garden. A woman's voice identified herself as Sophie Dawson. Before she said another word, Bobbie felt a sickening premonition like a wave of nausea flood through her.

Officer Cadet Cole Dawson had been found in his garage, hanging from the rafters by his belt, wearing full RAF service dress. A simple three-line note, "Sorry. I love you. It's not your fault." stuffed into his pocket.

Bobbie's whole body shook as she hung up. She leant against the patio table, knocking over a vase of flowers. As she watched Tammy through the patio window flipping through the papers, one thought thundered in her head.

With Flynt and Dawson both dead, would she be next?

46

While the CCTV footage from the slip hadn't provided the case-breaking evidence the team had hoped for, it did prove there were two men working together.

"Anyone recognise these two?" Manx asked, freezing the video. The footage was grainy: the cameras had been installed before high-definition recording equipment was the norm and the lens was foggy.

"Those bastards could be anyone," Nader huffed.

Manx let the footage play to the point when the vessel left the slip and motored towards Beaumaris, disappearing left of frame.

"No name on the boat, either," Nader said.

"At least we can confirm we're looking for two suspects."

They all turned as PC Priddle bounded through the doorway with the enthusiasm of an excited puppy.

"You took your time," Manx said. "Stop off for a bacon bap?"

He waved a slip of paper he was holding like a trophy and sat down in the nearest chair. "DNA results from the blood Morris found on the dock."

"Make my day and tell me it's a match for Collins."

"Not Collins. They ran it through the national database, no matches either."

"Then why do you look like the cat who got the bloody cream?" Nader asked.

Priddle leaned back casually in his chair. It tipped slightly too far back as he sat. He caught himself before gravity got the better of him and planted his boots to the floor. "I had an idea," he said.

"Bring on the dancing girls," Nader grunted. "The lad's had an idea."

"I asked Bevan to check on any familial DNA."

"What's that, then?" Nader asked. "Familiar DNA?"

"It's familial, not familiar, sarge," Morris corrected him. "We learnt about it in basic training. It's how they caught the Golden State Killer, that sicko who killed thirteen people in the 1980s?"

"A bit of light bedtime reading, eh, Minor?" Nader quipped.

Morris paused for only a second; she was becoming well-practised in the fine art of not rising to DS Nader's bait, though at times it took a large chunk of her willpower to hold her tongue. "They took DNA from one of the crime scenes. There were no matches, so they reckoned it was a dead-end; whoever the killer was hadn't been arrested for any other crimes. So, they checked to see if a close relative with a DNA match had been arrested. Turns out his uncle was in the system, so they created this family tree and arrested the sick bastard a few weeks later. Turns out the killer was a copper, a sheriff."

Nader folded his arms. "Right, so if this bloke's brother, uncle or grandmother's DNA's in the database we could find a match?"

"Not his grandmother," Manx said. "Familial DNA only works with Y chromosomes, men." He turned to Priddle. "So, did Bevan find a familial match?"

"Em, no," Priddle said. "Said it was going to take a few days, went on about his reputation, due diligence and that, but here's the good part. He confirmed the DNA from the joint we found in the van is from the same family as the blood Morris found on the slip, which probably means the men are related."

"That's something, I suppose," Manx said. "Did Bevan give any indication of when he'd have the results?"

"To hell with that, we'll be waiting ages for Bevan to pull his finger out," Nader snapped. "We should be out there, rattling cages, not waiting for bloody handouts."

"No reason we can't do both," Manx said.

Nader shook his head. "Waste of bloody time, if you ask me."

"You have a better idea?"

"Yeah, I do," Nader said, his face flushed. "Round up all the nasty bastards we know who wouldn't give two shits about knifing a copper. Got a few I'd like to question outside the interview room."

"Excellent example you're setting," Manx said. He gestured to the rest of the team. "You lot, get back to work. Nader, you stay."

As the team left, Manx dragged a chair and sat across from Nader. "What the bloody hell was that about?"

"Just saying, like, they're brutal bastards whoever did that. Didn't take to the woman much myself, but she was the boss–"

"Still is the boss," Manx reminded him.

Nader's skin tightened around his knuckles like the taut head of a snare drum. "I want to catch 'em, boss, that's all."

"You're not special, Nader, we all want that."

"Yeah, but the courts these days? Too many bastards get off on some technicality. We spend all this time investigating then something gets fucked up and they're back on the streets cocky as you like bragging how they got one over on the system."

"You, talking like this. That's what'll fuck things up, compromise the case we're building."

"But still, one of our own..."

That phrase again – the one that settled like cold stones in Manx's gut. Problem was, he knew where Nader's head was at, had felt the same emotions after reading the report on CeeCee Cartwright's death; suicide. Manx's less official version? Not. Bloody. Likely. CeeCee wasn't the suicidal type, never had been.

"Don't do anything that's going to make me regret not taking you off this investigation. Your record on this kind of thing hasn't exactly been squeaky clean."

"Why keep me on it, then, if I'm such a bloody liability?"

"Because, Nader, I need every officer we can spare, even a hot-head like you. You're angry about Troup, we all are, but this case gets closed by the book. We do things the right way."

Nader stood, hitched up his trouser belt. "Yeah, and you've always done things the right way, boss?" he said. "That why you're back here and not still down in London, cracking the big cases?"

Manx sensed his own rage stirring but kept it on a low simmer; there was enough tension in the room without adding to the mix.

"Just ask yourself this question," he said. "When DCSI Troup recovers, how are you going to look her in the eyes and tell her you went off on some maverick crusade that compromised the whole investigation and her attackers are walking around, like you said, 'cocky as you like'? Tell me that."

Nader took a deep breath. "Dunno, boss," he said, leaning his hands on the desk. "How are you going to look her in the eyes if we don't catch the bastards?"

As Nader walked out, the duty sergeant walked in. "Got a woman in reception," he said. "Says her name's Bobbie Matthews. Insists on talking to you. Says she'll wait as long as it takes."

47

After Bobbie finished speaking, Manx gathered his thoughts. The woman has been lucid, laid out her suspicions in an organised fashion, but still something troubled him. Maybe what her psychologist had told him at the hospital concerning Bobbie's trauma was colouring his attitude. Or maybe it was her emotional detachment, as if all this were happening to someone else, and how her eyes locked on to his as she spoke; they were the eyes of someone haunted by something, something Manx couldn't begin to fathom, at least not yet.

"What am I meant to do with this information?" he asked. "There's no evidence to support what you've implied. Commander Flynt's death is still under investigation. This Cole Dawson you mentioned? Cause of death hasn't been determined, and even if it does turn out to be suspicious, Lincolnshire is out of my jurisdiction."

"What about the car that ran me down?"

"We're still investigating. Could have been someone with a bellyful of booze. If that's the case, we'll track them down and they'll be arrested."

"Commander Boyd? He didn't tell you I'd talked to him."

"We'll be addressing that with the commander when he returns our calls," Manx said, an irritated edge to his voice. He'd already left several messages with Boyd's assistant with no response. He was beginning to feel like the desperate, dumped boyfriend.

"They're lying, you know," she said.

"Who? Who's they, Bobbie?"

"All of them. Flynt, Boyd, RAF Air Command... the government."

"The government?" Manx said, his eyebrows arching. "You'll need to be a bit more specific. Names. Titles. Any previous form."

Bobbie stiffened. "I can see you're not taking this seriously. I'm wasting my time. I should take this to a more senior officer with experience in more complex cases."

Manx met Bobbie's defiant stare with a steely glare of his own. "My seriously understaffed team is currently investigating a suspicious death and dealing with the aftermath of the vicious stabbing of a colleague, who is still in critical condition. And let's not forget some nasty little toe-rag kidnapped a local politician and we're in the process of turning over this whole island looking for him. So yes, your conspiracy theories are a bloody waste of time; mine not yours. Now, before you leave, there's one question you can answer for me."

Manx slid the printout of the photo he'd taken at the Sadiq's home. Bobbie's hands gave a momentary tremor as she looked at the photo of her and Danvir on their wedding day.

"How? How did you get this?"

"Were you aware the van once owned by your father-in-law, Mohsin Sadiq, was used in the attack in Menai Bridge?"

"No. I was not. And I don't see the relevance or why you would ask me about something I have no connection to."

"Your husband, he was killed last year. I'm very sorry, that must have been terrible for you. But you can understand why I have to ask the question."

"No, I really don't," Bobbie said, folding her arms.

"Here's another question. The night of Commander Flynt's death. Did you follow him to Benllech?"

Bobbie quickly pushed back her chair and stood. "I came here to give you information about a serious military cover-up, and now I'm the criminal? I'll see myself out," she said, turning her back on Manx and slamming the interview room door as she left.

Running down the station steps, muttering to herself, her anger reaching peak boiling point, Bobbie checked her phone: several missed calls and a voice message from Tammy. She listened to the message three times, the words failing to sink in. By the time she'd reached the cemetery, the words had sunk in with horrifying clarity.

"Who would do this?" Bobbie said, kneeling at Danvir's gravestone, the words "Paki Scum" spray painted across the marble in red paint. At the base of the stone, the flowers that Bobbie made sure were fresh each week were thrown from their vases and trodden into the gravel.

"I don't know, Bobbie," Tammy said. "Sick, that's what they are, just sick."

Bobbie traced her finger along the engraving; 'Danvir Sadiq. Dedicated son. Loving Husband. Died serving his country.'

Died serving his country. That epitaph crawled its way under Bobbie's skin. It sounded as hollow and meaningless as the cruel words sprayed across it.

Tammy began to clear up the flowers and setting the less damaged back into the vases.

Bobbie grabbed the flowers from Tammy's hands. "Leave it. He was my husband, not yours."

"I was only–"

"Give me some space, Tammy, for God's sake," Bobbie said, her voice raised, face flushed and close to tears.

Tammy laid down the flowers and backed off. "Yeah, of course. Call me later, eh?" she said, walking back to her car, leaving Bobbie kneeling at the graveside.

That night, sleep came to Bobbie in fits and starts, interrupted by fragments of dreams, memories, and wild leaps into her subconscious, where she waded, knee-deep, through a thick marsh that seemed as endless as it was deep.

On the ceiling, figures, like shadow puppets, took to the stage, played out their scenes then exited. Danvir, James Flynt, and Commander Boyd flickered like old film, their features distorted and blurred as if the celluloid were melting as it passed over the projector's worn teeth creating spectral blooms that floated around her bedroom. Cole Dawson, though, came to her in brilliantly rendered colour; lips blue, face pale, wounds around his neck red and raw, body swaying like the pendulum of a grandfather clock; leather creaking against wood as it brushed against the rafters.

The dull thud of his body cut from the belt and falling to the floor startled her awake. She lay there for several minutes, limbs rigid, eyes wide open in the darkness. Call Me Andy had been right about one thing. She could sense it now, her shadow soul, could almost reach inside herself and touch it. But it wasn't a shadow; not anymore. It had matured into something greater. It was a sky full of thunder clouds with no cuts of blue or breaks of sunlight, just blackness; dense and relentless. And like thunder, the breaths in between its beats were becoming shorter and shorter, until there were no breaths anymore, just a darkness that swallowed all in its path.

At around 5am she stepped out of her bed expecting the heaviness that had greeted her most mornings. Instead, she had a clarity and focus that was as close to a religious experience as she was ever likely to get. With the sunrise flickering behind the tree branches in her garden, she made herself a coffee, sat at the kitchen table, and thought about making a start on the papers she'd brought home from the base. One of the press releases she'd been editing, red-lined with Commander Boyd's suggestions, fell to the floor. She picked it up. As she glanced at the contents, another moment of clarity seared clean across the morning.

This was it. The sign she was sure would reveal itself. The starlings, Flynt's death, the bull in her path, the car running her off the road, Cole Dawson's apparent suicide, the vandalising of Danvir's gravestone; they were all signposts along the way, guiding her here to this moment.

Bobbie picked up her phone and dialled.

"I'm ready to help you," she said, her voice barely above a whisper. "But we do things my way."

48

If Manx could have bothered himself with the concept of a to-do list, that morning it would have included three action items: a meeting with the North Wales Coroner, Richard Hardacre; a long-awaited meeting with Commander Boyd; and, at the end of the day, dinner at his mother's house. His sister had called last night to remind him she still had a box of his "stuff" and if he wanted any of it, this was his last chance. He couldn't imagine what "stuff" Sara referred to; it had been over thirty-years since he'd left home. Out of curiosity he agreed to drive over. He'd at least get a decent meal; no doubt served with a side-order of guilt and a slice of humble pie for dessert, which he'd be required to swallow without complaint.

At 11.30am, Richard Hardacre sat in his garden. He wore a panama hat and was sipping a gin and tonic from a large, bulbous glass, nibbling on a cut of cheese and looking as if the troubles of the world were far from any of his concern. Manx walked across the lawn. He was greeted with a subtle tip of Hardacre's hat.

"Hatching your evil plan for world domination, Hardacre?"

"As usual, Manx, you've lost me."

"The Bond villain look? All you need is a cat and a bad accent, and you'd have had me at 'I've been expecting you, Mr Manx'."

"Droll. Take a seat."

"So, why the summons to the lair?" Manx asked, pulling up a chair and shuffling into the shade.

Hardacre poured more gin over the ice in his glass. "Day off from the cold slab of the morgue, Manx. I'd offer you a drink, but I suspect you'll say you're on duty."

"I'm not the cocktail type."

"Why doesn't that surprise me? Listen," he said, putting down his cheese knife and laying a folder on the table. "My friend, the geologist? She's put the cat amongst the pigeons, Manx."

"Do geologists do that? Wouldn't they be more likely to throw rocks at glass houses or something?"

"Strained metaphors aside, Manx, take a look at this." Hardacre placed two photographs on the table. "Exhibit one. The rock fragments found under our victim's fingernails contain the expected amount of limestone, native to the cliffs around Benllech."

He laid down another photograph. "Now, the fragments I excavated from said victim's head wound? Turns out they're not native to that area. My geologist friend confirmed these fragments are from blueschist rocks. A few hundred million years old, mind you, but widespread all over Anglesey."

"But not at Benllech beach?"

"Unlikely."

"Does she know where?"

"Like I said, blueschist is one of the most common rocks on the island. However, simple deduction concludes–"

"Flynt couldn't have struck his head on the rocks at Benllech," Manx interrupted. "Killed elsewhere, then driven there, maybe?"

"Or the killer was already in possession of the murder weapon and chose to batter our victim's skull close to where we found him. It would have been my preferred modus operandi, spares the effort of and mess of transporting a dead body in the boot of the car."

Manx stood, and rolled up his shirt sleeves. "I was right, you're a criminal mastermind, Hardacre. A real-life Scaramanga."

Hardacre squinted. "Just don't tell the wife, she'll be wanting to know where I stashed my ill-gotten gains." He took a sip of gin. "Good luck with all this, Manx. I suspect with this and that kidnapping situation your summer holiday's on hold for a while."

"I'll live it vicariously through you, Hardacre," Manx said, heading back to his car.

Commander Boyd had requested to meet off-base. Manx had reluctantly agreed – he wasn't going to hand him another excuse to delay. He pulled the Jensen onto several hectares of freshly cut fields just off the A55, passing three large billboards welcoming him to this year's Anglesey Agricultural Show. He drove past a crew of men ramming fence posts marking out the show perimeter, while a few hundred metres away a large crane lifted the poles supporting the main show pavilion. He parked and walked to the only other vehicle close by, a black Range Rover.

"Don't want me snooping around the base, commander?" Manx said, making himself comfortable in the passenger seat.

"If I was the suspicious type, I'd think you'd have something to hide."

"I thought you lot thrived on suspicion," he said, pronouncing the words "you lot" as if they fell sour on his mouth. "I'm told RAF Valley has always been heavily involved with the Anglesey Agricultural Show, hence my presence. What can I help you with?"

"One of your officers, Bobbie Matthews. She told me she'd informed you several days ago she'd seen Flynt driving from his home the night he disappeared, and here I am having to chase you down to verify those facts."

The commander tapped his fingers on the steering wheel. "Flight Lieutenant Bobbie Matthews is... how shall I put this delicately? Mentally unstable."

"That was delicate?" Manx said.

"I assume she informed you she's being transferred to a psychiatric hospital at the end of the month?"

"She neglected to mention that, but I'm still curious. Did she tell you about seeing Flynt that night or not?"

"I have no recollection of such a meeting."

"So does that mean it didn't happen, or you just forgot? Busy man like you, I expect you're in meetings all day."

The commander pursed his lips. "No recollection means it never happened. Now if there's nothing else, I've got a security audit to conduct," he said, gesturing at two RAF officers walking from the showground. "What with the Duke and Duchess opening the show this year, the pressure's on to oversee their safety."

"Heavy lays the crown, right?" Manx said. "Do you know why Bobbie Matthews wanted to speak to Flynt that night?"

"Not a clue. Now if that's all," the commander said, checking his rear-view mirror and starting the engine.

Stepping out over the running boards, Manx turned to face

the commander. “Oh, you should probably know, new evidence came to light today that strongly suggests Commander Flynt’s death wasn’t an accident. We’ll be stepping up our investigation a gear or two. Expect a visit from myself and my team in the next few days.”

Commander Boyd waited for Manx to reverse out of the grounds before selecting the Bluetooth function on his dashboard and calling the number he’d stored simply as “JC” in his contact list.

He coiled his fingers tight around the steering wheel as the call connected. “Seems Bobbie Matthews is a bigger problem than we imagined,” he said, giving the two RAF officers the two minutes hand gesture. “I wouldn’t book your ticket back to London just yet.”

49

The sun was leaning low over the horizon, dusk yet to descend when Manx arrived at Alice's house. He was sitting at the kitchen table, picking at his tofu stir-fry as if hoping to unearth something meatier amidst the greenery: Sara had apparently committed to No Meat Mondays: bad timing on Manx's behalf.

His mother spoke. "Nice of you to come, Tudor. We don't see enough of him, do we, Sara?"

"No, no we don't," said his sister, spearing a chunk of tofu as if it were prey and throwing Manx a short snip of a smile.

"No more late-night wanderings I hope, Mam," Manx said.

Alice looked at Sara, confused. "I don't know what you mean. Sara, what is he talking about?"

"She doesn't remember a thing," Sara said.

"All for the best, huh, Mam?"

Alice drifted for a moment, her gaze floating through the kitchen window to the cottage two fields away. It was as if she remembered fragments but couldn't attach them to her memory in any meaningful way.

Manx noticed his seven-year-old nephew, Dewi, gawking intently at him from across the table.

"You don't look like my dad," the boy finally announced.

Manx glanced over to his sister.

"He wouldn't, would he?" Sara said. "Uncle Tudor is my brother, not your dad's brother, so he's going to look like me, not like your dad."

Dewi took in the information and studied them both through squinted eyes. "He doesn't look like you, either," he said.

Dewi wasn't the first to make that observation. Manx had the leaner, taller bearing of his mother. Sara took after their father; shorter and stockier. They did share the same colour eyes; slate-grey, steely, untrusting.

"Of course, they do. I gave birth to them, I should know. But your aunty, Miriam?" Alice said, leaning closer to the boy. "You never met her; she was the best-looking out of all my children. She was a gift, you know, a gift from God."

Manx and Sara looked at each other and shrugged. There was no competing with ghosts; they'd given up trying decades ago.

"You'll get to meet her when she comes home," Alice said, snapping her napkin tight in her lap.

"Where is she?" Dewi asked.

"A beautiful place." Alice's eyes drifted. "A paradise," she confirmed, satisfied that it was indeed true.

Dewi thought for a moment "If it's that beautiful, why would she want to come back here?" he asked.

Silence lay heavy across the table. Some questions were just too hard to contemplate, let alone answer. Sara collected the dishes solemnly, as if retrieving church collection plates, while Manx rolled up his sleeves and stacked the dishes into the sink.

~

Just after 7.30, dishes cleaned and dried, Manx said his excuses and headed upstairs to examine the box of "stuff" Sara was so eager to offload. As he walked along the landing, he passed Miriam's room. He hesitated, then slowly opened the door. Alice had kept the room just as Miriam had left it, as if she expected her daughter to return. Manx doubted his mother had even stripped the bed and laundered the sheets since that day. He hovered around the door, unable to raise the willpower to enter; maybe his mother was right, some things should remain undisturbed. He clicked the door back into its frame.

In Sara's bedroom, he tore the masking tape from the top of the box. The artefacts were a time-capsule from the last three years Manx had spent at Cwm Tawel; ages fourteen to seventeen. A faded collection of beer mats; a pack of custom-gauge steel guitar strings – unused; a stack of old school notebooks and a copy of *New Musical Express* with The Specials gracing the cover that month. However, two objects did pique his curiosity; a scuffed Pentax 35mm camera and a RC 2500 radio with a built-in cassette recorder, which seemed like a relic from a long-lost civilisation.

He reached for the camera; it felt sticky, as if coated with dried saltwater. When he placed his thumb over the advance clicker, it made a grinding sound. He flipped the camera over, shook out the grains of sand and tried again. The plastic gave one final click, then stopped. He wound the spindle tight, opened the back and retrieved the roll. If there were any place on the island that still developed film, he'd take it in; he was curious to see what was on there, but equally hesitant. Maybe thirty years on, the images had dissolved to mere ghosts on celluloid; he'd amassed enough ghosts in the past few decades and wasn't looking to add to his collection.

He pocketed the roll and plugged in the recorder. The Memorex C90 cassette was nearing the end of its life expectancy; he could almost see through the thin magnetic tape as he held it to the light. He clicked the tape into the spindles. "Chuck E's in Love" by Rickie Lee Jones was reaching its final chorus. 1979, Manx guessed. The same year Miriam was lost to them.

The following song was a disco-infused version of "Light My Fire". Time hadn't been kind to the remix; the production sounded paper-thin, propelled by a monotonous, manufactured drumbeat. He was about to press fast forward when the song abruptly ended. It was followed by a rustling noise, then a girl's voice that sent a shiver so deep down Manx's spine he doubted he could have stood up straight even if he willed himself.

Miriam. She'd likely found the cassette recorder in Manx's hiding place; an old shoebox slid under his bed. She began to sing. He remembered the track; she'd been singing it the whole summer: "I Don't Like Mondays" by the Boomtown Rats. It was a blast of nostalgia that sucked the wind right out of him. It was as if she were here in the room, singing just to him. He secured his back against the wall.

Miriam's voice took him right back to that day. The day Manx had one job to do – look after his sister – and he'd failed. Failed her in the worst way possible.

And it was all because of a girl. Nothing, at the age of sixteen, was more important than "a girl", certainly not watching his younger sister. The girl's name was Frankie; large, trusting brown eyes, skin that tanned like some exotic plant in the summer and a smile that sent Manx's heart fluttering some three feet above his chest. He'd been infatuated with Frankie since she had arrived as the new girl in school one year previously. Her family had moved from Liverpool to Anglesey when her father was transferred to the Wylfa Nuclear Power Plant. Frankie had a cool, alternative edge; everything the girls at his school aimed for, but for the most part, failed. Frankie and

Manx had bonded over a mutual love of the Patti Smith Group and anything released on the Two-Tone record label. Frankie was also a committed fan of black; black clothing, dyed-black hair and black eyeliner – the darkest she could find in Woolworth's cosmetic aisle. Manx thought Frankie the coolest girl, outside of Debbie Harry, he'd ever set eyes on. Looking back some years later, Manx would have admitted Frankie was his first love; the kind of first love that never fails to leave a scar somewhere on your heart.

That day, Manx had driven Frankie and his sister to the beach in his mother's ageing Ford Anglia, which he'd taken without her permission. When he picked up Frankie from her local bus stop, the day was brimming with sunshine and promise. Miriam sat in the back, her bucket and spade resting on the beach towel in her lap, singing "I Don't Like Mondays" as if trying to commit it to memory. Manx and Frankie sat up front, holding hands and stealing glances at each other as the tilt of sunlight shone through the car windows.

Sometime during the heat of the afternoon, he and Frankie had wandered off into the shaded privacy of the sand dunes. On a Wednesday, the beach was all but deserted save a couple of families picnicking nearby. Miriam had made friends with one of the children, a boy called Martin. The family had never come forward when the alarm was raised later that evening; maybe they never heard it or had their own reasons for not talking to the police.

When Manx and Frankie returned, Miriam was gone. Manx doubted he'd ever felt anything so sickening as that sensation before or since; his world had shattered around him and there was no way to pick up the pieces and fix it back together again.

It had been over thirty years; it was as if the air itself had taken her. Barely a day passed when Manx didn't think about Miriam and, if he was offered the chance to do it all again, how he'd never take his eyes off his sister that day; not for one second. But he'd learnt that life rarely offers do-overs, and the best he could hope for was to someday find some answers that would bring closure to his family. He guessed that life didn't owe him that sort of guarantee either, but it wouldn't stop him from trying.

"She always had a good singing voice," Sara said, leaning against the door frame. Manx wasn't sure how long she'd been there. "National Eisteddfod material, Mam always said," she added, a hairline crack breaking through her voice.

"Did you know?" he said, gesturing at the recorder.

Sara shook her head and reached for her pack of cigarettes. "Christ, it's like she's here in the room with us." She shuddered.

Manx wiped his hands over his face. "We can't tell Mam; she won't be able cope."

"That'll be the first thing we've agreed on for a while," Sara said, throwing open the window and lighting a cigarette. Over the Snowdonia mountains the sky was turning colour, thin strips of orange peel littering the low clouds.

"Can I hear it? All of it?" Sara said, sitting on the edge of the windowsill and blowing the smoke into the blue twilight.

Manx pressed rewind. They both sat in silence as Miriam sang, neither of them wanting to break the spell. They replayed the tape five more times, hoping they'd catch some clue, or some answers. There were none to be found.

As Manx left, he felt more tired than he had in weeks. Spending time at his mother's house always had this effect on him, but tonight it was infinitely more pronounced as if the ghosts in the house had finally found a way to latch on to him and were intent on tightening their grip. There was only one cure for those kinds of feelings, and it came in a non-prescription bottle of single malt, Isle of Islay scotch, preferably room temperature with a single ice cube.

The thought of a few stiff drinks before bed fortified him as he drove the twenty-minutes back home, the familiar turns and twists of the roads blurring past, canopies of ancient oak trees swaying overhead. He imagined, if he drove fast enough, he could avoid the grasp of their branches. Or maybe that, like hoping to one day find the truth about Miriam and finding closure, was also nothing but wishful thinking.

50

As Logan Collins was dragged from the coal shed, something sharp and cold was thrust into his lower back; a gun, or a knife maybe? Something that nicked into his flesh and hurt like hell, that was for sure. His eyes burned as sunlight burst through the fabric of his blindfold. He stumbled, legs weak, as Melvin urged him over the cobblestones. The loud creak of a door opening, and Collins found himself in another room. This one he sensed was larger with more light and air circulating around the space. Colder too.

"Sit," Melvin grunted, pushing him onto a chair.

He took the chair; it felt good to rest against something other than bricks. In one swift motion, the tape was ripped off his mouth.

"Water?" Collins asked, his lips dry and stinging. "Please."

His request was met with the sharp rim of a plastic bottle at his teeth and the sweet relief of water slipping easily down his throat. "And the blindfold?" he croaked.

"All in good time."

A new voice? A woman's voice.

She spoke again, clear and precise. "Mr Collins, you're going to do exactly as we say. Do you understand?"

He nodded.

"No," she said, voice slightly raised. "I need to hear, verbally, that you understand my instructions."

Collins cleared his throat. "Yes. Yes, I understand." His voice was dry and cracked. Although he could feel the words form in his mouth, they sounded as if they were spoken by a stranger.

"In a few minutes we will remove your blindfold. In front of you there will be a camera and below the camera a sheet of paper. On that sheet of paper are words that you will read out."

Collins swallowed hard. "What words?"

She ignored the question. "We will give you exactly two minutes to look over the words then you will speak them. Is this all clear to you?"

Collins nodded.

"I need–"

"Yes. Yes, it's clear. I read out the words, you record me. What are they, your ransom demands?"

No reply, just footsteps, the smell of sweat and the reach of thick fingers working to untie the knot. The relief of the blindfold's release was short-lived. He caught a glance of the woman's face, barely enough time to make out her features, before she was set into shadow behind the beam of a dazzling spotlight. He squinted, trying to make sense of the words printed below the camera lens.

"Can you move the light?" he asked.

The woman tilted the beam a few degrees and stepped to her left. It was a smart move. Even as Collins craned his neck, attempting to make some kind of eye contact, she was still cast in shadow; an amorphous form looming behind the beam.

As his eyes grew accustomed to the light, he focused on the

words – four paragraphs that killed whatever hope he had remaining. "I-I can't read this," he stammered.

The woman spoke. "You're mistaken. You seem to think you have some leverage in this situation. I assure you, you do not."

"No one will agree to this, it's madness," he muttered.

"Then you'll die, here. Alone."

"Can I at least see your face?" We can talk, maybe figure out a way we all come out of this thing without anyone getting hurt. Surely, you must understand this won't end well for you."

"Typical bloody politician, can't stop fucking talking." That was Melvin's voice. He'd stepped closer, dragging the weapon he'd held earlier across the soft tissue around Collins' neck.

"If I read this, I'm signing my own death warrant," he said, his neck muscles taut, wire tight. "I refuse."

Melvin took a few steps back, placed his foot in the crossbow's stirrup, cocked the mechanism, slid the twenty-inch 400 grain carbon fibre bolt into the rail, and steadied himself to take the shot.

A stiff twang echoed off the walls as the crossbow limbs released their pent-up energy and propelled the bolt at 300 feet per second from the tiller.

Pain was too soft a word for what Collins felt next; it was pure agony, and it radiated in thick swathes of nausea through his body. As the initial shock wore off, he looked down. The bolt had made clean entry through his foot and into the floor. He felt the salty spill of tears as he watched blood pool inside his loafer.

"Now we understand each other, Mr Collins, I recommend you read the words. Unless, of course, you'd prefer Melvin to reload and continue firing until you comply."

Despite the searing shock of pain pulsing up from his foot to every cell in his body, Collins read the prepared script. The woman made him repeat it another three times until she was satisfied with the conviction of his performance.

"You'll never follow through with this," he said, sitting back.

She stepped forward, her face still silhouetted against the blast of light, and knelt by his feet. "People die all the time. You'll be missed, but in time forgotten," she said, grabbing the nock and yanking the bolt clean from his foot.

Collins' scream was feral; a guttural wail that seemed to emanate from some deep, primal place.

"Your death will simply redress the balance."

Back conversing with the dark night of his soul in the coal shed, Collins thought on her words. She sounded seriously disturbed, operating on a far more dangerous level than Ronnie and Melvin. They were in over their heads, given time he could have maybe pitted them against each other, persuaded them to let him go. But the woman? She had an agenda; an unwinnable one as far as he could tell. He was no longer an irritant in the hands of a couple of opportunists. He was now a hostage with a price on his life; a price he was sure nobody would be willing to pay.

51

Byron Gates had spent the day transcribing what Reaper had told him and cross-checking the information against the redacted papers sent to him several months ago. He was running through the events in his head when something Reaper had said made him sit up; about having "taken everything from her". It sounded as if she were talking about more than her career – a lot more.

He wondered if she had been completely honest with him. Did she have an alternative motive, or a personal axe to grind? He was no stranger to some personal axe grinding of his own, but she'd also insisted he approach the media, which would leave him exposed. He'd agreed to her terms – the story was worth the risks – but just over twenty-four hours later he was having second thoughts. There were too many anomalies, too many questions he'd failed to ask.

He logged on to his secure browser and searched for an article he recalled reading when the incident was first reported. It was deep in the hyperlink hierarchy by now, but after some digging, he sourced the original article on the mirror.co.uk website. The headline had the hallmark of the publication's expected jingoistic outrage; "IS Murder Our Boys!" He looked closely at the names of the six men killed that day, searching for clues. One of the names on the mournful rollcall of young, dead men caught his attention; Danvir Sadiq, along with his photograph and an obituary stating he was survived by a thirty-eight-year-old wife, also a serving RAF officer, and his parents, who lived in Bangor, North Wales.

He took a minute to check his map application. Bangor was less than ten miles away from where he was staying; he remembered seeing the road signs as he drove here. A kernel of an idea began to form. He searched for Danvir's Facebook profile. It had been, as he expected, memorialised, with a single photo of Danvir's face and the word "Remembering" preceding his name. He scoured around for any reference to the legacy contact who had frozen the profile in time; there was none. Instead, he searched through the messages left on the page, and cross-referenced the names with another Facebook search in a new tab. He got a hit on one of the names, Tammy Povey, a Facebook friend of Danvir's who lived on Anglesey.

He searched through Tammy's feed. She was an avid poster, at least three per-day, and mostly photographs taken at some new restaurant or expensive-looking wine bar. Clicking around for several more minutes, he finally found the needle in the haystack; a wedding photo with the caption; "Danvir and Bobbie finally tie the knot!" written under. It was taken underneath the gables of a church, the camera catching the storm of confetti as it swirled around the bride and groom. Byron dragged the photo to his desktop, opened his editing app, and enlarged the image. It lost some detail in the process, but he was nearly one hundred per cent sure this was the same woman he'd met with two days ago. The angular features, the slight build, the small, circular birthmark above her right eyebrow.

On the bedside cabinet, his phone pinged. He checked the

incoming message. Reaper was requesting a second meeting: she had some additional information she was sure he'd want to hear. *Good*, Byron thought, typing his reply, he had some information of his own he was keen to ask her about. The meeting was set for later that day, at the Porth Wen Brickworks, on the northern lee of the island. He confirmed he'd be there, 7pm.

During the three hours before then, Byron made his preparations. As he structured his theory – things always seemed to make more sense once he put fingers to keyboard – the pieces fell into place, though he still had one unanswered question. Was Bobbie, if that was even her name, a grieving widow looking for someone to blame for her husband's death? Or, had she ventured beyond that now? And people like Byron would become collateral, sacrificed for Bobbie's mission.

The troubling thought was still at the back of his mind as he drove to the meeting point.

52

The Bee-Hive kilns were circular in design, covered with domed roofs, and supported with brick and iron bands. They'd been constructed in 1852 when Porth Wen's sole function was to manufacture silica bricks that could withstand the vast heat generated by the furnaces powering Britain's steel production. Less than a hundred years later, the plant had shipped its last cargo of brick and was abandoned to the vagaries of the Anglesey weather and the Irish Sea's caustic bite. It was now a scheduled historic monument, but because of its remoteness received few tourists. Was this why Reaper had wanted to meet here? She either suspected they were being watched or else she wanted to meet Byron far away from any witnesses. Neither alternative was of any comfort.

He was standing in the belly of one of the kilns, peering through an archway looking out to the ocean. Several metres below, the waves cymbal-crashed into the slick, black rocks, while a salt-tinged breeze whistled through the cracks in the stonework as if calling out to lost souls.

Byron leant against the kiln wall. He was glad of the rest: his knees were complaining from the cross-country trek; at least forty-five minutes from St Patrick's Church in Cemaes over a rough, stone-strewn pathway that hugged the coastline. Dusk was already bearing down, casting its dim light over the crumbling winding house and old crushing sheds. Rising from the small crescent-shaped bay, the lines of the funicular, which was used to transport the raw silica from the docks to the plant stood out like scars of an old addiction in the overgrown dirt. To his left, the tall chimney seemed perfectly preserved in time; a testament to the skill of its Victorian engineers. It cast a shadow, like that of a long finger, pointing over the wild scruffs of grass.

Byron took a sip of tea from his flask and checked his watch. 6.58pm – she'd be here soon, Reaper seemed like the punctual type. Unless, of course, she was already here, observing. The thought produced his second shiver of the night. He wondered if it was wise coming here. But he was a journalist, at least of sorts, more of a truth-seeker, and Byron Gates didn't turn his back to the truth, no matter how uneasy it made him feel.

He turned as he heard footsteps scrambling down the bank behind him. He screwed the top back onto his flask. Reaper walked towards him, dressed as she was when they first met, but without her shades. As she drew closer, he was one hundred per cent sure it was the woman he'd seen in the wedding photograph.

"Byron," she said, moving closer. "I have a task for you."

"What kind of task?"

She reached into her jacket pocket. Byron stiffened, backed away a couple of steps.

"What? A gun? Is that what you were thinking?"

"Um, no, it's just–"

"What I have is far more compelling than a gun to your head," she explained, holding a USB thumb drive between her fingers.

Byron glanced at it. "Yeah? Like what?"

"I have some communication that requires distributing. Communication we can't risk sending through the usual channels."

"Usual channels?" Byron's mind had already jumped to the word "we". Who the hell was "we"? The question would have to wait.

"YouTube will provide us with a wide exposure, but we can't risk the North Wales Constabulary tracing its origins."

Byron's mouth ran dry. "The police? I'm not sure–" he began.

"Yes, you are sure, Byron," she insisted.

He collected his thoughts. "You want me to post whatever's on that thumb drive so no one can detect where it came from?"

"You did assure me your network was, I think your words were, 'military-grade'? Multiple VPNs and non-static IP addresses?"

Byron squared his shoulders. "Only amateurs use VPN socks," he said, cockily. "If I want to send something undetected, I use a pawned system, hijack at least four devices all over the world, make them zombie machines, no way to detect where it originates from."

"I knew you were our man," she said, stepping closer and handing him the USB.

He turned it over in his palm. "What's on it? Some kind of malware code?"

"Nothing that complex. Just a short video."

"I-I don't want to get into any trouble," he stuttered.

"Oh, you don't know?" Bobbie said. "You're already in trouble. There's a significant digital dossier on Byron Charles Gates in RAF Central Intelligence. Photographs, documents, everything ever uploaded to your website. I'd call that trouble."

"Old news," he said, trying to sound nonchalant. "If they were going to prosecute me, they would have done it by now."

"Prosecute?" Bobbie said. "Far more efficient to have you

eliminated. You do this for me and I can point you to the location of that digital file and you can destroy it like it never existed."

The wind chose that moment to pick up, baffling around the kiln's stonework with an urgent menace. The flask in Byron's hand was shaking. He laid it down. "And if I don't do this? This task?"

Bobbie looked behind her. From the shadows a man appeared, his crossbow primed. She nodded. The bolt cut through the air at speed, landing millimetres from Byron's boots and scattering a handful of dirt in the air as it made contact with the soft earth.

Byron jumped back, contemplated running, but saw the man had loaded another bolt into the tiller and raised the weapon a few feet higher so it was now aimed directly at Byron's chest.

"Tonight," Bobbie said. "Do it tonight, or we'll make a visit to the Rose Cottage Bed and Breakfast. If for some reason you're not there, we'll make a house call on your mother at 31 Burlington Avenue, Waddington. Is this clear to you, Byron?"

He nodded. She couldn't have been any clearer.

"No," she said. "Tell me, in words, that this is clear to you."

Byron wiped an arm across his forehead. "Yes. Yes, it's clear."

"Good work," she said. "We won't meet again, but if we do, you can be guaranteed my partner's aim won't be so generous."

As Bobbie turned to leave, Byron steeled himself. "I'm sorry," he said, blurting out the words.

Bobbie turned, her eyes seeming to scan right through him.

"About your husband, Danvir. It was a terrible accident."

She stood for a moment, processing the information.

"But I don't think it's fair you're taking it out on innocent people, like me, Bobbie," he said, heavily stressing the last word.

She smiled, tight and controlled. "Innocent? A man I know

would have an answer to that," she said. "Let he who is without sin cast the first stone. I'll look forward to your decision."

She turned to leave, the man following close in her shadow.

Byron immediately regretted saying anything. Had he shown his cards too early? Admitting he knew her name and her motive? He imagined the information would have given him some currency to negotiate with. He was wrong. She wasn't the negotiating kind.

As he staggered over the path back towards his car, the twilight was quickly obliterated by darkness. He used the flash-light on his mobile to guide him along the narrow path, stumbling a few times over the rocky outcrops. He took a break at one of the benches along the way, felt the USB drive in his palm and contemplated throwing it into the ocean. It was a stupid idea; another Byron Gates fantasy doomed to failure. This wasn't programming code, hacking around servers or posting anonymous documents anymore. He'd walked into a situation where he was way out of his depth and he'd been confronted with a choice, which was really no choice at all. If he wanted to live to see his home again, his mother, his friends, he'd have to do as she demanded.

The thought churned his stomach as he looked over the blackening landscape, the sound of the ocean crashing like broken bones onto the rocks behind him. Reaper, Bobbie, was out there, somewhere, watching his every move.

He'd never been more certain of anything in his life.

53

"My name is Logan Collins. I've been asked to speak these words by the Welsh Nationalist Movement, Meibion Glyndŵr. To ensure my return, they have two demands, which if not met, will result in a swift and violent response.

"Eighteen months ago, the Royal Airforce launched a drone strike, Operation Vanguard, on a convoy of insurgents travelling south of Mosul, Syria. In the aftermath of this attack, six RAF officers were also killed. The official report on this incident cites the second explosion as an attack by enemy combatants. This is not true. The report was falsified. Our demands are simple. A redaction of the validity of the report by the RAF, with full disclosure of the events. Truth and transparency.

"Our second demand is for the Anglesey County Council and the National Assembly for Wales to write into law safeguards limiting the sale of homes as rental properties for all of Wales.

"You have seven days to comply. If after seven days, these demands are not met, I will be executed. I know the police will attempt to locate me, but the longer you waste your time, the more lives will be put in danger. Act now, swiftly, and no one else need die."

Manx froze the video just before Logan Collins' terrified expression faded to grainy black. The incident room fell into silence as the officers absorbed the information. At 10.30pm, the core investigation team may have been bleary-eyed and beat from their day shift, but Collins' words were like a jolt of caffeine to their system; they were now attentive, primed; anxious.

"Looks like he's half-dead already," Nader said.

"A dead man talking," Manx agreed, wiping a hand over his face. "Right, what do we know about this Meibion Glyndŵr outfit?"

"Active in the late eighties and early nineties," Nader said. "They were named after Owain Glyndŵr who led the Welsh rebellion against the English. Died in 1530, or something."

"Yeah, and that's their flag," Priddle said, pointing at the four lions outlined on red and yellow squares serving as Collins' backdrop.

"I'm not the most patriotic Welshman in the room," Manx said, "but doesn't the Welsh flag have a red dragon?"

"The red dragon on green and white, wasn't officially recognised as the Welsh flag until 1959," PC Priddle explained. "And Owain Glyndŵr died in 1415, sarge, but nobody's really sure because there were no records of him after 1412. Vanished, apparently, or went into hiding."

"Oh, right you are, Professor Priddle," Nader said, chuckling. "Got a cold case you want to chase up, then? The vanishing of Owain Glyndŵr. Last known sighting on a battlefield back in 1412. We're appealing for witnesses anywhere in the vicinity."

"No, just interested in history, that's all," Priddle said.

"How the hell does this help us find Collins?" Manx asked.

"It makes sense, though, doesn't it?" Morris said. "They set holiday homes on fire back in the day too."

"They did a bloody lot more than that." Priddle's voice rose an octave as he talked. "They sent letter bombs to English MPs, planted bombs on powerlines and water plants. Fire-bombed over 200 homes owned by the English, and estate agents all over England too. I don't think they killed anyone, though."

"More through luck than judgement, maybe," Manx said. "If we've got a resurgence of Welsh nationalist militants burning down holiday homes, how the bloody hell is this connected to the RAF and this Operation Vanguard?"

"If what Hardacre says is right and Flynt was killed, he could be the connection," Priddle offered.

"I'm not seeing it," Manx said. "Let's assume the two men on the slip are members of Meibion Glyndŵr." He pointed at the CCTV print out. "Originally, they'd planned to use the go-to terrorist-approved move of ramming a moving vehicle into their target. The plan changed, they kidnapped Collins, we hear nothing for five days, then they post this video. I'd expect the demand for the change in housing laws, but the second demand, Operation Vanguard, it's not fitting the motives."

"It's like two birds, one stone," Nader said.

Manx turned to the board. "We're looking for a connection between the RAF and Meibion Glyndŵr. Flynt is dead, Commander Boyd's only been here on the island for less than a week. Which leaves us the only other serving RAF officer who's involved, Bobbie Matthews." Manx pointed to the photo of Bobbie and Danvir. "She saw Flynt the night he disappeared. When she came to see me, she was very agitated, on edge."

PC Morris searched her notes, then spoke. "Sir, I didn't think anything of it at the time, but when I was researching Bobbie Matthews, that name 'Operation Vanguard' cropped up. It's when her husband was killed. The dates line up."

"Good. That's the connection we've been looking for," Manx said. "If Bobbie Matthews blames the RAF for the death of her husband, then that's a bloody big motive. And, if we can tie Flynt to Operation Vanguard, that's another motive. Either Bobbie Matthews was right in what she told me, or she's very clever at covering her tracks and she killed Flynt and kidnapped Collins."

"She's got to be working with someone, someone from the island," Nader offered.

Manx wrote the words Meibion Glyndŵr on the board. "We need records on this lot from back in the day," he said. "Arrests, anyone under suspicion or affiliated."

"Aye, good luck with that," Nader said. "We weren't exactly high-tech back then, and the archives got moved twice. Who knows what the hell got lost?"

"Evidence, witness statements, DNA, we need the lot."

"Won't be any DNA," Nader said. "Not back in the day."

"None that were tested. But any physical evidence might still contain some residue. If we get a match with the two samples we've already analysed, the closer we are to finding who did this."

Manx was about to extend the team one of his end-of-briefing pep talks to keep them focused, when DCI Canton entered the room. "Ellis," Manx said, looking up. "Good news about the extra officers I requested, I hope?"

Canton forced a thin smile. "Couple of gents requesting to speak to you. They don't look like the types who take too kindly to 'come back later'."

54

As Manx and Canton walked into the station conference room, Commander Boyd looked agitated, eager to dispense with pleasantries and get down to business. "Obviously, these demands are ridiculous," he said, looking over at Jack Carlisle. "The RAF will not be releasing any documents pertaining to this or any other incident."

"Completely out of the question," Carlisle agreed, as he leant back and smoothed down his tie.

"But you know the incident the kidnappers are referring to, this drone strike? Operation Vanguard?" Manx asked.

The commander's posture stiffened. "I wasn't directly involved, but yes, I have been briefed."

"Right you are," Manx said, fixing his gaze on the commander's eyes which struggled to meet his own. "But why here? Why is all this happening at RAF Valley? The only obvious connection is James Flynt, but he's not likely to come forward with any new information anytime soon."

The commander glanced at Jack Carlisle, who, with a subtle nod of his head assured him he had permission to speak further.

"I can only confirm what's already in the public domain.

James Flynt was transferred to RAF Valley. Before that, he was an overseer at the unmanned aircraft ground control station at RAF Waddington, Lincolnshire."

"Was he connected to Operation Vanguard?"

"Disclosing that could put our servicemen in danger."

"Of course," Manx said, wearily. "And was this the same incident that an RAF medic..." he rechecked his notes. "Danvir Sadiq was killed?"

"I couldn't possibly–"

"No need," Manx interrupted. "These online news archives are a godsend, saves us a lot of wasted man hours." He dumped a thick wad of printed articles on the table. "I visited Danvir's parents on a related matter. Nice couple, heartbroken as you can imagine. As it turns out Danvir's widow is Bobbie Matthews, who we've already talked to. She's big into her conspiracy theories."

"Which is why her transfer to the VA facility is being fast-tracked," Boyd said. "The sooner she receives help, the better."

"Bloody big coincidence, though, isn't it?" Manx said. "Flynt killed, Bobbie Matthews in a hit-and-run, and now a ransom demand relating directly to the RAF and her husband's death? But here's the thing, I'm not a big believer in coincidences. Now, facts and hard evidence, those are the kinds of things I can put my faith in." Manx opened his palms. "Commander, do you have any of those you can share with myself and DCI Canton? Because we're running against a deadline and I have no doubt these people will follow through on their threat. Do you have any information that might help me stop those threats before we're sending out a coroner's van to pick up Logan Collins' body from a ditch somewhere?"

Boyd was set to speak when Carlisle, who'd been silent for the past few minutes, spoke. His tone was icy, controlled. "It appears we've reached an impasse, gentlemen," he said. "Commander Boyd is bound by the Official Secrets Act. Both of you have a serious hostage situation and its aftermath to contend with. Maybe there is some information we could share that would help in your investigation."

Manx folded his arms across his chest. "I'd have preferred to hear that a week ago, but I'm listening."

"The person you should be interrogating," Carlisle said, reaching into his briefcase and laying a folder on the table, "is Byron Charles Gates."

Manx glanced at the photo. A surveillance shot of an overweight, bearded man with a bad sunburn. Sitting next to him, Bobbie Matthews.

"Byron Gates?" Canton said, scanning the file. "Says here he lives in Lincolnshire."

"His primary residence, yes, but our intelligence confirms Gates has been here on Anglesey for several days."

"Why is he important to you?" Manx asked. "Has he made any threats?"

"When an enemy of our country moves within five miles of the people I'm tasked with protecting, I get twitchy."

Manx doubted if Carlisle got twitchy about anything. "What's his connection to my case?"

Carlisle flipped over one of the pages. "Byron Gates operates a website called DronewatchUK. He's a ghost in the machine. He receives sensitive military documents from service personnel who think nothing of betraying their country, then publishes said documents on his website."

"You're the military: can't you just shut him down?"

"We have, many times, but fifteen minutes later the site's back online, masked behind a wall of non-static IP addresses and hijacked devices." Carlisle paused, directed a frosty look in Manx's direction. "The same technical expertise it takes to upload a video and make its origin untraceable."

Manx processed Carlisle's words. His theory was plausible, but he remained unconvinced. "Just so I understand this. You think Byron Gates kidnapped Logan Collins and is now holding him hostage to force the RAF to release information about a drone strike that happened thousands of miles away, over a year ago?"

"People like Gates find it hard to move on."

"Has he made any credible threats?"

"You know as much about his threats as we do," Carlisle said, "but we do have his location." He handed over a handwritten note.

"You won't mind if I take the file?" Manx asked.

"Not at all. We have copies."

"If you know his whereabouts, why don't you just pick him up yourselves?" Canton asked.

Carlisle nodded. "Gates is still a civilian, in the eyes of the law he's done nothing illegal. We can't prove he uploaded the documents: he's a master of obfuscation. The North Wales Constabulary has enough evidence to pick him up and question him for twenty-four hours at least. We'd, of course, also need to question him once he's in your charge."

"Of course you would," Manx said. "Maybe you'd want to haul him off to Guantanamo too, while you're at it?"

Canton quickly jumped in. "Inspector Manx will personally take care of it. If this Byron Gates character's our man, we'll know soon enough."

Carlisle tugged down on his jacket sleeves. "You should also know Gates has become increasingly desperate of late. Multiple postings, ranting blog posts."

"Big jump, though," Manx said. "Blogging to kidnapping?"

Carlisle's eyes narrowed. "We suspect Gates is on medication or maybe even off his medication to escalate matters to this severe a level. We are not prepared to gamble with the life of the second in line to the throne. Neither I suspect, inspector, are you."

Manx internally flinched at the implication. Carlisle's world view was solidly black and white; you were either with him, or you were against him. Manx was still debating on which side he'd fall.

"Oh, one more thing," the commander said, gathering his cap. "Valley is on lockdown until this is resolved. We've informed the commercial airlines that share our airstrip of our decision."

"Can you do that?" Manx asked.

"It's the Ministry of Defence," Carlisle confirmed. "There's little they can't do. Bottom line, there really is no value in having the local police coming and going from the base as they please. It's simply not practical."

"And what about Bobbie Matthews?" Manx asked.

"We suspect they may be working together," Boyd said.

"Matthews and Gates? How so?"

"A picture paints a thousand words," Carlisle said, nodding at the photograph.

"If that's the case, I'd like to speak to Bobbie Matthews immediately, base lockdown or not."

"So would we," the commander said.

"Ah," Manx said. "One of your own gone AWOL?"

"I'm sure with the efforts of the North Wales Constabulary it won't take long to locate her," Carlisle said.

"We're a little busy right now, what with this kidnapping and a few other ongoing investigations."

Carlisle's eyes were two grey ice-blocks set against cold white. "I suggest we all leave here on good terms, our goals aligned."

"Our goals?" Manx asked.

"Neutralising the threat to our country's security."

"And finding Collins before they put a bullet through his head," Manx said, throwing Carlisle a cold, hard stare of his own.

"Of course, same goals," Carlisle replied, easing out of his chair and extending his hand. "Best of luck."

Manx and Canton watched the black Range Rover HSE pull out from the station car park, its metallic paintwork gleaming.

"You buy all that?" Canton asked.

"Buy it?" Manx said, glancing at Carlisle's dossier. "I buy it's a distraction, but that's not what they were selling us."

"Worth following up."

"I'll send someone to check out Gates."

"Good man. Same place tomorrow, early?"

"No other place else to be, Ellis."

Manx lifted the thin dossier from the table. It felt weightier than it should, as if its pages were bloated with the same doubts and reservations that had settled heavy on Manx from the moment Jack Carlisle opened his mouth and spoke. He suspected a restless night was in store. Seven days? The silent ticking of the clock was already counting down, he could sense it deep in his bones.

55

Andrew Pierce drove back from the RAF housing in a daze. He'd headed over to Bobbie's house as soon as he'd heard the news reports and seen Logan Collins' terrifying video. The house was deserted, locked up as if she'd never been there. He'd knocked on a few neighbours' doors; nobody had seen Bobbie for days.

He headed south east along the A55, turned on the A545 into the town of Beaumaris, and pulled up in the car park overlooking the Menai Strait, the ruins of the old castle behind him. He passed the small turret-like entrance at the pier and walked the whole length before resting at an empty bench.

The day was thick with tourists enjoying the sunshine and career-opportunist seagulls cackling above, ever on the scrounge for their next meal. This was the cadence of the everyday world, and Pierce felt three steps out of sync with its rhythm. He'd failed Bobbie, and that burden lay like cinder blocks across his heart. The demands Logan Collins had spoken came back to him as he looked over the green ribbon of the strait. "The truth about Operation Vanguard". It was all Bobbie had ever wanted; what she deserved. Maybe he could still help her; save her, even. But for that he required a large, unambiguous gesture.

He reached for this mobile and searched for a number. After several rings it was answered. He explained the situation clearly and precisely. Several moments of silence were followed by a deep resigned sigh, and clear instructions on the time and place to meet.

56

Byron Charles Gates had been a conscientious child, quick to defend others against perceived injustice. Some might have called him a snitch; Byron would have simply called it redressing the balance of justice. In the playground, he'd caught enough beatings for his tattletale leanings. Not that a blackeye or bloodied nose had deterred him: if anything it had strengthened his resolve. But by the time Byron had entered upper school, he towered several inches above his peers and had filled out like a prop-forward. He suffered little bullying after that summer-long growth spurt.

The kids just simply ignored Byron now, called him Wacko Byro behind his back. It never bothered him; he was happy keeping to himself, spending hours alone mastering every video game he could set his thick thumbs around. Bored with playing, he began programming his own games, writing code, then when in college, collaborated with a group of like-minded misfits who taught him the basics of cyber hacking. After that, his course was set. Not that he'd done any of it for the money. Byron had loftier goals than holding peoples' computers for ransom or selling stolen credit card numbers for a few quid a pop. His targets were the multi-national corporations which acted with impunity when it came to paying their corporate taxes, dealing in illegal arms trades or funding terrorist organisations. It was around that time, the early 2000s, when Byron had launched DronewatchUK. He had a new enemy in his sights now, the industrial, technology and military complex.

In Byron's mind, the drone strikes sanctioned by the RAF were no different to the mass carpet bombing of Berlin and Dresden during the Second World War. Back then, tens of thousands of innocents had suffered at the hands of the military gods. People were still suffering their wrath, albeit thousands of miles away in remote villages across the middle east and Pakistan. He had a duty to tell the world the truth: if only the world were listening.

Watching the video, he'd been conflicted. There was an insane bravado in forcing the RAF's hand, but the hollow look in the politician's eyes, the way he talked as if he were already dead and had found himself in hell, had shaken Byron. Not that he had much choice, Bobbie had made that clear.

After he'd uploaded the video – fake Gmail account, several high-jacked devices in Macau, Odessa and Lagos, and eight different IP addresses pinging across three continents – he'd conducted a far simpler hack; locating Tammy Povey. If he could speak to her, gather some intelligence, he might gain some leverage, something he could use to bargain for his life if the time came.

He wrote down her address on the stationery in his room: those kinds of records were best kept analogue. He left fifty pounds on the bedside table, plus a five-pound tip. After stuffing his clothes into his backpack, he flipped open his laptop, logged on to his TOR browser. Bobbie had already threatened him with his life, and, as she'd told him, the RAF possessed a hard drive full of evidence against him. What if they had eyes on him now, were tracking every mouse click and keystroke? The words "rock and hard place" came to mind. He needed a failsafe, a backup if the worst happened.

He clicked to the Duck Duck Go search engine, scanned the *North Wales Daily Post* online edition for the past week and found the officer leading the investigation: Detective Inspector Tudor Manx. Next, he accessed the public-facing website of the North Wales Constabulary. Manx was stationed at Llangefni, no personal email address, but there was a general email where members of the public could send in questions. The subject line, it informed him, should include the officer's name and the words, "Just Ask A Copper."

Byron laughed. Just ask a copper for what? Protection from Bobbie? Immunity from prosecution if the RAF were tracking his every move? No, he needed to be smarter, several steps ahead.

He pasted what he'd written earlier; everything he suspected about Bobbie, her threats, how she forced him to upload the video; how he feared for his own life. Before sending, he hesitated. Was he showing his hand too early again? If Bobbie found out, he was done for. Clicking back to his TOR browser, he pasted the contents to his secure email server, adding a specific time and date for the email to be sent. He just needed to stay safe a few more days, then this would all be over, and he could go back home. If not, he'd have something to use to bargain for his life.

Live long enough? Bargain for his life? How in God's name had it come to this? Three days ago, he was at home, minding his own business, playing pinball; his only concerns generating extra income from his computer repair business and his mother's health. Today, he was putting a plan in place in the event of his death; or more specifically, his murder. He pushed the grim thought to the back of his mind, grabbed his backpack and drove into the warm Anglesey night.

57

Melvin's day had started badly. He'd woken up at 5am. During the night, a knife blade had somehow twisted a path inside him and was carving up his lungs like meat on a butcher's block. The thick phlegm of blood he'd coughed up while sitting on the toilet seat had seemed unreal to him, as if it had been exorcised by someone else, someone weaker, someone who wasn't Melvin Powell, Gwynedd County Welter-Weight Champion; The Great Welsh Hope. He'd had a good laugh at that word, hope. When hope was just about gone what else was there left other than to laugh at how ridiculous the word sounded on his lips?

At the kitchen table, Lydia had laid into him about how he looked thinner, paler. Was there something wrong? Something he needed to tell her? It riled Mel, being questioned about anything before he'd finished his first mug of tea of the day. Lydia's questions had made him edgy and defensive – Lydia didn't do subtle. He'd left the flat before finishing his breakfast, thrown half a glass of juice at the wall, he wasn't proud of that, but the woman could really push his buttons when she set her mind to it.

Adding to his dark mood, a paint job he'd bid on for an office building in Holyhead had fallen through. Someone had undercut his quote; no doubt one of those cowboy operations that had sprung up on the island recently, Polish or Ukrainian lads, scruffy, homeless-looking sods, knocking on doors, offering to work – any kind of work – for a few quid an hour, or shining tyre walls at the local car washes. They were likely trafficked in through Holyhead and living ten-to-a-room in a half-demolished farmhouse out in the middle of nowhere, where the coppers wouldn't come knocking.

With nothing better to do, he'd driven to Cemaes Bay to work on his boat. She needed a fresh coat of wood varnish and the motor needed cleaning out if he had any hope of selling the vessel. He was crouched over the engine, cleaning between the thin grooves of the spark plugs when he heard someone calling his name. He looked up, lifting the bill of his cap to see the bulky, anxious figure of Stan Thomas standing at one of the mooring cleats.

"All right, Stan, bit early for you, isn't it? Bookies don't open till eleven, or do you do all that online gambling these days?"

Stan looked around as if he suspected someone had followed him. He took out a late-morning copy of the *North Wales Daily Post* from his pocket "Is this you, then?" he said, waving the paper at Mel. "You and that lapdog nephew of yours?"

"Don't know what you're talking about, mate," Melvin said, widening his stance on the boat's floor to steady himself.

"Come on, I wasn't born yesterday." Stan edged closer to dockside. "Step too far this is, mate. Setting fire to a few houses to make a point, that's what we signed up for, but kidnapping, death threats? We all agree, it's too far, too bloody far. We've got wives, kids, grandkids some of us. What the hell are you thinking?"

Melvin looked down, ran an oily rag through his fingers. "Liberation or death, brothers till the end?"

Stan laughed. "We're not bloody kids anymore. Grow up, eh?"

Melvin threw the rag to the floor. "What are you doing here, Stan? I'm busy," he said, his anger swelling, but he wasn't going to show that, not to Stan Wilson. He held it back, kept it locked down, waited to see how the conversation played out.

"Came to tell you it's done, mate. All that Meibion Glyndŵr stuff, all done with. If you don't stop, we're all agreed, we're going to the police, tell them everything."

Melvin stretched out his arm. "Give us a hand up."

Stan hesitated.

"What? You think I'm going to drag you into the fucking water? Come on, help me up."

As he reluctantly stretched out his arm, Melvin grabbed Stan's wrist and hoisted himself from the boat and onto the dockside. The moment his boots hit dry land, he snatched back his arm and pummelled his fist hard into Stan's solar plexus.

Stan felt his stomach push into his backbone, his legs buckling. He fell, his knees taking the brunt of the landing. Setting his hands either side of him, he vomited a pool of clear liquid onto the dockside.

"Listen," Melvin said, speaking calmly into his ear. "You start mouthing off, any of you, there's going to be trouble. Go home and I'll forget you threatened me. Can you do that, Stan? Or do you need reminding what I was like in the ring, back in the day?"

"You're not right in the head, Mel," Stan said, barely exhaling his words. "Bloody mad, off your rocker."

"Aye, you might be right, there," Mel said. "Now, you go back and tell the rest of them, if I go down, they all go down, and not just for the fires. That clear enough for you, Stan?"

He nodded and hauled himself up, his legs barely supporting his body. "It's not going to end well, Mel, none of this, I can tell you that now." He spat on the ground and turned his back.

As Stan walked away, his gait slow and pained, Melvin climbed back onto his boat. End well? Of course none of this was going to end well, not for him at least. Not that it mattered. Best to go out with his arms high, fists raised, not pissing in a hospital bed, his dignity ravaged to nothing, his body and mind numbed solid by painkillers.

He pressed the start button on the engine. After a few sputters it cracked to life. *Fuck Stan and the rest of them*, he thought as he threw off the casting rope and headed towards the open ocean. He had a true cause to fight for now. He'd made a promise to Bobbie, one he wasn't about to break just because Stan Thomas was crapping in his knickers. If there was a bitter end, he'd see it all the way through to that final destination, he owed her that much.

58

DI Tudor Manx's morning had started at 2.15am with a head full of theories that dead-ended at every turn, and the relentless ticking of a time bomb counting down at the back of his mind. The day was made worse by a visit from the North Wales Constabulary Chief Press Officer demanding a statement and a time and date for a press conference with himself and Canton. Manx had given her the brush off; he could delay the request a few days, and right now he'd take any breathing space he could get.

"Papers are having a bloody field day," Nader said as Manx walked into the incident room. "What with those dead starlings – by the way, my money's still on the jet fuel – and Collins' kidnapping. They're quoting all these old Welsh academics, even got an interview with Dafydd bloody Iwan."

"That'll boost his record sales," Priddle offered.

"Always a silver lining," Manx said. "Anything on Gates, Priddle?"

"He checked out of the bed and breakfast."

"When?"

"The landlady, Mrs Rose, went up to his room yesterday

evening, his door was wide open, no sign of him. Said he left fifty quid and a fiver tip on the bedside table."

"Conscientious type, then?"

"How do you mean?"

"People doing a runner don't usually leave payment plus tip."

"Yeah, I suppose," Priddle said. "Oh, Mrs Rose took his car registration. He was driving a Toyota Prius."

"Make sure we get that number to dispatch. Send it out to every station and patrol car on the island."

"Do you think Gates is responsible for this?" Morris asked.

"The RAF and Carlisle are hot under the collar for us to apprehend him, but we have no evidence other than he has the technical skills to anonymously upload a video to YouTube, which most teenagers with half a brain cell could probably pull off."

"Do we have any other suspects?" Morris asked.

Manx turned to the incident board; it made for dismal reading. Two weeks after the discovery of James Flynt's body, they should at least have a prime suspect, but every lead had fizzled to nothing, and with RAF Valley now off limits Manx felt he was investigating with two hands tied behind his back and his feet stuck in quicksand.

"I could rattle a few more cages," Nader said. "Been on this island long enough to know most of the nasty toe-rags out there. Bring them in, turn them upside down, see what shakes out."

Manx conducted a mental count to ten. He didn't need this from Nader, not today. "I want you focused on what I asked you to focus on, Nader: the archives on that Meibion Glyndŵr outfit."

Nader cocked his head towards the corner of the room.

"That's it?" Manx asked, looking at the three thin carboard boxes stacked on top of each other.

"The archives flooded a few years back. Lost boxes of evidence to water damage, that's when they moved the record-keeping over to Colwyn Bay."

"I looked through it already," Morris said. "I can start tracking down some of the names this morning."

"Yeah, good luck with that, Minor," Nader said. "Probably moved away years ago, or dead and buried by now."

"Or they might not have done anything," Priddle said, a hesitant edge to his voice.

"Oh, aye, know that for a fact, do you?" Nader snapped.

Priddle shuffled awkwardly in his seat. "Some people reckon the whole thing was a set-up, by the government."

"Oh, classic Priddle, this is," Nader chuckled. "Can't wait to hear the professor's latest bloody theory. Go on then."

Priddle pushed against his chair and pulled back his shoulders. "It's not just a theory, sarge," he said. "The English government paid these blokes to stage the attacks, so it made the Welsh look bad, like we were all terrorists, like the IRA."

"That right?" Nader said, chuckling. "And I heard the Titanic hit an iceberg planted by the Germans and Owain Glyndŵr was seen having a pint down the pub last week with Princess bloody Di."

"That's as barmy as starlings killed by jet fuel and sound-waves," Morris said, with a smile.

"Fascinating as this is, conspiracy theories from forty years ago are not top of my list of priorities today. What I need from you, Morris and PC... sorry, what was your name again?"

The young constable, red-faced with the wisp of a ginger goatee, sat up straight. "Pritchard. PC Bryn Pritchard."

"What I need is for you to sift through those evidence boxes like you were panning for gold. The big shiny nugget you're searching for is any forensic evidence with a high probability of containing DNA – clothes, blood stains, fibres, weapons found at the scenes – and send them over to Bevan's team for analysis."

Manx directed his next question at Priddle. "Any updates from Bevan on that familial connection we requested?"

"Nothing yet."

"Lurk outside his bloody door if that's what it takes. The clock, Priddle, and the rest of you, is ticking." He took his pen and pointed to the board. "We need to find Bobbie Matthews, quick."

"Is she connected to this Byron Gates?" Priddle asked.

"The RAF seem to think so." Manx pinned up the surveillance photo of her and Gates. "With RAF Valley on lock-down until this blows over, our hands are tied."

"If she lives in the RAF housing, not in the barracks, then it's not on the base," Nader said. "Fair game."

"Then, move on that. Search the electoral register for her address. Ask around, maybe the neighbours saw something."

"Got it, boss," Nader confirmed.

Manx turned to the seven-day calendar and timeline he'd scribbled onto the incident board late last night: in the cold light of day, it looked as if it were drawn by a drunk. "For the next six days, we live and breathe this timeline. All leave is suspended, we'll be working long shifts, and before you ask, yes, Canton has approved all overtime."

Looking over the already exhausted team, Manx imagined they'd need every reserve of stamina and fortitude before this was all over.

59

Andrew Pierce had opted for casual civilian dress that morning: trousers, an open-neck shirt, and a blue linen blazer. The outfit was designed to attract as little attention as possible: just another passenger boarding the 9.05am Bangor to London train, with a change at Crewe, final destination, Lincolnshire.

At 1.35pm, he sat at the Costa Coffee at Lincoln station, ordered an extra hot flat white and waited for his contact to arrive. He sensed a flicker of nervousness. This wasn't his style – setting up clandestine meetings to procure classified information – but these were extenuating circumstances. The unnerving sensation that he was close to losing Bobbie for good was like a deep, gaping hole in his chest.

Turning the screws on an old colleague had been more challenging than he expected. After several reminders of how far he'd stuck his neck out for him and a not-so-subtle hint that Pierce had kept a record of "certain evidence you wouldn't want to come to light", eventually William Baker agreed to meet.

Baker was a commissioned officer before moving to the MoD, where he'd made fast progress climbing the Whitehall career ladder; Pierce recalled he'd always had a nose for which way the political winds were blowing. Early in their career, Pierce and Baker had been stationed together and had become close friends. Baker was a hard drinker; the Oliver Reed level of drunk but without the charm or charisma. Baker was driving home late one night after an afternoon-long bender in the local pub when he hit a cyclist; a young lad no more than twenty-three; one of the civilian contractors at the base. Baker hadn't even stopped, just continued as if he'd hit a stray badger or fox. The lad had suffered through a long, drawn-out coma before his heartbroken parents signed the paperwork and his vital organs were removed and helicoptered out.

Baker began to fall apart soon after and had come to Pierce for guidance, either spiritually or mentally; it made no difference, Pierce was still training, not yet ordained as a chaplain nor fully qualified as a clinical psychologist, but the prospect of trying to "fix" Baker was too much of a temptation to resist. After all, it was the reason God had put him on earth; to heal the wounded.

Pierce had recorded all of their conversations, mostly for his own training. As the sessions progressed, Baker formed his own, warped, narrative around what happened; a narrative that absolved him of all blame. It was then, his morality already compromised, that Pierce realised the recordings could be useful in another way. He wasn't yet qualified to treat anyone, so any patient–doctor confidentiality was irrelevant. If he confessed to the Base Commander how he'd got the recordings, he'd face disciplinary action which could see him drummed out of the service along with Baker. Instead, he kept seeing Baker and recording their sessions until one day Baker declared he'd found salvation in God's word, and God had chosen to forgive him. Pierce's counsel was no longer required. He doubted Baker had found any kind of salvation, divine or otherwise, but Pierce had kept the recordings for over fifteen years, figuring some day they might be used as leverage. Today was that day.

Baker, as expected, was punctual. He sat across from Pierce with a grunt and a look that suggested his attendance was only marginally less unpleasant than root canal surgery.

"You look older," Pierce said. Baker's hair, what remained of it, was a dirty shade of grey. His pallor was of someone who had spent long, tedious hours under the artificial glow of fluorescent strip lighting in some dank basement office.

"Let's dispense with the pleasantries, shall we?" Baker said, taking a small USB drive from his trouser pocket and looking around him before placing it under a napkin on the table. Pierce palmed the object, slipped it into his jacket pocket and handed Baker an envelope containing the session recordings.

Baker got up to leave.

"No catch-up, Bill?" Pierce asked.

Baker shook his head. "Some other time. Maybe never. Is never good for you, Pierce?"

"Why meet here? It's a long train ride from Whitehall."

Baker sighed, eyes rheumy and narrowed. "Confidential Air Command matters to attend to. Way above your pay grade." He stood, placed his palms on the table and loomed over Pierce, his top lip moist with sweat. "If this ever gets out, I'll make it my personal mission to destroy you. With any luck I'll never see your face again, and you best hope you never see mine."

"That Whitehall job's made you paranoid," Pierce said. "Still accepting God as your saviour, Bill? Or are your allegiances more secular these days?"

Baker emitted a short grunt. "You always were an insufferable prick, Pierce," he said, before turning his back and scurrying out like a dog with its tail between his legs.

By 7pm, Pierce was back at his office. He slipped the drive

into his PC. He clicked on the folder titled simply "_VG" and waited for its contents to reveal themselves.

A single PDF document opened up. The name "Operation Vanguard" was typed across the top and the government protective marking, "Top Secret" – suggesting it contained information which could cause serious harm if compromised – was stamped in large block lettering across the front.

Before reading, he looked up as the lights from an incoming aircraft illuminated the office. Something wasn't right. He glanced at the back of his office door where he always kept his chaplain's vestments and clerical collar; they were missing. He could have sworn he'd hung them there after his service last Sunday... or perhaps he was mistaken, and he'd left them back in the vestry at Valley church. No matter, he'd go over there tomorrow and make sure.

He focused his attention back to the document and began reading.

60

Byron Gates had spent the night in his car. It wasn't the first time. The afternoon he spotted a black Range Rover parked across from his house he'd made a rapid escape and headed for a secluded spot near Lincolnshire Wold. He'd hidden out there for three nights; it was all his body could handle. His back was sore for a week after. When he returned, the Range Rover had gone; if it was ever there in the first place. Sometimes Byron's mind liked to play tricks like that; little pranks to keep him on his toes.

Today, when he woke, he was greeted with a similar twinge of pain, but this time accompanied by a spectacular sunrise streaming like a wash of yellow corn through the windscreen. He'd parked at Dinas beach, a sheltered bay, accessible only by a one-track road. At 7am, the car park was deserted, save the chorus of cormorants and seagulls cracking the dawn wide open with their cries.

He switched on the radio. The news was still broadcasting coverage of Logan Collins' video. He felt guilty, as if he were somehow to blame. He chided himself for feeling that way; this was all Bobbie's handiwork. If nothing else, it confirmed he'd made the right decision to stay off the grid – Bobbie wasn't one for idle threats, that was for sure. After pouring himself a few tepid mouthfuls of coffee from his flask, he entered the address he'd copied to his mobile and headed towards Beaumaris.

When he pulled up outside Tammy Povey's home, a large detached house with a wide driveway and what looked like a brand-new Mercedes C250 parked outside, the sun was in full bloom, a scattering of benign white clouds floating high in the blue. He knocked three times, rang the bell twice. He was set to leave, call back later, when the door was pulled sharply open. Tammy, hair tousled, eyes half-closed, stood in the doorway. She tied the belt of her red dressing gown around her waist.

"This better be bloody good, waking me up on my day off," she said, barely registering Byron's face. "Where do I sign?"

"Em..." he began, scrunching his brow in confusion.

Tammy tugged the lapels of her dressing grown across her chest. "No package? I don't get my new oil delivery until September. Who are you?" She stepped back, shook her head. "Oh, not with the God Squad, are you? Jehovah bloody Witness or something?"

"Huh? Um, no," Byron stammered.

"No," she confirmed, studying Byron. "Too bloody scruffy."

"I'm a friend of Bobbie's."

"Yeah," she said, checking out Byron's dishevelled, nerdy appearance. "You look like you might be, but why are you here?"

Byron hadn't anticipated this question. In fact, he hadn't anticipated much of anything, least of all questions. It was a spur of the moment decision, coming here; he could have kicked himself for not being been better prepared.

"Well?" Tammy pressed.

"I was wondering if you knew where she was?"

Tammy shrugged. "Home. Or working, all she ever does."

"And where does she live again?"

Tammy folded her arms across her chest. "If you were her friend, you'd know that."

"We lost touch, a while ago."

"What did you say your name was?"

"I'm just trying to reconnect with Bobbie."

Tammy set both her palms against the door, pushing it closed. "Try Facebook, like a normal person."

Byron wedged a boot in the doorway. "I don't mean to scare you, honest, but I think Bobbie might be in trouble. I'd really like to speak to her."

"Trouble?" Tammy smiled. "If anyone can handle trouble, it's my sister. Now, if you don't get your foot from my door, I'm calling the police," she said, slipping her mobile from her pocket.

"Sorry to have bothered you," he said, pulling his foot away. He felt the draft on his face as Tammy slammed the door. No matter. He'd obtained one vital piece of information he wasn't expecting. Bobbie was Tammy's sister.

It was a start. He'd uncovered a small nugget of hope, some leverage he could use when the time came. The thought gave him some comfort as he started the engine and searched for his next hiding place. Someplace isolated. Someplace Bobbie wouldn't find him.

61

After several heavy fist pummels on the front door, DS Nader walked around to the back of the house. There were two ground floor windows, one looking into the kitchen, the other looking into the dining room. Both had the curtains drawn tight as blindfolds. The garden was small with a square patch of lawn and flower beds framing the edges. The Indian stone driveway was also empty, save a wet pool of engine oil. He crouched down, touched the thick black solution. Fresh; maybe a recent engine leak.

"She's not buried under the driveway, if that's what you think."

Nader stood, his knees creaking like a pair of rusty door hinges. "And who are you, love?" he asked, looking over to a woman speaking to him from behind the white sheet she was pegging to the washing line.

"Bloody neighbour, aren't I. Who do you think?" she said nodding towards the house. "Candice. Everyone calls me Candy."

Candy was in her mid-thirties, Nader guessed, hair-colour

straight from a bottle, outfit courtesy of Primark; attitude honed on the council estates of Valley.

"You know the woman who lives here?"

"Depends on who's asking, don't it?"

"Detective Sergeant Mal Nader, North Wales Constabulary," he said, taking out his badge.

"Closer," Candy said, beckoning him with her hand.

Nader stepped forward.

Candy leant her thick forearms across the hazel hurdle fencing. "Yeah, I know her," she said, wiping her hands down her oversized pink Juicy Couture T-shirt. "Bobbie Matthews. Why? What's she done? Already had some bloke asking about her a few days back."

"Oh, aye, who was that then?"

"RAF type, from the base. Didn't tell me his name."

"Did you ask?"

"Mind my own business, I do."

"That right?"

"Yeah, it is. But I feel sorry for the young girl, yeah?" she said with a solemn shake of her head. "Widowed at her age. Thank God mine's out of active service." Candy leaned forward, lowered her voice. "Mind you, some days I wish they'd deploy the useless lump a few thousand miles away, leave me in peace."

"Did you know Bobbie Matthews well?" Nader asked.

Candy shrugged. "She wasn't the get-to-know-you-well type, if you know what I mean. Kept herself to herself, bit miserable if you ask me. Mind you, I bet it weren't easy for her, settling down here in RAF housing after what happened. Most of us wives have been here for years. We stick close, like. Not that we didn't invite her over – drinks, cards, that kind of thing – but she was always too busy. Well, after a while you stop asking, don't you?"

"Have you seen her recently?"

"Her car's not been there for a couple of days, and I've not caught sight of her around the village for a week now."

"See her down the local?"

"Like I said, she wasn't the 'meet me down the pub' type."

"Anywhere you know she might have gone?"

Candy thought for a moment. "She kept herself to herself, and I'm not one to pry. But she did mention she had a sister over in Beaumaris."

"Did this sister have a name?"

Candy paused. "Tammy. Yeah, Tammy, that's it."

"Good, Candy," he said. "Thanks for your time."

"You lot going to find that bloke before they kill him? Not much for politics, but he's got a wife and kids," Candy asked, her voice raised as if she wanted the whole housing estate to hear.

"We're doing the best we can."

"And those dead birds. Want to know what I think?" she said, crossing her arms across her chest. "All the radiation from those mobile phones, got to be."

"Well, when we know you'll know," Nader said, turning his back and walking back to the service car.

"Oh, yeah? Great bloody comfort that is," Candy said, shaking her head and pegging her sheet firmly to the washing line. "Radiation. Hot tip, that is, mate."

Nader continued walking.

"Hey! You're bloody welcome," Candy called out.

62

Tammy had opened the door to her sister earlier that evening. Bobbie had stood under the porch light, kitbag flung over her shoulder. Bobbie would often turn up on Tammy's doorstep, stay for a couple of nights then leave without a word. She'd learnt to live with it by now; well, not exactly live-with-it, more like roll-with-it. That kind of attitude became second nature when you were Bobbie Matthews' sister.

"You can use the spare room, but you're making your own bed, mind."

Bobbie had agreed to the terms with a sharp nod and walked upstairs. By the time Tammy had turned from the doorway, Bobbie had already closed the bedroom door. It was another three hours before she emerged to join her sister in the kitchen.

"You look like you need a stiff drink," she said, as Bobbie threw herself onto one of the kitchen chairs.

"Tea's fine, thanks."

"Yeah, of course it is," she said, flipping down the switch on the kettle. "Want to tell me what this is all about?"

Bobbie stretched out her legs and shoved both her hands deep into her hoodie pockets. "Not now, Tammy, I'm knackered."

"Suit yourself, but if you're kipping here you need to talk to me. I've had it with this sulky teenager act."

Bobbie shrugged. "Yeah, just give me time, okay?"

"Is this about Dani? Having one of your bad days?"

Bobbie shrugged.

"You can talk to me, you know, about what happened."

"Been there, tried that."

"Yeah, I'm not talking about some grief counselling thing. We're sisters. We grew up together. Remember, we used to tell each other everything. No secrets."

Secrets? The word made Bobbie want to laugh. Tammy might have thought Bobbie was still the sullen teenager she remembered growing up, but Tammy hadn't matured that much either. She still believed in some adolescent fantasy of a girlish sisterhood that had never existed; at least not that Bobbie remembered. Truth was, neither of them had been the sister the other needed. They were sisters in name only, separated by the genetic traits of two different fathers. It should have drawn them closer, but instead those differences had thrust a sharp wedge between them.

"You heard about that poor bloke who was kidnapped?"

"Hard not to."

"I always thought this place was too bloody quiet; now I could do without all the stress to be honest."

"Careful what you wish for, right?" Bobbie said.

A few seconds of silence was broken by a sharp kettle whistle. "Oh, I almost forgot," Tammy said, sloshing hot water over the teabag. "Some bloke called round this morning looking for you."

Bobbie stiffened, but kept her composure as Tammy sat and slid the mug across the table.

"What bloke?"

"Didn't say. Said he was a friend of yours. Scruffy-looking sod, big beard, nervous too. Looked like he didn't socialise much."

Bobbie straightened her back. "What did you tell him?"

"Didn't tell him anything, just sent him packing."

Bobbie pushed back her chair and stood, wiping her hands down the front of her hoodie.

"Where are you going? You just got here."

"Sorry, I've got to–" she said, cutting her sentence short before rushing upstairs.

Bobbie slammed the bedroom door and stuffed the clothes she'd just unpacked back into her kitbag.

Tammy flung the door back open. "Who was he?" she demanded, stepping into the bedroom. "What did he want?"

"He's a nobody, just a creep."

"Oh, like a stalker you mean? Had one of those myself, once."

"Yeah a stalker, just like a stalker," Bobbie said, hauling the kitbag over her shoulder.

"He said you were in trouble, Bobbie. Is that true? Are you?"

Bobbie's stomach snarled into a stiff ball of wire. More questions. Tammy had more questions than Call Me Andy. Didn't they realise she was tired of talking, tired of being lied to? She took a step forward, ready to shoulder-charge her sister if necessary.

"No," Tammy said, blocking the door and folding her arms. "Not until you speak to me. Why did he say you were in trouble? Is it about Dani? How he died?"

The sound of her husband's name on her sister's lips was like the twist of a knife in Bobbie's chest. Tammy had always called him Dani, as if she were too lazy to take the time to learn how to pronounce his name correctly. Bobbie snapped out her arm, wrapped her sister's wrist in her hand and pressed hard with her thumbs. Tammy groaned with pain.

"Jesus, Bobbie!" she said, stepping aside and rubbing her wrist. "If you want to go that badly, just go. But you don't get to come back. This is the last time."

Bobbie dropped her kitbag, turned to face her sister and stood to attention as if presenting herself on the parade square. "Danvir. My husband's name is Danvir Mohsin Sadiq. He died in a missile attack in Mosul, Syria, but I don't know anymore if that's true or if it's a cover-up, or if I killed him. I've been relieved of my duties and will be sent to a VA psych hospital for rehabilitation for as long as they see fit to keep me there. Everyone else involved in Operation Vanguard is now either dead or lying about what really happened. It has fallen on my shoulders to exact the punishment and redress the balance of justice. Necessary killings in a necessary war."

"What the hell are you saying, Bobbie?" Tammy asked, the pain in her wrist replaced by a more unsettling feeling; fear.

Bobbie lifted her kitbag. "I am not in denial, Tammy, I'm living with the echo of what I did every single minute of the day. My house reminds me of Danvir. My job reminds me of him, the base, the uniforms, the bloody wives in the housing, everything. There has to be justice, right, Tammy? A balance? I wanted to explain this all to you later, when I'm in a better place. All I asked for was time, but you're just like Maggie – 'Keep calm and carry on, get over it, Bobbie, move on, Bobbie, cheer up, Bobbie, it might never happen, Bobbie.' But you know what, Tammy, it did bloody well happen."

"Jesus–" Tammy began before Bobbie interrupted.

"Happy? Good conversation, sis?"

Tammy's words were stuck somewhere deep in her throat. If she'd managed to speak, she was sure her words would have tumbled into a mess of incoherent noise.

Bobbie bolted down the stairs, pulling the door hard into its frame as she left. In the resonance of the slam, Tammy had the unshakeable feeling that her sister was heading into something dangerous; something there was no coming back from. The sensation sent a sudden chill pulsing to her core.

63

The following day, Manx pushed through the mob of reporters, microphones and news cameras blocking his way up the station steps. The questions were the same as yesterday and the day before:

Have you located Logan Collins yet?

Has anyone been arrested?

Will the RAF release the Operation Vanguard documents?

Is the North Wales Constabulary failing in its duties?

When will there be an official press briefing?

How is Logan Collins' wife dealing with the stress of her husband's kidnapping?

That last question was a new take, Manx thought as he shoved open the station door. Entering the reception, the question suddenly made sense. Danica Collins – back pin-straight, hands fixed on her lap – sat on one of the chairs. She was composed but had the pallor of a woman who was a stranger to sleep. She stood, smoothed down the front of her jacket and looked directly at Manx; her eyes had the same other-worldly clarity he'd noticed when they'd first met.

He turned to the duty sergeant. "Interview room two free?"

The sergeant checked the monitors and nodded.

"Follow me, Mrs Collins," Manx said, buzzing open the door and leading her into the brightly lit corridor.

"Just so you understand, I did not come to hear platitudes," Danica said, gracefully easing herself into the chair.

"Truth is, I have none to give you, Mrs Collins," he said, sitting across from her.

"Do you still think my husband is being held on the island?"

"Most likely, yes."

"It's not that large."

"One person, 260 square miles, and limited police resources–" Manx began.

"So, what are these resources actually doing?" she interrupted.

"Our job, Mrs Collins. Investigating."

Danica dropped her hands to her lap. In that moment, she looked fragile; a woman navigating her own personal hell. "When my husband was first taken, do you remember what you told me?"

She didn't wait for Manx's reply.

"You told me most of these situations are resolved. The victims are returned, unharmed. Nobody gets killed."

Manx had a vague recollection. It was only a few days back, but it already felt like weeks ago.

"So, let me ask you," she said, leaning forward. "Do you still believe that's true?"

Manx's hesitation was the only answer Danica Collins required. She held herself stiffly as if she were controlling every muscle in her body, and if she relaxed any of them, she might fall apart at the seams. She dragged back her chair and stood.

"Mrs Collins–"

"Words don't interest me, inspector," she said. "Actions.

Finding my husband, bringing a father back to his children, those are the only things that matter now."

As she pulled the interview room door closed behind her, Manx leant back. "Jesus Christ," he muttered to himself.

Back in reception he glanced through the window at the commotion outside. Danica Collins was addressing the cameras. Manx couldn't hear what she was saying, but he was damned sure she wasn't thanking the North Wales Constabulary for the sterling job they were doing in locating her husband. As he turned to head into the break room to pour himself a tepid coffee before digging through the evidence again – his life was turning into a macabre version of *Groundhog Day* – DS Nader rushed in from the incident room.

"Boss!" he said, waving a slip of paper in his hand. "Bobbie Matthews' sister's address. Got her photo off Facebook. She's a bit of a looker, too. Wouldn't have to ask me twice. I'll head over there now."

Manx took the paper. "No," he said. "I'll go. Could do with some fresh air and a change of scenery."

Nader's face fell a few millimetres, then he smiled. "Maybe for the best. The woman probably wouldn't stand a chance once I turn on the old Nader charm."

"Nailed it, as usual, sergeant," Manx said. "Now maybe you use some of that charm to solve these bloody cases. Call me with anything new."

64

Tammy Povey was having none of it. She sat at her breakfast bar, arms folded tight. "Don't know why you're asking about Bobbie, I hardly ever see her," she said, staring defiantly at Manx.

"When did you last see your sister?"

"Half-sister," Tammy said, snapping her dressing gown cord tighter around her waist.

"Your half-sister. Have you seen her recently?"

"Is she in trouble or something?"

"How well do you know her, Tammy?"

"What kind of question is that? We've known each other all our lives."

"That's not what I asked," Manx said, sensing her unease as she shuffled and brushed a length of hair from her face. It was early in the morning and Tammy Povey had obviously had no time to attend to her typical make-up routine, but Nader had been right: Tammy was a looker, striking even; sparkling blue eyes that locked on to his when she talked; high, perfectly sculpted cheekbones; skin that seemed to glow in the morning light streaming in through the kitchen window. She had the sort of energy Manx found himself drawn to; a natural confidence he'd always found attractive. Tammy had it in spades, and he could sense it sparking across the table as she crossed her legs, revealing a sliver of thigh, and looked at him as if she were waiting to be impressed.

"You can live with someone all your life and still not know them," he finally said.

"Oh, like those women married to serial killers you mean?" she said, pointing her coffee cup at Manx. "Don't buy it myself. I'd sniff that out in a heartbeat and any woman who tells you otherwise is lying. There, you can have that insight for free, Inspector Manx."

"I'll remember to include it in my memoirs," Manx said, laying out the printout of Bobbie and Byron Gates on the table. "Do you know this man?"

Tammy picked up the photo. "Yeah. Well I don't know him, but he called around here looking for Bobbie a couple of days ago. He looked shifty, so I sent him packing, almost called you lot, actually. Who is he?"

"His name's Byron Gates. We have reason to believe he and Bobbie are working together."

Tammy narrowed her eyes, causing her nose to scrunch in a way that made Manx smile. "How do you mean working together? And why are you smiling like that?"

Manx continued. "Logan Collins' kidnapping–"

"No. No," Tammy interrupted. She stood and walked to the opposite end of the kitchen. "Bobbie's been upset recently, but she's getting help. She's checking into a psychiatric hospital in a couple of weeks. You're barking up the wrong tree. What about that Gates bloke? He looked the shady type to me."

"Do you know where she is, Tammy? A place she might feel safe? Friends she's close to that wouldn't hesitate to help her out?"

"Friends?" Tammy said, shaking her head. "This is Bobbie we're talking about."

"No friends?" Manx said. "Seems unlikely."

"Then, you don't know Bobbie," Tammy said.

"No," he agreed. "I don't, but you do."

He stood and handed Tammy his card. "If she contacts you or you think of any place she might be hiding, call me. We want to find her before anything bad happens. I want to keep Bobbie safe. Whatever she's done, we can work through it, make sure she gets the help she needs. Do you understand, Tammy?"

"I think so." She twirled the card around her fingers. "Thank you," she said, flashing another dazzling smile his way: one he'd happily have pocketed and taken home with him if he could. "You're all right, you are."

"Nicest thing anyone said to me all week," he said.

"For a copper," Tammy clarified, this time her smile wider, a playful glint in her eyes.

"For a copper," Manx muttered to himself, shook his head and saw himself out.

65

Collins was running, or was he dreaming he was running? He could no longer discern what was real and what his imagination had cooked up to keep him sane. All he knew for sure was that the ground under his feet was soft and someone was calling out to him from behind a beam of light. The smell of slurry was potent, the sky dark but clear – it seemed bigger than he remembered it, as if it had expanded in the days he'd been blindfolded.

As he ran, Collins' foot sent a shock of pain searing through to his bones – a stark reminder of the bolt Melvin had fired into his flesh. The bandage they'd provided to wrap his foot and the disinfectant they'd poured over the wound to stop it festering wasn't working; he could tell by the stench and the blackening skin that it was already infected. For a glorious moment, he wondered if this was all just some nightmare and the agony, the shock, the sheer terror, were all being played out in his imagination. But, if that were true, wouldn't he have woken by now, safe in his bed, his wife sleeping beside him? As the voice shouted at him to run faster, it didn't seem to Collins he'd be waking up anytime soon.

Melvin Powell wasn't one for dwelling on regrets, but what he'd done in the snug of the Lantern Arms less than an hour ago? That, he did regret. Not that the bloke wasn't asking for a slap in the mouth; he was and then some. It had begun innocently enough, some light-hearted banter then the man, who was old enough to know better, latched his attention on to Lydia with a crock of half-arsed compliments and a mouthful of filthy jokes he must have heard in one of the rougher pubs around Holyhead docks.

As the evening slipped into night, the man began downing whisky like water. At around what must have been his seventh or eighth double, a switch seemed to have flipped in his brain. When Lydia walked around the front of the bar, he grabbed her around the waist, pulling her in for a full-on lip kiss. Melvin knew Lydia could handle herself but had kept an eye on the situation just the same, twisting a damp beer towel around his fist as he watched. When the bloke pawed at Lydia's blouse buttons, asked her to show him her tits, then called her an old tart when she refused, Melvin's patience had finally snapped. He'd climbed over the bar grabbed the bloke by the shoulder, spun him round, looked him directly in the eyes so the man understood exactly what was coming his way, then ploughed his fist into his face.

The bloke didn't talk much after that.

Instead, he'd swayed for a second as if he were processing the hammer that had just pummelled his jawbone, fallen backwards and landed on a table of empty glasses which had shattered to the floor. Lydia had screamed at Melvin, shoved him out of the pub, shouted something at him he couldn't hear because by that time the blood in his ears was roaring like thunder.

That was an hour ago. He'd cooled down since then – the

joint had helped ease the dull thud of his pulse against his skull. He leant against the wall behind the pub. He was letting the pressure get to him – that wasn't smart, not when things were still in motion.

His sickness was harsh enough to contend with, but the situation with Logan Collins wasn't helping. The video had been Bobbie's idea, a good one too, better than having to kill the bastard. He couldn't deny punching that bloke's lights out earlier had made him feel more alive than he'd done in months, but it wasn't fair to Lydia. The pub was her livelihood, it would be all she had, and he had no right to lay into one of her customers like that. Lydia would have calmed the man down, put a lid on the situation without raising a hand. Regrets? Yeah, he had a few. He heard voices coming from the field near the coal shed. He stubbed out his joint and walked over.

The padlock was hanging off the latch, the door knocking lightly against the frame in the slight breeze. He peered inside; no sign of Collins. Looking over the field behind the pub, he noticed a light breaking through the darkness. He pushed open the gate and called out to his nephew – no reply. He called out again, this time louder. He heard a faint "Yeah?" in the distance.

"What the fucking hell are you up to?" he asked, marching towards Ronnie.

Ronnie held the crossbow low at his hip, directing the beam towards a dark figure wandering aimlessly in the distance. "He was complaining he was getting cramps. Wouldn't fucking shut up, so I told him, ten minutes, but you stay where I can see you."

"We discuss these things, Ronnie," Melvin said, poking him in the shoulder.

"Oh, yeah? Like Collins' fuckin' YouTube video? Don't remember much discussion 'bout that."

"That was different: someone had to fix your fuck-up."

Ronnie ran a sleeve under his nose. "Yeah, you and her come

up with that idea, did you? Bloody stupid, if you ask me. You're no better than her errand boy."

Melvin's blood thundered in his ears. It would have been easy to floor his nephew, but he'd already made one mistake tonight. He was about to direct Ronnie to shove Collins back in the shed when he heard the ground rustle behind him. He turned.

"What's all the noise about, Mel?" Lydia said, squinting in the intense beam of the lamping light.

As Logan Collins stumbled back across the field towards them, Lydia gasped. "Jesus, Mel, is that...?"

Mel debated lying, but there was really no use, not now. "So now you know," he said. "Ronnie, get him back in the shed."

Lydia took a few seconds to process. "What the hell have you done, Mel?" she said, her voice straining.

"Kept your nose clean and out of this, that's what," he said, stabbing his index finger in her face. "And I can still do that, if you keep quiet, forget you saw anything."

Lydia brought a hand over her mouth and watched, eyes saucer wide, as Ronnie shoved the crossbow into Collins' back and led him back to the shed. "I don't know. This isn't making any sense, Mel. This was all you? You and Ronnie?"

"Now you know, nobody's going to do something stupid like call the coppers."

"You've got him locked up in a bloody shed, for God's sake, Mel," Lydia said, turning back to walk towards the pub. "It's not right, none of this. I'm calling the coppers."

"You're not going anywhere," Melvin snapped, grabbing her wrist in a tight grip.

Lydia spun on her heels. "Oh, going to clock me one too, like you did that bloke?" She stepped close, her face inches from Mel's. "I knew you lot were up to something, but this? Takes the bloody biscuit. I don't want any part of it. I've got the pub to think about."

"Aye, and that's why you'll keep your mouth shut. If the brewery finds out, they'll throw you out on your arse, get someone else in to run the place."

"I can't, Mel, I just can't..." Lydia said, sensing the pull between what she knew was the right and the cold, barren truth of Melvin's words. A voice to her left startled her from her thoughts.

"I really recommend you revise your position, Lydia."

Lydia shook her wrist free and looked at the woman, who she was sure she recognised; a customer but not a regular. The woman slipped her kitbag from her shoulder, letting it drop on the grass.

"Do you understand what Mel just told you?" Bobbie Matthews said, walking towards Lydia. "What that implies?"

"Mel?" Lydia said, turning. "What the hell is going on?"

A swathe of light crossed the three of them as Ronnie returned from the shed. He stopped and shone the beam directly into Bobbie's face. "What the fuck's she doing here, Mel?"

Bobbie brought up a hand to shield her eyes. "Put down the light, Ronnie."

"Not even a please?" he said, waving the beam across her face, as if searching for something in her features that would give him some clue as to the hold he was sure this woman had over his uncle.

"I've had enough for one night, Mel. Who is she?" Lydia said. "Coming here, telling me how to behave on my own doorstep."

There was a momentary glance between Bobbie and Melvin, an understanding that now was as good a time as any.

Melvin took a breath. "Her name's Bobbie Matthews," he said, his voice low, almost a murmur swallowed by the night.

"And?" Lydia pressed – there was more to her than just a name; she could tell by now when Melvin was holding back on her.

"She's..." he looked to the ground, then pulled back his shoulders as if to give the words more emphasis.

"She's my daughter."

"Shit!" Ronnie said, shining the beam directly in Bobbie's face, this time looking for something more tangible, some familial similarity. "You told me you didn't have any kids."

Melvin pressed his hand on the crossbow lamp, directing the beam to the floor. "Well, shows how much you know. And before you say anything else, Bobbie needs a place to stay, I told her she could have the spare bedroom in the cottage."

"As if," Ronnie said, spitting. "That's my home. I get to say who stays there or not."

"You start paying rent, you can call it home. Until then, Bobbie stays in my cottage, no arguments."

"For how long?" Ronnie asked sulkily.

"As long as she bloody well needs," Melvin confirmed. "Now, let's go inside, I need a bloody drink."

66

Lydia dragged a chair to the head of the kitchen table and sat.

Bobbie and Ronnie positioned themselves either side of her with Melvin sitting five feet across the stretch of old pine. He seemed like a stranger to her now; a stranger with his feet under her table and a space in her bed. *Not for much bloody longer*, she thought as she lit up a joint, tapping her fingertips on the table.

"Right, who wants to start," she said, inhaling a dense plume of smoke.

Silence; save the shuffle of feet over a hardwood floor.

Lydia waited, looked each of them in the eyes. They all avoided her gaze, except for Bobbie, who met her eyes with an equally resolute stare of her own. It unnerved Lydia – it was the sort of look that seemed to penetrate through to someplace she wasn't prepared to have exposed.

"No one?" she said a few moments later. "Right, then I'll start. You kidnapped that politician, locked him up, and now got him to say all those things on camera. How's that for my starter for ten?"

"Correct," Bobbie confirmed.

"And you," Lydia said, pointing. "Are you Mel's daughter?"

"Also correct."

She took another drag. "So, any other kids you haven't told me about, Mel? A second family somewhere?"

"It's not like that," Melvin protested.

"Oh, what is it like? Spill the beans, eh."

Melvin opened his palms. "It was a lifetime ago, Lyd," he said, sitting back. "I knew Bobbie's mother, Maggie."

"Seems you did a lot more than bloody well know the woman."

"Maybe I can help," Bobbie said. She reached into her kitbag and took out a pile of letters wrapped in an elastic band. "These were my mother's," she said, setting the bundle on the table. "They're letters between her and Melvin. It took me a few months to figure it all out, but Melvin is my biological father."

Lydia turned the letters in her hand. "Tell. Me. Everything."

Bobbie relayed as best she remembered what her mother had told her and what she'd read in the letters. Melvin added his own punctuation of the odd head nod and low grunt as Bobbie spoke. After she finished, Lydia shoved the letters back across the table.

"Bloody closed book you are, Melvin Powell," she said, shaking her head. "But it's all water under the bridge, none of us were angels back in the day, but that bloke you've got locked up? You're letting him go, tonight. No argument."

"We can't do that," Bobbie said.

Lydia slapped her hand on the table. "You will bloody well do it, or I'm calling the police, no two ways about it. Understand?"

Bobbie leant forward. "I don't think you understand, Lydia. Our mission is incomplete, and don't forget you've implicated yourself just by talking with us."

Lydia looked at Melvin. "What does she mean? Tell me what she means."

Ronnie drummed his fingers on the table. "Don't be fucking stupid," he said, shaking his head. "She means you're just as fucked as the rest of us if the cops find us."

Lydia took a moment, leant close to Ronnie. "I wasn't asking the monkey," she said, blowing a thick plume of smoke in his face. "I was asking the monkey's uncle."

Melvin spoke through gritted teeth. "If the police come, they'll say you're part of all this, probably lose your licence. It's like you keep saying, this pub's all you've got."

"And," Bobbie said, leaning back, "you'd need us to back up your story that you were innocent in all this."

Ronnie exhaled a loud whistle. "Fucking hell! Cruel bitch, you are. No doubt you're a Powell through and through, yeah?"

"I didn't ask for this. None of it," Lydia said, running a hand through her hair.

"You've got Ronnie to thank for that," Melvin said. "My nephew, the criminal mastermind, left us no choice, did he?"

"Oh Christ!" Lydia said, her eyes wide, a hand shooting to her mouth. "That copper, the one that was stabbed? That was you?"

Ronnie couldn't resist a faint smile of pride. "She was asking for it. The bitch pepper sprayed me. She got what was coming."

"That does it," Lydia said, reaching for her mobile.

Bobbie placed her hand over Lydia's wrist. "Not the smartest strategy for you right now, Lydia, trust me."

"Oh yeah, what are you going to do, tie me up? Shove me in the coal shed along with that other bloke?"

"If necessary," Bobbie said, pressing her thumbs down hard on the veins on her wrist.

It wasn't the answer Lydia was expecting. "Mel?" she said, a creeping sense of desperation in her voice.

"Sorry, Lyd, she's right. We've come too far."

"Jesus," she snapped. "All this over the English buying holiday homes? You're no better than those bloody Muslim terrorists."

Bobbie exerted a heavy and sustained pressure on Lydia's carpal muscle. "This is different," she insisted. "Very different."

Lydia stared into Bobbie's eyes, hoping to find some kindness in there, an ounce of female bonding, but there was none, just a blank, cold emptiness. "What happened?" she asked. "What happened to make you like this? So... I don't know, cruel?"

"When you've lost everything that mattered to you, then you're qualified to ask me that question, not before," Bobbie said.

"Look, I don't know what happened, love, who made you like this, but I can't let you destroy my life, Mel's too. It's not right." She turned to Melvin. "Why? I just don't understand, why?"

"She needed a father's help," Melvin said, nodding in Bobbie's direction. "I wasn't around for her growing up."

"Help for what, for God's sake?"

"She's family. She needed my help, end of story." As he spoke, Melvin's chest tightened, a hard fist bunching around his lungs, squeezing the life from them. He gripped his fingers around the table and attempted to inhale, but all he could do was cough; cough as if his whole insides were rattling loose. He wiped a napkin across his mouth and coughed large globules of blood onto the white.

Lydia's face paled, the pieces falling like shrapnel, into place. "It's to do with all this, isn't it? Whatever it is that's wrong with you."

"Melvin has stage four small cell lung cancer," Bobbie said, flatly. "His condition is terminal."

"Oh God," Lydia said, her chest suddenly heavy and tight. "I knew it, I knew something was wrong. Why didn't you tell me? You should be in hospital, chemotherapy or something."

"No," Melvin said, finally wrestling his coughing under some control. "I do this my way, my rules."

For the past few minutes, Ronnie had remained silent, absorbing the information. Now he stood, pulled back his chair and walked towards the kitchen door. The three of them watched as he slammed shut the door.

"He didn't know, did he?" Lydia said.

"It's how Mel wanted it," Bobbie explained.

Lydia's anger rose to a sharp boil. "You should be ashamed of yourself. He should be resting, not messing around with whatever you've got him involved in. You just told me you were his daughter for Christ's sake. You're using a sick man for your own ends."

"Enough, Lyd," Mel snapped. "I'm my own man, nobody forced me into anything. I'm doing this for me, understand?"

"No, no, Mel, I don't understand, none of it." Lydia's eyes were moist, stinging from the effort it took to hold back the dam of tears.

"I'm a fighter, it's in my blood."

"But cancer, Mel, you can't punch your way out of that."

"I'm not going down without a fight."

"So, this is what this is all about? Well, let me tell you, Melvin Powell, you're fucking delusional. What's the plan? Go out in a blaze of glory like some kind of bloody hero?"

Melvin wiped a hand across his lips. "Better than the alternative. Everybody pitying me, looking at me like I'm already dead. Leave it alone now, what's done is done."

Every bone in Lydia's body wanted to reach over, shake Melvin, slap his face; wrap her arms around him like she'd never let go. She did none of this; she was wasting her breath, that was clear. She knew by now when to let a thing go. But there was still the matter of Collins; that she wouldn't let go so easily.

"That bloke you've got locked up, you're letting him go, tonight," she said, staring at Bobbie.

"I've already told you, that's non-negotiable."

"You bloody well will or I'll call the police myself."

"No. No you won't," Bobbie said, grabbing both of Lydia's wrists as if she were about to lead her in prayer. She embedded her thumbs deep into the veins. "In a few days, this will all be over. We'll move Collins, no one will ever know he was here. If you call the police, I can't guarantee you won't be implicated. If you still refuse to co-operate, you will force my hand, which will not end well for you. Do you understand what I'm telling you, Lydia?"

Lydia looked at Melvin, her eyes pleading; pleading for something he was unable, or unwilling, to grant her. It was the moment she knew it was over; Melvin, her protests; everything. She wasn't one to cry, hadn't cried for years, decades even, but the sheer hopelessness of her situation hit home, hard. She nodded, the spill of tears running down her cheeks, cutting rivers through her concealer and through to her foundation.

"No, Lydia," Bobbie said, pressing harder, looking harder into Lydia's eyes. "Tell me, in words, that you understand my instructions."

"I... understand," Lydia whispered. "I understand."

67

"'Stand by Your Man', 'Apartment 9', 'D.I.V.O.R.C.E', which is probably her most ironic song as she went through five husbands," Manx said, forking a chip from a shallow pool of malt vinegar.

"Impressive," Tammy said. "And Bobbie Gentry?"

Manx paused. "'Ode to Billy Joe', 'Mississippi Delta', and she recorded a blinding version of 'Gentle on My Mind'."

Tammy wiped her hands on a napkin, applauded and reached into her purse to hand Manx a fiver. "You named three songs by each of them. You win, inspector."

"Keep it," Manx said. "Buy me a pint next time."

"Next time?" Tammy said. "You're confident."

Manx forked another chip and smiled. They were sitting at Red Wharf Bay watching the retreating tide as twilight fell over the boats anchored like toys in the sand. Behind them, the Ship Inn was bustling with tourists clamouring for space at the outside tables, the bar four deep, the young waiters struggling to keep up with the orders. Manx stole a glance Tammy's way; she looked even more striking than the last time he'd seen her. Her jeans, skin-tight; the black leather boots, expensive; the beige cashmere hoodie which she'd zipped up to just under her neckline, hugging every curve from her hips to her chest.

"So, what do you do when you're not trying to con impressionable men out of their money?" Manx asked, fixing his attention back to why they were here in the first place.

"That's just my hobby," Tammy said, laying down her fish and chip dinner on the bench. "I'm a regional manager for a well-respected bank. Loans, financial products, fraud; all very exciting. Youngest regional manager and first ever woman to supervise the whole north west territory, by the way."

"My turn to be impressed."

"You should be," she said. "You're on a date with a very powerful woman. Some men get very intimidated. Are you intimidated, inspector?"

"By the fact you just said we're on a date, or that you're a powerful woman?"

Tammy smiled. "I'll have to be on my toes around you."

"Top of your game," Manx agreed, taking a swig of beer, then asking the question he'd been waiting to put to Tammy all evening. "Tell me about Bobbie."

"I knew you had an ulterior motive asking me out."

"Call it two for the price of one, in my advantage," Manx said.

"You already know the important stuff. Bobbie transferred back here last year after her husband, Dani, was killed. She wasn't the same after that. Not that she was ever the life of the party, but she really withdrew into herself. She had all these counselling sessions, they helped a bit, but I couldn't see her getting any better. Then there was the incident at the pub."

"What incident?"

Tammy explained how Bobbie had turned on the young RAF auggie and forced him to apologise. "Not that he didn't deserve it mind, but it was like she snapped or something."

"Does she have many friends?"

"She's always been a loner, private. Our mam, she drilled it into us, 'don't depend on a man, they'll only end up disappointing you.' Probably the best thing she ever did for us, but I think Bobbie took it too far, she was too bloody independent. That's why we were so surprised when she got married. It was like the two of them against the world: her and Dani." Tammy took a deep breath. "What happens when you find Bobbie?"

Manx took a swig of beer. "That all depends. The longer she puts off turning herself in, the worse it gets. Do you know where she is, Tammy? Any ideas at all?"

"I wish," Tammy said, shaking her head. "I wish I bloody well knew. I can't believe she'd do something like this, she's always been so dedicated to the bloody RAF, it's not like her. I just want this to be over, I want Bobbie to be safe, get the help she needs."

"We all do," Manx said. As he spoke, he recognised a familiar voice from the opposite side of the car park: Ashton Bevan calling after his wife, Sherry.

"Shit," he said, throwing the remainder of his cod and chips into the nearby bin. "Let's go."

"Go? Go where?"

Manx didn't answer, took her hand and pulled her from the bench.

"Okay, mister take bloody charge all of a sudden," she said as he guided her to a small hidden area to the side of the pub where the narrow footpath leading from the town of Pentraeth ended.

"Christ," Tammy said, settling her back against the wall and looking out to the car park. "What was that all about?"

He watched as Bevan and Sherry walked arm in arm along the seafront. "Someone I'd rather not bump into right now."

"Wife? Jealous ex-lover?" she asked, looking to the car park.

"Neither. Just the local town bloody crier."

"So, you're embarrassed to be seen with me?"

Manx turned, realised there were just a few inches of air between them: that and a thick crackle of electricity that he could almost run his fingers through. "Correct," he said, looking into her eyes. "I'm ashamed to be seen in public with an attractive woman."

Tammy tilted her head slightly. "Attractive?" she said, hooking her fingers around his jean pockets and pulling him closer.

"If that doesn't offend your whole independent woman thing."

"No. I'm not offended," she said, lifting her lips to meet his.

Manx ran his hands over Tammy's waist, her hoodie rising until his fingers caressed soft skin. She drew a hand around the back of his neck and pulled him closer, kissed him like she had no intention of stopping. For a few minutes it was all there was in the world: him, Tammy, the warm summer air on their skins.

After a few minutes, Tammy pulled back and flicked a strand of hair from her cheek. "You forgot one," she said and began to hum a tune. Manx immediately recognised it from the first three bars.

"Written by Bacharach and David," he said, kissing her neck. "UK number one for Bobbie Gentry, 1969."

"Bingo," Tammy said, smiling as she hummed the first few lines of "I'll Never Fall in Love Again."

"Am I meant to read something into that?" he asked, moving to kiss the nape of her neck.

"You're the copper, you tell me," Tammy said, pulling Manx's face closer.

68

That morning, it wasn't a corn-yellow sunrise nor the cormorants hungry cackle that woke Byron Gates. In fact, the sun was yet to break the back of the Irish Sea when he was woken by an urgent clanking noise; something heavy and metallic falling in a steady clank, clank rhythm against the glass. His eyes finally gaining focus, he looked through the windscreen to the sunrise casting an orange glow over Aberffraw beach, a half-mile long stretch of sand protected by a ridge of dunes sheltering the bay from the main road. The beach was rarely busy and, a few minutes after dawn was populated only by a group of hardy windsurfers floating like bait bobbins as they waited for the wind to fill their sails.

Byron barely had time to register the metal clanking at the glass was the tiller of a crossbow, before a blast of light filled the car with a cold, white glow followed by the urgent pull of the door handle and a simple command.

"Byron, exit the car. Now." The voice was chillingly familiar. That curt, military tone that left no space for misinterpretation or reading between the lines – Bobbie Matthews rarely used more words than were necessary.

He lifted his hand to his brow. "Why? What do you want?"

Byron could have sworn he heard Bobbie's impatient sigh from behind the glass. "Just exit the vehicle, Byron, like I requested."

The vessels in Byron's head thumped. These were the commands of a bully; a woman who used others to get what she wanted, wielding her own brand of justice. He folded his arms across his chest, shook his head and kept his gaze fixed through the dirt-ridden windscreen. He heard the muffled speech of two people debating next steps, followed by a tense, uneasy silence where Byron wondered if they'd maybe given up and left him the hell alone.

He should have known better.

Seconds later, the silence fractured as a crossbow bolt shattered the driver's side window and embedded itself with a sharp twang in the innards of the car's navigation screen.

Message received, Byron brushed the shards of glass from his lap, exited the car and waited, shivering in the cold dawn air, his feet clad only in his socks. Bobbie Matthews stood a few feet in front of him. To her right, the same man he'd seen that night at the brickworks slipped another bolt into the tiller.

"Now we understand each other, we need to talk," Bobbie said. Kneeling at the right wheel arch, she reached inside and extracted a metal object. "If you were wondering how I found you," she said, turning the object in her palm. "That day we first met, and I informed you I'd checked out your car to make sure you weren't being followed? That was a lie. Well, more of a half-truth. You were being followed, but not by who you thought."

Byron shivered, felt his throat coat with sand as Bobbie dropped the tracking device and slammed the heel of her boot down hard on the thin metal casing, crushing the internal circuitry.

"Why can't you leave me alone? I did what you asked."

"Correct," she said, leaning against the car's bonnet. "But you overstepped your mandate. What do they call it, overachieving?"

"I–" Byron began.

Bobbie moved closer, stepping the full weight of her boots onto the toes of his right foot. Byron exhaled a sharp groan as his metatarsal bones bent under the compression. "You visited my sister. I don't remember that being part of your mission, in fact, I'd say you went rogue on me, Byron. Snooping around my private life? What were you hoping to achieve? Leverage you could use to find me then what? Threaten me? Blackmail maybe?"

Byron clenched his teeth, felt the cold metal of the crossbow urging into the nape of his neck.

"I thought we had an understanding, but I see now I was wrong. Who knows who else you've spoken to, the police? Should I expect a knock on my door soon, Byron? Should I?" Bobbie pressed down harder on his foot.

"No, I... I wouldn't," Byron stammered.

Bobbie looked Byron up and down as if sizing him up for the correct dimensions for his coffin. "I can't trust what you tell me, and that's unfortunate." She stepped back, releasing the pressure. "People always disappoint you in the end, don't they? But no matter, for every cloud a silver lining, right? It just makes the decision to terminate you that much easier."

Byron's hands trembled. He had words, things he wanted to say, but sentences failed to form, thoughts resisted any attempt to render them coherent.

"I see you're upset, Byron, only to be expected, but I'm not completely without mercy." She stuffed her hands in her pockets. "Are you aware of what we call enemy combatants who escape a missile attack?"

Byron shrugged. "Lucky?" he said.

Bobbie smiled. "Good one, Byron, but no. They're called

squirters. These men, these terrorists, would hear the sonic boom from the missile launch some thirty thousand feet above them, or notice the red laser point reflecting off their truck window, and they'd realise they had twenty-seconds to get the hell out of the blast zone or get blown to a thousand body parts." She paused, allowing him to take in the information. "I'm going to extend you the same courtesy, but in your situation, let's make it forty seconds: you don't look like you're in much shape for sprinting."

She nodded to Melvin, who flipped on the spotlight and shone the beam directly into Byron's eyes.

"Forty seconds," she said, gesturing to the long ridge of dunes stretching like the spine of a sleeping dragon along the beach. "Who knows, we may never find you, and you get to live. Either way it's the best option you've got right now. A forty-second head start."

Byron looked at Bobbie hoping to find some trace of humanity in her eyes; there was none. She may as well have been wearing the same sunglasses she wore on the first day they met; her eyes seemed tinted with a similar darkness. His options, he figured, were as limited as they came, but maybe there was a chink in Bobbie's armour, a gap where some light could penetrate.

"You and me, we're the same."

"Really?" she said, with a slight cock of her head.

"We both want justice. It's all I've ever wanted. You, forcing the RAF to release the truth behind Operation Vanguard it's the same, can't you see that? We're on the same side, Bobbie, we want the same thing, it's just our methods are different, that's all."

Bobbie studied his face for a moment: a moment when Byron thought a glimmer of light might have snuck in. He was wrong; no light was strong enough to penetrate that darkness.

Bobbie was a black hole, a place where energy came to die and, alongside it, hope.

"I can see how you might think that. But the difference is you haven't lost everything that mattered to you. So, no, this is not an even playing field. I have nothing left to lose, you however, do."

"I know the truth," Byron lied. "What really happened that day. Let me go and I'll show it to you, all of it."

Bobbie stepped back. "I wish I could believe you, Byron." She checked her watch and began to count.

Her voice was like the boom of a starting pistol. Byron looked quickly around him, then ran. As he stumbled through the wet sand, heading towards the dunes, Bobbie Matthews' voice was thick and precise, counting down to Byron's fate.

"Thirty-nine. Thirty-eight. Thirty-seven..."

69

There was something about skirting so close to death that made every nerve in his body pulse with life. The irony wasn't lost on Byron Gates as he scrambled over the marram grass sprouting from the sand dunes. He could shelter there for a few minutes before the cruel shaft of the spotlight caught him, compelling him to run across the no man's land that led to the next sheltering point.

They were gaining fast, footsteps crushing the undergrowth beneath them, every splintering twig seeming to echo closer, then closer still. His breathing laboured, his lungs squeezed of air. Bobbie was right, he was in no condition to run, not for this long and this fast. His body, never a loyal friend, was failing him just when he needed it most; needed it to keep him in motion, keep him alive.

He scrambled up the dune on his hands and knees. Grains of sand burrowed like ants under his fingernails. With one final wrench on a stub of marram grass he made it to the peak, lay face-down across the sand and took a moment to regulate his breath, which seemed like swallowing razor blades as he took in the morning air.

The top of the dune gave him a good vantage point to scour the landscape. The light was changing fast, sunlight falling across the terrain in uneven shafts through the low foliage of cloud. The dull greens and browns of the terrain were awash in a glow of orange, making it harder to discern shapes, especially any human forms stalking over the undergrowth. For a moment, he imagined that maybe they'd given up on the chase, let him live.

It was the second error of judgement concerning Bobbie Matthews that Byron had made that morning.

He turned to face the open sea as the sun struck down on the ocean's broad shoulders in stark white rays. If he ran fast enough, dug deep into that reserve of fuel, he could make it to the ocean. He'd always been a strong swimmer, maybe he could swim along the coastline, drift far from the beach to some hidden cove. What was it that Bobbie had said? A head start? A chance to live?

He rolled down the dune, sand grains filling his eyes. At the beach level, the ground was damp but solid. He stood, rubbed the back of a hand across his eyes.

As he looked out to the ocean, contemplating the hundred-metre hinterland between him and the water, a thought occurred to him; he would have liked to have tried windsurfing. It seemed the kind of pastime that compelled you to go with the flow, surrender to the forces of nature. All his life it seemed he'd been doing the opposite, pushing back against forces more powerful than himself. All that resistance seemed futile now, a waste of a life. But if he could make it to the ocean, maybe he'd be rewarded with some kind of redemption, a second chance.

As he ran, his feet sinking into the sand, the sunrise burst through the clouds in a magnificent coat of orange. But that kind of beauty was not Byron's to enjoy. Not today.

His pain was sharper, more immediate than any perfect sunlit Anglesey morning, cutting through the splendour with the precision of a perfectly aimed crossbow bolt burying itself deep into his neck.

70

The ratcheting of the zip around Byron Gate's face was a fitting punctuation mark for the morning's events. His body had been discovered by the windsurfers after they'd noticed plumes of black smoke rising from behind one of the sand dunes. By 11am, Byron had been zippered into a body bag, hauled into the back of the coroner's van and driven to the morgue. Surrounding the burnt-out remains of his Toyota Prius, several CSI techs in body suits were gridding the scene and combing diligently through the evidence left behind in the ash and tangled metal.

Lead CSI Ashton Bevan walked towards Manx and presented him with a clear, plastic evidence bag. "Pretty cut and dry on cause of death," he said. The bag contained a single blood-stained crossbow bolt. "Did you know the victim?"

"Only by reputation."

"One of Anglesey's most wanted?"

"Someone obviously thought so," Manx said, looking over to the vast expanse of rolling ocean and glistening sand. Aberffraw never failed to leave a Miriam-sized hole in his gut. She'd disappeared close to the spot they'd found Byron Gates. His mind flashed back thirty years; a day as warm as this one, the tide retreating; a girl who was there, then suddenly she wasn't.

"Bad memories, Manx?" Bevan said, his eyes scanning the inspector as if looking for clues.

Manx said nothing.

Bevan pushed a little more. "This is where she disappeared, right? Your sister?"

Manx sensed the familiar pangs of irritation that appeared whenever Bevan was within striking distance. This was Bevan's go-to interrogation technique: throw some seemingly off-hand remark with the implication he knew much more than he was letting on in the hope Manx would fill in the blanks. Manx was too tired, running too low on patience to engage. He was about to walk away, talk to the techs busying around the carcass of the car when he noticed DCI Canton stumbling towards them over the uneven terrain, his forehead already glistening with sweat.

"Morning, Bevan," Canton said, wiping a handkerchief across his brow. "Busy enough summer for you lot?"

Bevan exacted a thin, forced smile. "I'd best be off," he said. "Idle hands and all that."

"Before you leave, any luck on that familial DNA we requested, what was it, three days ago now?" Manx asked.

Bevan pursed his lips. "I understand you're under an immense amount of pressure, Manx, what with that kidnapping and all these fires and still no results to speak of, but–"

"Simple question, Bevan. Do you have the results or not?" Manx interrupted, sensing his fists clench under their own will.

Canton noticed and put a hand on Manx's arm. "Easy," he said. "We're all on the same side here, isn't that right, Bevan?"

Bevan squinted, as if debating the veracity of Canton's remark. "Should have something for you tomorrow."

"Fair enough," Canton said. "Right, Manx?"

"Am or pm?" Manx pressed.

"If, and when, we get a match, you'll be the first to know," Bevan said, before turning and heading back to his van.

Canton guided Manx several metres away and spoke in a low whisper. "I just left the hospital half an hour back."

Manx's stomach flipped. He'd had enough bad news for one day.

"The consultants reckon she'll pull through, but it's going to be a long haul. Several months of rehab with no guarantee she'll return to duty at the end of it."

"Vera was lucky."

"I prefer to think someone's looking over the good ones," Canton said, with a soft smile.

Manx debated arguing with his DCI – there was sure as hell no one watching over Miriam the day she vanished – but let Canton's remark drift off on the morning breeze.

"Any thoughts on all this?" Canton asked, waving his arm across the beach as if he were trying to wipe it clean.

Manx had thoughts, plenty of them, but none that added up to anything solid. "We can rule out Byron Gates as the kidnapper."

"Which leaves us with no prime suspect."

"He was never top of my list."

"Tell me you do have someone you're looking into, Manx?" Canton said, with an edge of concern.

"Bobbie Matthews. This all leads back to Operation Vanguard and her husband's death."

"And the attack on Vera?"

"It's connected, but Bobbie Matthews can't be working alone. Friends, family; who the hell knows. She's somewhere here on the island; someone's providing her refuge."

"What about that familial DNA?"

"It's a long shot. Even if the database throws up a connection it could take weeks to comb through all the relatives."

"We don't have weeks, Manx. We've got a few days at best."

"Four," Manx confirmed.

"Then you're putting a lot of faith in Bevan turning up something with that DNA match. You hopeful he'll deliver?"

"If it's what you want to hear, Ellis, yes I'm hopeful we'll find a match. Feel better now?"

Canton shook his head. "Not remotely."

"No, me neither," Manx said, and trudged away past the smouldering wreckage of Byron Gates' car.

PART III

KILL SHOT

71

Police work, or "coppering" as Manx often called it, frequently threw up days like this. It wasn't like the movies or TV police dramas where the clues came in neatly, perfectly timed sequences. Real coppering was far more unpredictable and looser around the edges. Days like this, when the investigation hit a dead-end, when the evidence trickled in or stopped completely, when promising leads fizzled to nothing (though he noticed the hotline received plenty of calls proffering theories on the demise of the dead starlings), those were the days that tested your mettle not only as a police officer but also as a human being. The frustration and long hours were by now etched deep into the faces of the investigation team. Manx likened it to having all the pieces of a jigsaw puzzle but with no reference picture to help figure out where the pieces belonged.

Long days, punctuated by pub lunches scarfed quickly, errands run to pass the time in the hope distraction might trigger some new insight; it hadn't. Manx had taken several trips to Benllech beach just to walk the scene, had come back with nothing but a headache from the sun's reflection beating off the ocean.

He'd taken the opportunity to visit the chemist and drop off the film he'd found at his mother's house. The young girl behind the counter had looked at the roll as if it were a curious museum piece and told him to come back in two weeks. *Those were the days*, he thought as he headed back to the station.

The team continued to comb through the evidence in the Meibion Glyndŵr cases looking for connections and any glaring red flags. There were none; at least none that were obvious. They'd tracked down three of the original members still living on Anglesey and brought them in for questioning. They all had solid alibis for the nights of each of the holiday home fires and the evening Collins was taken hostage. The remainder were either deceased or had left the island decades ago.

Manx considered petitioning for a warrant to search RAF Valley, but that required permission from the MoD, which he was unlikely to secure. He'd even contemplated turning up at the base without an appointment, but imagined he'd be turned away at the checkpoint with nothing to show for it but a wasted couple of hours and a several gallons of petrol drained to fumes. His discussion with his DCI had been equally fruitless. Canton reminded him that "being an arrogant prick" wasn't sufficient evidence for a warrant. A fair point. Flynt has died off-base and Manx's team had interviewed, twice, all the personnel the commander had given them access to. Boyd was under no obligation to furnish them with any further information.

Manx had spent the last two evenings sitting on the patio of the Pilot Inn until it became too cold, then headed inside for a nightcap, followed by several more malt-coloured nightcaps back home, accompanied by his John Prine playlist; it was always John Prine when an investigation took this kind of downturn. Prine's lyrics had always cut to the quick, were more like mini movies than they were songs. Manx was hoping he might be blessed with a similar clarity, a flash of incisor-like insight. It hadn't happened.

The one bright spot was the call he'd received from Tammy. She'd wanted to talk about Bobbie. It was past closing time and Manx suspected she might have been a little tipsy. *Pot, kettle, black*, he'd thought as he put her on speakerphone and poured another drink of his own. Tammy hadn't given him much more information than he already knew, but the desecration of her husband's grave was news to him. She'd also regaled a story of her having to sneak Bobbie into the house on the evening of her seventeenth birthday, worse for wear after downing one too many rum and blacks. It was the only time she'd ever seen Bobbie drunk. "I liked Bobbie like that," she'd said. "She should have been drunk more often."

He figured Tammy had wanted to talk, and he was happy to let her do so.

"You're a good listener," Tammy had said, some hours later.

"For a copper?" Manx had replied.

"For a copper," she'd agreed, before hanging up.

As Manx walked into the incident room the following day, the smell of sweat, cheap cologne and desperation hit him fat in the face. Five additional constables had been recruited, along with several community support officers who were given administrative tasks and were expected to keep the core investigation team fed and watered. When he received a call from Ashton Bevan requesting a meeting at the Bull's Head, Manx would have typically told Bevan to get off his arse and drive over to the station, but after a morning trawling through the same evidence for what felt like the hundredth time, he was ready to blow off the cobwebs.

"You look like something my cat threw up," Bevan said, as Manx pulled up a stool next to him at the bar.

"You're a born charmer. Did you get a match on my DNA?"

Bevan took a sharp sip of his lager shandy. "Can't rush these things. I'm not about to put my reputation on the line for you, no matter how desperate your investigation."

Manx ordered a pint of the local cask ale. "If this is another quid pro bloody quo tactic, I should warn you I'm running on three hours sleep, a headache that could down a horse and an itch to punch a hole in the nearest wall. Just so you know."

"Got it," Bevan said. "I'll cut to the chase. The DNA from the blood found on the slip at Menai Bridge threw up an interesting match." He took a piece of paper from his jacket pocket and laid out the DNA analysis. "A familial match to someone already in the database, very probably a close relative."

"And?" Manx asked, taking a gulp of beer.

"One Dafydd Merion Powell. Sentenced to four years for arson on a holiday home near Trearddur Bay back in the early eighties."

Manx took the paper in his hand. "Bit early in the decade to be collecting DNA samples, wasn't it?"

Bevan smiled, pulled, like a magician from a hat, a plastic evidence bag, inside a black leather glove. "Thanks to some stellar work from my team, we located a splinter of fingernail in the right index finger cavity. Normally, the hard cuticle contains little useable DNA, but today must be your lucky day, Manx."

"I'll head off to the bookies, then, wager a tenner on a hundred-to-one outsider while you get to the bloody point."

Bevan pursed his lips and continued. "There was still some soft tissue attached to the nail, along with a several spots of dry blood on the inside of the glove. Best guess, he tore off his fingernail on a wall or barbed wire, put on his gloves to protect the finger then dumped them soon afterwards, the nail still inside. When we ran the DNA through the database, it threw up a match. This Dafydd Powell character was involved in an altercation–"

"Altercation?" Manx interrupted, taking a long sip. "What's that a euphemism for these days?"

"Aggravated assault. He sent some unlucky bugger to the A&E with a ruptured eardrum and a serious mandibular fracture; broken jawbone to you, Manx."

Manx let the insult roll off his back, this time. Bevan had delivered him the first glimmer of light in a case that had had him stumbling around in the darkness for days.

"The victim refused to press charges, no doubt scared he'd come back to finish the job, but Powell was required to provide a DNA sample, hence the match."

"So, the DNA from the slip is a relative of Dafydd Powell?"

"Yes, but don't go hanging out the bunting just yet. This is familial DNA. I did some cursory research and it seems the Powell family bred like Catholics."

"Bred like Catholics? Christ, don't go surrendering your seat at the peace talks just yet, eh?"

Bevan ignored the barb and continued. "It would take some time to trim down the whole family tree, time I suspect you don't have."

Manx quickly downed the remainder of his pint. "Then we go directly to the source," he said, picking up the bag and resting his empty glass on the bar.

Bevan laughed. "You think a convicted criminal is about to surrender one of his own family to the police force who got him four years jail time? Good luck with that."

"All I need is a little luck, Bevan. The rest I can handle."

72

Ronnie Powell had perfected the art of sulking; could have won a gold medal for it if it were an Olympic sport. He'd spent the day riding his quad bike across the fields, determined to put as much space as possible between himself and Bobbie who'd moved into the spare room in Melvin's cottage: his cottage. He couldn't bring himself to call her Mel's daughter – he would have choked on the words. But it was nothing compared to the anger he felt at Mel's betrayal. *Cancer? Terminal?* He couldn't shake the weight of those words. They were terrifying. There was only one other word that followed those, and that was *death*.

Cancer. Terminal. Death.

He came to a sharp stop at the peak of a hill and cut the engine. Why hadn't Mel told him himself? Why confide in her and not him? He lit a joint and looked over the fields. It reminded him of the days he and Mel would greet the dawn together after a night's lamping. Two men against nature, relying on some primal instinct that was strong in them both; a bonding as powerful as father and son; stronger because Mel had chosen him, chosen to raise Ronnie as his own. All that was good as gone now, what with Bobbie on the scene and Mel's diagnosis. He still couldn't comprehend it. His uncle was a bull; stronger than anyone he knew, could down any man he wanted with a single punch. How could energy and power be snuffed out so easily, laid to rest? But he'd witnessed the very same last night, Mel's strength flooding out of him as he coughed blood into his handkerchief.

He wiped the sleeve of his camouflage jacket across his eyes, looked down at the damp spots on the fabric. Tears? The last time he cried was that afternoon when Mel rescued him from the beating Dafydd Powell was inflicting on his son. Ronnie had made a promise to himself that night, one that he'd kept ever since. He wouldn't give anyone the satisfaction of making him cry; not ever again. His father would have been proud, he thought; proud that his fists had done their intended work.

As he felt the tears sting the back of his eyes, he let them drip like raindrops onto his jacket. If his father could see him now, he'd laugh at him, give him the beating he deserved. But maybe he could do that himself, take away the pain.

He clenched his fists, raised his arms, began pummelling his forehead until his head swam and ghostly orbs floated in front of his eyes.

The pain felt good, though, felt it was what he deserved. An old familiar friend come back to visit.

73

Dafydd Powell was a rough sort, hewn like a tree trunk, his face wizened like old bark. His face bore the scars of blows that had found their target once too often. At ten that morning, he either reeked of the scotch from the night before, or the chaser he'd had with this morning's coffee, Manx couldn't decide.

"I'm innocent," Dafydd said, slotting a cartridge into his Beretta S686 twelve-gauge. The gun had seen better days; the wooden barrel chipped, the chrome receiver scratched. He raised the sight, aiming at a paint can at the bottom of the garden. He drew back the trigger. The can ricocheted off the wall with a dull metallic thud.

"I haven't accused you of anything," Manx countered.

"Not yet you haven't." Dafydd dropped the gun to his waist and unlocked the barrel. "Been a pillar of the community since I moved out here," he said, gesturing to the miles of wilderness stretching out from his back garden to the foot of the Snowdonia mountain range. "Don't get into any trouble."

"Don't expect there's much trouble to get into," Manx said, scanning the rolling green fields and craggy outcrops of slate, which even in the heat of a summer afternoon held on to a cold and inhospitable chill.

"Why the house call?" Dafydd asked. "The shotgun's legit. You can ask the missus." Dafydd had a defensive way of talking, as if he were trying to pre-empt any questions about to be hurled his way.

Manx decided on the direct approach. "Meibion Glyndŵr," he said, allowing the words to hang a few seconds.

Dafydd settled the shotgun on the table next to him. "Another bloody lifetime."

"Was it?"

"I served my time, no more to be said."

"No stirrings of the old patriotism, Dafydd? One last fight for the great cause? What did they call it at the time? Wales Rising?"

Dafydd stabbed his finger at Manx. "Oh, I get," he said, nodding. "The answer's no fucking way. I haven't been back to the island for years. You're wasting your time, mate."

Manx took the plastic evidence bag from his pocket. "Recognise this?"

"A glove? Christ, you lot must be desperate."

"Your glove," Manx said, laying the bag on the table.

"Never seen it before."

"It's evidence from that holiday home fire you were convicted of in Trearddur Bay."

"Like I said, mate, I'm a reformed character."

"No doubt, except for that aggravated assault charge two years ago. Where was it again? Caernarvon?"

"The bloke made it all up, dropped the charges."

"But you provided a DNA sample."

"Had no choice, did I?" Dafydd said, his fists bunching. "Look, are you getting to the bloody point anytime soon?"

"All right, Dafydd, let's do that," Manx said, poking the evidence bag. "Your DNA, which we obtained from the soft nail tissue inside this glove was a match to the sample you provided at the Caernarvon police station."

"So what? Can't be convicted of a crime twice now, can I?"

"But here's the thing, Dafydd. We found further DNA evidence at a more recent crime scene on Anglesey."

"Well, that won't be mine. Unless you lot planted it."

"It belongs to a relative of yours. A very good match according to forensics. I need to know who that relative is, Dafydd. Problem is, you've got a big family. It's going to take us a while to interview the whole clan, time we don't have."

"Oh, takes the biscuit, that does. You, coming up here asking me to snitch on my own family."

"Expedient, that's all. Cards on the table, anybody spring to mind?"

Dafydd stroked his chin in a mock-thoughtful manner. "My old gran," he said. "Bit of a hell-raiser in her time, she was. Ninety-three now, mind you. Lives over in the old people's home in Menai Bridge. Got her number inside if you want it."

Manx reached down and picked up Dafydd's shotgun. "Nice piece, looks vintage."

"She's a few years old, aye."

"So, how long was it you served at her majesty's pleasure?"

"Four years. They let me out after three for good behaviour. But you already know that."

"Can't get much past you, Dafydd," Manx said, turning the shotgun in his palm. "Now here's another question. How did you obtain the licence for this?"

"Applied for it, like anyone else," he said, tugging at the front of his T-shirt.

"That right?" Manx said, laying the shotgun back on the table. "As far as I recall, and I might be wrong as I'm a little rusty on the details, but Section 21 of the 1968 Firearms Act prohibits anyone from owning a firearm if they served a sentence longer than three years. Are you aware of that?"

Dafydd jerked his shoulders back.

"Wouldn't take more than a phone call," Manx said. "Have an officer come over, confirm you obtained that licence under false pretences; if you even have a licence. That's another jail sentence, maybe a big fine to go with it. So, what do you say, Dafydd? One name and I'll be out of your hair."

"You coppers are all the same," he said, slamming two shotgun casings on the table. "Fucking bastards, the lot of you."

"I've been called worse, and from people a lot scarier than you. Now, give me a name, Dafydd, one name and you can keep shooting tin cans off a wall until the cows come home."

Dafydd bit his lower lip, raised his finger to his left eye which Manx had just noticed didn't move in its socket, as if it were stuck in a single focal plane. "Twenty per cent vision," he said, gritting his teeth. "Doctor reckons I'll be blind in five years."

"What's that got–?" Manx began, before Dafydd interrupted.

"Fuckin' family," Dafydd said. "Tough love they call it, yeah?"

"Who, Dafydd?" Manx said, sensing he had Dafydd on the back foot, and was about to leave himself wide open.

"My brother," he said, spitting on the floor.

"You had a falling out?"

"You're a sharp one."

"Name?"

Dafydd clenched his fists. "Melvin. Melvin Powell."

"Address?" Manx asked.

"No idea. Haven't spoken to him for over twenty years."

"It's a start," Manx said, turning to leave.

"Oy!" Dafydd called out as Manx walked towards his car. "If you find him–" he began.

"He doesn't need to know it was you," Manx said.

"I don't give a fuck, tell him if you want. I've waited long enough to get payback for what he did."

"Then what?"

"If he's got a lad there with him – he'd be in his twenties by now – go easy on him, eh?" Dafydd slipped two fresh cartridges into the barrel. "Melvin likes to be top dog, has to be in control. God knows what the hell he's turned that boy into by now."

Dafydd turned away, brought the shotgun to his good eye and fired at some phantom target deep in the countryside. The shot ricocheted like the resonant toll of a bell echoing off the thick slate mountains.

74

Ronnie watched Bobbie from the old, battered armchair in the corner of the kitchen. He hadn't spoken to her yet, at least not properly, other than a grunt or mumble when he passed her in the hallway or waited for her to get the hell out of the bathroom so he could take a shit.

For the past hour she'd been assembling a quadcopter drone, the sort Ronnie had seen on YouTube. As she slipped the propellers from their protective cover and laid them carefully on the table Bobbie spoke. "Are you going to sit there watching?" she asked, directing her focus to attaching the propellers to the four motors positioned at each corner of the rig. "Or are you going to help?"

Ronnie shrugged. "Suppose I could," he said, looking around as if he expected someone to chide him for offering. He put down the strip of wood he'd been whittling and joined her.

"Hold on to the main body while I attach the pushers."

Ronnie did as he was asked while Bobbie reached for the smaller propellers and secured them at opposite corners of the drone.

"DJI Inspire Quadcopter," she said, noticing Ronnie's interest in the packaging.

"Yeah, I can read," Ronnie mumbled.

"Commercial grade," Bobbie continued. "Twenty-seven-minute flying time, dual-frequency signalling, maximum speed fifty-eight miles per hour, four rotors, auxiliary battery pack and capable of carrying several pounds of extra weight."

"That meant to impress me or something?" Ronnie said. "Just a big bloody toy, isn't it? Uncle Mel won't be happy you're wasting time playing around."

Bobbie leant over and tightened the final screws on the landing gear. "You're close with Mel, right?" she asked.

Ronnie sniffed, ran the back of his hand under his nose. "Brought me up like I was his own."

"Must have been nice," Bobbie said, double-checking all the components were secure. "Was he a good dad?"

"Better than my own, but he was a right fucking bastard, so I don't have much to compare, really."

Bobbie nodded, grabbed the drone around its belly and lifted it so the sunlight streaming in from the window reflected off the silver casing. "Ever flown one of these, Ronnie?"

"Nah. Seen them on the internet, like."

"Come with me," she said, heading towards the front door. "Let's get you in the pilot's seat."

It took Ronnie around twenty minutes to get the hang of keeping the drone airborne and landing without crashing. Bobbie had taught him the basics; how to focus on the navigation screen streaming the live video while at the same time directing the drone's flight path and pitch with the buttons and small joystick on the slave controller.

"Just like a video game, this is," he said, unable to resist a smile as he manoeuvred the quadcopter several hundred feet skywards, then swooped it down low over the outbuildings and the old stable.

"The military ones aren't so different," she said, looking up.

"Yeah? You flown them, like?"

"I was an unmanned aircraft pilot," she said. "Flight Lieutenant in the RAF."

"Why did you leave, then? Cool job like that."

"Long story."

Ronnie looked down at a red flashing alert on the screen. "What's it doing?"

She looked over. "The battery's about to run out."

"Should I land it?"

"No need," Bobbie confirmed. "It senses when it's low on power and returns to its base location before it runs out. Take your fingers off the buttons and watch."

Ronnie watched nervously as the quadcopter descended, carving a slow, graceful path back to him before landing itself softly at his feet, the propellers coming to a gradual stop.

"Brilliant, that is," he said, squatting as if he were about to pet the drone like a good dog for returning to its master.

"Few more hours flying time and you'll be fully prepared."

"Prepared? Prepared for what?"

Bobbie picked up the drone and flipped it belly side up. "The insurgents we attacked with our Reaper drones," she said, removing the ancillary battery pack from its housing. "They eventually took to giving us a dose of our own medicine. All they needed was a drone, a strong phone signal and a forty-millimetre grenade stuffed into a small plastic bottle. They'd fly them as close to the target as they could, usually an allied convoy or small military base, and drop the grenades from as low as they dared to fly. The damage was never that significant, but that wasn't the point. Their goal was to spread fear, keep their enemy guessing. When you think about it, that's the true definition of terror, isn't it, Ronnie? You never allow your enemy to relax, not for a second."

"Couldn't you just shoot them down?"

"Good question," she said, screwing the cover back on the battery housing. "They could, but there was always the possibility of civilians being caught in the explosion. Eventually, we developed drone hunters; guns that fired out nets to drag the drones someplace safe before destroying them."

"Make's sense, I suppose," Ronnie said, shrugging. He fidgeted with the controller, flicking the thin joystick with his thumb. "So, why are you telling me all this?"

"It's obvious Mel is in no condition to partake in a plan requiring this level of focus." She looked Ronnie directly in the eyes. "But you, Ronnie, you're a natural. All those video games you've been playing? You can finally put those skills to good use."

"Is this to do with Logan Collins?" he asked.

"A large, unambiguous statement is required. The RAF has chosen to hide certain truths. They need encouragement to release that truth into the light. Do you understand?"

"Aye, maybe," he said.

Bobbie placed a hand on Ronnie's shoulder. "I know this has all been a shock to you; me, Mel's cancer, it's a lot to take in. But you can do this. You might not like me much, Ronnie, and we can work on that, but that doesn't mean we can't work together to make your uncle proud. I hate to say this, but it might be the last chance you get to make that happen."

Ronnie thought for a moment, took in everything Bobbie was telling him. Maybe Bobbie was right, this was the way to make Mel proud, pay him back for all he'd done for him.

Bobbie smiled. "I'm leaving this in your charge now, Ronnie," she said, handing him the drone. "Keep it somewhere safe, not here. When I'm done, I'll give you the package it's going to be carrying. Are you ready for this, Ronnie? Can I count on you?"

Ronnie looked down at the quadcopter and nodded.

"No, Ronnie," Bobbie said. "Tell me in words that you are ready and willing to carry out your mission."

Ronnie looked up. "Ready?" he said. "I was born fucking ready."

75

Manx attached the Google earth photograph to the incident board. "Tŷ Gwyn, cottage in Church Bay, home address of Melvin Powell. One of three Melvin Powells on the island, the only one related to Dafydd Powell."

DS Nader huffed and threw his copy of Melvin's briefing document on the desk. "No priors, no link to Meibion Glyndŵr. You sure he's our man?"

"Maybe he was never caught," PC Morris said. "Got lucky."

"Lucky or not, here's what we do know," Manx said. "Dafydd Powell was an active member of Meibion Glyndŵr from '81 to '87. He served a four-year sentence in Wrexham prison for burning down a home in Trearddur Bay in 1987. On his release, he moved a few miles outside Llanberis, where, he assured me, he's lived the life of a hermit ever since."

"So he says, yeah?" Nader snarled.

"Powell senior is not our man," Manx said pinning a photograph of Melvin on the board; a low-resolution portrait taken several years back for the "About Us" page on Mel's Paint and Plaster website. "Our person of interest is his younger brother, Melvin Powell. According to the reports, back when people actually read newspapers, Melvin was your regular teenage troubled child until he found his salvation in boxing."

Manx pinned up another photograph; an old black and white print of Melvin, gloved fists raised high, scowling at the camera, eyebrows raised, one side of his mouth curled into a menacing snarl, and the headline "The Great Welsh Hope" running across the lower third of the frame.

"Unfortunately for Melvin, that career path ended at the age of twenty-two when his motorbike lost an argument with a tractor reversing into the main road. A year later, he set up Mel's Paint and Plaster, which he's been running ever since. Now, let's play out this Powell family drama for a minute. Melvin's twenty-two years old, all his dreams just crashed and burned into the rear end of a Massey Ferguson. He's angry, pissed off. Boxers at Melvin's level don't just lose that fighting instinct. He needs to find another outlet for that energy and I'm betting house painting's not going to cut it."

"He joined Meibion Glyndŵr!" Morris said.

"It's highly probable Dafydd Powell recruited his younger brother. Melvin's young, idealistic, and more importantly he wants to prove that he's still got it, that he's still the 'Great Welsh Hope'. As Morris pointed out, it was probably dumb luck that he was never caught, but he'd have learned the best way to start a fire and how to leg it out of there without being caught."

Manx continued. "Take a close look at the house," Manx said, pointing at the aerial photograph. "Two miles off the nearest main road, hidden behind a copse of oak trees, several outbuildings–"

"That's where they're holding Collins!" Morris interrupted.

"Bloody hell!" Priddle said. "We've found him."

"Don't go planning the celebration beers just yet. It's a good lead, but as of now it's still unconfirmed."

"So, what's the plan?" Nader asked.

"We probably have three people hiding out in that house. Melvin Powell, Bobbie Matthews and an unidentified male, the one captured on the CCTV from the slip at Menai Bridge. We'll enter the property three hours from now. No sirens, no flashing lights, no helicopters. We don't extend them the courtesy of an early warning. The authorised firearms officers will do the door breaking and general scaring the holy crap out of the occupants; we'll follow behind and make the arrests. We'll position several officers around the perimeter of the property, including the back door, side entrance and outbuildings. The only way anyone's getting out of that house is in the back of one of our armed response vehicles."

As Manx gave the team the remainder of the itinerary, the incident room door swung open. "Someone to see you, boss," the desk sergeant said, standing in the doorway.

Manx looked up. "Is it important?"

"Bloke reckons so. Works over at the RAF base."

76

Andrew Pierce slid the folder across the interview room desk. "What Bobbie Matthews is demanding," he said, sitting back.

Manx slipped out the paperwork and read the headline: Operation Vanguard, Top Secret. "How did you get this?"

"It's not important. What is important is that Bobbie sees this and that you don't tell anyone how you got your hands on it. Not ever."

"How long have you been holding on to vital evidence, Mr Pierce?"

He shrugged. "I didn't know what to do. If I took this to the press, then I may as well paint a big target on my back. I thought this was the safest option."

"You're risking a lot for a patient."

"Bobbie's more than a patient," Pierce said, blushing slightly. "She's a friend, a good friend, and she deserves to know the truth."

"And the truth sets us free?" Manx said.

Pierce leant back, steepled his hands. "Let us not love with words or speech but with actions and in truth."

Manx failed in his attempt to resist a heavy sigh. "Are you sure you don't know where Bobbie Matthews is hiding? You two seem close and you obviously risked a lot to obtain this classified information."

"If knew, I'd tell you. Don't you think I'd have taken this straight to her so she could stop all this. I only ever wanted to help her. I'm not stupid, I know what can happen, she'll spend most of her life locked away for what she's done. But she deserves to know the truth."

Manx thought. The man seemed genuine enough, his reasoning plausible, but still there was something about him, something that Manx couldn't put his finger on.

"She's your patient. How likely is she to go through with her threat to kill Collins?"

Pierce thought for a moment. "Honestly, it makes no sense. Her trauma is directly related to the death of her husband and her obsession with getting to the truth of Operation Vanguard, which, when you read the report, you'll see she was right to pursue. It's the RAF she's angry with, not some local politician."

"So why threaten him?"

"Her judgement maybe clouded. Trauma can severely damage the mind, rational thinking takes a back seat."

"Isn't it your job to treat that kind of thing?"

Pierce flinched. "These things take time. James Flynt was impatient to have her shipped off to one of our veteran's hospitals. She should have stayed with me; I could have helped her. Read the report," Pierce said, standing. "But you'll never be able to tell anyone what you've read. It's a burden you'll have to live with."

"Any other words of wisdom? More evidence you haven't told me about?"

Pierce thought for a moment. Manx guessed he was debating whether to keep talking or not.

"One thing," Pierce said. "It's probably nothing, but I noticed something was missing from my office."

"What thing?"

"My clerical garments. I always hang them behind my door. I think maybe Bobbie saw me enter the keypad code and remembered the number. I should have changed it, but I didn't imagine–"

"Seems like a strange thing to take. Did she have a religious conversion or something? A come-to-Jesus moment?"

Pierce shrugged. "We can but hope. Anyway, I thought you should know."

Manx looked at the folder in his hand. "No plans to leave the island any time soon?"

Pierce shook his head.

"Keep it that way," Manx said.

"And the report?"

Manx felt its weight in his palm. "Leave it with me," he said.

After Pierce left, Manx took his time. He read the report three times to make sure all the details had sunk in. Pierce was right; he couldn't show this to anyone. The consequences would be too great; way above Manx's pay grade.

In a way, he wished he hadn't read it. If they did find Bobbie before the deadline, could he even hand it over? And if he did, what would be the repercussions for him? For Pierce? If Bobbie didn't read it before the deadline, the consequences could be equally dire.

Devil. Deep blue sea, he thought. *Manx caught somewhere in between.*

77

Bobbie, by now, had learnt to trust her instincts. They'd been honed over the years, sharpened and battle-ready, like a constant surge of electricity to be accessed at will.

As she stepped from the cottage for some air, a similar sensation she'd felt the day she'd entered the ground control station for the last time overcame her. She should have trusted her instincts that day. Tonight, she wouldn't make the same mistake.

She looked to the sky. The moon, a half-opened eyelid, seemed to be watching her. Speckled around the moon, the clusters of stars were like peepholes where more eyes were watching. Somewhere in the highest branches of the oak trees, the hollow call of an owl. Behind her the restless rustle of a fox or badger burrowing through the nearby hedges. A light wind scattered a litter of leaves along the driveway, then settled again as if it were just in rehearsals for its main performance at some later date.

There was something else out there too. This wasn't the nocturnal clock awakening the night's predators, it was man-made not nature born. There were eyes all over her, she could sense them.

Three hundred metres to her right, something caught her attention. Not a sound, more of a glint, like the soft glow from a mobile phone screen high in the trees. Or maybe it wasn't in the trees at all. She traced her eyeline across the canopy of branches. As the light extinguished, she concluded it came from the top of one of the poles carrying electricity into the cottage. Whatever the source of the light was, it was nothing natural that was for sure. And every instinct told her it was coming for her.

78

"We're leaving," Bobbie said, running back into the cottage, gathering up her all her clothes, and throwing them into her kitbag.

"Leaving? Where to?" Melvin asked, groggily. He'd been dozing for the past hour, his reactions slurred and blunted by fitful sleep and alcohol. They'd all decided that Mel's cottage was the safest place for the next few days, and besides, Lydia had thrown Melvin out on his ear the night he'd confessed. Bobbie had made a point of visiting Lydia the following day. It was just a precaution; a reminder of the consequences of blabbing her mouth to anyone, especially the police.

"Someone's out there," Bobbie said, slipping her arms through her jacket sleeves. She reached into the pockets, took out her black beanie hat, pulling it tight over her head. "We need to move, now."

"Paranoid, you are," Ronnie said, turning his attention away from the TV; another one of those reality shows that was pretty far removed from any reality Ronnie had ever encountered. "We're in the middle of nowhere, there's always something out there this time of night. It's nature, yeah?"

"No, you don't understand," Bobbie said, throwing Ronnie the hoodie he'd left dangling on the kitchen chair. "We're leaving now. Someone's out there."

"What do you mean, someone?" Melvin asked, looking through the window into the thick darkness. "Looks clear to me."

"Trust me," Bobbie urged. "I saw a light, something."

"Probably lampers," Ronnie said, increasing the volume on the television as the presenter revealed the unlucky contestant leaving tonight's show. "Bastards hunting on our patch."

"Too early for lampers," Melvin said, an edge of concern in his voice. "Not much to kill this time of–"

Melvin's sentence remained unfinished.

It was punctuated by the clatter of fifteen kilograms of steel pummelled against wood. Mel span around. The front door buckled as the steel enforcer made easy work of the frame. That was followed by a loud voice instructing them to fall to the floor, hands on heads, eyes closed, any weapons dropped and shoved towards the door.

Before they could comply, the house was plunged into darkness.

Bobbie and Ronnie fell to the floor and crawled towards the back door. Melvin's reactions were running slower. He put it down to the five cans of beer he'd drunk earlier, and maybe the cancer. Yeah, he'd blame whatever happened next on the cancer.

79

Ronnie followed Bobbie's lead, scuttling along the floor. A bright strobe of light pouring from a torch skimmed the kitchen window like a searchlight.

"Is there another way out?" Bobbie asked.

Outside, the commotion was building. The anxious barks of dogs, the scent of prey heavy in their nostrils.

"Yeah," he said. "Up the back stairs. The window opens to the old stable roof. We run across, jump down on the other side."

"You're sure?"

"Did it all the time when I was younger. Piece of piss."

Bobbie weighed up her limited options then agreed.

They rose from the floor, crouched low, like panthers, and ran. Ronnie stopped at the foot of the stairs. "Mel? Where's Uncle Mel?"

"I thought he was behind you."

"We can't leave him."

Bobbie debated. Going back was a suicide mission. She knew it, Ronnie knew it. Not that it made the decision any easier.

"Mel will be fine," she said.

"But–"

"Ronnie!" Bobbie snapped. "Mel can look after himself, he's probably found another way out. Now, come on, let's go."

Ronnie hesitated, debated with himself. *Yeah, Mel had probably got out already*. He'd see him when this was all over. He was a hundred per cent sure of it. Maybe ninety per cent. Maybe a little less.

80

Melvin Powell had never considered himself the sacrificial type. He was barely religious: what with having his dreams crushed at the age of twenty-two, then forty years later having his life cut short by cancer, and with nothing to show for the years in between, it tended to blunt belief in any kind of god.

All Mel had really understood was fighting. In the ring there was no grey area. You fought to win, and to win you had to surrender to your instincts. In a fight, he'd have a spilt-second to predict the punch his opponent was about to unleash, where it would land and how to defend against it. He'd been good at that. On his best days, he could almost see his opponent's glove move in slow motion, catch the tell in his eyes that signalled Melvin to expect an uppercut, right hook or body blow before his opponent had decided himself.

Tonight, that kind of primal instinct was beyond him.

He heard the ominous rolling of a CS tear gas grenade scraping across the floor, then exploding in a plume of grey, foul-smelling smoke. He drew his arm across his eyes as the gas escaped, seeping under his eyelids. Seconds later, the specialised firearms officers team rushed in, bodies crouched, helmet visors pulled low.

"On the ground! Now!" The voice was loud, but somehow lost in the distance, as if it were calling Melvin from beyond the sea. His ears were ringing, noise swirling and roaring. He looked for Ronnie and Bobbie through the dense smoke. Nothing. Maybe they'd made it out. He hoped they'd made it out.

As one of the men moved closer, Mel lashed out with his fists. But the strength wasn't there, never would be again. His fist landed somewhere in the officer's upper arm, barely making an impact through the Nomex suit.

Melvin felt a strong grip on his shoulder, pushing him to his knees. He coughed, the gas stinging his eyes and seeking a way into his lungs, coiling around them like a snake.

By the time the smoke finally cleared, he had been dragged by his collar from the cottage and into the brittle night air. Around him a sea of blue lights twitched nervously. The man holding him hauled Melvin to standing, shoving him towards one of the police vehicles.

"This your man?" the AFO asked, slipping off his visor.

DI Manx took his time to study Melvin Powell. "It's him," he said, stepping forward. "Logan Collins. Take us to Logan Collins."

Mel looked up at the tall, lean copper demanding something from him he was not ready to surrender, at least not without a fight.

"Don't know what the fuck you're talking about, mate," he said. "And before you ask me anything else, I want a bloody solicitor."

81

The police dogs stalked the perimeter of the cottage, stopped in their tracks, raised their heads and barked furiously at the stable roof.

"Shit!" Bobbie muttered, looking down at the swarm of blue and white lights and the sheen of anxious fur stalking below.

Ronnie inched his way towards the far gable.

"No, Ronnie!" Bobbie grabbed his belt.

He reached into his pocket, pulled out a set of keys. "I'll distract them, you jump down, meet me at the gate by the far field."

Before Bobbie could protest, Ronnie had flipped himself over the guttering and was gone. A cacophony of raised voices followed by nervy spotlights scanning the cottage walls and yard. Then, the sputter of a four-stroke engine peaking to maximum revs.

Bobbie scuffled the length of the roof, hesitated only briefly before jumping, landing in a crouched position on the grass, then made her break towards the iron gate that led to the fields beyond the cottage. Ronnie was waiting, engine ticking over, lights killed: he knew this terrain like the back of his hand.

Bobbie mustered all her strength and sprinted. Her scent caught in their nostrils, the dogs pursued her like wolves hunting their quarry, snapping in the darkness; she could almost sense their hot breath on her neck. They were close, but she'd make it.

She jumped on the back of the bike, wrapped her arms around Ronnie's waist. One of the dogs had made fast progress, teeth nipping at Bobbie's heels as she secured her feet on the footplates. "Go. Now! Go!" she shouted.

Ronnie slammed the throttle. The tyres churned up splatters of mud as they dug into the soft ground. The dogs' barks faded into the night as they sped across the fields.

"Where?" Ronnie asked. "Where the fuck do we go?"

Bobbie didn't hesitate. "Lydia," she said, brushing the hair from her eyes. "She set us up. She needs to face the consequences."

82

Manx, Nader and DCI Canton observed Melvin Powell and his court-appointed solicitor through the interview room mirror. After several minutes, Melvin stood, walked to the glass, checked his reflection, and adjusted the top button on his shirt.

"Looks like the bastard's getting ready for his bloody close-up," Nader said.

"Or preparing for his performance," Manx said, studying Melvin's mannerisms. They were deliberate, nonchalant even, as if he were preparing to enjoy himself as tonight's main event.

"We've let him stew long enough, lads," Canton said, checking his watch. "And no deals without authorisation," he warned.

"Got it." Manx picked up his coffee mug and watched as Melvin ran a hand backwards over his hair, tightened the elastic around his ponytail and nodded in satisfaction.

"Right, Nader you're with me. Let's see what My Little Pony has to say for himself."

83

Bobbie shoved Lydia Jones onto the kitchen chair and leant in close. "We all have one big regret in life, don't we?" she said, slipping the sleek crossbow bolt from her jacket and setting it on the table. "Something we'd like to go back and change. What do they call it, a re-do? What you did, Lydia, I suspect that will be your life's biggest regret, don't you think?"

"You know nothing about me, love, nothing," Lydia snapped, twisting her cordless phone in her hand. She'd been trying to call Melvin for hours, must have left him twenty messages, each one more desperate than the last. But she wasn't about to put that desperation on display, not to her.

"I know you called the police, gave them our location."

"Where's Mel?" Lydia asked, looking to the door as if she expected him to barge in and end all this. But she knew better, knew by now that knights in shining armour were in short supply for women of a certain age, if they'd ever existed at all.

"Mel had things to arrange, isn't that right?" Bobbie said.

Ronnie lifted his head from the crossbow he was spit-polishing with his sleeve. "Yeah, he'll be here later," he confirmed. "Soon as."

Lydia looked at them both. She'd been lied to often enough she could almost smell it on people, and these two, thick as thieves, feet under her table gave off a rotten stench. She gripped the phone. "Maybe I'll call Mel, see what he's got to say for himself."

"Not recommended," Bobbie said, laying the phone on the table and driving the bolt into the flimsy plastic casing.

"You ruined him," Lydia said. "God knows he was no angel, but you? There's something dark in you, love, dark and cold."

"Like the grave?" Bobbie said, extracting the bolt from the innards of the phone. "You don't like me much, do you? I suppose I'm what they call an acquired taste. Isn't that right, Ronnie?"

Ronnie nodded. "Aye, mates now though," he said.

"Go to hell," Lydia snapped.

"Been there, done that." Bobbie lifted the bolt and caressed it gently down Lydia's cheek, then placed the tip on her lips, parting them slightly. "You alerted the police, gave them Mel's old address. Did it feel sweet on the tongue, Lydia, exacting your revenge?"

Lydia exhaled an anxious chuckle. "I haven't known you long enough to miss you, love, so get off your bloody high horse. Don't you think the police would be here now, waiting, if I'd told them?"

"You were the only person who knew where we were. Logic concludes it must have been you."

"I don't know how many times... it wasn't me."

Bobbie nodded, stood, buttoned her jacket.

"Leaving, are you?" Lydia said, a tremor of relief in her voice. "Be on your way. I don't want to see your face round here again."

"Leaving?" Bobbie said, reaching for the rope she'd asked Ronnie to bring from the quad bike. "I'm not the one who's leaving, Lydia."

84

"No. Bloody. Comment."

Two hours into Melvin Powell's interrogation, those three words were beginning to set Manx's teeth on edge; punching into his nerves like a dentist's drill. *No. Bloody. Comment.*

"Come on, man," DS Nader said. "Change the bloody record for Christ's sake."

Melvin smiled. "No. Fucking. Comment."

Nader shook his head and kicked the table leg.

"I'll ask you again, Melvin," Manx said. "Where are you holding Logan Collins?"

Melvin shrugged, offered another cocky smile which instantly reminded Manx of Dafydd Powell – the same slight upturn to the right of his lips, like a lopsided snarl.

Manx sat back, decided on another approach. "Do you know how we found you, Mel?"

"Yellow pages?"

"Your brother, Dafydd. Couldn't wait to shop you, some family dispute back in the day he wanted pay back for. Know anything about that?"

For the first time, he observed a small tell: a flicker of a twitch in Melvin's right eye, as if he were flinching from an incoming punch. "Can't choose your family. Haven't seen him in years, surprised he's not dead. Thought his liver would have given up on him by now or someone put a knife in his back." Melvin exhaled a loud cough that rattled his ribcage.

Mel's solicitor, Ffion Owens, late forties, all business, slightly overweight and an attitude that had immediately raised Manx's hackles, spoke. "My client requires water before answering any more of your questions, which, I don't need to remind you, you are legally obliged to provide him with." Ffion was an old hand at this, had been on the circuit for a couple of decades representing the likes of Melvin Powell.

"No, you're right, you don't need to remind me," Manx said, nodding towards the two-way mirror. Melvin coughed again; Manx wondered if it was all part of the act. He had his solicitor convinced, that was for sure. Manx sat back and adopted a tone a shade more compassionate. "Mel, you don't look the picture of health. Not the Great Welsh Hope you once were, eh?" He shoved the old newspaper clippings towards Melvin. "Are you sure we can't get you something else? A towel maybe, so you can throw it in before you fuck this up too?"

"Fuck off. I'm not talking."

The incident room door opened. PC Morris walked in, handed Manx a slip of paper and placed a cup of water on the table.

"Good news, at least for us," Manx said, glancing at the paper. "The DNA we found at the boat slip is a 99.9 per cent match to yours. Want to enlighten me as to how it got there, Mel?"

Melvin took a slow sip of water. "What boat slip?"

"The one owned by Peter Whinstone. Ninety-seven Beaumaris Road?" Manx turned his laptop screen and played Melvin a repeat performance of the security camera footage. "That was the same evening my detective chief superintendent was stabbed. You were less than a quarter mile away from where it happened."

Melvin shook his head. "Nah. Shadows, mate. All you've got there is shadows."

"So why is your DNA all over that slip?"

Melvin looked at Ffion. She thought for a moment then nodded. "Painted the bloke's conservatory. He asked for a quote for refinishing the wood on the deck. I looked it over, gave him a quote, end of."

"We'll check it out. Morris, if you wouldn't mind," Manx said.

As Morris left, he sat back. "Okay, let's play this out. You knew the slip was unused because you'd been there a few weeks before, but your grand plan went tits up, didn't it? Whoever was driving the van you stole from Ali Kalpar decided to take Collins hostage. Is that what you and Bobbie were arguing about on the slip?" Manx gestured at the screen. "What you were going to do with the bloke?"

Melvin's right eye repeated the same twitch it had betrayed a few minutes ago.

"Didn't think we knew about Bobbie, did you? How did you persuade her to get involved in all this? You can't be lovers, that would be an image I'd find hard to unsee. Friends maybe? Though God knows why she'd be hanging around with a low-life like you."

Manx saw Melvin's fists tighten, noticed how dense they were, pale, as if no blood was reaching the knuckles.

"If not friends, definitely not lovers, then what?" Manx stood, paced the room, hands in his pockets. "Must be family, right? Somehow, some way, you and Bobbie are family? Am I warm?"

"Stone, fucking–" Mel began. Before he could finish, another kind of fist formed. This one was vice-tight, grappling around his insides, choking the bronchi and lobes into narrow passages where the air struggled to fill his lungs. He brought a hand to his chest, his breathing now more of a crippled wheeze.

Manx sensing an advantage pushed harder, reached for a tissue from a box on the table. "Come on, Mel. All this holding stuff in, it's not doing you any favours, let it all out. Tell me where you're holding Logan Collins, I guarantee you'll feel better."

Mel slapped a hand on the table grabbed the tissue and coughed a thick wedge of blood onto it.

"Where is he, Mel? Logan Collins? What's your connection to Bobbie Matthews? How did you murder James Flynt? Why stab Vera Troup, then kidnap Collins? Was it you who put a bolt through Byron Gates' neck?"

Mel was doubled over, slipping off the edge of the chair, using the table to support himself. "Fuck you," he wheezed.

"Inspector Manx!" Ffion shouted, standing and putting her arm around Mel's shoulder. "I can't tolerate this–"

"Not acceptable," Manx said, walking around the table, squatting next to Melvin, whispering in his ear. "Come on, Mel, it's over for you now, you know it. Spit it out. Where are you holding Collins, Mel? Where. Is. He?"

Melvin did spit it out. Coughed a thick chunk of blood-tainted phlegm over Manx's shirt. "Christ!" he shouted, stepping back and grabbing a handful of tissues to wipe himself down.

By the time Manx had turned back around, the Great Welsh Hope was regaining his strength; at least for now. "Don't worry, I'm not contagious," he said. "And fuck you and your stories. I know nothing."

Manx shoved his chair hard against the table. "Pausing interview with suspect Melvin Powell at 9.16pm. Inspector Manx leaving the interview room."

Manx flung open the gallery viewing room door, slammed it behind him and grabbed another handful of tissues to wipe the blood.

"All going to plan then?" Canton said, turning from the screen, his face three shades more flushed than usual. "What the hell were you doing in there? Trying to get the whole case thrown out?"

Manx flung himself onto the nearest chair, then scooted back as Morris and DS Nader made their way in.

"Powell's right. He did a paint job for Peter Whitestone back in early July," Morris said. "And Whitestone did ask him to quote for refinishing the slip. Sorry, sir."

Manx stood, placed his palms on the two-way mirror and shook his head. "He's lying. That cocky little shit is lying his arse off." He slapped hard on the glass.

"You need a confession, Manx," Canton said. "The DNA only confirms he was on the slip at some point, which he's already admitted to. The CCTV footage is worthless. If Bobbie Matthews was hiding out in that cottage, then she's long gone by now, and unless we find the words 'Bobbie Matthews was here' finger-painted in one of the rooms, there's no way to prove she was even there; neither her DNA nor prints are in the system."

"What about the other bloke?" Nader asked. "He's got to be helping Bobbie Matthews."

"Got away on a quad bike," Manx said, leaning his back against the glass and taking a deep, calming breath.

"Here's the deal, Manx," Canton said. "And I'll tell you this before Ms 'by-the-book human rights solicitor' in there reminds you. You've got twenty-four hours to either release him or charge him. With the evidence you've got, I doubt you'll secure an arrest warrant. I don't like it any more than you do, but if by nine o'clock tomorrow night Melvin Powell's still giving you the 'no bloody comment' line, and we haven't found any credible evidence to charge him, he walks."

"We ask for an extension," Manx said. "Kidnapping and attempted murder on a senior police officer, they've got to grant us more time to secure the evidence."

"Give it your best shot, Manx," Canton said. "You might get thirty-six hours, if you're lucky."

Manx looked through the mirror as Melvin Powell strutted the room and checked out his reflection.

He didn't look like the confessing type. Not even close.

85

Manx stared at the bottle of Springbank as if it were his mortal enemy. What was it they said? Keep your friends close and your enemies closer? Manx pushed the temptation of his enemy to the farthest end of the breakfast bar. It was far too dramatic a gesture; the bottle was still easily within arm's reach, his name floating flirtatiously in the scotch's honeyed depths.

It was 11.45pm. Manx had thrown in the towel with Melvin Powell an hour before, decided to tackle the weaselly bastard first thing tomorrow morning with a fresh head and a few hours of sound sleep. He'd kept his drinking to his rationed two fingers of scotch, one ice cube, repeated three times; a ratio he'd worked out over the years that would help take the edge off and still avoid the foggy mire of a hangover. He quickly sorted through his post; two bills, three new credit card offers, a request for a donation to the RNLI, and a flyer for Thursday's Anglesey Agricultural Show.

Most of his mail dumped, donation envelope filed for later, Manx flipped open his laptop and searched his music library, opting for the shuffle feature; tonight, he'd let fate roll the dice. "Hard Luck Story", a track from one his favourite alternative country bands, Whiskeytown, played over the speaker. The irony didn't pass him by as the song's propulsive, freight-train rhythm filled the tiny kitchen. "I gotta bucket full of tears and a hard-luck story," Ryan Adams sang as the song reached its chorus.

"Amen to that," Manx mumbled, raising his glass to the ghosts, present, past and future, who had suffered the same biting sting of failure. The raid on the cottage had barely been rescued from total disaster by the capture of Melvin Powell, but two other suspects, one of which had to be Bobbie Matthews, had escaped. That wasn't what he'd call "mission accomplished" by any means.

At precisely 11.59pm, as he nursed his last ration of scotch, a loud ping from his computer interrupted his playlist. He clicked on his email app. There was a forwarded email from the North Wales Constabulary Just Ask A Copper account; the first and only one he'd ever received. He checked the sender's address: ByronGates@dronewatch.uk

The hairs on Manx's neck spiked. It wasn't often he received emails from a dead man. He read the first few lines:

For the attention of Detective Inspector Tudor Manx.

If you're reading this email, I'm more than likely dead. The cause will be murder, and the person who killed me will be Flight Lieutenant Bobbie Matthews. If you're investigating her already, this won't surprise you, if you're not, then I'd recommend finding her as soon as possible. Here's what you need to know about Bobbie Matthews...

Manx read the rambling dissertation. Much of it Manx already knew; Operation Vanguard, the kidnapping of Logan Collins; Byron had obviously spent hours formulating conspiracy theories of his own. He went on at length about how Bobbie had forced him to upload the video, how he'd searched her, found the motive to her actions, how he'd visited her sister Tammy.

Reading Tammy's name, Manx almost resisted the urge to call her, but the scotch was making him feel more cavalier than usual. Tammy answered on the third ring, pretended to be annoyed, but then agreed that she too was finding it hard to sleep and yes maybe she could come over, talk, pass the time.

Thirty minutes later, Tammy sat in his kitchen, pouring the gin she'd brought with her into a glass, having guessed correctly that Manx's larder would be woefully bare of her drink of choice.

"Did Bobbie ever mention anyone called Melvin Powell?" Manx asked, watching Tammy bring the glass from her lips: lips he was desperate to reacquaint himself with, but he resisted temptation, at least for the moment.

Tammy shook her head. "Why? Is he important?"

"Just a name, that's all."

"I can't get my head around all of this," she said. "I keep thinking if there was something I could have done differently or said differently. If I'd been a better sister, then she wouldn't have done any of this."

"There was nothing you could have done. Bobbie set her own course."

"And you really think she killed Byron Gates?"

"Or had him killed," Manx said.

"Christ, I don't know which scares me the most," Tammy said, putting down her drink. She took a deep breath and wiped her hands across her eyes. "I'm sorry," she said, composing herself. "Bobbie was always a little strange, you know. When we were kids, she had to win every game we played, she'd get into a huge strop if she lost. In the end, I'd just let her win, just for some peace. I didn't care, it made her happy, anyway it was just a game, no harm done."

Tammy placed her palms flat on the table, looked at the wall clock; 12:53am. "I should go," she said, screwing the top back on her bottle of Aber Falls Botanical Gin.

Manx sensed the gesture was at best half-hearted. "Stay," he said, almost without thinking.

Tammy sat back and smiled. "Stay? The night? With you?"

"No one else here."

Tammy thought for a moment. "It is a bit late to be driving home, I suppose," she said, leaning across the breakfast bar.

Manx leant in to meet her gaze. "Can't be too careful these days, maniacs on the road," he said, moving his face closer to hers.

Her lips parted slightly, shaping a seductive smile. "You'd think the police would do something about that."

"I have connections," he said, running a finger down her hair to her neck. "I could have a word."

"Then there's the gin, probably over the limit by now."

"I hear there's patrols all over the island this time of year." Manx breathed in the heady bouquet of her perfume and pressed his lips against her cheek. "I'd hate to have to come and bail you out."

"Well, that settles it," she said, her lips brushing his. "I expect you have a spare bedroom I can kip in?"

"Single bed, very uncomfortable, you wouldn't sleep a wink."

Tammy nodded. "Is that right? And the sofa?"

"Lumpy as hell. You'll have back problems for weeks."

Tammy sat back, dragged the hair from her face and placed

her palms on the table. "I don't usually do this on a second date, just so you know."

"Technically, it's a first date," Manx said. "That evening at the Ship Inn was you helping the police with their inquiries."

"And tonight?" she asked.

"If you continue to resist, I might need to keep you here overnight, continue the interrogation."

Tammy stood. "Well then, Inspector Manx, I'd hate to disappoint the North Wales Constabulary."

Most of their clothes were torn off and discarded to the floor before they'd reached Manx's bed. There was little talking. Skin pressed against skin; fingers entwined in fingers; limbs wrapped around limbs. Faint moonlight spilling in from the window shone across Tammy's body, casting a milky aura over her skin. In that moment, Manx doubted he'd ever seen anything more beautiful, and if he had, it was so long ago the memory had by now faded to dust.

Forty-five minutes later, their bodies recovering, a sheen of sweat covering their skin, Tammy shuffled close to Manx and draped her arm across his chest. "There's a problem," she said.

"I'm open to most requests," he said, drawing her closer.

Tammy lightly slapped his chest. "If we're going to do this again, I can't keep calling you inspector."

Manx smiled. "Tudor," he said. "Tudor Manx-Williams."

"Tudor," Tammy whispered. "Very regal." She said his name again. Then there were no sounds, just the steady breathing of deep and satisfying sleep.

Manx was maybe three hours into the best sleep he'd had for weeks, months even, when he woke with a striking thought that had made its way into his subconscious while he slept.

He slipped quietly from the bedroom, headed to the kitchen and opened his laptop. He replayed, at low volume, the video of Logan Collins reading out the demands, scrubbing to the section where he said "no one else need die". He replayed it several times. He hadn't noticed the significance before. Why reference other people dying when the only threat had been to murder Collins?

He recalled the conversation with Andrew Pierce. "Bobbie was angry with the RAF; it makes no sense for her to kill Collins." *No, of course it made no sense*, Manx thought as he sat back and ran a hand across his mouth, which still tasted of Tammy's skin and lipstick. What if threatening Collins wasn't all Bobbie had planned? He looked to the wall opposite at the Moelfre Lifeboat calendar he'd bought for half-price a few months back. He checked out the month of August and scanned backwards through the days.

Summer Bank Holiday, August 26th; RNLI Open Day, August 14th; August 7th, the day after tomorrow – The Anglesey Agricultural Show. He remembered his father, Tommy, taking him there one year. Or, more precisely, dropping Manx off then picking him up several hours later stinking of beer, fags and pig roast.

Manx thought for a moment, his brain slowly catching up with the tingling sensation he always felt in his neck when he was close to finding a breakthrough in a case; it was like the slow drip of water seeping through cracks in a wall.

He reached behind him into the bin and pulled out the flyer for the Anglesey Show he'd thrown in there earlier. He flattened it on the table, flipped it over, and read the list of events. One caught his eye. The official opening to be performed at 11.30am by their Royal Highnesses the Duke and Duchess of Cambridge.

Manx sat back down, reached for the bottle and took a hearty mouthful. That tingling he felt earlier was now a fully-formed tsunami of certainty. The threat to Logan Collins was real, but it wasn't the only threat. Bobbie Matthews had something else planned. Collins had been a convenient coincidence, a decoy.

If he was right, and he hoped to God he wasn't, he had twenty-four hours to find out what Bobbie Matthews had planned and stop her. But right now, at 3.33am, the night still thick, the sun two hours away from rising, he had no shadow of a doubt the odds were stacked firmly against him.

86

How Melvin Powell could hold in his smile a curl of menace and a kind of lopsided goofiness was a mystery to Manx. But there it was, staring him right in the face at eight in the morning, along with the refrain that was beginning to loosen the nails from Manx's fingers:

"No. Bloody. Comment."

Manx pressed his palms on the table and towered over Melvin. "Just tell us. We know Bobbie's planning something at the Anglesey Show. Tell us what it is, and maybe we can talk to the CPS, get you a deal."

"I don't think you can promise anything, Inspector Manx," Melvin's solicitor, Ffion Owens, said as she walked in. She took the chair next to Melvin and threw her briefcase on the desk as if throwing down a gauntlet. "And you don't have the right to question my client without me in the room. Anything he told you will be inadmissible in court."

"That's a relief," Manx said. "Because if I hear 'no bloody comment' one more time I might lock myself up in one of our cells. Now, I'll ask you again, what's Bobbie Matthews planning?"

"No–"

"Bloody comment. Got it," Manx said. He stormed out of the room, slammed the door behind him, and joined Canton in the viewing gallery.

"It's a bloody stretch, Manx," Canton said as Manx walked in. "Even for you I'd say this is a big leap of imagination."

"Not that big," Manx said, sitting. "Collins had no real value for Bobbie. He's a means to an end. She kills Collins, she's gained nothing, just taken the life of some local politician. Her target is the RAF, always has been. If she launches some kind of attack tomorrow, the day the royals open the Anglesey Show, that's going to make the RAF look like a bunch of incompetent fuckwits. If she can't get the truth she's looking for, then she's going for full-on humiliation."

"Do you think she's capable of this?" Canton asked, his tone reflecting he was slowly coming around to Manx's theory.

"Her clinical psychologist seemed to think so."

"Shit," Canton said, shaking his head. "We can't go to the press with just a bloody hunch. Imagine the panic, and don't even think about the RAF being embarrassed. If you're wrong about this, we'll both be hung out to dry like this morning's washing."

"We don't start with the press," Manx said, grabbing his coat and car keys. "Well, are you coming or not?"

"You are pulling my bloody leg, aren't you?" Morgan Lloyd, chairman of the Anglesey Agricultural Show, said, throwing himself into the leather chair parked behind his obscenely large mahogany desk. "This is a joke? A prank?"

"I believe the threat is genuine," Manx said.

"What threat?" Lloyd asked, rubbing a palm over his broom-bristle moustache and pointing a stubby finger at Manx. "This sounds like something you've just pulled out of your arses."

"Could we quote you on that?" Manx said. "I'm sure Collins' wife and the local press would be over the moon."

"This Anglesey Show," Lloyd said, "we're expecting 60,000 people. I've got farm machinery manufacturers from all over the country already here, including Massey bloody Ferguson who are sponsoring the opening night dinner."

"I understand–" Manx began, before he was interrupted.

"Let me tell you, inspector, unless you can present me with a specific threat, there is no way in hell I'm cancelling my show. But, if you're offering to add a few more coppers on the field, I'd be happy to take them. God knows the North Wales Constabulary hasn't offered up anything much in the past."

Manx's blood pressure rose a couple of notches. "Some co-operation wouldn't go amiss."

"Other than cancelling the show, how can I help you?"

"We want to search the showground tonight, when it's quiet so no one gets wind."

Lloyd nodded. "Anything else?"

"Increased surveillance on the day. Undercover officers."

"Still on the hush-hush," Lloyd said. "I won't have any of my exhibitors spooked."

Manx and Canton agreed.

"Good," Lloyd said, standing and gesturing it was time for them to leave. "Now, as they say, gents, the show must go on."

87

After dropping Canton back at the station Manx made a quick call, briefed the team on the morning's events, and put Nader in charge of organising the explosive-detection dog team to search the showgrounds. Half an hour later, he was back in the Jensen, coasting the A55.

He pulled into the showgrounds. The fields were bone-dry, the earth hard, grass yellow-tipped and brittle. As Manx and Carlisle walked, several articulated lorries the size of tanks off-loaded their heavy-metal: row-crop tractors, combine harvesters, rotary tillers, earth movers and the like were driven off their semi-trailers and reversed, engines spluttering, into their pre-assigned lots.

Carlisle waved away a blue bottle buzzing near his face. "I'd say it's wild speculation, Manx. Our intelligence hasn't picked up any chatter, and you're not in possession of a specific threat."

"You're not the first one to point that out."

"Then maybe the universe is trying to tell you something," Carlisle said, stopping at one of the fence posts. "What makes you believe the royals might be targeted?"

Manx didn't have a concrete answer for that, he was running

on instinct; that trickle of static at the back of his neck that told him he was right. "Prince William? He's an honorary air commandant as well as a lieutenant commander, correct?"

"Amongst other military ranks from the Navy and Army."

"Take that to its logical conclusion. Bobbie Matthews is demanding the release of highly sensitive military information–"

"Which will never see the light of day," Carlisle interrupted.

Manx continued. "She's issued a threat timeline that ends on the opening day of the Anglesey Show – tomorrow – which the royals are scheduled to officially open."

"Could be a coincidence, completely unconnected."

"I don't think you really believe that, otherwise you wouldn't have agreed to meet me. If the end game is to make the RAF pay, or embarrass them in some way, then there's no better target than a senior member of the royal family serving at Valley."

Carlisle looked towards the expanse of land that stretched in a carpet of wide, uninterrupted green. "And if you're right?"

"Believe me, Carlisle, I'd be happy if I was wrong, but there's a bloody good chance I'm not."

Carlisle let Manx's words simmer for a few moments. "I've known them long enough. They don't like disappointing their public. Building goodwill here on the island is important to them."

"You need to make them listen."

Carlisle swatted another fly buzzing near his face. "I don't *need* to do anything, but I'll take the information under consideration. Without a specific threat, there's nothing I can do. Unless, of course, you lock this down and make an arrest before tomorrow."

"There's always that," Manx agreed.

"Settled, then," Carlisle said. "I'll pass on your concerns. If the North Wales Constabulary neutralise the threat before the

Anglesey Show, then situation normal, we move ahead as planned. If, by the end of today, you're no further on in your investigation I'll strongly insist they cancel their appearance."

Manx considered pushing him further, but figured he'd reached as close to a compromise as he'd get from the man.

"It's my best offer," he insisted.

Manx shoved his hands in his pockets and agreed.

"Good man." Carlisle tugged on his shirt cuffs. "Seems you were right about Byron Gates," he added.

"Lot of good me being right does him now," Manx said.

"We work with the intel we have not the intel we wish we had," Carlisle said. "Threats to our national security need to be neutralised, I'm sure I don't need to remind you of that. I'd wish you luck but seems we're well beyond relying on luck by now. I'll expect your call when you've found Bobbie Matthews."

Manx watched Carlisle climb into his Range Rover and drive away. Several hundred metres away, the deep rumble of heavy farm machinery engines sent a shudder through the ground and into Manx's boots. It was like the tiniest of earthquakes, faint enough to be of no consequence, yet held within it a sober reminder of its power and the destruction it was capable of unleashing.

88

Logan Collins imagined he must be veering close to delirium, maybe even a razor's edge away from insanity. It had probably only been a few days since he'd been here, a week at most, but it felt like this was all there ever was; all there had ever been.

He was thinking on this when a thin shaft of light cut through his blindfold. "Melvin?" he asked. He hoped it was Melvin, not that cruel kid, Ronnie. But hope was a fleeting thing, engineered to take flight in an instant. That instant came in the form of Ronnie's voice.

"Got you some company, mate," he said, yanking down Collins' blindfold. Ronnie shoved the woman, forcing her to sit. "No touching, mind you, she's Mel's bird. He'll put another bolt right in your bollocks if you start feeling her up."

Ronnie's giggle was childish and cruel as he left. But at least there was one saving grace, he'd neglected to pull Collins' blindfold back in place. Collins blinked a few times, his eyes adjusting to the light. He looked at the woman. She didn't look scared, she looked defiant, more than defiant, angry; top of the boil, furious, angry.

"What the bloody hell are you looking at?" Lydia snapped, kicking to free the ropes which were bound tight around her ankles.

"Em, nothing," Collins said, his voice dry, barely audible.

"Good," she said. "Got any ideas on how to get out of here?"

Collins shrugged, showed her his hands, bound tight with duct tape and rope.

"Typical bloody politician," Lydia said. "Not one decent idea between the lot of you."

89

It was a probability Bobbie had to consider, no matter how grubby or disloyal it made her feel. Melvin had now been in custody for over twenty-four hours and she had no idea what he might be telling the police. She was sure he wasn't the kind of man to betray his family, though what did she really know about him?

What she did know was this. The man hadn't hesitated when she told him she suspected she was his daughter. He'd smiled, said he could see the family resemblance borne out in the sharp, angular features of her face and the way she held herself, proud. "You hold herself like a fighter, Bobbie," he'd said. She did wonder if it weren't for his terminal diagnosis if Melvin would have risked so much. But that was a question she couldn't dwell on. She was resolute now, determined to ensure Danvir hadn't died in vain and someone would pay for his death.

She walked into the kitchen of Lydia's flat. Ronnie was at the kitchen table flipping through an old photo album. Bobbie passed behind him. "You both look young in that one," she said, pointing at a picture of Ronnie and Melvin standing at the cottage gate, crossbows cradled in their arms.

"First time we went lamping," he said. "Shot three rabbits and a fox that night."

Bobbie placed a hand on his shoulder; it felt like the right thing to do, even though that sort of gesture made her uncomfortable these days, as if whatever shadow cast within her grew weaker with human contact. Tomorrow that shadow needed to be strong, stronger than ever; stronger even than her.

She pulled her hand back. "We should run through tomorrow's strategy."

"No need. Got it all in here," he said, tapping his forehead.

"And the quadcopter?"

"Stored it in the back room where we had the meetings: no one ever goes in there."

"Is the battery fully charged."

"Will be by tomorrow morning."

"And the vehicle?"

Ronnie sighed. "Nicked one. Old Ford Transit from outside a chippy in Bangor."

"Good," Bobbie said, pacing the room like a caged animal.

"Sit down, you're making me nervous."

"There's a lot to be nervous about."

"Nah," Ronnie said, raising his right hand, making a fist, then circling it in sweeping motions before releasing the fist and emulating the sound of an explosion. "Piece of fuckin' cake."

Bobbie left him to his memories and walked into the bedroom. She took out her combat flying suit from her kitbag and laid it out on the bed, smoothing out the creases with her palm. Next to the suit, she placed the medal she'd earned for her role in the RAF's Operation Shader in Iraq and Syria. She should have been awarded more medals, a lot more, but the RAF had only recently began awarding the operations service medals to drone pilots: this after years of lobbying. It was yet another example of how the RAF had treated drone pilots like herself, and another reason the RAF should be held accountable. Successful kill strikes were still kill strikes, no matter if you made them from three feet away with a rifle, 10,000 feet above from the seat of an F150, or 3,000 miles away from the flight deck of a ground control station. Taking out the enemy was still the objective, and she'd done her job better than most. The service had chosen to repay her with one token medal and the suspension of her combat-ready status; for that, they needed to pay. Holding the silver medal between her fingers, the Queen's face rendered in profile, it suddenly seemed less like a medal and more like a fairground consolation prize; the plastic toy when she'd failed to hook the duck and win the goldfish.

She shook, tossed the medal into her bag, stepped into her flying suit and pulled up the zipper. She hadn't worn it since that day in Waddington. It felt heavier on her now and it was still thick with the smell of the ground station. That was over a year ago, her ground zero, and now that journey was coming to its conclusion.

When she'd forced Collins to speak those words, she hadn't imagined this day would finally come to pass. She'd been convinced – or maybe had just convinced herself – the RAF would have given in to her demands, but instead they'd offered nothing. That decision had left her no choice. Pointless deaths had to be avenged, injustices redressed. Maybe, as Byron Gates had suggested, they weren't so different. They were both seeking justice, both fighting a power far greater than them. But Bobbie wasn't different from Byron because she had nothing left to lose, she was different because she'd sought to redress that injustice and not just posted documents on a website that mattered to no one. Byron Gates had been nothing more than a messenger, and the fate of messengers had been written in cliché for hundreds of years.

The same was true of Call Me Andy. He was a messenger of a

different sort; one who was there to merely rubber stamp the decisions made by the command. Unlike Byron Gates, who'd betrayed Bobbie, Call Me Andy had at least tried, and for that his life could be spared. Before she'd left the base for the last time, she'd gone over to his office with the intent of giving him at least the courtesy of a goodbye, but he was out for the day according to his calendar. Before she left, she'd noticed his chaplain robes and white collar hanging on the back of the door.

Now, she took them out her kitbag and laid them out on the bed before trying them on for size.

90

The following morning, a thick layer of grey, soupy mist had settled over the showgrounds, stretching across the fields and farmland both sides of the A55 artery. The earth underfoot was firm to the shoe, the dampness of the dawn tweaking the saturation of the grass rendering it a brilliant green. Twenty-five miles south east, rising 3,500 feet, Mount Snowdon's jagged peak was set clear against the blue. Behind the peak, a belt of low morning cloud brushed with the barest hint of a flame-red sunrise sketching its way into the day.

The showground was already a bustle of activity. Prize bulls, magnificent and proud, were led from their trailers to holding pens. In the animal enclosures, farm hands applied the final touches to the show horses, looping brasses over manes and brushing coats to a show-quality shine. To the north of the main arena, the salespeople added the finishing polish to the already sparkling metal of the farm machinery they'd been sent here to sell.

Around the perimeter, the explosive-detection dogs, noses to the ground, tugged hard on their leads. Meanwhile, Manx's team combed the food tents and craft stalls, paying specific attention to the main stage, where the royal couple were set to appear in a few hours. Each officer carried a photograph of Bobbie Matthews with strict orders not to approach and to alert Manx if she was spotted.

As Manx walked into the administration tent, Jack Carlisle was already there; had been for some time it seemed, sipping tea with the show chairman Morgan Lloyd, who was flipping through a thick wad of tickets.

"Counting your chickens?" Manx asked.

Lloyd sat back, hiked up his trouser belt. "Best year yet, I reckon. Seventy thousand, give or take."

"Let's hope that's all it's memorable for," Manx said.

Lloyd huffed and went back to flipping through his ticket receipts like Fagin tallying his takings after a fruitful day's pick-pocketing.

Carlisle settled his mug on the table. "A word, Manx?" he said with a subtle nod. "Outside."

"If you're about to ask me if we've received a credible threat, I'm not in the mood. I'm knackered and my team's worn down to a nub."

"I'm not saying you're right, Manx, but we have strengthened security," Carlisle assured him. "The royals will arrive in the first Range Rover, myself and my security detail in the other. We'll be in communication as we approach, and I've placed three under-cover officers ready for when the gates open at zero nine thirty hours. They'll only be in communication with myself and my team. Arses well and truly covered. And one thing, Manx, this all better be more than a hunch, or you'll have the whole damn royal security detail wanting your head on a silver platter."

"I'd feel a hell of a lot better if they'd cancel the appearance all together," Manx said. "Save us all the headache."

"If we allow the terrorists to dictate the rules of the game, they win, Manx," he said, turning to leave.

"One question, Carlisle," Manx said. "What does a win look like in your book?"

Carlisle turned back, paused. "Easy, Manx, it looks like this." He motioned across the breadth of the showground towards the crowds shuffling through the entrance gates.

Manx got his point; business as usual, living in freedom, only gets to happen because of people like Carlisle, and in his world, there were no grey areas. You either understood that or you didn't.

91

Ronnie pummelled his fists against the wall of the Transit van and shouted. "Stop fucking kicking, or I'll put another bolt through you myself!"

Silence followed as Logan Collins complied.

Ronnie was parked on a hill overlooking the showground. At 9am, a long tail of traffic was backed up to the town of Gaerwen, three miles east. The warm weather meant big crowds for the show this year. Ronnie almost felt envious. *Yeah, it would have been champion on a day like today, walking the showground with Mel, checking out the big farm machinery and trawling the beer tents until closing time. Next year. There was always next year.*

Kneeling, he carefully unwrapped the package Bobbie had given him last night; a steel pipe bomb, eight inches in length, three inches in diameter and sealed at both ends with brass caps.

"This is very volatile, Ronnie, don't fuck about with it," Bobbie had instructed him. "Handle it the wrong way and it will blow your head off and scatter your limbs in all directions."

His hands were calm, still as rocks, as he attached the device to the auxiliary battery compartment. He ripped off two strips of duct tape with his teeth, then fixed the pipe to the drone. The final step was the trickiest. In the centre of the pipe was a narrow hole filled with two, four inch long fuses which Ronnie connected to the motherboard of the quadcopter via two wires; one to carry the signal from the control panel to the drone, the other to detonate the five pounds of tightly packed explosive material stuffed with masonry nails. Once that was complete, he took the screen from his backpack and secured it to the A-frame above the control panel.

Stepping back, he fired up the main motor. The four propellers oscillated slowly at first, then quickly gained velocity. As he hovered the drone a few feet above ground, an alert beeped on the screen. He checked the message. Something about a low battery. That couldn't be right. He'd had it on charge all night. He was certain he'd plugged it into the correct socket – the one Melvin told him to always plug the kettle into – the only working socket in the old building.

Yeah, he thought as he navigated the quadcopter fifty feet skywards, he was a hundred per cent sure he'd plugged it into the right socket.

Or maybe ninety per cent sure. Or maybe a little less.

92

"Any sign of Bobbie Matthews?" Manx called out over the radio as he walked the grounds. A chorus of "negative", "no boss", and "no guv" came back over the radio.

As he clicked off, DCI Canton, his bald head shimmering in the heat, walked over. "Christ, Manx," he said, taking out a handkerchief and dabbing his brow. "Are you sure about all this. We've been here two hours and no sign of the woman."

"Don't you start, Ellis. Carlisle's already laid into me."

"Maybe he's right. What if Bobbie Matthews is halfway to the bloody Algarve by now, laughing her arse off." He took out her photograph. "We've got twenty officers patrolling the grounds, plus Carlisle's lot. If she was here, someone would have spotted her by now. She's not a master of bloody disguise."

Disguise? The word triggered a flash in Manx's mind. He nudged his brain into reverse gear. Andrew Pierce. The interview room. Three days ago. What the hell was it? It seemed like an off-hand remark at the time. Then it hit him, square in the eyes.

"A vicar," he said. "Bobbie Matthews stole the chaplain's uniform, or whatever they call it."

“Vestment,” Canton said. “A clergy’s vestments.”

Manx clicked on his radio and alerted the team on the updated description for Bobbie Matthews.

93

People trusted vicars, priests, men of the cloth, which made it a lot easier for Bobbie Matthews to pass through the heightened security cordon that morning and into the showground.

Officers charged with searching for persons matching Bobbie's description would have passed her by without a second glance. She resembled a man of God; briefcase in hand, as if she were off to conduct some emergency exorcism, hair scrunched under a hat, black robe flaring behind. The white clerical collar was the finishing touch that left no doubt that Bobbie was who she claimed to be.

Along with Call Me Andy's Sunday best, she'd also taken an RAF radio comms device. That sort of hardware was easy to smuggle out of the base. Weapons, on the other hand, required signing out, paperwork filled in, permissions granted. No matter, she was resourceful. Building a home-made explosive device was hardly brain surgery these days; there were hundreds of pages dedicated to the subject on the dark web. She'd presented the finished device to Ronnie late last night.

Bobbie had then driven by the showgrounds to conduct a final scout. When she arrived, her gut had told her something wasn't right. There were too many cars parked for that time of night – specifically, too many police cars. She'd driven past, decided it was too risky, and headed back to the Lantern Arms. The same unsettling thought she'd had last night came to her this morning as she passed a stall selling Welsh dragon belt buckles similar to the ones Melvin wore. Had he confessed? Given the police the time and location? Or had the police, smarter than she'd given them credit for, figured it out for themselves. Of both scenarios, the latter seemed most likely – Melvin was a lot of things, but he wasn't a traitor. Either way, she'd need to be vigilant; she still had work to do, elements to lay in place.

She headed to where the royal couple would be addressing the crowds later. Several dogs were sniffing around the stage. She waited for the handlers to pull them away, then slipped her briefcase under the stage, making sure it stuck out enough for someone to notice. She snapped some photos with her phone and texted Ronnie. They would give him some solid visuals for his mission.

Ronnie had been a fast and eager learner, but he'd be anxious by now, which is why Bobbie had secured a timing device to the drone. Instead of triggering the explosives manually, Bobbie would send a text when the target was in range. Ronnie would set the countdown for ten minutes, pilot the drone fifty feet above the target and hover it in place until the timer hit zero. It was a failsafe mechanism, she'd told him, in case the digital trigger she'd rigged onto the control board failed to engage.

Her explanation was half-true. Manual triggers could be unreliable, especially if the signal was corrupted between the control panel and the quadcopter, but the key reason was

Ronnie himself. If he was compromised, or bottled out at the last moment, this ensured the mission would be completed, with or without him.

94

Five miles away, at Llangefni police station, Melvin Powell's solicitor Ffion Owens was arguing with PC Bryn Pritchard, a sickly-looking young man, still six weeks away from completing his twelve-week mandatory constable tutoring programme. Canton had assigned him to manage the reception while he and the senior officers patrolled the showgrounds.

"The North Wales Constabulary has a legal obligation," Ffion stated. She checked her watch. "In ten minutes, the thirty-six-hour detention ends and you'll have to either arrest or release my client."

"To be honest, I'm not really familiar with the case," Pritchard said, tapping his pen on the desk, trying to recall if he'd studied anything similar in classroom training a few months back. His mind drew a blank. "I don't think I can just release him," he said – more of a question than it was a statement.

"Listen," Ffion said, checking his name and number. "When I inform the Crown Prosecution Service that PC Bryn Pritchard, collar number ID 1271, failed to release a member of the public after the statutory, legally permitted time, whose feet are they going to hold to the fire? DI Manx? DCI Canton?"

"I wouldn't know anything about that," Pritchard mumbled. "They only brought me in today, I'm usually over at Beaumaris. Don't get many arrests over there like, pretty boring actually, get the odd drunk, tourists lost their wallet or something–"

"PC Pritchard," Ffion interrupted. "Unless you want to trigger a lawsuit, I recommend that within the next eight minutes you release my client."

"Em..." Pritchard muttered. "I should probably call my DI, just to make sure, like."

"You do that."

Ffion checked her messages as Pritchard dialled Manx's number, mentally crossing his fingers he'd pick up. The call went straight to voicemail.

"No reply," he said, hanging up. "Probably busy."

"Great detective work. I can see why the force snapped you up. Now, let me help you out here, constable," Ffion said. "You can legally release my client under a Released Under Investigation document. You are familiar with the procedure?"

Pritchard span his mind back several months to a lecture on arrest and release procedures. "Yeah, I'm not bloody stupid."

"Let's leave that open for discussion," Ffion said, smiling. "You sign the document and my client is released within the thirty-six-hour window. The North Wales Constabulary is still within its power to bring my client in at any time for further questioning. And, you've seen the state of the man, he's hardly a flight risk."

"Aye, I suppose," Pritchard agreed.

"It's the morally right thing to do. That's something they wouldn't have taught you in training," Ffion said with a slim smile.

Pritchard sighed. “Wait here,” he said, and trundled out of the reception area, wondering where the hell they kept the Released Under Investigation paperwork.

95

By the time the news of Melvin Powell's release reached Manx the metaphorical horse had bolted the metaphorical stable: Melvin could have legged it anywhere, but Manx's instincts told him he would want to be wherever the action was. Rather than spend the next five minutes giving Bryn Pritchard the mother of all bollockings, Manx hung up and focused on his next steps.

With all his key officers patrolling the showground, he'd left the station woefully undermanned; it was like he'd pushed all his players forward, leaving no one in defence and the goal mouth wide open. He was in no doubt Melvin was heading over here and was about to alert the team when Nader's voice bled in over his radio.

"Boss, I think we've found something," he said, his words tripping out fast and anxious. "There's a briefcase under the stage. Weren't there when we looked twenty minutes ago. I've got a bad feeling about this. Me and the lads–"

"Secure the area, right now!" Manx instructed. "Move the crowd as far away from the stage as you can."

"I'll try my best." Nader's breathing was hurried. Manx could almost picture the clammy sheen of sweat forming across his DS's upper lip.

"Keep a lid on any panic. And Nader, I've just been informed Melvin Powell's been released from custody. If he's making his way here, keep a look out, and tell the rest of the team."

Nader clicked off the airways without responding. Scanning the area, Manx was suddenly and acutely aware of the large crowds now congregating. The voice of the show announcer booming over the PA system gave him an idea. He ran, elbowing his way through the crowds. A crackle of static broke through the radio, followed by Jack Carlisle's voice.

"Danny Collins and Daphne Clark on route. ETA five minutes."

Manx responded. "We have a level critical threat situation. Advise driving Danny and Daphne back to home base." Manx chose his words carefully. He was certain Carlisle would understand and react to the phrase "level critical" – an attack was imminent.

A brief moment of silence followed by Carlisle's measured tones. "Negative. Vehicles are stuck in traffic, no way to execute a safe retreat."

Before replying, Manx recalled a backroad the team had identified last night that ended where the animal transporters and trailers were parked. He gave Carlisle the directions, picked up the pace and made a direct line to the announcer's stage.

Winking Wynn Williams, a local celebrity with a predictable line in corny patter, jumped out of his seat as Manx bounded onto the stage. "Hey, steady on," Wynn said, his laughter forced. "Seems we've got someone looking to take over my announcing duties. Are you in the union, son?" Another nervous chuckle.

Manx shoved his Police ID in his face, cupped his hand over the microphone, and spoke to Wynn in a low, urgent tone.

Winking Wynn Williams nodded slowly, his face now three shades redder, and cleared his throat. "Erm, ladies and gentlemen, no need to panic, like, but the North Wales Constabulary have asked me to make this very important announcement..."

96

D*anny Collins and Daphne Clark?* The code names were almost comical, Bobbie thought, as she adjusted the volume on her RAF radio. She'd overheard the airmen mention the code names in the canteen. Danny Collins and Daphne Clark. The royal code names were always based on the initials of their titles; Duke and Duchess of Cambridge: DC. *That would need to change after today*, she thought, *or be nixed all together if Ronnie had his shit together*.

The sound of the announcer's voice over the PA system caught her attention. The police had obviously found the brief-case. She smiled and texted Ronnie: "Danny and Daphne on the road."

As Bobbie walked towards the livestock carriers and horse trailers at the western side of the showground, she had the distinct sense someone had eyes on her. By now, she'd learned to trust that instinct, embrace it. She continued, her pace unchanged, but her senses on high alert, her mind already set on a strategy.

97

Detective Sergeant Mal Nader didn't have a strategy, it wasn't his style. What he did have was a scorching anger, like a severe, unquenchable heartburn raging in his belly. Melvin Powell had been released. What he'd predicted to Manx had come true. He could just imagine Melvin Powell, strutting out the station doors, pleased as punch with himself. If he saw him now, he wouldn't hesitate to punch the bloke's lights out or zap the bastard with his taser, to hell with the consequences.

When he spotted Bobbie Matthews a hundred or so metres away, dressed in a black robe and clerical collar, he was in no doubt she and Melvin Powell were the reason DCSI Troup was in hospital holding on to life by a fingernail. She wasn't just his DCSI; she was a wife and a mother. His anger burnt brighter and fiercer as he thought of her daughter; that poor kid, having to watch her mother suffer like that.

As he watched Bobbie Matthews slip behind the line of animal transporters, he clicked the talk button on his radio, held it down, was about to inform Manx and the team, then decided otherwise.

No. He could handle this without calling in the bloody cavalry. A slip of a girl dressed like a bloody vicar? No two ways about it, he could take care of that problem.

He released the talk button and followed Bobbie Matthews; his fingers gripped tight around his baton.

98

After initiating the countdown, Ronnie navigated the drone east towards the showground, gradually increasing the elevation as it flew. He checked the screen as the drone glided, effortlessly it seemed, over the fields. For a moment, he was lost in the high-definition, brilliant greens of the island where he'd spent all his life. Watching the live feed from this perspective, he realised how special this place was. He could never imagine living anywhere else; it never even crossed his mind. He was deep in this thought when he heard a voice behind him calling his name.

He froze, turned slowly around. "Christ, Mel," he said, with a tremor of relief. "I nearly shit myself. When did they release you?"

"About an hour ago."

"You should be resting. Me and Bobbie, we've got this."

"I'll rest when I'm dead," he muttered, as if he were making a promise to himself.

"Nah, you should be resting now, Mel. Save your energy for the celebrations, yeah? Few pints, open a bottle of Penderyn."

Mel walked towards Ronnie. "Give me the controls, boy. That's my job." He coughed, straining.

"You're in no fit state, Mel," Ronnie said, glancing nervously at the screen. The warning had appeared again; low battery. "Just hang back. Me and Bobbie, we've got this under control." He turned the screen towards Mel "See, six minutes, then it's done, we made our point. Six minutes, we'll be legends, Mel, bloody legends."

But Melvin wasn't listening. As he stepped closer, the familiar look in his eyes made Ronnie's blood run cold. It was a look that said he wasn't going to take no for an answer. A look that had all the chilling hallmarks of another family member, his own father, Dafydd Powell.

When the punch struck, Ronnie didn't even see it coming.

99

Leaving Winking Wynn Williams in a state of agitation, Manx headed across the showground. He hoped Carlisle had taken the back road and was safely parked. If the briefcase contained any kind of explosive device, they'd be well protected behind the wall of livestock transporters and trailers.

As he walked, a loud buzzing sound, like an angry swarm of bees, stopped him in his tracks. He brought a hand to his brow and looked skywards. A deep pit hollowed out in his chest as he tracked the bright glint of metal circling as if it were searching for its target. He grabbed his radio. "Carlisle, find a way out of there, now!"

"Negative, Manx, the access road's blocked."

"Then head towards the showground."

"Are you serious? You just informed me there's a bomb there, and you want me to drive right to it?"

"It's a decoy. Bobbie Matthews planted a decoy."

"What the fuck is going on Manx?"

"There's a drone circling the showground. I don't think it's here taking footage for tonight's news."

A short pause of static over the airwaves, then Carlisle spoke. "Thanks for the intel, Manx."

"Thanks for the intel?" Was that it? It seemed like a gross underreaction, Manx thought as he kept eyes on the drone. The good news was it was heading away from the crowds. The very bad news was that it was travelling at high velocity directly towards Carlisle and the Royal Protection Squad.

100

DS Nader trod carefully at the rear of the livestock trailers, the stench of fresh slurry in his nostrils. He'd lost sight of Bobbie Matthews, but he was sure she was here, hiding. His hunch was confirmed when from inside one of the trailers the troubled neighing of a horse caught his attention. He moved closer, squatted, and checked out the pile of clothing left on trailer's ramp; a black robe and a clerical collar.

He felt suddenly vulnerable, as if he were being watched. Back in his army days he'd have his 9mm LA91 Browning close to hand, but today he was armed only with his collapsible baton, a can of CS incapacitant spray, and the X26 taser that all team members were issued with last night. If it came to it, he'd use them all.

That chance never came.

Before he sensed somebody had crept up behind him, he felt the cold sting of a steel bolt into his neck and a hand pull back on his hair.

"One wrong move and this ends up severing your jugular. Understand?" Bobbie Matthews said, urging her point further into his neck.

Nader nodded.

"No," Bobbie said. "Say the words. Say you understand."

"I... I understand," Nader confirmed. "I understand."

"Good. Let's walk," Bobbie said.

101

Ronnie wasn't sure how long he was out, but it couldn't have been more than a minute. His cheek was sore as hell, his mouth sodden with the metallic taste of blood. He lifted himself up.

Melvin now had control of the drone. He seemed lost in his own world. "You better stay there, unless you want another smack in the mouth," he said, barely turning to look at his nephew to confirm he'd comply; that was a given.

Ronnie leant on the front of the van and wiped the blood from his lip. "You know what you're doing with that thing?"

"Bobbie showed me," Melvin said. "Who'd have thought it, eh? A kid that smart in the Powell family."

Ronnie craned his neck to study the screen. The countdown clicked down to four minutes.

"What's that sound?" Melvin asked as the control panel emitted three urgent, short beeps.

"Low battery, I think," Ronnie said. "But I charged it up yesterday, so it's probably just on the blink."

The beeps stopped. Melvin smiled. "Going out fighting, yeah? Just like I always said I would."

"Yeah," Ronnie agreed. "Like a champ, Mel," he said, spitting a glob of blood on the ground. "Go out like a champ."

102

Manx ran to where Carlisle had positioned the Range Rovers. They were parked to form a point, like the apex of an arrow, engines running, primed for either a rapid escape or the back-seat occupants were demanding their creature comforts of air conditioning; not that he could see beyond the tint of privacy glass.

Carlisle stood in front of the vehicles talking into his mobile, nodding, as if confirming a command he was confident he could follow through on. Set around him were four of his men, Glock 17s in hands, eyes scouring back and forth between all compass points.

"Standing your ground, Carlisle?" Manx shouted. "Your call, but I think it's the wrong one." He looked up. The drone was barely a pinprick of light in the blue, but the sound was still there; a menacing, insistent hissing of rotors.

Carlisle ended his call and fastened the middle button of his suit. "We'll take it from here, Manx. Thank your officers for all their support. I'll make sure the royals are aware of your dedication to their safety and well-being."

Manx was still processing Carlisle's words when a sudden

movement to his right made him turn – Bobbie Matthews, dressed in her combat flying gear. To her left, DS Nader, his face pallid, eyes wide open; a crossbow bolt secured at his jugular.

Carlisle's men turned with a speed and efficiency that took Manx by surprise and trained their weapons on Bobbie.

"If you think you can shoot faster than I can stab, go ahead," she said, standing her ground some ten metres away.

The security detail gripped their fingers firmer around their weapons and waited for Carlisle's order – a barely visible shake of the head. A non-verbal signal they'd no doubt rehearsed for these kinds of emergency situations. The men relaxed their stance a degree.

"What do you want, Flight Lieutenant Matthews? What are your demands?" Carlisle's voice was calm, precise.

"Now you ask?" Bobbie said. "The RAF had their chance. The deadline has passed."

"I'm not RAF, neither is that officer you're holding hostage."

"Leverage is leverage," she said, urging the point of the bolt deep enough into Nader's neck to draw a trickle of blood.

"Boss?" he mumbled. No pre-arranged signals required; his face told all the story Manx needed to know; Nader was terrified.

With her free hand, Bobbie checked her mobile and permitted herself the luxury of a thin smile. "In precisely four minutes, a quadcopter drone will drop a hundred feet and detonate five pounds of explosives wrapped in a pipe bomb directly on those two shiny Range Rovers over there. I expect the collateral damage to be significant, especially to that precious cargo you're carrying in the back seats. You could attempt to get away, but what with that security incident in the showground and the line of cars bottle necking all the escape routes, I doubt you'd get far. Oh, and of course, this police officer would see none of that because he'd be too busy trying to stem the flow of blood from his neck. He'll do this for around a minute before realising he's going to die."

Carlisle slipped his phone into his jacket pocket. "Five pounds of explosives?" he said, his tone calm and considered. "Anything within a hundred metres off the blast radius will be destroyed, including yourself."

Bobbie smiled. "My death is of no consequence. I have nothing left to lose."

Manx was taking all this in, his eyes darting around from Carlisle to Bobbie, to Nader, to the security detail who were becoming twitchy, stances no longer relaxed, Glocks primed. Manx observed that their hands were rock-steady, holding not a tremor of doubt that if the order came, their triggers would be pulled. The stand-off continued for another minute. Manx broke the silence. Maybe there was a way to end this; lives saved, no one killed.

"Don't you want to know what happened, Bobbie?" he said, reaching into his jacket pocket to retrieve the printed copy of the report Andrew Pierce had left with him. "Operation Vanguard? The truth?"

"Manx, what are you doing?" Carlisle said, his voice wire tight and fringed with caution. "I thought we requested you to leave."

"He's not going anywhere," Bobbie said, urging the steel another few millimetres deeper into Nader's neck. Another slow ooze of blood.

"It's all in here," Manx said. "What happened after the strike, how your husband died."

"You're lying," Bobbie said, her eyes narrowing, her hands betraying the slightest tremor.

Manx could see she wanted to believe. Wanted to know all this had been worth something. "You didn't kill Danvir, Bobbie. It wasn't you."

The sound of her husband's name was like ice dripped down Bobbie's spine. Before she could make sense of Manx's words, the drone plunged downwards, reappeared fifty feet above them, propellers slicing through the still morning air. Three of Carlisle's men quickly trained their Glocks on the quadcopter, the other man keeping his aim sure and steady on Bobbie's upper body.

"You shoot, you still lose," Bobbie said, checking the countdown. "It blows, we all blow."

"You don't need to do this, Bobbie," Manx said, his throat tight, neck muscles tensing. "Fly the drone into the fields and I'll read you the report. If, after that, you still want to kill us all, go ahead, do it." He showed the first page of the report to Bobbie.

"You're out of order, Manx," Carlisle said. "You have no authority to negotiate."

"Neither do you," Bobbie snapped back.

Manx could see Bobbie was debating, deliberating her choices as the drone gained altitude and veered back over the showground.

"Good. Good, Bobbie," Manx said. "Fly the drone as far away from here as you can, and we'll talk. I'll read you everything that's in here. Everything."

"No," Bobbie said, glancing nervously at her mobile, trying to get some clarity on the situation. "It's not... it's not me. I don't have control. It's flying itself."

103

Ronnie turned as he heard the hiss of propellers travelling closer. The drone was sweeping in at high velocity back to its base. That wasn't the plan. Mel must have got confused, messed up the controls. He ran over.

Melvin was lost in his own world; unaware he was piloting the drone back to its launch point.

"Mel! What the fucking hell are you doing?"

Melvin seemed hypnotised by the screen, watching the fields rendered in brilliant high definition as the drone flew above them.

Ronnie made a grab for the control panel. Melvin's elbow pummelled him hard in the ribs, sending him reeling. He stumbled back up, checked the countdown and felt his stomach lurch.

Twenty-nine seconds. Twenty-eight...

Bobbie's words came whirling back to him, loud and clear. "Five pounds of explosives, Ronnie. Enough to scatter your limbs in all directions, Ronnie."

Mel turned to his nephew, his brow creased in confusion. "What the fuck is it doing?" he said, stabbing the screen like a frustrated child trying to get a device to do its bidding. "It's not listening, and it's beeping again."

A bolt of realisation hit Ronnie between the eyes. Mel wasn't piloting the drone. He'd ceded control some two minutes ago when the last bar of power had dipped under three per cent.

His mind raced back to the afternoon Bobbie had taught him how to pilot the quadcopter. *When the battery pack runs low, it automatically takes its feed from the auxiliary battery pack.* But there was no auxiliary battery pack. That had been removed and replaced with explosives. With no power source, the drone would pilot itself back to the base station like a faithful dog fetching a stick.

"Mel! We've got to get the fuck out of here, now!" Spit sprayed from Ronnie's mouth as he screamed. "Now, Mel, drop the fucking screen!"

Fifteen seconds. Fourteen seconds.

Ronnie lunged at Melvin, managed to grab a handful of his T-shirt before his uncle struck his fist like a hammer across Ronnie's cheek. Ronnie felt the teeth rattle in his mouth, the familiar rust of blood on his tongue. He stumbled backwards, just managing to keep his balance. Through the floaters and popping points of light fogging his vision, he glanced at the screen:

Ten seconds. Nine seconds.

"What's going on, Ronnie? What the fuck's going on?"

Those were the last words Ronnie heard from his uncle. Melvin was still poking at the screen as Ronnie made his decision. He could stand there, alongside Mel, have his limbs blown from his body, or he could run.

Six seconds. Five seconds.

Before Ronnie turned his back, he watched the drone land perfectly at Mel's feet, the whir of the rotors slowly fading. This was it. The twelfth round, the final bell; Mel refusing to back down, prodding the screen as if his strength alone could will it into submission.

Ronnie almost tripped over his feet as he ran. He hurled himself against the rear of the van, as petrified as the day his uncle had rescued him from Dafydd Powell, except this time there would be no saviour. He clenched his fists, brought them to his mouth, tried without success to stop the skin on his bones from shaking.

104

The explosion was a sonic boom of heavy thunder on the horizon. A thick cloud of grey smoke mushroomed into the blue. The Transit van seemed like something spat up by the ground as it catapulted skywards, its metal catching the sunlight before it landed on its side, doors and windows blown out, wheels spinning uselessly in place.

Bobbie turned to the chaos, attempting to make sense of what the hell had just happened. In that split-second Manx noticed a red laser dot float across her forehead like a freshly bloomed blemish.

"No!" Manx shouted. "Don't–"

His protest was too late, and futile. From the rear window of one of the Range Rovers, a long-range rifle took the kill shot. It struck its target with absolute precision.

Bobbie Matthews' head snapped back. Blood sprayed from the single bullet hole. Her fingers flexed open, releasing the bolt. She crumpled to the ground, her combat suit seeming to deflate as she fell. Beside her, DS Nader dropped to his knees, wiping Bobbie's warm blood splatters from his face.

"Nader! Are you all right?" Manx said.

"Never been better, boss," the DS said, rubbing a warm smear of blood off his shirt.

Confident Nader was safe, Manx turned his attention to Carlisle. "You didn't need to–"

"Yes. Yes, I did," Carlisle confirmed, taking out his cell phone to relay the message that his mission was complete; orders carried out. "My job is to protect. I did that job. The world is a safer place without Bobbie Matthews in it."

As he spoke, a flash of realisation burnt bright in Manx's mind. Carlisle was far too careful and calculated to take this level of risk. He threw down the report and rushed towards the Range Rovers.

"Manx! Do not–" Carlisle warned.

"I don't take my orders from you," Manx said, pulling open one of the back doors. He stepped back as he came face to face with the muzzle of a SIG SG 550 assault rifle. He looked down. A red laser point hovered over his shirt, directly above his heart.

"Manx!" Carlisle shouted. "Do not give me a reason."

Manx ignored him and flung open the back doors of the other vehicle. The back seats were pristine; empty.

Carlisle took a deep breath and signalled for the marksman to stand down. He complied, pulling the door shut.

"Did you really think I'd endanger the life of the royals?"

"So, you lied?"

"Loose lips and all that. I couldn't reveal any intelligence that would have jeopardised our operation."

"What operation?"

Carlisle leant his back against the front wing of the Range Rover. "What people like you will never understand, Manx, is that our country is at war, and will be for the foreseeable future. There won't be any Victory Day parades when this is all over, and do you know why, Manx? Because it won't ever be over. These fundamentalists don't just wave a white flag, surrender and shuffle back to whatever hut they crawled out from. Fighting is all they know; all they'll ever know. This is the new reality of war; poor, uneducated jihadists sending women and children strapped with explosives to their deaths with no notion of what victory looks like beyond a vague notion of the world kneeling in terror at their feet. I, for one, am not willing to let that happen, neither was Bobbie Matthews. She'd been on the front line of that war, seen more death in a few short years than any of us will see in a lifetime."

"Then why kill her? She would have stood trial, been put away for life on the evidence we had."

"You're forgetting one thing, Manx," Carlisle said, gesturing at the Operation Vanguard report. "She would never have stopped searching for answers, and once she found those answers we couldn't risk her leaking them to the press or whoever. We need the public and the press on our side if we're to make any progress in ending this."

Manx gestured to Bobbie's lifeless body. "So, you used us to bring Bobbie out in the open so you could kill her? That makes you no better than the bloody terrorists."

Carlisle spoke deliberately as if he were explaining a difficult concept to a child. "In my experience, traitors rarely repent for their sins; there was no cure for what ailed Bobbie Matthews. Prison would have been little deterrent to someone of her persuasion, let alone a low security psychological hospital. I'm sure you're more than familiar with how lenient our justice system has become, what with the Courts of Human Rights and the hurdles we have to jump over to make any charge stick. It's a sad reflection of the times we live in when the people who threaten our freedom are granted the same protection as everyone else."

"All equal in the eyes of the law," Manx protested. "And what about Flynt? Did you silence him too?"

"There was no need to. He got the promotion he wanted; we gained his loyalty. You should look closer to home if you're looking for who killed Flynt," Carlisle said, gesturing towards Bobbie.

"And Cole Dawson?" Manx asked.

"I believe the official cause of death was suicide. Hardly a surprise, the man was a drunk with severe battle trauma. We tried, but he wasn't ready to accept our help."

Carlisle directed his men to fall back. "We did good work here today, we neutralised a terrorist, a danger to our country, we should be proud of that."

"Proud?" Manx countered. "She was a widow looking for the truth and you killed her."

"And now, no doubt, she's found whatever truth she was seeking," Carlisle said, stepping onto the Range Rover's running boards. He took one final look over the fields, the spirals of grey smoke rising over the horizon.

"Looks messy," he said with a grimace. "Good luck with the clean-up."

105

Five days after Bobbie Matthews' death, the summer heatwave broke, bringing with it a heavy downpour that soaked the island for several hours. The rain fell hard on the fields where the Anglesey Show, for that year, had been cancelled. Afterwards, the air seemed fresh to the touch; a presage of a new beginning. At least for some. For others, the time for new beginnings had passed.

Manx gazed through the window of Gwynedd Hospital, watching the last of the grey clouds scuttle west as if being pursued by the incoming blue. Three floors below, the media presence had dwindled to a single BBC Cymru crew. After the initial flurry of media attention, the news cycle had moved on.

People, as they were often compelled to do, had also moved on. In a few weeks, the memory of Bobbie Matthews and the "Showdown at the Showground" as the newspapers had christened the incident, would begin to fade. Six months on, few people would be able to recall the name of the other victim, nor the name of his nephew who had barely escaped with his life and was now waiting for his trial date, cuffed to a bed inside the Ashworth high security hospital on Merseyside.

The names Melvin and Ronnie Powell would, however, remain present and clear in DI Manx's memory for years to come, as would the name Logan Collins.

Collins himself had been lucky; a word he would keep returning to as he ramped up his political ambitions come the autumn. The rigid structure of the Transit van had functioned like a steel cage protecting Collins from the worst of the explosion, though he hadn't escaped unharmed. He was bounced around the van like a human pinball as the shockwaves struck the metal. The Transit's gear lever, shorn from the transmission, had buried itself into Logan's right thigh. His left leg had fared far worse, crushed under the heavy weight of the front seats as the van flipped and landed on its side.

Manx had spoken to Collins' wife, Danica. The conversation had not gone well. Danica had remained calm, listened to Manx, before turning those narrow, feline-like eyes on him in a manner that suggested Manx could burn in hell for all she cared.

"You are the reason my husband will never walk again. You are the reason he's in a wheelchair; a cripple. You assured me these things rarely happen, victims return unharmed. You were wrong. I believe you and your team did not do enough to find my husband. We will make sure you pay for that, no matter how long it takes. Remember, Inspector Manx, you have blood on your hands."

Days later, those words were dark echoes in the back of his mind. *Blood on your hands*. Maybe she was right, but Danica Collins was not in possession of the full facts, never would be.

Hours after the explosion, a man had been flown by helicopter from Whitehall to RAF Valley and was driven directly to Llangefni Station. The grim-faced civil servant, William Baker, several pay grades elevated from Jack Carlisle, had sat Manx and Canton in one of the interview rooms and laid out in no uncertain terms what they could or could not release to the public. As

Manx expected, Carlisle's name and any reference to the Royal Security Squad were to be kept out of all and any press releases. "This falls on you," Baker had explained. "The North Wales Constabulary takes full responsibility. That, gentlemen, is how it will be."

Baker had also demanded they hand over any copies, both digital and printed, of the Operation Vanguard report. "I suspect you won't want to perjure yourself, so I won't ask how you came in possession of these," Baker had said, slipping the papers into his briefcase.

Manx had accepted the demands with little protest. Hours after the incident, his emotions were raw; capitulation came easy. As Danica Collins had said, he had blood on his hands. He couldn't see or touch it, but he could sense it, like an invisible film across his skin.

Lydia Clarke; her name had come across his desk a day later when she was found in the coal shed behind the Lantern Arms. The driver from the brewery had heard her screams as he was hauling beer kegs off the back of his lorry. She was Melvin's lover, she'd told Manx; she'd told him a lot more too, happy to keep talking to save her own skin. When she revealed, almost in passing, that Melvin was Bobbie's biological father it was the final piece of the jigsaw falling into place. Melvin wasn't only on a mission to go out in a blaze of glory, he was expecting some kind of redemption by helping his daughter uncover the truth she was so desperate to find.

When the dust had settled, and memories of that day began to fade like the last faint ripples across a pond, the name that would haunt Manx the most was that of Bobbie Matthews; the young widow searching for truth. She never got to hear that truth; unless what Carlisle had hinted at was true, and wherever Bobbie was now all would have been revealed and she would be at peace. As comforting as that thought was, it took more faith than Manx had the capacity for.

To hint that Bobbie Matthews was as much of a victim, as some of the more liberal-leaning papers and online commentators had suggested, was a stretch too far in Manx's book. If nothing else, her death had pointed a glaring light on the trauma suffered by military personnel who may have been thousands of miles away from the line of fire, but their trauma was no less real than if they'd stood eye to eye and taken a life.

Some weeks later, the BBC broadcast a *Panorama* documentary "Behind Friendly Lines" about that very subject, along with interviews with former drone pilots, their faces obscured under shadowy lighting. If he could have seen their eyes Manx wondered if they'd be haunted with the same emptiness he'd seen in Bobbie Matthews' eyes? Manx could never condone her actions, but at the same time, he couldn't condone her murder. She should have stood trial, where the truth would have come to light. But that was Carlisle's objective when he ordered the kill shot; to keep that truth hidden, locked away for good.

There was plenty Bobbie Matthews didn't know about what had happened after she left the ground control station that day. Flight Commander James Flynt had immediately called the Waddington Base Commander, who in turn had contacted the Chief of the Air Staff, the highest ranking official in the RAF. His call to the Defence Secretary, head of the MoD, had escalated the situation to the highest level of government. Within thirty minutes of the strike, a strategy was formed, a plan put in place; orders carried out without question.

A secondary, more detailed, battle damage assessment conducted by British ground troops had found the cause and origin of the secondary blast. There were no enemy combatants in the vicinity and none of the debris had the markings of usual IS weaponry. What they did find was the blown-out remains of three large propane cylinders buried seven feet underground, packed solid with explosives. The destruction was so complete it was impossible at the time to discern if they'd been stored by insurgents or planted by the allied forces for use later as a massive IED in an attempt to beat the enemy at their own game.

It wasn't until the formal forensic report came back the following day that the provenance of the explosives was verified. The debris contained traces of RDX nitroamine and dioctyl sebacate; two of the core components and a binding agent found in most Unites States Armed Forces explosive devices. British-made explosives typically contained cyclonite and lithium grease.

Several days of tense negotiations followed between the MoD and the United States Joint Operations Command. If the findings were leaked, it would have looked bad for both sides; made them look at best careless, and at worst incompetent. Neither was a good option when trying to win the hearts and minds of the public in the war on terror. What did win hearts and minds was outrage. Outrage directed through the right channels to sympathetic newspaper editors.

It took a few days at most for the British tabloids to attach themselves to the story of six young RAF medics blown up by Muslim terrorists. It was the kind of spin that sold papers and bolstered the government's position on utilising drones in the fight against terror. Manx remembered Byron Gates had used the phrase "false flag" several times in his rambling communication; he was half right. The RAF hadn't deliberately killed their own men to further their cause, but they had used a tragic accident to their advantage, with no thought as to the lives ruined in the process.

If Bobbie Matthews had been furnished with the truth at the beginning, then maybe none of this would have come to pass; James Flynt and his wife would be enjoying retirement; Logan

Collins would be standing at the podium, not bound to a wheelchair, as he delivered his campaign speeches; Byron Gates would have continued his fight against injustice; and Bobbie Matthews would have lived, given herself the chance to properly grieve for her husband and, over time, may have come to forgive herself for something that was never her fault.

Manx turned from the window, the burden of the last two weeks still bearing down on him, and looked into Vera Troup's room. The hospital auxiliary staff were busy stripping sheets and blankets from the bed, preparing the room for the next occupant.

"She'd like to talk you," DCI Canton said, walking into the waiting room. Five days on, he still looked ragged and worn out; Manx guessed he'd fared no better himself, but there was something more serious in the way Canton held himself. The slump in the shoulders the weariness in his voice, made Manx think there was something more at play than sheer exhaustion. His mentor and friend looked older; the job maybe finally taking its toll on him.

"She's asking for the name of that St John ambulance volunteer," Canton said, sitting down with a groan. "Reckons he saved her life; she'd like to personally thank him."

Manx nodded. *Hugh Jones deserved that recognition*, he thought. The man had stepped up, done his job without complaint; saved a life. He should be damned proud of that, certainly a lot prouder than Manx was feeling about himself right now.

"How's she doing?" Manx asked, sitting in the chair opposite.

"Weak, gets tired quickly, but there's one thing for certain, her days as a DCIS are over."

"She said that?"

"Not in so many words, but when something like this happens your priorities change."

Manx nodded. "And you, Ellis? Stepping up?"

"I daresay that ship's sailed," he said, his voice betraying a slip of resignation. "I'll hold down the fort, but they'll want someone with some juice still left in them. They've already retained a talent recruitment company and I doubt my name's on their radar."

"Everything changes," Manx said with a resigned smile.

"We all jump back on the merry-go-round and just hope we get off at a better place than we got on, right, Manx?"

Manx thought for a moment. "Problem is, Ellis, I don't remember ever getting off the bloody ride in the first place."

106

ONE MONTH LATER

The short service for the scattering of Bobbie Matthews' ashes was an intimate affair conducted at Cable Bay beach in the late afternoon. Manx stood next to Tammy; Mohsin and Rida Sadiq stood to his left. Rida seemed to tolerate his presence but arched her eyebrows and glanced at her husband when she saw Tammy slip her hand into Manx's.

Few words were spoken. Tammy set a small speaker on a rise of marram grass and took out her phone. "(What's So Funny 'Bout) Peace, Love & Understanding" by Elvis Costello and the Attractions drifted on early evening breeze. It seemed like a solid choice, Manx thought. He hadn't got to know Bobbie, but he imagined she wasn't the kind of woman who would have approved of an overly sentimental pop song to mark her passing. After the track faded out, Tammy reached into the urn, took a handful of ashes and let them fall from her palm. They floated away on the cool evening breeze; a life scattered to the winds.

Tammy and Manx headed back, taking the pathway leading to the car park. As they walked, Manx noticed a lone figure in RAF service dress standing at the edge of the beach. He told

Tammy he'd call her later that evening and made his way towards the man.

Andrew Pierce shuffled uncomfortably as Manx approached. "They didn't have to kill her," he said, looking over the white caps skimming the ocean surface. He had Bobbie's headset in his hand, his fingers rubbing over the cheap gemstones.

Manx had no response; at least none that had any merit or one that didn't contradict his own feelings about Bobbie's death. He turned up his jacket collar as a gust of wind blew up from the beach, bringing with it a smattering of sand.

"You always imagine there was something more you could have done, an extra mile you could have walked," Pierce said, wiping away an errant grain of sand caught in the corner of his eye.

"Bobbie made her own decisions. She chose a bad road to go down. It was never going to end well for her. I think she knew that," Manx said.

"She deserved to know the truth. It would have set her free, I'm sure of it." Pierce exhaled loudly, barely holding back his tears.

"Do you believe the truth sets any of us free?"

"I have to believe, or what else is there left?" Pierce looked at the headset and began picking off the gems one by one. The rainbow of colours caught the light for a moment before they fell to the ground and were lost in the beige carpet of sand.

When Manx reached the car park, two cars remained; the Jensen and what he assumed was Pierce's Mitsubishi Outlander. Walking past, he noticed a thick wedge of masking tape wrapped around the driver's side wing mirror. He ran his finger along the edge. The mirror toppled to the right, the tape pulling at the seams. He peered inside; Pierce's cap was set on the passenger seat.

He reached for his mobile, called the station and asked Nader to meet him here as soon as. Then he called Ashton Bevan. "James Flynt's cap? Did you check it for any DNA other than Flynt's?" he asked, peering through the rear windscreen and at the fleece jacket in the boot.

Bevan replied they hadn't.

"Do it," Manx said. "And while you're at it, look for any blood traces."

He hung up and looked over at Pierce, still plucking at the headset as if he were picking out daisy petals: *she loves me, she loves me not*.

107

Andrew Pierce was calm, resigned almost, as he sat in the interview room. He'd agreed to come in and "help with our inquiries," as Manx had informed him. "You're not under arrest, but any information you have could prove to be useful." Pierce attempted to be evasive, but Manx could tell his heart wasn't in it. Unlike Melvin Powell a few weeks back, Pierce looked the identikit picture of the confessing type. It was only a matter of time before he folded. That was fine by Manx, he was in no rush, Bevan's team was still combing over Pierce's car for the evidence Manx needed to hammer home the final nail on Commander James Flynt's murder.

"How long had you been in love with Bobbie Matthews?"

"From the moment I met her," Pierce said, matter-of-factly.

Manx slid the printout of Bobbie's wedding day across the desk. "When her husband died, I'm sure a small part of you saw that as an opportunity to make the moves on Bobbie. A familiar shoulder to cry on?"

"It wasn't like that."

"Tell me, what was it like?"

"Bobbie was special, I'd never do anything to hurt her."

"But you did hurt her, Pierce. You ran her down in the middle of the night. Lucky for her you were there to pick up the pieces."

Pierce shrugged. "Are you going to charge me for that?"

"What was your end game, here? You'd be her guardian angel? Her protector? Someone she couldn't live without?"

"Bobbie never needed a protector."

"That must have hurt, the rejection?"

Manx turned as the door swung open. PC Priddle walked in, handed Manx a Manila folder, then scooted out.

"Let's talk about James Flynt. You didn't agree with his decision to transfer Bobbie to a psychiatric facility?"

"We were making progress; it would have been like starting all over again for Bobbie. She didn't need to go through that."

"Is that why you killed him?"

Pierce's Adam's apple rose and fell like a sewing machine bobbin, his breathing shallow and hurried. "I didn't–"

"The tyre prints we found next to Flynt's car are a perfect match to your Mitsubishi Outlander."

"There must be hundreds of cars with the same tyres."

"Thousands," Manx confirmed. "But that's not the evidence that's going to put you away, Pierce." He pulled out a plastic bag from the folder. "We took these rock fragments from the fatal wound you made in Flynt's skull when you struck him with the rock you were carrying in your jacket pocket."

"I'm not sure what–" Pierce began.

"We're sure, and we've got the science to prove it." Manx flipped over a signed document from Mary Bedford, Department Head, Geological Oceanography at Bangor University. He took his time to explain to Pierce how the fragments in Flynt's skull couldn't have come from Benllech beach. "So, how did fragments of blueschist rocks get into his wound, Pierce? Any idea?"

Pierce's brow glistened with a layer of slick sweat.

Manx leant forward, held Pierce's gaze. "I'll save you the time and energy of coming up with a lie. You called Flynt, made up some specious reason for meeting that time of night. You knew it was a long shot persuading him to change his mind about Bobbie, but you had a backup plan. A murder weapon you picked up somewhere. Maybe from your back garden? The base? Who the hell knows? That's not important. What is important is that once you put that rock in your pocket with the intent of killing Flynt, that's as close a definition to premeditated murder as it gets."

"I... I think you're reaching," Pierce muttered.

"We also found blueschist fragments all over the passenger seat of your car. And the fleece jacket you kept in the boot? In the right-hand pocket, we found the exact same fragments. I think you carried the rock on the front seat, then put it in your jacket pocket when Flynt arrived. Again, premeditation."

"That doesn't prove very much," Pierce mumbled.

"Not by itself. But that's not how evidence works. We like to package it all up, so the CPS has a very clear understanding of why you should be arrested."

Manx turned his laptop to face Pierce and pressed play on a short video clip. "This is CCTV footage of your car leaving Breeze Hill public house in Benllech at 9.45pm. You also have no alibi for the remainder of that evening other than sitting at home, alone. Now, you can see for yourself how my case suddenly becomes very persuasive. I have motive; traces of what we believe is the murder weapon in your car and on your clothing; and you were in the vicinity of the murder when it happened with a paper-thin alibi that's not going to hold water in front of a jury."

"I think I'd like a solicitor," Pierce said, shuffling like he'd just found something sharp sticking out of his seat.

"Good idea," Manx agreed. "Once they're briefed, we can legally request you provide us with a DNA sample."

"I'm not saying anything else until my solicitor get here."

"Fair enough," Manx said. "But here's what we did figure out. Flynt was wearing his cap when you struck him. Do you know how we know that?"

Pierce shrugged.

"Our forensics lads found traces of blood splatter on the outside rim of the cap, which means he must have been wearing it when you delivered the fatal blow. You then returned the cap to Flynt's car to make it look like he'd gone for a late evening stroll with every intention of returning. Now, when we collect your sample, what do you think are the chances we'll find some trace of your DNA on that cap? A skin flake, blood; a strand of hair? Or you could just save us all the time and confess. Your call, Pierce."

Manx gathered his things, stood and turned to face the door.

Pierce sniffed loudly, ran the back of a hand under his nose. "Bobbie just needed someone to care for her. She needed a friend," he said, looking off into the distance, as if trying to convince himself.

Manx turned. "With friends like you, eh," he said, and left the room.

108

When Manx arrived back home later that evening, daylight was still in bloom. It would be another thirty minutes before darkness fell completely, but for now the sky was a ribbon of dark blue etched with deep orange. As he reached his doorstep, he noticed a small package with a note attached.

Thought you were probably too busy to pick up your photos. Pay me next time. He glanced at the signature – Gina Roberts, Benllech Chemist – and looked out over the roofs of the small housing estate towards the fields. To the east, a flock of starlings flitted, swooped, and spiralled in an impossible, intricate dance. The old farmer, Walter Edwards, had been right; the murmuration was beautiful, and at the same time hauntingly unfathomable. The deaths of the hundred starlings had been equally enigmatic, but six weeks on, the experts had concluded the flock had probably entered a dive murmuration to avoid a severe weather incident or a raptor, and were unable to pull back quickly enough to avoid hitting the ground. When Manx had read the findings, his thoughts immediately turned to Bobbie Matthews. That had been her fate too. The last year of her life had been one long, free-falling tailspin that she was destined to never pull back from and recover. For that, she'd paid the ultimate price. Before heading inside, Manx watched the remainder of the starlings' performance until the flock extended its final curtain call, bowed, then vanished like a brush stroke into the watercolour complexion of dusk.

In the house, he peeled off his jacket and slipped off his shoes, exhaustion and hunger hit him like two trucks at once. It was only an hour later, after nuking and devouring a lamb biryani he'd excavated from his freezer and chugging several bottles of Kingfisher, that he found the courage to open the package. Part of him hoped the roll of film would be completely blank; nothing to see here, no gut-churning reminders of that day, but he doubted Gina would have gone to the trouble of hand-delivering an envelope of black prints.

He stacked his plates in the dishwasher, shoved the plastic container into the bin, twisted the top off another beer and called Tammy. Their conversation was subdued, gentle even, both too tired to talk long. They hung up after about ten minutes, both agreeing that grief was sometimes best shared alone, in reflection. He promised to call her tomorrow.

He walked to his spare bedroom, slipped the brightly coloured envelope from its plastic and flipped through the photographs. His initial suspicions were correct. There were no date stamps nor geo-tag information back then, but there was no doubt they were all taken on the day Miriam had vanished. Most of the photographs were of a seventeen-year-old Frankie, his girlfriend at the time, smiling and mugging to camera. Most would have been instantly relegated to the trash icon in today's Instagram-filtered world, he imagined. The other thought he had glancing at Frankie's youthful, almost childlike face, was far more visceral: *Where the bloody hell did the time go?*

He took a swig of beer, wiped his mouth, and shuffled through the photographs. The remaining shots were all scenic; a teenage Tudor Manx's sorry attempts at art, no doubt trying to impress Frankie. They looked humorously forced: a discarded Coke can set into the sand, the ocean blurred in the background; a blade of marram grass, bright green and mostly out of focus; a close-up of Frankie's black polished fingernail resting on her choker necklace. He'd always tried too hard around Frankie, imagining he was never cool enough for her. He wondered if Frankie, like him, had left at the first opportunity? Or, had she hung around, married, found herself with three kids, a dog, and a mortgage? Frankie never seemed the family type, but then again, people change.

He flipped quickly through the remaining pictures, hoping that maybe he'd taken one of Miriam that day, but he hadn't. One photo, however, caught his attention. A wide shot of Aberffraw beach, a car parked on the old stone bridge crossing the river. He pulled the image closer; a midnight-blue Jensen Interceptor, he was sure of it. Someone was leaning on the bonnet. It must have been his father, but the face was too blurred to be sure. Why would Tommy have been at the beach that day? His father never mentioned it, not once, as far as he could recall.

Manx taped the photograph to the whiteboard on the bedroom wall; it had now become his personal incident board. He'd created the collage of clippings soon after he'd been transferred to Anglesey and begun receiving cryptic text messages concerning Miriam's disappearance. Ten months later, the wall was a jumble of old newspaper clippings, faded photographs of his sister, and texts he'd screen-grabbed and printed out – origin unknown and sent via a cryptophone; anonymous and untraceable. He was convinced someone on the island was sending the messages, but were too scared to come forward, preferring to leave clues, like breadcrumbs, for him to follow or maybe to drive him into some kind of obsessive madness; Manx was still debating.

He took another slug of beer. The photograph made no sense. Was it taken on a different day? Not likely. Why didn't Tommy mention he was there? Manx had combed the cold case files often enough to know his father had never mentioned it. So, what was he doing at Aberffraw beach the day his daughter vanished, and why hadn't he provided the police with a statement to that effect?

Manx slid down from the bed, sat on the floor, and pressed his head back against the mattress. He hadn't spoken to Tommy in years. The last he knew his father was living outside of Cardiff. He'd always made a point of keeping tabs on Tommy; nothing too overt, just a subtle check-in via the police database every few months. Now, it seemed to Manx, would be the time to reconnect. But not tonight, nor tomorrow; next week maybe. Tommy wasn't going anywhere, hadn't moved for years, and besides, he was sure answers as important as these were worth waiting for; worth taking the time to prepare the right questions that could bring him a step closer to the answers he was searching for.

Whether those answers would provide him the closure he wanted, of that he was less sure. He knew from experience the wide gulf that existed between the answers you assumed were the truth and the truth itself: sometimes they met in the middle, more often than not they were miles apart.

THE END

ACKNOWLEDGEMENTS

A huge thanks as always to my wife, Laura, for her unwavering support and patience. A massive thanks to my dear friend Gloria for her insight and attention to detail. And for saving my arse on numerous occasions, a big thanks to my diligent and eagle-eyed editor, Clare.

Printed in Great Britain
by Amazon

59269252R00253